The author, a former professional mariner, came from a long line of policemen beginning in 1860 and ending in 1954. His introduction into written story-telling came when he was aged 15. At that age he wrote a story about a mystery aboard a yacht. This story achieved a house mark, one of the only two he gained. As the headmaster congratulated him so the author received a severe reprimand from the English master for using the word 'grub' instead of the word 'food'. Notwithstanding the reprimand, the author went on to write non-fiction magazine articles for maritime and in-house publications with books on wartime ships and ship building, 19th century village education and a history of horticulture. This is his first book of fiction.

W.F. Kim-Henry

THE BARE ENIGMA OF MURDER

AUSTIN MACAULEY PUBLISHERS™
LONDON * CAMBRIDGE * NEW YORK * SHARJAH

Copyright © W.F. Kim-Henry 2024

The right of W.F. Kim-Henry to be identified as the author of this work has been asserted by the author in accordance with Sections 77 and 78 of the Copyright, Designs and Patents Act 1988.

All rights reserved. No part of this publication may be reproduced, stored in a retrieval system, or transmitted in any form or by any means, electronic, mechanical, photocopying, recording, or otherwise, without the prior permission of the publishers.

Any person who commits any unauthorised act in relation to this publication may be liable to criminal prosecution and civil claims for damages.

This is a work of fiction. Names, characters, businesses, places, events, locales, and incidents are either the products of the author's imagination or used in a fictitious manner. Any resemblance to actual persons, living or dead, or actual events is purely coincidental.

A CIP catalogue record for this title is available from the British Library.

ISBN 9781528940511 (Paperback)
ISBN 9781528940771 (ePub e-book)

www.austinmacauley.com

First Published 2024
Austin Macauley Publishers Ltd®
1 Canada Square
Canary Wharf
London
E14 5AA

Chapter 1
The Life and Machinations of 'D' Division

The fitful spring sunshine made patterns on the parade room floor as the windows let the alternating sunshine and then clouds pick up the shining boots of the ten men and two women lined up facing a desk bearing the control room message logs.

At 1:45 pm precisely, the hall echoed to the sound of 'Parade, parade 'shun' came the order from the tour sergeant followed by the order 'Present your appointments'.

As one the twelve men and women then held out their pocketbook pen and, for the smart ones a pencil with their truncheons, short ones for the women, warrant cards, handcuffs and whistles.

The sergeant then turned to the duty police inspector who was sitting at the desk seemingly studying his hands and in no particular hurry to perform his 'Oh, so trying' task as he told the hovering ever-watchful staff sergeant when he slowly lifted his buttocks from his comfortable chair.

"Ready for your inspection, sir," intoned the sergeant in a voice barely concealing his irritation at having an inspector there at all. It was noticeable that on the early tour the inspector was missing until, at the least, 7:30 and thereby avoiding the 5:45 a.m. tour parade carried out by the sergeant without supervision.

The inspector lifted his eyes from the floor and made his way to the rear of the assembled constables and looked from their footwear to their hair. He then walked to the front and looked at each person likewise from bottom to top. He turned away spoke softly to the sergeant and sat down again pushing the message books towards the sergeant.

The sergeant ignored the books and picked up his board with the details of the patrols and point duty locations that his men & women would perform during the next eight hours. He then issued the order, "Stand at ease," then walked to each person and told them their destiny which each constable wrote in their pocketbook. Amongst other duties, he ordered two of his men to patrol the dock area of the city and liaise with the security guards at the docks and following the whispered instruction of his inspector admonished one of them for the length of his hair.

"Att-en-shun left turn, dismiss." With these words from the sergeant, the late tour parade was over.

And as he walked away from his arduous duty, the inspector turned to the staff sergeant and said, "Staff, how busy are you today?"

Before answering the staff sergeant thought of the ancient adage, "Always look busy or someone somewhere will find you a job and not to your liking."

"I'm very busy working out a roster to accommodate the reduction in working hours from forty-four to forty-two hours a week, which bye-the-way is yet another job which you idle sods have offloaded on to an idiot like me. OK, what do you want me to help you out with?"

The reply was, "Could you spend an hour or so down at the docks later on today and visit the men down there, liaise with the guards and sign off their logbooks and perhaps kick arse just to keep them on their toes?"

"Not asking much are we?" replied the staff sergeant followed by, "You owe me one chum, in fact, more than one. Are you going to ask for time off or just legging it when the corridor Mafia go home?"

The corridor Mafia related to the occupants of the offices along the main corridor from the control room containing the central offices, the offices of the superintendents, chief inspectors and the senior Criminal Investigation officers.

"Legging it," was the straightforward reply from the inspector.

The staff sergeants parting comment as he made his way to his office behind the control room was, "I do hope that she is worth getting caught for!"

Staff Sergeant Hamish Fergusson went into his office closing the door softly behind him, had a good stretch then casually looked at the jumble of papers on his desk, sighed deeply and lighted his King Edward cigar and almost fell into his chair with the thought running through his mind, "Another day another dollar."

Into the third draw on his cigar, the door opened with the Tour sergeant stood there. "Missed a trick?" he enquired before proffering the control room logs and message book and the sergeants diary for Staff to initial as having read and understood.

Fergusson then initialled the relevant page. "Anything to read?" Mr Fergusson enquired.

"Bugger all," came the reply.

So, with confidence in his sergeant, he scribbled his collar tab number in the comments column then said, "After tea, I will be going to the docks to see your chaps down there."

"Why is the white collar not doing it?" came the question from the sergeant.

"Your inspector will be unavailable after tea, or to be precise immediately after the Mafia have gone home," came the reply.

"Authorised or just legging it?" enquired the sergeant of Staff Sergeant Fergusson.

"Legging," was the brief reply.

Inadvertently taking a deep inhale of the cigar smoke, the sergeant let himself out of the office door with the observation that "He'll get his arse scorched one day 'specially if you stop covering for 'im."

A little smile crossed Fergusson's lips as he thought, covering for him? Slowly, slowly catchee monkey. Knowledge both positive and even negative is power in any language or occupation particularly policing.

Looking at his wristwatch Fergusson noted that it was only twenty minutes after two, then had another stretch and deep puff on his cigar before booking a car to use on his visit to the docks later.

Booking a car was problematic as the Yard manager who was responsible for all outside the station works and transport availability was a former constable now a civilian who did his very best to annoy or obstruct those who had been in authority over him during his service days.

"Staff here, Mr Prudow, please have a car or another vehicle available for me about 6:00 p.m.," which seemed to be a reasonable request.

However, the request was met with the truculent statement from Prudow, "I ain't got no cars or anyfink else except a bike. We 'as six cars per shift, one for point duty relief, one for patrol change, two for CID and two for the senior white collars, and the God almighty you might fink you is but you ain't 'aving the super's Jag, see. I'll 'ave a bike yer for ee at 6:00."

"You will have the inspectors car available for me at 6:00 p.m., Prudow, as he will have no further use for it; is that understood?"

Prudow finished the exchange with, "I was a PC with 'im; he was an idle sod then and nothing 'as changed 'as it?"

The click of the receiver was the only reply Prudow had. Fergusson presumed that he was referring to the duty inspector.

The docks security was maintained by their own guards with the dock owners paying for regular patrols of their dock and sheds and overall supervision of their guards by 'D' division officers. Staff Sergeant Fergusson parked the police car alongside the security office then went to the police hut nearby and let himself in to find constable 263 Dobie having his sandwiches inside. A brief talk ensued relating to patrols, the location of his mate and where he intended patrolling during the remainder of his tour.

Fergusson went out to speak to the guard at the dock entrance. In the course of the conversation, a car stopped as it was about to leave the dock. The driver wound down the window and hailed the staff sergeant with, "Hey, Hamish, long time no see, not chasing international rogues anymore?"

The car driver was one of the immigration officers for the port. Fergusson's face brightened up as he recognised his chum from their youthful time together at sea before embarking on their subsequent careers. He went across to the car and the two got into a conversation of past days at sea and their present occupations.

"When was our last job together? Enquired Dick Young. The Yank stowaway heading for Ireland so say to study the Book of Kells," was the reply. That blighter was heading for the IRA no doubt about it was Dicks considered opinion. He continued, "But we got him, the only downside was that the taxpayer had to pay his airfare back to the States, but that's the way it goes."

As the staff sergeant looked up so the involuntary blaspheme was uttered as he declared, "Christ."

In a hushed voice, he then asked, "What is that?"

Dick craned his head around to see in the direction that his chum was looking towards the dock.

The gate guard just gaped as a person, almost as an apparition appeared walking in the middle of the dock road. The person was over six feet tall, very skinny, dressed in a beret an off white raincoat reaching down to the lower calf then a gap before the bare legs carried feet in thick socks in sandals.

As this whatever approached the staring men at the gate it smiled and despite a maritime career as well as a police service of nine years, never had Hamish Fergusson witnessed such an unnerving sight.

The person opened their mouth and gave a very broad smile with their teeth being stainless steel.

After the really frightening smile, the person reached into the pockets of the raincoat and produced what turned out to be packets of Russian cigarettes and exposed a huge gold bracelet on its wrist.

It was at this point that it became obvious that the person was female and unable to speak English as she gestured for the men to accept the cigarettes. Staff Sergeant Fergusson put on his best British incorruptible Police persona. "No, thank you, ma'am," he told her as he waved his hands in a sign of rejection.

She again proffered the cigarettes and the constable who had by now joined the group began to put out his hand. His hand only got as far as a third of a stretch before he noticed the look of his staff sergeant, not a look to be taken lightly if he wished to continue a promising career at 'D' Division under his staff sergeant. Hands are promptly withdrawn! However, the dock guard was not so hesitant not only did he grab one packet, he had both without a hint of any guilt. The woman gave another terrifying grimace and headed down the road out of the dock.

Turning to his chum the immigration officer, the staff sergeant informed him of the fact that he had heard of people, particularly Russians having steel teeth but the sight of them for real was very unnerving, to say the least.

Dick Young then told him, "She is one of three radio operators, and I suspect the ship's commissar; she silently appears whenever I interview the ship's master or officers and don't be fooled by the smiles and hand gestures; she does understand and obviously speaks English. Whenever I said anything contentious she would then gabble in Russian. Strangely, although I do not speak Russian my instinct is that Russian is not her first language in that she sometimes has to keep repeating her conversational words with her fellows aboard the ship. I have met her aboard the timber boat on previous occasions but I haven't seen her ashore before. Just mind that she doesn't bite you Hamish, happy days."

As he went to drive away the staff sergeant stopped him and asked for a copy of the crew list of the Russian 'Timber boat'. Reaching into his briefcase, Dick produced a crew list and underlined the woman's name written in English Helga Weismuller.

The staff sergeant then walked with the constable around his patrol patch, not a popular course of action with this particular constable and even less so with his men and women when he was a Tour sergeant with twelve people to supervise and enough guile to keep the inspector off of his back.

In his day as a constable, it was unusual to see a sergeant the whole shift. In those cases, the order of the day was, out of the earshot of the inspector, keep your book open and your mouth closed. In layman's terms, it translated as to make no entries in your pocketbook and say nothing until your patrol is completed. Then the constable would present his or her pocketbook to be signed on a blank page at the time to suit the sergeants non-existent patrol and the constable would then make up his patrol diary to suit the place of the sergeant's mythical visit.

The only upset to this arrangement was if the PC attended an incident without his sergeant however, a smart sergeant could get around this by creating his own make-believe potentially more serious detraction to his duty of supervising his men.

The springtime evening was beginning to fade as they approached the Lock gates. Halfway across Fergusson became aware firstly of the Russian vessel berthed stern to the adjacent Dry-dock and then of a man on top of a ladder against the post of one of the arc lights surrounding the sea lock. Addressing his constable he told him to enquire who this chap was and what was his business up a lamp post. "Oh, he is a ship photographer, I have met him before photographing ships." After a pause the constable continued, "He is very good, staff."

"I am well aware that photographers can be very skilled and arty but going up a lamp post does not appear to be either skilled or a particular art form," the staff sergeant declared.

The PC went over to the man and asked him to come over and see his staff sergeant.

"Good evening, sergeant, I'm John Crocker. I am a ships photographer." With that, he produced a licence from the dock company authorising him to photograph in and around the docks system out of normal working hours and to offer any photographs to the Company free of charge and free of copyright.

"Fine," said Staff Sergeant Fergusson, "so kindly explain why you were up that arc light pole?"

Proffering his card to Staff Fergusson the photographer said, "My card, this is my home number."

The photographer explained that his intention was to mount cameras on the four poles which would cover the expanse of the locks. When a vessel went into locks from the dock he had a system in place to remotely set off each or all the cameras to record the slow descent of the vessel below the walls of the dock.

This idea was to capture all the differing reflecting lights sky and water from four different angles. If the weather was suitable he intended to use the same system for vessels entering the locks. If it all worked he would hold an exhibition for a different vessel in the four seasons of the year hoping that there would be snow in the forthcoming winter.

The staff sergeant enquired which vessel he hoped to photograph?

"The Russian timber boat, she is due out tonight on the rising tide if it works on her I will then try it on the big refrigerated cargo liners." He concluded with the opinion, "They are beautiful ships."

"Good night and good luck," were the parting words from the staff sergeant as he and his constable made their way to the nearby transit shed where the constable made up his pocketbook including the meeting with the photographer under the supervision of his sergeant. The staff sergeant took his book and in the fading light read what he had written noting, in particular, the fact that he was supervised by his staff sergeant when dealing with the photographer.

The staff sergeant let a smile cross his face as he read the cop-out should anything go wrong with the photographer. He was tempted to say to the constable, "In the event of anything going wrong you will say, Oh no, your honour; at the time of the incident, I was under the direct supervision of my staff sergeant but thought better of it. In similar circumstances some years ago, he might well have done the same."

His mind went back to the time with two other constables he was sent to break up a fight between Norwegian and German seamen in the street outside of a pub. Blood and guts were everywhere with bodies lying in a quite haphazard arrangement all over the road and pavement and the sergeant arriving on his cycle at the scene and without looking to his left or right, carefully cycled in and around the bodies then he continued cycling into the pitch-black night.

Not a word or sign that he has seen or heard anything untoward. This was a sergeant who had been decorated for bravery at Arnhem and after capture had simply walked away from his captors back to the British lines. When Hamish and the other constables returned to the station the sergeant was sitting at his desk behind a copy of the 'Times'.

"Cor sarg, that was quite a dust-up outside the Goose and Garter," said a very naive constable. The paper slowly lowered until two very dark eyes and even darker eyebrows appeared and the voice, a deep baritone said with a certain menace.

"How many prisoners are in the cells?"

The reply came from the night tour control room constable, "None sergeant."

The Times was lowered once again, and the baritone voice asked, "What reference is there in the control logs and message books?" The Times returned to its original position.

Again from the control room officer, "None sergeant."

For the third and final time, the 'Times' was lowered, and the baritone voice declared, "There is no record of any incident outside of any Public House. Refreshments will now be taken."

That should have been the last word but the stupid constable began, "But sarg you...."

Hamish dragged him out of the office before he could dig his own grave. After the naive constable had been removed from the presence of the Sergeant he was told that (1) never call that sergeant 'Sarg', (2) do not interrupt that sergeant when he is reading his 'Times', and (3) expect to be given crap jobs for the rest of the week. And surely the dire prediction came to pass.

Smart arsed little bugger, he'll go far that boy thought Fergusson as he signed the constables oh, so accurate pocketbook.

As he left the constable he told him, "Be at the gate at 9:45 p.m., and I will take you and your chum back to division."
With that, he left the constable and went looking for his mate who if he had walked his beat in the usual fashion would be about a ten-minute walk away. Eventually, he found his man and signed his pocketbook and gave him the same instruction about being at the gate to be returned to the police station.

The staff sergeant made his way back towards the entrance gate of the dock looking at the Passenger/cargo liners at each berth and wondering if he would have been better off staying at sea. Every time that he came to the dock the same thought crossed his mind and when he had business on a particular New Zealand trading liner only to find that the captain was his chum at sea the temptation to go back unsettled him for months on end.

At the gate, he found a new guard on duty and he spent a good half an hour chin-wagging with the guard and heard much of his life story as the guard in between stopping and enquired into the purpose for a vehicle leaving the dock and collecting a pass if necessary and checking the vehicles entering the dock and the nature of their business. Staff thought, "I bet this guard wishes me in hell for standing here causing him to work rather than sitting down just waving the traffic in and out on a Friday evening."

The staff sergeant was busy looking down the road for the appearance of his constables as they finished their patrols when he heard a vehicle pull up at the inward barrier. Turning to have a curious look at whatever was behind him, he was fascinated to see a white Morris Commercial van at the barrier. Staff did a double-take as he was drawn to the passenger when she smiled at the guard as the driver explained that he was the agent for the Russian timber ship Ordjonykitso and as the vessel was about to sail he was returning a radio officer to the ship and complete the paperwork before she sailed.

Staff was amazed to see the gate lights reflecting off of a full set of steel teeth. He was desperately trying to remember the woman's name to enquire if she had enjoyed her time out of the dock to let her know that he knew exactly who she was and see if she answered in English or understood what he had said. As he struggled to find where he had put the crew list it dawned on him that if she was a radio officer she would have understood English anyway.

The guard lifted the barrier and the ancient van drove into the dock. "Did I hear aright that he claimed to be the agent for the Russian vessel?" Fergusson enquired of the guard.

"Yup," was the reply.

Staff then asked, "Who is he and who does he work for?"

The reply came, "Jones & Stallard so he said. He is a regular agent for both the Russian and East German ships. He's been here for ages."

The staff sergeant then said to the guard, "I can't imagine a Shipping agency using a Morris Commercial van of possibly 1954 vintage as a conveyance for their agents. When it comes out make sure that the vehicle is searched and the identity of that chap is discovered."

He continued, "That passenger, have you seen her before?"

The guard replied, "Yeh, she regularly comes in on that ship."

"How come if she is often here that your mate who was on here about eighteen hundred hours had never seen her before?" Staff asked the guard.

"Dunno," was the short reply that was then cheerfully followed by, "I won't be yer when they come out."

"Then tell your relief that I will check if the vehicle has been checked and who the driver is OK?"

Truculent silence was all that staff was met with, he then emphasised with a noted display of authority, "I said OK. Do you clearly understand?"

Reluctantly, the guard acknowledged that he did understand.

The staff sergeant picked up his constables and returned then to the Station where he checked the night tour men with the Tour sergeant before going to his office taking off his jacket, lighting a cigar and relaxing in his chair before going through the paperwork that has amassed during the two to ten shift and filling in his diary which included every detail of his visit to the docks.

As he was about to make his way home he remembered his instructions relating to the white van at the docks and rang up the security hut. Yes, his instructions had been followed, and the instructions were given to the gatekeeper, but up to then, the van had not reappeared. He then made a note in the Tour diary to check that his instruction at the docks had been followed and to ring up Jones & Stallard and find out if they employed the man and if an old white Morris Commercial was theirs.

With a cheery wave at the Tour sergeant as he locked his office, knowing that someone somewhere would have a key to his door and desk and be in there overnight to read what was written about them or anyone and anything else, he let himself out of the building for the weekend.

All was quiet and in good order on a fine and bright Spring Monday morning when at exactly at 8:54 dressed in uniform except for a hacking jacket replacing the uniform jacket Superintendent Fredrick Cole approached the Divisional Police station door climbing the steps he made his usual grand entrance, shot his cuffs, nodded his head to no one and pursed his lips as he approached the control room counter. Sliding back the glass doors he thrust his head through and depending whether it was one of his men, the over forty-fives or a 'bit of a kid' he would enquire in a soft tone or a harsh tone, "Anything new?"

If it was 'his' men, he would address them by their Christian name, to the rest before they could answer him he would have turned on his heel and walked towards his office passing the Divisional office en route.

At the stable office door, there would be the same performance, if his chum Jake was in there he would pass the time of day, anyone else he would just ignore. The unlocking his office door would correspond with the arrival of the chief inspector/acting superintendent at the office next door. No sign of recognition would be acknowledged between them.

Superintendent Cole, often called 'Old King Cole', after entering his office would unlock his wardrobe hang up his hacking jacket and put on his uniform jacket containing his precious medal ribbons. Sitting at his desk he would rescue his desk keys from his trouser pocket and unlock the desk drawers.

Quite why he went to such trouble with his keys was a bit of a mystery. Access could be obtained to all of the superintendents locked places, particularly by his chum Jake in the clerk's office. It was custom and practice in the police station that every one of sergeant rank had an illicit set of keys to all doors, desks and filing cabinets. No self-respecting senior sergeant would survive without the ability to censor, destroy or change any files kept about them or a negative assessment of their ability without being able to covertly tamper with such documents to improve their lot.

After Supt Cole had opened his desk drawer he would get a packet of Capstan Full Strength cigarettes and light up taking a deep lungful of tobacco smoke then spend the next thirty seconds doing his best to bring up his lungs. As the first coughing spasm subsided so in would saunter Chief Inspector Stuart Thomas, and with his foot, he would hook the leg of the chair to position the chair between the superintendent's wardrobe and his desk.

He would sit on the chair search his pockets for his tobacco pouch, then find his pipe in the other pocket and after filling and lighting it lean back in the chair with legs outstretched and ankles crossed and except for lunch and lavatory visits, there he would remain all day unless a major incident occurred hence his unauthorised title of 'Olympic Torch', as is the case with a torch, the chief inspector/acting superintendent never went out.

When major incidents or fractious prisoners occurred C/I Thomas excelled without shouting, waving of arms or, God forbid, physical involvement. The words Calm and Collected should be engraved on his tombstone.

Whereas Cole was belligerent, confrontational and loud so Thomas was the exact opposite both achieving their aims in their own characteristic ways. That being said it was not unknown when his position or involvement was questioned for Tommo to explode which on the rare occasions that it did happen cheered his men considerably and always achieved the desired goal.

"Morning, Fred, morning, Tom," came the reply as they settled into their roles for the day.

"Is he in?" enquired Cole.

"Yes, just after me," replied Thomas. They were referring to the Divisional chief superintendent who had an office suit off of the main lobby the title suit meant that he had a dressing room, sitting room very large office with comfortable chairs for guests and a lavatory, a shower and his personal secretary.

All in all vastly superior accommodation to the chief constable. The chief superintendent was, as befits a former wartime submarine commander, a quiet man and a Knight of the Realm who allowed his senior officers to run his division as they saw fit subject to occasional adjustments on the tiller at his behest.

A knock at Cole's office door heralded Jake from the office with the logs and message books for inspection by the superintendent.

"Thanks, Jake," said Cole.

"Anything I should look into?" Jake replied.

"Nothing much, a couple of prisoners fighting over an old slag, We had a complaint from the docks that a vehicle was impeding cargo work and could we get it moved…"

Jake was stopped in full flow as Cole interjected, "Move a vehicle in the dock." His voice rose as he continued, "What in the bloody 'ell do they think we are, tell them to move their own bloody vehicles. Christ whatever next, they'll ask us to escort dockers home on payday, bastards." That ended the conversation.

Staff Sergeant Fergusson began his day at 8 o'clock and read the message books and logs as he settled down for an hour of peace and quiet before the 'white shirts' arrived and no doubt would then spoil his day. At 9:15, he mistakenly thought that his day could be reasonable after he had established that the Shipping Agents Jones and Stallard did not own a Morris Commercial van and had their agent was aboard the Russian vessel fifteen minutes before it sailed.

They had no knowledge of a van or a man posing as their employee. With this information, the staff sergeant made out a brief report and was taking the copy to the CID room for their attention. As he passed the office of Cole he heard a not unusual loud shout "Staff," a pause, then "Come here now." He put his head around the door noting the crossed ankles of Mr Thomas. Looking straight at Cole and said, "Sir?"

Cole hesitated then continued, "I've just been told by Jake that the docks are complaining that a van is in the way. Now I read that our men have reported this vehicle twice this weekend and nothing has been done about it. Why not?" Before answering Staff Sergeant Fergusson looked around the corner at the chief inspector and said, "Good morning, sir." Thomas looked up and replied, "Good morning, my boy. Everything alright?"

"Yes, thank you, sir. Depending on the reaction of the super when I tell him that I have not been here all weekend," replied Fergusson.

"Oi, I'm sitting 'ere and this superintendent is not some third person Fergusson, whether or not you were 'ere at the weekend is no excuse. You've been 'ere for an hour and I say again why has nothing been done about it and why have you done nothing about it in the past hour?" Staff went to open his mouth to reply when Cole interjected with "Not read the books, have you? What have you been doing?"

Staff replied, "I have been investigating the van and its alleged association with a Shipping Agency and I am about to put this Billy-do on the desk of CID," a long pause then added "Sir."

Cole, part defeated once again by the staff sergeant, noisily and copiously cleared his throat as he dismissed the staff sergeant with the words, "Get on with it then." As the staff sergeant turned to go the chief inspector gave him a wink as he chewed on the stem of his half-burnt pipe of tobacco.

Superintendent Cole and the staff sergeant had come to grief several years before when Fergusson was a constable and Cole was a new inspector on the 'A' division. Cole made a demotion creating mistake and PC Fergusson witnessed it. Fergusson never said anything about it but Cole spent the rest of their time together trying unsuccessfully to get some mistake or misdemeanour against the then constable to equal the 'Account'.

It must have been a shock for the superintendent when appointed to the 'D' division to find Staff Sergeant Fergusson with his own office and a very comfortable chair in residence. It did not help the situation when the chief superintendent introduced Cole to his staff including Staff Sergeant Fergusson and in so doing remarked on his "Notable maritime and academic career."

Hamish went into the CID office to deliver his note and saw the detective chief Inspector looking rather glum.

The broad smile from the staff sergeant was not reciprocated by DCI Broadweir. "Shall I go out and come in again Harry?" asked the staff sergeant. He continued, "Your face looks like something akin to a slapped arse chum."

Harry opened his mouth to reply and for a second no sound came. He coughed and said in the most dejected voice, "As of now I am going to headquarters. That's a doddle of a job why so sad, we'll give you a good CID send-off. You'll be incapable for a week," said Hamish and then enquired "when are you going?"

Harry's lips barely moved as he said, "Now."

"Bloody Hell, why?" asked Hamish "What have you done?"

"Nothing," came the reply, Harry continued, "Something has gone badly wrong at HQ and the detective chief super is in with Cole and the boss now. I'm to hand over my files to my DI now and go to HQ by noon."

"I'm so sorry to see you go chum and genuinely I will miss you and thanks so much for your support in dealing with." At that point, Hamish jerked his thumb at the now-closed office door of Superintendent Cole.

"Any time you want anything from down here please let me know." Turning to the detective inspector, Hamish concluded with "anything you want please just shout."

"All I need now is to find out who my new DCI will be," Ron Wilkins said. "He won't be as good as Harry that's for sure, oh, bugger it all." With a flailing of his arms, the conversation in the CID office came to an end.

On his return journey past the superintendent's office the concerned staff sergeant, purely by chance, of course, heard as he walked so slowly past the unusually closed-door Cole shouting, "No, Bill, I ain't 'aving it, you're taking him away for no good reason and replacing Broadweir with a DI. If this goes on I will end up with a DC in charge of CID. Anyhow, what does the silent one have to say about it?"

The silent one was the divisional Chief Superintendent, Sir Simon Bates, DSO & Bar DSC. The inherited title, Knight, thus 'Sir' was not used as a title in normal police work.

The detective superintendent replied, "When I told him he said to inform you and any operational alterations would be dealt with by you."

Cole replied, "I bet he did but I ain't having a…?"

At that point, the staff sergeant was aware that he was being watched by Jake from the office stable door and decided to saunter towards his office.

Jake looked at the staff sergeant and said, with much sucking of teeth and the 'knowing' look, "If you want to know the full story you can ask me later."

"Balls," was the reply to the offer which as usual would come with very long strings attached.

Hamish went into the control room with the registration number from the Morris van and told the control sergeant to 'run the number plate through the Police National Computer and the Licensing people for a name and address.

He went into his office and lighted a cigar, plonked himself in his chair and a timid knock came on his door, it opened and Mrs Briggs, a tiny bent lady, one of the station cleaners of indeterminate age came in with "A cup of coffee for you dear." Mrs Briggs was a true British stalwart. Hamish knew that she had retired years before he arrived and was working there quite illegally and was not on the payroll or insured but paid through petty cash which Jake and his sergeant in the office fiddled from 'Expenses'.

Mrs Briggs appeared to have no relatives and lived in council accommodation and her police station was her life and all the sergeants and officers were her friends and they worshipped her. It was a different side to policing that the public never saw and even less believe.

Even Chief Superintendent Bates chose to ignore the fact that Mrs Briggs was probable nearer ninety than eighty. No questions were ever asked but everyone in authority prayed that Mrs Briggs would not die on the job. Imagine the falsification of evidence should that happen.

As Hamish lifted the cup to his lips so his door was pushed open and one of the control room officers came in with the response to the checks for the Morris van. "The vehicle is not on PNC, but at Licensing, it is registered to a Maurice Van White of 238 Windrush Hill."

Staff Sergeant Fergusson looked at the constable as the constable looked at him. They burst out laughing then looked again at the details of ownership.

The staff sergeant broke the mirth with the observation that this was a wind-up if ever he had heard one. "Maurice Van White, the owner of a Morris van? Surely even a bonehead at Licensing could see that this was a non-runner."

"Yer staff, that was a beauty, a non-runner." And with that, he burst into what appeared to be uncontrollable laughter.

The staff sergeant came out with the observation that the address was also rubbish when he said 238 Windrush Hill. That's tripe, Windrush Hill ends at 180, "I know that as I was keeping a watch on 180 when I was in a cold stinking van during my days in the Street Offences Squad watching for old whores using it as a brothel. If the duty inspector is around get him to see me please."

"He's 'yer sarg, I'll get him. If the office door had been closed the opening of it would have been somewhat akin to the grand entrance in a Wagnerian opera. The duty inspector threw himself in and declared in a voice loud enough so that all in sundry in and around the control room could hear him put the staff sergeant in his allotted pigeon hole.

"Since when did a staff sergeant summon an inspector to see him. I am your superior, not your lackey. Now apologise." Staff Sergeant Fergusson still in his comfortable chair looked at the puce faced inspector and equally loudly replied "I do apologise for treating you as my lackey and I will try my best to erase my memories of your indiscretions," long pause then, "Sir."

Now can we get on with the matter in hand another long pause then 'Sir'.

"We have a van at the docks which the superintendent is concerned about. The particulars of the owner are rubbish and fraudulent and I was about to ask you to authorise the van to be forced open to ascertain if there are any details of the owner inside but I will go to the superintendent and ask him if you will not authorise the opening," Hamish told him. Another long pause followed by the demeaning rendition of 'Sir'.

"Alright," the inspector agreed, "open it with minimum force." As he turned to leave the office Fergusson said "I am not the Tour sergeant, you'd best instruct him to deal with it promptly." The long pause then 'Sir' to a by-now empty doorway. The inspectors head reappeared and he said in a quiet voice, "Will you stop giving me bloody orders?"

"Sir," was the totally meaningless reply.

As the inspector left so another body, namely that of Jake from the office appeared and threw a piece of paper on the desk with the explanation that it was with the fondest love from the super. "Sorry it's a bit late should have done this last week."

Hamish unfolded the note and it commanded him to roster all campaign medal-wearing constables and sergeants on to the day tour on 22 May for annual parade and inspection by some 'Worthy' or other.

This day was the day of the year for the superintendent. He was able to wear his array of medals and escort the 'Worthy' proffering knowledge of each display as the recipients of the attention of the 'Super' and the 'Worthy' stretched themselves taller and pulled in the age-induced ever-increasing paunches. The superintendent had a general dislike of any mariner, with the staff sergeant naturally included and in particular any wartime serving mariner. By the virtue of them serving in all theatres of war in some shape or other they, pro-rata, had more campaign medals than the other two services.

In order that the mariners did not steal the show with their well-earned 'ironwear' displayed in the front row, Cole had them relegated to the second and if possible third row so that the Army and Air force were the star performers. Hamish smiled to himself as he thought of the former Sergeant Major Cole at the parade as he barked, "Front rank… shun," and with his swagger stick under his arm, he would escort the 'Worthy' along the rank until two thirds along he would poke his head through the front rank to holler, "Second rank… wait for ittt… shun."

Almost every year the various 'Worthies' almost jumped out of their socks or stockings at this unexpected bellow. When a third of the way along the second rank Cole would put his head between two in the front rank and holler, "Front rank… front rank staaand at ease."

This performance would be repeated through the ranks of officers. The truly galling part of the Parade was when he brought the 'Worthy' back to the Saluting podium there would be the chief superintendent with more than double the medal of Cole waiting to greet whoever.

These parades were a nuisance to those involved and particularly to Fergusson and his rosters but they did sometimes have a humorous side for the men and when the tales circulated throughout the entire Division.

A fine example was when the 'Worthy' was so drunk that Cole had to hold him up as he inspected the men and finally gave up after the third rank had been done. His speech was a three-minute repetition of five words which included a fine body of men. After a whisper from the boss, he stuttered and out of the blue muttered, "Women, women, wo… men." He then collapsed into the chair.

On another occasion, a vertically challenged mayor spent his inspection standing on tip-toe to look at the medals. The incident that really caused great difficulty in the men of the second rank maintaining a straight face was when a titled lady was inspecting them and her knicker elastic failed and a pair of expensive French-looking silk unmentionables followed the laws of gravity. Without hesitation and never breaking step, the lady simply stepped out of them and seemingly unperturbed carried on her inspection.

Imagine the poor officer whom she next chose to stop and talk to trying his best not to openly laugh as she enquired of him, "Just how do you manage to keep your end up in modern policing?" C/I Thomas, part of her entourage, swiftly bent down and recovered the underwear unsuccessfully trying to conceal it between his unworn brown kid gloves and yet still keeping his swagger stick under his arm.

The chief inspector endured with good grace the continual ribbing about his part in the recovery of the ladies knickers. Some of the printables included. "Did they fit you, sir? Are you sure that you returned them to her ladyship, sir? Did she blush when you handed them back, sir? Are you sure that Mrs Thomas knows that you have another woman's drawers in your office, sir?"

The truth of the handing back was simply that he handed the knickers to a woman sergeant and after the inspection and speech, sans knickers, the sergeant offered the lady the ladies facilities and there the hand over took place. A source of reliable rumour has it that when the lady was reunited with a small part of her wardrobe she pulled up her dress, looked at her unfettered nether region and said, "Well, well, fortunately, this is not the winter; thank you, my dear!"

Staff Sergeant Fergusson was at a crossroads of administration, did he get on with trying to fit a forty-two-hour week into the same system as the present forty-four hours or move all the Tours and day men who had medals into a two-hour slot on 22 May while his mind was still wondering what was going on in CID and the superintendent's office.

Chapter 2
Enter Ma'am and Murders

His conflict of rosters times the matters along the Mafia alleyway was brought to a halt with a gentle knock on his door. For some unknown reason, probably the pressure, he barked, "Enter."

The door opened and he lifted his eyes from the mess of paperwork before him and saw a very attractive woman standing in the doorway with the sunlight from the control room outlining her tall lithe figure.

"Hello, Hamish, can I come in?" the woman asked. "Well, I'll be buggered," Hamish spluttered as the woman said, "I sincerely hope that you will not be buggered on my account, my dear. Well, can I come in?"

Hamish gasping for breath said, "Close the door," and signalled her to a chair to the side of his desk.

"Freya Douglas Gore Hamilton if I am not mistaken," he uttered, followed by, "delighted that I am to see you but, what are you doing in this backwater? Are you here for work or just to please me? I haven't set eyes on you since October." Detective Inspector Freya Douglas Gore Hamilton replied with a laugh, "Is this meeting too soon dear?" Then she told Hamish Fergusson, "You look harassed. Relax now I am here.

As far as anyone knew, Hamish and Freya first met at the Hendon training school as probationers. They had a very close association and worked together through the two-year probation period for Fergusson and six months for Freya as she'd spent eighteen months at Oxford on a Graduate police scheme. As a 'fresher', she met Hamish with him in his final year, studying without any subsidy before they met up again and joined the 'A' division. Whilst there they had many adventures and were considered a pair by many including sergeants who did their best to ensure that they worked different shifts which did make dating difficult but not impossible.

The two of them just sat looking at each other. Freya broke the silence when she said, "I wonder just who you have upset to still be a Staff Sergeant?" Hamish replied, "I have been offered an inspectors job for about four years but this job suits me at the moment. Here I have much more power than any inspector. I can make their life hell if I chose to."

"How?" She asked.

"I have the position to control all of their men and I determine just who they get all the good or all the bad or if the inspector tows my line, the good 70% the bad, 30%," he said with no little amount of satisfaction.

"My power comes from having something on everyone from recruit to divisional superintendent. While they shout and flaunt their ranks above me, like the clerk Jake, I can embarrass or break any of them whenever they are no longer of use to me 'Furthermore dear' he added 'I am not a Freemason, a certain first-class passport to officer rank, or for that matter, some sergeants rank as well."

Freya then said, "My Father's a Freemason and you know it Fergusson; careful just what you imply." He looked at her and laughed as another silence came between them.

The silence was broken when after all the intervening years he brought up the subject of their probation and the need in the Force that all officers should have a swimming certificate in lifesaving. "Do you remember old sergeant Roles the swimming instructor? What a bugger he was forcing us into that freezing water at seven and chasing a brick in uniform."

"What made you think of that?" she asked.

He told her, "I think that it was the first time I took any notice of your craftiness."

"Why?" She again asked. "Because you WPCs must have had the longest continuous periods in history. In the months that I spent in those baths, you and your mates were always sat at the end of the pool in full uniform while the rest of us froze.

Every time Roles asked why you were not swimming, like parrots you all said, "Time of the month sarg'. It stuck in my mind. Did you get your cert?"

"The reason that we were allegedly on our periods was simply to drag out our time away from work which after teaching generations of us, Roles must have been well aware of. When we were threatened with being chucked out of the Force if we didn't get our cert suddenly our periods were not such an issue," she concluded.

Another silence ensued only broken when like an embarrassed schoolboy he told her, "I note your promotion since we last met in October. What are you now about twenty-eight? And a Detective Inspector, quite a meteoric rise particularly for a woman in so short a time."

"Acting Chief," Freya interrupted to correct him. Hamish, ignoring the interruption continued, "It is strange that other than our special annual day, in all these years we have never worked or really been together."

"Why?" Freya asked. Then she continued, "For my part, I kept clear of you, and I suspect that you kept away from me for much the same reason.

"What has come up?" he asked her, "I've come here to…"

Before she could answer his question the office door flew open and Cole barged in. Fergusson looked at the puce faced officer with the vein in his temple protruding and plainly throbbing and said, "Thanks for knocking, sir."

"Where is that roster for the parade?" shouted Cole.

Hamish, with Freya making this surprise visit, was in no mood to put up with Coles temper. He replied, "It's not even looked at yet and won't be for a couple of days."

The superintendent looked as if he was about to explode, "Why not you've been sitting on it for a bloody week and I want it now, d'ya hear? Now bloody sergeant, now. You sit behind a desk all bloody day and do bugger all, you're useless. I've had it up to here, and it's only halfway through the morning, and now, they are ordering me to have another bloody woman in the station so I don't want any excuses from you. Be in my office in ten minutes."

Hamish replied, 'If you will take a breath."

The superintendent interrupted, "Take a bloody breath. I'll squeeze the breath out of you, you conceited bastard, my office in ten minutes." Fergusson stood up behind his desk and thrusting out his jaw said, "Your message was only delivered to me less than half an hour ago by your dear friend Jake so how in the bloody hell could it be ready in ten minutes?"

Cole looked startled and promptly changed his attack as he was flogging a dead horse with his roster argument.

"And bloody women as well, what sort of a sodding Division am I supposed to be running? They'll have a bloody crèche down here next." Hamish interrupted the diatribe with the observation. "You already have women here, sir, so what is your objection?"

"She's a woman running the CID, a bit of a kid so say. She's got access to everybody. I expect she slept with the chairman of the Watch committee or the chief constable or both, she's too young to have got there otherwise." As the original temper spasm of Cole subsided he took his bulging eyes off of Fergusson and saw Freya who had been in plain sight by the side of the desk all along.

"Oh, sorry, ma'rm, I did not know you were there, very sorry I hope you will excuse my French." Freya gave Cole her most radiant smile and said "Of course. Could you lean down a bit so I can see your insignia of rank?" Cole duly bent his shoulder towards her, "ah, yes a superintendent I see, you are forgiven, I didn't hear you say a bloody thing. You really are a most charming man, almost good enough to sleep with," she concluded with another radiant smile which usually overwhelmed most men but with 'Old King' Cole, most unlikely.

Cole, with a very strained grimace, nodded at her and left. "Door," Fergusson shouted after him and lo and behold, the door was silently closed.

Hamish and Freya looked at each other and under the preceding circumstances burst out laughing then he asked, "Are you the woman he is moaning about?"

"Yup," she replied. "That's me for better or most likely worst."

"God," he uttered, "you're in for a baptism of fire."

She replied, "Never mind sleeping with the chairman and probably all of the watch committees with the chief constable chucked in, I have my own methods with overbearing men; all of my career, I have been fighting against the mindset of dinosaur-like Cole.

He still believes that women officers are just here for 'Women and babies'. "Do you remember when we were on that detective course in that old mansion at Bristol?"

He nodded adding, "Kingsweston."

She continued, "A woman detective chief superintendent from the Met gave us a lecture dealing with maggots coming out of the anus of a human as an aid to determining how long a person was dead."

He said, "Not to be forgotten but not of much use nowadays with modern science."

"Yes," she said and continued, "At that lecture, I decided that if she could do it in the Met, I could do it here, and I am referring to rank not maggots from a deceased bottom!"

She paused then continued, "I have got where I am not through sex with everyone or anyone but through dealing with people like Cole as I have just demonstrated. Imagine the psychological hurt he will suffer when I present myself at his door as acting Detective Chief Inspector Freya Douglas Gore Hamilton. To put it crudely, he will know that I have him by the balls now and that I can twist them at my time of choosing. Standing up she brushed herself down and said, "In answer to your original question, I'm replacing Harry Broadweir. Now for your chief super, I hear that he is a sweetie, is that right that he is known as the silent one? Then after him an interview with my new friend Super' Cole. Oh, and what of my staff, any duds?"

Hamish took a minute to think then said, "No, but they need a firm hand, Harry was too lenient with them and did their work for them. By the way, what is the crisis at HQ?"

She smiled and said, "Too many high ranking officers had their fingers in the money pot from selling seized booze and fags. When it was wanted for evidence in court it wasn't there. They are only suspended at the moment pending further enquiries. If they manage to squeeze out of it your chap will be sent back here and I will get out of your hair and go back to HQ."

She opened the door and as she went through it said, "Au-revoir darling, look me up some time, we have such a lovely history."

With a gay wave and a skirt shimmy caused by the provocative swing of her hips, she was gone for now.

The pity was that he did not know how long she would be with the boss so would not know when, he by chance, of course, would find himself outside the office door of Cole when she would confront Cole as the new Acting Detective Chief Inspector commanding 'D' Division Criminal Investigation Department.

A bang on the door heralded the appearance of the control room sergeant. "Yer staff has he completely gone off his 'ead?" in reference to Superintendent Cole.

"Whatever do you mean sarg?" Fergusson asked.

With a certain relish, the sergeant said, "He was absolutely spitting tacks when he came through our door and into yours. He came along the alleyway shouting about you being a useless bastard and some effing woman coming 'yer and how she would wish she hadn't come 'yer when he had finished with her the hatchet-faced lesbo and with that he almost fell through your door. I bet he was surprised with that woman being in your office, did you know, that woman?"

Hamish asked the sergeant, "Did she introduce herself to you at the counter?"

He replied, "She just asked if Staff Sergeant Fergusson was in the station and if he was could I direct her to you."

"Why did you not phone me, as usual, to ask if I wanted to see her?" enquired the staff. The sergeant answered, "I dunno, she was a bit of alright and my mind was not in gear, sorry staff."

Fergusson then told the sergeant that the woman was the new head of CID. The look of absolute astonishment on the sergeant's face was a picture to savour as the sergeant got his face under control and he said, "She's too attractive to be who she is."

He then paused and then stated, "She's probably younger than my daughter. I have heard about her but never seen her but she obviously knows you staff."

Fergusson was about to say that they had a history but changed his mind and said, "We were probationers together."

After that bit of information the sergeant thought, "If she is the boss of CID, it doesn't say much for your career as just a staff sergeant." Continuing that thought the sergeant went back to his control room.

In the passage of time, a knock came on Fergusson's door and in walked Chief Inspector/Acting Superintendent Thomas. "If I don't tell somebody, I shall split my gusset," he told the staff sergeant as he gently closed the door.

"I've been working with Fred for about twenty years now and I have never known him totally lost for words." With this as his introduction, he settled his backside in the chair, got out his 'Baccy', filled the pipe and puffed away.

At this point, the staff sergeant decided that he too could have tobacco in the form of his beloved King Edward. Both sat back in their chairs and Tommo began; "I was in Fred's office when a manly thud came on his door, it was closed as we were discussing 'The silent one'."

"Come," shouted Fred, he was not in a good mood anyway; apparently, you upset him particularly and he picked on 'the damned great signet ring you wear'. I think the word used was ostentatious. I don't think you two see eye to eye; anyway, he shouted, "Come."

The door opens and his mouth literally fell open, it was a young woman standing there. All the time his hands are waving but nothing is coming from his mouth. Behind this girl is the Boss and as they walk in 'Sir, the silent one' tells Fred that this girl is the new head of our CID. How in the hell Fred didn't faint on the spot I'll never know.

The Boss looked at Fred who by now was damned near green and asked him if in his office was it not courtesy to greet a new colleague with a handshake? Fred put out his hand but still could not get any words out.

In the meantime, I stood up and took her hand and introduced m'self.

She reciprocated by telling me that she is the DI acting DCI and replacing Harry and hoped that we could successfully work together. Mind, how in the hell a slip of a girl could even be a DI never mind acting DCI is a mystery. By now Fred is back in his chair and I can see beads of sweat on his face.

The Boss looked at him and said that he looked so ill that he must go home and rest at once, Fred tried to protest presumably about either being told that he looked ill or because he was being sent home but only part words came out. I thought that he was having a mini-stroke.

Fred just got up out of his chair pushed aside the Boss and the girl and stumbled into the corridor and walked to the foyer I was behind him. Then he stopped, put his hands in his pockets and I suppose realised that he still had his uniform jacket on. I told him that I would get his jacket from his locker and this time he pushed me aside and got his own jacket out of the wardrobe and went home. On reflection perhaps we should have sent him home in a car for safety, but I have only just thought of it."

Hamish had burned quite a large amount of his cigar by the time Tommo's story had unfolded. "She told me that she had worked with you and was looking forward to rekindling the association. What association did you have with her?" Mr Thomas, with a sly smile asked. Staff had another long puff at his cigar while he had time to think of a holding response before telling Tommo anything. He finally decided what sanitised version of their history that he would tell his chief inspector.

"We joined about the same time and later attended the detective training school at Kings Weston House but she was recruited by the Regional Crime squad before graduation and I went into the street offences squad and then an attachment to the Met because of my alleged expertise in ships' cargo and the laws pertaining to it. Other than years ago when we arranged to meet once or twice a year, I've had no work connection with her until now. We used to holiday together once but not recently, and that's that!"

"She has a quite cultured manner of speech, well-educated I suspect," Thomas gave his opinion to the staff sergeant.

Hamish did not reply immediately, he needed time to think about just how much information to give about Freya and then said, "You're probably right, sir. Yes, well educated no doubt."

Tommo puffed on his pipe and gave a sideways look at the staff sergeant and said in a very matter-of-fact fashion. "Her manner of speech, naturally female, is not altogether unlike yours, did you go to a good school?"

Before 'staff' could answer, he continued, "Some months ago I looked up your confidential record only to find a good proportion had been harvested into the staff sergeants barn including your schooling record. He concluded with the question, "Well, what do you have to say, staff sergeant?"

"Purely by chance, sir. I was assisting the clerk in updating the probationer's records and the 'senior officers' file fell out and surprisingly yours fell to the floor and in picking it up I noticed, accidentally you understand, that all of your annual conduct and ability files until you were made inspector did not exist. I immediately returned them and as I closed the file, I am sure that it wasn't my imagination, but it might have been, that there was a picture of a Massy-Harris combined harvester with a sign pointing to 'The Barn', sir !"

Chief Inspector/Acting Superintendent Thomas allowed a little smile to cross his lips as he rose from his chair placed his still smoking pipe in his pocket and left the office softly allowing the sound of the word Touché to escape his lips.

Staff Sergeant Fergusson was contemplating the choice between taking lunch in the canteen or getting out of the toxic atmosphere of the Police station and going down Timaru street and into a pub for a ploughman's. The Ploughman's won the argument. He went into his locker and exchanged his tunic for his jacket and leaning over the control room counter he was about to tell them that he was away for an hour at the pub if anyone wanted him when the control room sergeant who was on the phone, held up his finger spoke a few words into the phone and as he put it down he called,

"Staff, don't go, need you." Fergusson was less than pleased when he was told that after waiting all morning for a locksmith to allow them into the mysterious white Morris Commercial van they had now got in and found a gagged and bound body of a white male. Could they have assistance?

"Tell the CID," Hamish told the sergeant and turned to leave.

"But staff, you were dealing with that van, we did the PNC for you this morning." said the puzzled sergeant. Fergusson then said "Bodies found bound and gagged or otherwise are the responsibility of the Tour sergeant and it is his decision on the avenues of inquiry to be made. Cheerio."

'CID' in a bored voice was the initial response the control room sergeant had from the presumed super-efficient 'D' division criminal Investigation Department. The sergeant passed on the information from the White van openers. The prompt order from the now awake detective was along the lines of making sure that the message from the scene of the presumed offence was accurately recorded.

Freya was introduced to her staff that were on duty by her senior detective sergeant but surprisingly no one enquired why she had replaced 'poor old Harry'. She was shown all the working parts of her new Empire which were displayed from their own clerk's office to the forensic laboratory with limited facilities appropriate for Divisional use.

Freya returned to her own office and adjusted her chair to suit her long legs, pulled herself up to her desk and started going through the drawers and cupboards. This exercise was not new to her, to the contrary, she had taken over at least three CID squads at short notice and it was quite remarkable the objects that she would find and in some cases having no relation to crime whatsoever including gambling slips, tobacco and pipes, football boots, unwashed underclothes, American pornographic magazines, broken watches, fancy dress items and in one station a delightful pair of woman's very brief and lacy, high legged briefs naturally, coloured black. When washed they fitted her to a 'T'!

"Ma'am, we got a suspicious death at the docks by the locks," Ron, her detective inspector, told Freya as he burst into her office. "Thank you, Ron," she answered, "please deal with it and do try to remember to knock when my door is closed. Use the pillar system to call me if you have to."

"Yes, ma'am," was the rushed acknowledgement as Ron with his DC then did a Starsky and Hutch exit from the station yard.

Freya rang the control room and asked for the new control room sergeant to read out to her exactly what the message was from the scene of a likely crime. When she had digested the message she asked if there were any records relating to the van. The sergeant replied to the effect that Staff Sergeant Fergusson had been dealing with matters relating to the van and had done a PNC and checks at the Licensing people and taken the details to her office earlier that morning, according to the control room logs.

Freya thanked the officer sat back and mulled over her next steps. Those thoughts led her into the CID general office. She shuffled the paper from the

'In' tray and eventually found the message from the staff sergeant. At that time she was not overly concerned with an unexplained death but the state of the 'In' tray was a matter of concern and would not be tolerated during her watch.

While musing over her next move the phone rang and on the end of the line was her detective inspector Ron Wilkins.

"I think that you might attend here, ma'am; it isn't unexplained; it is murder or at best manslaughter as far as I'm concerned and a barbaric one at that." Freya enquired if he had called the forensic team and Wilkins answered in the affirmative.

As she put on a coat the thought did cross her mind that this incident could be her baptism of fire before she had been in the building four hours. Quite a lot had occurred to her in those few hours and the only pleasing bit was brief but to her happy reunion with 'her Hamish'. Her first difficulty was that she had no idea where the entrance to the docks was. After asking Mr Thomas where the gate was he offered to navigate for her.

DCI Thomas was not a man to be particularly impressed about almost anything, probably with the exception of his son getting a good university degree.

However, when Freya went into the station yard she approached a Bristol 407 in deep maroon and opened the door. Her navigator just stood there until she said, "Please close your mouth, a passing fly might go in, sir." With that, Thomas got in and rested his anatomy in the cream leather seats as Freya started up the superb hand-built luxury vehicle and made a tyre screeching exit.

"Without being too personal," Mr Thomas asked, "just how do you earn enough money to buy a vehicle like this?"

She replied with a laugh, "A rich daddy goes a long way with all aspects of life, and no in answer to your unasked question, my father is not the chairman of the Watch committee or the Home Secretary. I got this job through bloody hard work and in so doing weeded out all the slackers at my level and most importantly those above me," she continued.

"If a woman complained about a male superior she would probably be ignored, moved, had her future promotion blocked or demoted. If a man makes the same complaint and backs it up with irrefutable evidence he is believed and action is taken. Strange, isn't it?"

After a seemingly long pause, the reply of Thomas was, "Mind your speed, you are doing forty-three miles per hour in a thirty limit, and 'Traffic' are very hot on speed and will nick you as quick as anyone else. The mayor's been done and Superintendent Pope on 'C' division and ahead of you is the dock gate and driving this car you will need to flash your card to get in."

Arriving at the gate, sure enough, the guard asked for identification and Freya did 'flash' her warrant card. In the time that she flashed it the guard plainly didn't and couldn't have looked at it before he waved her in.

"Where now?" she enquired and Mr Thomas directed her amongst all the bustling vehicles and people.

"Busy place," she ventured to him.

His reply was, "Watch your car, some of 'em here about would consider it a strike for socialism if, very regrettably they drove a forklift into this capitalists classy conveyance."

"I'll neuter the blighters if they even touch it with their hand," she replied and Thomas was inclined to half believe her.

The first sign of the 'incident scene' was the blue and white tape tied to a downpipe of the transit shed and the leg of a nearby crane along with the forensic van and the car of Ron Wilkins. They both got out of the car and immediately Freya went to a constable and detailed him to stand by her car and protect it, never mind the presumed murder.

She went to the rear doors of the van and looked inside at what at first glance looked just a bundle done up with tape and chord. Closer inspection around the forensic team showed that it was a person in a crouching position bound with the chord and tape, blindfolded and gagged.

She turned to Ron and said "Not much I can do here except to get in the way of you and the forensic men. When they have finished get the body up to the morgue and bring in Professor White to do the post mortem as soon as possible. No, on second thoughts don't bother, I will have a chat with him when I get back to the office."

She looked around for the chief inspector only to find him on his knees looking under the near side of the van. "Ron will have the van lifted onto a lorry so that forensics can deal with it in the yard," she told him.

"What are you doing under there?" Freya asked Tommo, "Mud and debris, a good start to any murder enquiry eh?" He replied. "Let Ron run this one," she replied. "I will get involved if necessary and deal with the press." As they went to get into the Bristol, Freya turned to Ron and told him "Get the staff sergeant down here before anything is moved to identify the van as the one that he dealt with." With that, the two of them returned to Divisional HQ rather more slowly than the journey coming to the docks.

Freya looked at her watch as she unlocked her office door, it was only ten to three, she'd had no lunch and not even a drink. She left her office went to the clerk's office and enquired,

"What is the situation with getting a cup of tea here?" Jake swivelled around on his chair and said, "Go upstairs and wake up Mrs Briggs and she will get you one ma'am," Freya thanked him and made her way up to find Mrs Briggs. She eventually found her asleep on the couch in the Recreation room. Perhaps to say she was surprised was an understatement at the obvious age and the diminutive size of Mrs Briggs.

Deciding not to awake the elderly lady she quietly walked away into the adjoining kitchen and searched around, firstly a cup but had to settle for a mug, then a further search for the tea followed by a search of countless drawers for a teaspoon. She was about to pour the water from the boiling urn when she became conscious of a presence at her elbow.

"What be you doin' yer an' oo be you?" Mrs Briggs asked Freya. "Hello Mrs Briggs," she said, "I'm the new girl in CID." She then held out her hand to Mrs Briggs who took it and looked closely at Freya before saying, "Youm be very pretty, oo did youm said you be?"

"I'm the new boss of CID," Freya replied. "I've replaced Chief Inspector Broadweir and…" before she could finish her sentence Mrs Briggs interrupted with the observation that "Mr 'arry were a lovely man. 'ee were very upset when 'e were chucked out." Tears appeared on Mrs Briggs cheeks which even upset Freya, she said to Mrs Briggs, "Yes, Harry was upset but he wasn't chucked out. He has gone to a much better job at headquarters but he did tell me all about you and just what a dearie you had been to him."

Both the fact and white lie cheered up Mrs Briggs who then pronounced, "I'll bring yer tea down to you Miss an' with a biscuit for 'ee. You shouldn't be makin tea a lady likes youm be." Then much to the rather disconcerting question "Youm must be the lady friend of staff 'amish then, 'ee be lovely too. So sad that 'ee seems so lonely wen 'ee 'ave youm. But 'taint none of me business Miss."

"Who claimed that I was the lady friend of Ham…?" Freya then corrected herself and said, "I mean Staff Sergeant Fergusson?" The prompt reply came from Mrs Briggs "Big Jake in the office, but ee be a gossip worse than wimmen."

Without a word, Freya returned to her office where a few minutes later Mrs Briggs delivered a cup of tea and a very welcomed biscuit. As she gently put it in front of her she said "Excuse I Miss, I just be a silly old skivvy. Sorry, I let me mouth run away with I."

Freya replied, "Not at all Mrs Briggs, it has allowed me to put a marker on this Jake, you have done nothing wrong thank you."

"Thank you, Miss." With these words, Mrs Briggs returned upstairs to prepare for her afternoon tea round.

After her brief refreshment break, Freya rang Prof White and introduced herself, his initial comment was to make the point that this was certainly a baptism of fire on her first day in the post. They then discussed the procedure for his examination, the recording of it and the cooperation between him and the Scene of Crime officers, SOCO, and forensic officers during the unwrapping of the corpse before he decided on the cause of death.

That now settled, she took a few minutes to think over the events of her first day and for the first time ever about the hundreds of cases and the dozen or so nasty ones that she had dealt with and with this new case she felt alone and a little vulnerable. She could really have done with a smile and a hug from Hamish. After thinking about such a scene she mentally returned to her position in her profession and decided that her girlish thoughts about Hamish was simply because of their meeting and talk earlier on. Mentally slapping her own face she brought herself down to earth and in so doing realised that she had not contacted the detective chief superintendent at HQ.

She promptly picked up the receiver and phoned his office. His clerk answered the phone and told Freya that the Super was on his way and not too pleased that he had not been told of the incident earlier. He only found out about it when the mortuary rang his office to ask if CID had any special requirements.

Freya was about to get up from her chair as her door opened and there stood William Gaunt, detective chief superintendent, one of.

"Good afternoon, inspector," he began as she was desperately trying to remove her clothes from the available chair. After sitting in her chair at the desk he continued, "We have known and worked with each other over many years, maid. I have always been very impressed with your work and total commitment to the job at hand. It is me who has promoted you and pushed your career along sometimes against harsh criticism particularly by the two chief constables we have endured since you came to us from the Regional Crime Squad.

Although most people don't know yet that this is only a temporary billet for you until we either get the squad of miscreants back on Division or I do some recruiting from elsewhere if they end up where I think that they should be. Such a move will ensure that the 'acting' words in your title will be put to bed as you will then be titled detective chief inspector and I will expect you to fill that role as you have done in your previous ranks.

However, not informing me the moment a suspected murder is detected is simply not acceptable particularly when I hear of it third hand. It will not happen again. Do we understand?" What else could Freya say but, "Yes, sir."

"Right, acting chief inspector, you have a story to tell me, do you not?" Again a 'Yes, sir' came from her and then she began the convoluted story up to the body being taken to the mortuary with the Post Mortem to be supervised by Professor White.

All the time Gaunt was nodding and his only comment was to say one word, "Complicated." With that, he vacated Freya's chair and headed for the door, he hesitated and asked, "It's none of my business but I am making it my business, maid. There appears to have been a lot of telephone time wasted by the control room staff here, particularly the control sergeant gossiping to his counterpart at my HQ.

Did you go to a staff sergeants office before going to introduce yourself to Chief Superintendent Bates and when you left the staff sergeants office did you call him "darling?"

"Yes, sir," she replied. At that point, Gaunt raised an enquiring eyebrow and lowered himself gently into the visitor's chair as she continued. "I did not intend to be disrespectful to Ch/Supt Bates, it was just that it was the first time in a working scene that I had the opportunity to see Staff Sergeant Fergusson since we were together with you as our chief inspector at Kings Weston on the CID course."

Gaunt then told her. "I remember that class, that was where I pushed you into the RCS before graduation but I don't remember any Fergusson, but then I saw hundreds of people over the years. Right, if it is all those years since you set eyes on him kindly do not give the great unwashed the opportunity to make mischief by gossiping about either this Fergusson fellow or anyone else. OK?"

With her final 'Yes, sir', Gaunt hauled himself out of the chair and other than a goodbye said not another word.

Freya sat quietly thinking over the past ten minutes and in particular the dressing down she had received from Mr Gaunt. This was the first time in seven years that she had been found wanting and she was disappointed in herself for laying herself open to criticism particularly from of all people, her mentor.

She was trying to fathom out quite why he had made such an off-centre point about Hamish. Their past was totally private so there could be no gossip about either of them as individuals or as a pair. Her thoughts were brought to a halt with a knock at her door and the head of CI Thomas appeared, "Everything going alright?" he asked.

She swung around in her chair and replied, "If I wasn't who I am and what I am and the senior rank that I am I would simply break into tears. What a first day with a strange team, in a strange 'Nick' with a strange and presumed murder on my hands and an alleged mysterious association with the station staff sergeant. Apart from that Mr Thomas, not too bad a first day."

"Don't be sarky," Thomas told her. "Just be grateful that it wasn't two murders."

"I'm sorry," Freya said, and meant it. She continued "You, Mr Bates, Staff Fergusson and the tea lady are the only welcoming people that I have met today. I didn't expect to be garlanded with roses but the raving of Mr Cole put a damper on things even before the rest of the day turned sour."

"Go home, have a stiff drink and go to bed," he told her. She replied, "I have to wait until Ron reports back. As for a stiff drink, I need food, not booze, other than Mrs Briggs biscuit I haven't eaten since an early bowl of porridge this morning."

CI Thomas cheekily said, "well at least less food keeps your figure trim." To which Freya told him, "You are a senior police officer, I am a senior police officer and such things as my figure should not be up for scrutiny, but please don't stop."

He finished the exchange with "Good night you trollop. See you in the morning for a better day tomorrow."

"Night," she replied as he left her in peace.

No sooner had Thomas left than Freya's phone rang with her DI on the other end. He told her that he had just left the morgue and undressed the corpse. He had supervised the Scene of Crime officers as they photographed the face of the corpse and as Headquarters as nearer to him he would wait for the SOCO or Scene of crime officers to process the photograph and before he went home he would have it circulated through the Missing person files at first then tomorrow if there was no positive identification there, then go onto the national police authorities and if that brought no response, finally the national press.

"Thank you, Ron, from what you have just said, I take it that there was no identification on him; don't come in too early tomorrow. I expect that you have had a basin full today and I will see you about noon," Freya told him. "Thank you, ma'am," he replied, "see you tomorrow."

With the end of the phone call, she picked up her bits and pieces closed the door and locked it knowing that some smart-arsed sergeant would 'raid' her office during the night tour. Getting into her beloved Bristol she went back to her penthouse in the city and hopefully, peace.

The following morning Freya returned to her office and sure enough, the hair that she had left in her diary was not there anymore. She thought, "He must have been a simple soul to have fallen for the hair in the book as he searched for a nice juicy bit of 'Gen' to boast about at the 2:00 a.m. breakfast on the night tour."

She then went down to the sergeant's office to see which sergeant was on the roster for the last night's tour and tonight's tour. The same name and number came up. Never mind murders she thought, "I'll nail that sergeant and give a warning to other miscreants that she was on to their nefarious conduct."

Back in her office, she typed out a notice "Sgt Collins, keep your sticky fingers out of my drawer and off my desk and do the duties that you are paid for. She then went to the clerk's office and handed Jake the note and said "Will you kindly laminate this paper and return it to my office." Jake studied the note and took another long look as if the twenty-four words applied to him which was exactly the motive of Freya knowing that after only one day in the station that Jake was the senior gossipmonger of all. The simple response of Jake was, ma'am.

Her team came in in dribs and drabs depending on when they went home after their enquiries into the murder and in some cases more mundane tasks such as the enquires into the missing phosphor bronze bearings worth thousands of pounds which entailed visits to every scrap yard in the city and quite a few beyond the city 'Walls'.

Freya was busy looking after the detective sergeants in the absence of DI Ron when she became aware of a figure in the doorway. The figure turned out to be one of the forensic scientists that she had seen the day before.

"Are you bringing me a problem?" she asked him.

He replied, "No, I would like to think that you might be glad to see me after I have told you a surprising development in yesterday's fun and games."

Freya took him into her office, showed him to his seat sat down herself and said. "You are going to tell me just who bound him up and killed him because the science has fingered him or her?"

He replied "Er no, not quite but, I have discovered one thing without any scientific training or sixteen years of digging every last morsel out of a case. It is a first for me and all that I ask is that you do not tell anyone else, particularly any forensic nerds what I am going to tell you."

Freya looked at him quite bemused by what he has so far told her and was eagerly waiting to find out what, judging by his last few words, that he had made a cock up over. "Unless I have to use what you are about to say to me as evidence, my lips are sealed. However, if you are likely to get into trouble simply write down the bits that you would not like given in court and I will massage the story to give the truth without hurting you, OK?"

With that assurance, the man appeared to relax in the chair and began his story.

"I was busy going through my processes on the clothes, bindings and body when the Scene of Crimes officer was trying to take the fingerprints of the body. Frankly, I was in his way and he was huffing and puffing and being a bit of a distraction to me. In the end, we came to an arrangement that if I took the prints and let him have them this morning he would get out from under my feet. He went home and I had the clothes laid out alongside the body. The trousers were there open at the fly with the inside of the waistband facing upwards and the end of the leather belt protruding. Finally, I finished my examination, and fortunately, I told my assistant that she could go home and that I would clear up.

As she left the morgue I remembered that I was supposed to take the prints and deliver the form to the SOCO first thing this morning. I arranged the fingers and the forms ready turned around to get the ink for the block and roller. As I did I wasn't paying attention and spilt the dye or ink and it fell on the waist of the trousers and the protruding part of the belt.

I naturally rushed to mop up the dye and as I was mopping it off of the belt an indented number revealed itself off the leather.

I promptly wrote down the numbers, and it was fortunate that I did as the dye completely obliterated the numbers within seconds. I decided that the numbers made sense as a phone number so this morning I rang it but got no reply. So here I am, ma'am."

Freya at first said nothing then burst forth with "How will you talk yourself out of the fingerprint dye fiasco?" He replied, "I'll say that the SOCO dropped the dye. He can't argue or they will want to know why it was me doing his job and he will be in it up to his neck."

Freya then took down the numbers that he had written down and told him that apart from the dye matter she would tell everyone what a truly exceptional man in finding the numbers in such an unusual location. With that endorsement of his genuinely clever detection, he bade her goodbye and left.

The moment that he was gone Freya dialled the number and as with the chap from Forensics she had no reply. She thought about the case and, in her experience, the unique circumstances in that the man was so bound up; not dissimilar a stone age sacrifice would have been. To her eye, there was, other than from the bindings, no particular marks of violence. However, a peculiarly placed phone number and in an abandoned van registered to a mythical person without an address was a conundrum.

The control room constable swivelled around on his chair in front of the switchboard and called to the control sergeant, "Got a stiff in the locks, so say."

"Well, either they have a body or they don't," the sergeant said.

"Which is it?" he asked.

The constable went back to his phone and then added, "It's the lock keeper he says that they have neaped the lock to scour the mud out and by the inner lock gates appear to be a body in the mud trapped by the gate fenders."

The control room sergeant casually wandered into the Tour sergeants office behind the control room and announced with a certain amount of glee.

Chapter 3
The Work Load of Ma'am Increases

"Had your breakfast yet?" a reply to the negative came back. "Too late now mate, you've got a body in the mud at the bottom of the inner lock gates, they have been scouring mud from the locks on a Neap tide. You had better get a move on before the tide turns."

The Tour sergeant picked himself up from his chair plainly and justifiably peeved at firstly having his planned morning totally ruined, his breakfast being a total illusion, reams of paperwork to get done and a shift to supervise before the home time at 2 o'clock if he was lucky. As the sergeant left his office to inform the now returned to duty and remarkably very quiet Superintendent Cole, he saw his mobile patrol officers coming through the door.

"Well done, lads," he told them with a broad and welcoming smile. "God, I know what's coming when the sergeant welcomes us with a smile," one of the mobile officers told the other one. "Cacky-poo has hit the fan and it's heading our way and it's too late to duck," the other constable unknowingly yet very accurately replied.

"Right lads," the sergeant told them adding, "A body in the locks by the inner gates, get the wire stretcher in case the body falls apart as you pick it up. Search it for identity and I'll send a van to cart it to the mortuary. If you move your arses you might be finished by two." With the end of the sentence hardly out of his mouth, a voice not heard since the preceding Friday rang down the alleyway.

"Where is the body, sergeant and why have I not been told yet?" demanded Mr Cole plainly now in a good demanding and by pitch, a threatening voice. The sergeant lied just to see the fireworks and the illusionary steam emitted from the ears of 'Sir'.

"I was just going to inform the inspector sir and I am sure that he would have informed you in due course." And decided to on a final 'Sir' to demonstrate total and sarcastic humility which would wind up 'Old King' Cole even more.

"Inspector, inspector?" The superintendent said and then gave the audience the benefit of his opinion about the competence of the duty inspector with, unbeknown to him, the inspector standing right behind him.

"A lot of bloody good he is, doubt if the blockhead knows where the dock is never mind the locks." Realising that there was someone behind him he turned and with not a hint of embarrassment continued "No use telling him, I will supervise you and see that everything is done properly, carry on."

The inspector in a voice loud enough to be heard by Cole as he returned to his office said, "Blockhead from that half-wit is quite a compliment, if he wants to supervise, that's up to him."

Following the sergeant's orders, the two 'mobile' officers went into the basement and collected the 'body strainer' equip themselves in rubber over trousers, long rubber gloves and manly 'Wellington's'. With their body collecting from the mud gear, they ventured into the yard to beg for a van from Prudow.

The usual performance took place with Prudow of the yard, the vehicle yard, concerning the availability of a van and every excuse was given by Prudow why the officers should not have a van.

They patiently pointed out that as their equipment displayed they were to collect a body from the mud at the dock and pointed out the importance of beating the tide.

The response from Prudow was as expected, 'e can wait, dead uns don't mind waiting and with a bit of luck 'e will float away again."

The yard door opened, 'Prudow' that well known bad-tempered sergeant major voice of Cole exclaimed, "Get a van, now and if you don't I will kick your miserable arse up between your shoulder blades, move now!"

Van keys were collected from his office and a truculent Prudow threw them at the constables. Following their superintendent, they made their way through the dock gate and through the hustle and bustle of waterfront life until they reached the locks where quite a group were standing on the lock gates looking down including both of the constables assigned to the docks on the early Tour. Pushing aside the assembled dockers, shipwrights, office girls etc Mr Cole led the way onto the locks where he was met by the dockmaster who pointed out the shape of a body in the mud thirty-five foot below them with one arm seemingly hooked in the permanent wooden fenders of the inner lock gate.

"I want a crane and a cargo flat to lift us down," Mr Cole demanded. Looking at the two constables on dock duty as they tried to slip away he called them back and ordered them to see the dry-dock manager and get him to swing his very large crane with the suitable length of reach over the inner lock gates. The other constable he dispatched to the nearby transit shed to collect a wooden cargo flat with netting sides.

Within five minutes, both the crane and the cargo flat were assembled ready to lower the two constables and the stretcher down into the mud of the mighty locks.

Mr Cole as befits his position in life took immediate charge of the situation issuing orders to the crane driver without the need for a megaphone or the appropriate hand signals which under the sad circumstances caused no small amount of mirth amongst the watching workers. The signal for up was a straight finger pointing to the sky with a Capstan Full Strength induced bout of coughing after an attempt to bawl 'up'; with the constables hanging onto the ropes of the flat with both hands as they went up in the world swaying with both the wind and the effect of the luffing of the crane, then down into the mud strewn depths the men on the cargo flat descended.

As everyone was busily engaged in watching the recovery of the body so the sergeant noticed a figure in a boiler suit amongst the throng. He made his way over to the figure of a scene of crime constable. Discovering that his purpose in the docks was to photograph a burglary scene in an office and lift prints the sergeant said to the officer, "How about photographing this scene, the recovery and grab a photo of the body and the face?"

"I only do that at the scene of a crime and as far as I can see this is probably just a 'jumper', and we don't do them," replied the SOC officer.

"If it's not a 'jumper' your snap's could land you with a commendation for the initiative," the sergeant very casually remarked.

With the prompting of the sergeant's words and reasoning, the camera bag was instantly opened and different models of the lens were fitted to the camera to make a comprehensive photographic story.

"Stop, stop, I bloody well said stop' shouted Mr Cole to the crane driver as the cargo flat slapped into the mud several yards from the body. The sergeant went to the side of his superintendent and quietly suggested that they borrow a 'Hatchman' from a nearby ship who could direct the crane driver in hand language that both understood? As Mr Cole turned to the sergeant, plainly to argue the point a man alongside the superintendent told them that he could direct the crane driver. Mr Cole, in his usual confrontational fashion then asked him why he hadn't offered his services before?

"Because I was waiting to see just what a balls-up you would make of it Fred and you certainly have. If I was the crane driver I would have come down and given you a good slapping for the words you used about him," said the hitherto anonymous bystander.

Superintendent Cole plainly shocked by the words used against him did a comical double-take, smiled as best he could and declared "'ello Bert, you win, get on with it and I'll stand you a pint in the club. "It'll be a short or two as well mate, don't you worry." demanded Bert, the chairman of the Working Men's club and probable saviour of the men on the flat.

The men on the cargo flat were marooned far from the body and shouting up to be moved a bit closer to the body and a few choice words about their superior which the wind did not muffle nor the depth below the gathered throng. If the superintendent heard the sentiments about him and the morals of his mother from the depths of the lock he gave no indication.

With deft hand movements, the crane guider soon had the flat alongside the corpse and the constables were then entangled in the nets as they tried to get off the flat and into the mud with the wire stretcher. Apart from the difficulties so far experienced they now found that when the lock was scoured, scour did not mean that all the mud was removed from the bottom of the lock as noted by the constables when they sank up to their thighs as they alighted from the flat.

Fortunately, thanks to the skill of the crane driver and the guiding hands, the constables were right alongside the body and then they attempted to use the stretcher. After a few attempts, they gave up and manhandled the body onto the flat with a separate struggle with the body entangled in the netting of the flat.

As the tide began to cover the mud so the crane lifted the cargo flat with its mud-covered occupants both dead and alive. As it came level with the top of the dock wall so Mr Cole became more vocal demanding of no one, in particular, to supply water to principally wash off the constables and possibly the dead person as well.

As if by magic more than coincidence one of the observers was a waterman with his hose going to fill up the tanks of a nearby vessel. He presented himself to Mr Cole and after coupling his hose to the fire hydrant washed off the constables whose major concern was not the mud but how they could indent for a new uniform. Their agreement on that course of action was interrupted by them issuing a howl of pain as the powerful jet of very cold water brought their conversation to an untimely end.

Superintendent Cole was now in charge again and revelling in his return to power after the enforced surrender to the crane directing skills of his drinking mate Bert. "Put the 'ose over it," he told the waterman indicating the mud encased body on the still muddy cargo flat along with the wire stretcher.

"Stop, stop," came a voice from the crowd as the Scene of Crime officer still busy taking photographs heard the order for the water to be turned onto the body. "You mustn't do that sir," he told Cole.

"You might be destroying evidence," he argued.

"I've dealt with more stiffs in my time than you've had birthdays sonny," Mr Cole insultingly told the SoC officer.

"Wash off the face gently like I said," ordered Mr Cole without, yet again, any hint of embarrassment at his change of instruction because he was brought up short by this very junior officer.

The waterman reduced the pressure and as the mud was washed from the face it became apparent that the body was of a male.

The photographer achieved a perfect photo as the face emerged from the mud as the by now freezing constables struggled to wrap the body in a tarpaulin and deposit it in the van for the trip to the mortuary. "Go with it and have a report on my desk before I go home and put these two," indicating the two very cold constables with his thumb "in some dry kit," the superintendent told the Tour sergeant.

"I am the Tour sergeant and I have my shift to look after and fill in all the sheets for them; I am six to two and will soon be off duty, sir."

"You will take the body to the mortuary and write out a report about this before you even think about going home," was the final word on the subject.

The two cold retrieving officers were dropped off at the station and taken in hand by the control room sergeant as the Tour sergeant went into the staff sergeants office and poured his heart out to Staff Sergeant Fergusson. Hamish Fergusson told him to clean himself up and get on with his shift duties and that he would take the body to the morgue and do the report. Almost physically grabbing two-day working constables off the pavement, Fergusson drove them and the filthy body to the mortuary.

With the still partly mud-encrusted stretcher, the constables carried in the body and with much shouting, gesticulating and abusive language from the mortuary attendants. They unwrapped the body from the tarpaulin and dumped it on the slab.

Hamish looked at the bloated face of the body and was very surprised to identify it as the man driving the white Morris commercial van he had last seen at the dock gate a few days ago. The staff sergeant told the constables that once they had removed the clothes they were to search them for any identifying papers particularly for Maurice Van White before allowing the forensic team to deal with the clothes and the body.

While his constables were dealing with that he walked out of the mortuary and lighted a King Edward and inhaled deeply. In his mind, Hamish was going through the events since the previous Friday evening when he had seen 'Iron gob' with this man in the white van.

His quiet smoke was interrupted by a shout from one of his constables. "Sergeant, oh, sorry, staff sergeant," he corrected himself. "We have more than just a 'Jumper' here. We reckon that he's been done." The first thought of Hamish was not for the dead man but for his expensive cigar.

He would have to throw away the almost unsmoked cigar in order to return inside the morgue to the body. Once a good cigar is extinguished it never tastes the same if it's re-lighted. Inside again the constables, mortuary attendants and forensic men were looking at the torso of the body.

"What have you found?" Hamish asked. The Forensic officer pointed to the left-hand side of the torso below the armpit and simply stated, "Puncture wound."

"Oh, bugger it," were the involuntary words escaping the staff sergeants lips as he thought, "Why did I volunteer for this?" Breaking his own rule of eighteen years; Never volunteer!

He turned to one of the muddied constables from the corpse and told him to ring the CID at the station and let them know that this may probably be a murder and let them take it over. Also to tell them that 'Staff' would put in a report concerning his involvement with the body and be now leaving it to the forensic team to deal with the clothing and dental profiling and to send a Scene of crime officer to do fingerprints and photographs.

After the phone call was made he collected his subdued constables for whom this may have been the first time that they were required to deal with a body for themselves. During training, they would have been taken to the mortuary and witnessed a post mortem with many fainting. This time it was them dealing with the body, not a nice experience for those of a more sensitive nature.

As they went to the car, DI Wilkins turned up. After the usual greetings, it transpired that Ron was here to witness the post mortem on the body from the white van. His response to the information about the body from the sea lock was, "Oh! Bloody hell, this is going to stretch us. Have you told the boss?"

"No," replied Mr Fergusson, and he continued, "that my dear chap is your task. It's a bit hard on her to have two stiffs in her first three days, very hard luck. However, I can save you a lot of leg work inasmuch as I am able to positively identify the person as the man I witnessed entering the dock last Saturday in the white van that your 'Thrust up Turkey' body was found in."

"How about giving us a hand Hamish, you were trained with her and you were embedded with the Mets Flying Squad for many months. Just the man to give us a hand." Ron Wilkins suggested.

"Not bloody likely chum," came the response. "There is one strange thing about his clothes. He was wearing a body belt a very unusual one with half-moon pockets. I've not seen such a thing before. It could have been adapted for something other than money. Over to you Ron, good luck and goodbye."

With a smirk, Ron asked him, "Your response would have nothing to do with my mistress would it?"

Hamish simply stared at him, made no response, got into the car as Ron's sergeant came out of the mortuary telling him that 'everybody' was waiting for him.

"Oh! Damn," Freya uttered as she took the call from the constable at the mortuary.

"Something wrong?" enquired Mr Thomas as he entered her office.

"Yes," was her tired response, "your man from the locks has a puncture wound to the left side of his torso under the armpit. She continued, "I've been here a couple of days and would you believe it I appear to have two murders during a very short time in post."

"Oh, damn!" she exclaimed again and said, "I'd better inform dear old Gaunt at HQ. I had a first-class cursing after he found out about the chap in the white van before I told him."

"Mind if I stay?" Asked Thomas. A nod was the reply as Freya was put through to her superior's office.

Acting Detective Chief Inspector Freya Douglas Gore Hamilton in a rather flat manner of speech recounted the litany of events to her boss. Her oft-repeated words as the phone call went on and on was 'Yes, Sir' time and time again. Mr Thomas eventually gave into a habit and tamped down the Gold Flake tobacco in the pipe bowl and lighted it as he stretched out his legs, crossed his ankles and seemed settled for the long haul of unfolding events.

"No, sir, all of the routine work is being carried out by the detective constables. Nothing is changing there, but with Ron, I will need a bit of experience to help out if as I suspect these cases take up a lot of time. What I need sir are two reliable detective constables to help with the leg work as the enquiries continue. No, Sir, thank you, I do know that he has an impressive record but at the moment I think it best that if needed I ask Superintendent Cole if he could loan me a couple of men or women with one more person manning the office.

Yes, thank you, sir, I will of course keep you informed."

"What was all that about?" Mr Thomas asked. She answered "As you will have gathered that was Bill Gaunt offering me any assistance in what has now materialised as two murders which may be linked. I have just been told by Ron that the staff sergeant has positively identified the body from the locks as one Maurice Van White if you can believe that name."

"Who exactly were you referring to when you told Bill that "He had an impressive record?" Freya gave him a composing eye-to-eye stare and said "You know very well who I was talking about, don't you?"

"OK, so my suspicions are correct," Stuart Thomas said, adding the question.

"What an old-timer like me can't understand is why both you and him are forcing yourselves to have as little contact as possible yet at this time you both need each other?" Before, with a twinkle in his eye mischievously adding, "in a professional capacity, of course."

"I'm off," Mr Thomas suddenly declared saying.

"You have a lot to do," he concluded as he left her office.

The phone then rang and it was Freya's Detective Inspector at the mortuary on the line. "The pathologist has just finished the post mortem and subject to further tests is of the opinion that our white van man died principally of chest compression causing slow asphyxiation and organ failure resulting in death. When the tests are completed he will give you full details in writing and a death notice for the Coroner."

Jake was leaning out from the stable door of the clerk's office when he saw the chief inspector leave the CID office and head towards the office of the superintendent, his normal perching place. Over his shoulder, after noisily sucking his teeth, he said, in a very conspiratorial hushed but noisy in tone to his clerk sergeant. "Thomas has just left 'her' office and gone into Fred's place. Strange that." From inside the office, the sergeant enquired what was strange about the chief inspector acting superintendent being in the superintendent's office?

With a sigh signifying just how tiring it was to deal with a dolt like his sergeant, he said in tones reminiscent of a mother gently telling a challenging child why he was not understanding something. "In most of my years here it would take nothing less than a bomb under his arse to prise Tommo out of that chair in Fred's office, but put an attractive young shapely officer class bird along the alleyway and for the first time ever he deserts his mate Fred and can now be found in her office.

I'm a bit surprised that he hasn't taken the chair from Fred's office along to hers yet. Thinking about it, I'll put a fiver on him taking his chair there within the week. If I see him when he goes home I'll ask him if his wife knows where his pipe brightly burns in the station?"

As Jake turned back into the clerk's office his sergeant, a very quiet man suggested that Jake should be more circumspect to his superiors to which Jake replied "Other than the 'silent one', I know every wart and carbuncle blemish and professional misdemeanours of all of 'em. At one time or other, they were all probationers under instruction from me. It's in all their interests to keep me onside. How do you think I got this job, it wasn't through the 'Secret society'." The sergeant, a 'Brother', put a mental marker on Jake for that unwarranted remark.

Jake, a very clever man academically with an inspiring general knowledge, did indeed have a gilded career as a constable. He had refused all promotions and would not accept responsibility other than that required by his rank. Like so many in this particular Division Jake had a distinguished war career in the Far East but refused to wear his medal ribbons on his uniform as he claimed many who were braver than him were never recognised with the medal for bravery that he had. And of course, this refusal to wear medal ribbons meant that on Annual Parade he was in the rear rows of constables much to the obvious annoyance of Superintendent Cole.

Annoying Cole was one of the joys of Jake's year along with meeting up with his friend, the captain of a South African ship, which called at the docks twice a year.

One such visit went down in Divisional history when Jake was a control room constable on night duty. He asked his Tour sergeant if he might have a couple of hours off to visit his chum at the docks. Nobody refused Jake anything, he had too much power, one word from Jack could seriously dent the prospects of any sergeant attempting to climb the ever-extending very greasy pole to the rank of inspector along with a white shirt and peaked officers cap.

Off Jake went giving strict instructions to his fellow control room constable who was reluctantly covering for him "Write down every message and point check on a separate piece of paper and when I get back I will copy it in the logbook. Be sure to get the times straight." Silence was the reply from the constable as Jake hitched a ride to the docks in a passing traffic patrol car.

At about 2:00 a.m., two different traffic officers delivered Jake back to the control room in a very inebriated state. The sergeant was called back off patrol because of the state of Jake and on entering the station enquired where Jake was? "In your office, in your chair and could be asleep," the constable replied with very raised eyebrows.

Sure enough Jake was as described with the exception being that he was awake and almost successfully persuaded everyone that he was as sober as any of them. The sergeant was not convinced and told his wayward control officer to sleep it off but be awake by five to fill in the logbook.

Jake then disappeared into the clerk's office for his nap. The moment that the sergeant resumed the patrol of his men Jake reappeared and told his stand into 'scarper' and Jake took over the control room.

It was pure good fortune for the night shift sergeant that he was unusually relieved by the early tour inspector and sergeant at 5:30, and went home with his relief's ensuring all the night men were back safely before dealing with their pocketbooks and sending them home.

Had he not been relieved early before the inspector went to check the logbook he would not have slept very well, if at all.

Just before it was time for the parade the inspector as usual went to collect the control room logbook. This logbook was protected from tampering by having numbered pages with the number printed on an embossed coat of arms. Like some of the constables, Jake had been relieved early and, despite not getting too close to the inspector or acknowledging the huge amount of alcohol in his system promptly exited the station car park.

"What in the bloody hell is this?" the inspector asked no one in particular as he raised the logbook lifting it to chest height swivelling around to show his non-existent audience what caused him to allow such involuntary language to pass his lips and him being a devout Christian of the Methodist persuasion "Look at this log," he almost screamed at his sergeant. "There will be the devil to pay for this. I've never seen anything like it, there will be a sergeant looking for another job later today plus an office clerk.

The Tour sergeant wondered exactly why his inspector was having a dose of the vapours, he soon found out as the logbook was thrust into his hands. He looked at it wondering just what was wrong with it.

His inspector was within seconds from foaming at the mouth as the situation presented itself to the sergeant as the current page number sixty-three came into view. The details of messages, duty point times and actions taken were written upside down in the book and the times were written back to front namely the beginning of the previous shift 10:00 p.m. was the final time entry, and the first entry in the log was for 5:45 a.m., a brief ten minutes ago.

Before any conversation could be made about the book, the inspector and the sergeant made a dash for the parade room where their constables were awaiting their parade prior to being at their point of duty by zero six hundred hours.

The inspector and sergeant returned to the Tour office and both sat down after finding it impossible to translate the details in the logbook to the constables. "Christ only knows what will happen when the white shirts get hold of this," said the sergeant.

"I can get quite angry when people and most of all my staff blaspheme and just remember sergeant that I too am a white shirt and that derogatory remark is also offensive to me."

"Sir," was the only reply and under the circumstances the only word needed.

The two men mused about what had gone on during night Tour and just how many heads would roll by 9:00 a.m. Their prophecy of doom was interrupted by the new control room sergeant producing an A4 sheet of paper detailing a log of all matters between '10:00 p.m. and 2:00 a.m.' on that morning which gave light to the entire night's activities in the control room.

As always the arrival of superintendent Cole heralded the start of yet another day in the administrative life of the 'D' division. The counter sliding glass doors were pushed open and the face of Mr Cole appeared and was promptly met by the duty inspector's face. Mr Cole, not expecting a face at the counter, gave a startled jump and before he regained his composure he enquired "Wadoyowan?"

"I have to show this to you sir and could you authorise the issue of another control room logbook please," the inspector almost pleaded. Cole snatched the book and went to his office soon, as usual, to be joined by Chief Inspector/Acting Superintendent Thomas.

The inspector, after giving the offending book to Mr Cole, made a hasty retreat from the building first telling the Tour sergeant and the day Tour sergeant, "I am off for an hour or so. I will re-appear about ten when the fan has hopefully stopped revolving.

With almost a skip and a jump, he was gone into the bright spring sunshine whistling a merry tune as mentally he rubbed his hands together at the thought of the pleasing prospect of nailing at least two policemen to the wall. He saw his purpose in life to persecute and if possible prosecute as many policemen as possible. His simple philosophy in life was to capture just one offending policeman was worth catching three criminals. What a superb example he was of a good Christian man upholding the ten commandments?

In good biblical parlance, 'Lo! And behold' Absolutely, nothing happened at all. A new message book was produced with virgin pages and it began with the changeover in shift from night shift to early shift that morning. No enquiry, no Court of Discipline, no forfeitures and no sackings- nothing. That was a classic example of the power of Jake even when he was at home probably with a first-class hangover.

Being told of this incident during her second day, only last Tuesday, the same day that Freya drew his attention to unauthorised ingress to her office and desk with a blatant tilt at Jake being one of the offenders, she decided to change gear in the knowledge in this station he was all-powerful, and as such, she needed Jake on her side in the certainty that likely battles will come between her and Superintendent Cole and there was no time like the present to sound Jake out.

She phoned down to the clerk's office and asked Jake if he could spare her a few minutes of his time. Quite how Jake managed to put the receiver down walk about twenty-five feet knock on her door and be seated by her desk impressed Freya and as Jake did not know the reason for the summons to her office she deduced that he guessed that she had nothing on him and that she could be a good source of gossip for him.

"I was going to say 'Take a chair'," she told him. "But I can see that such an invitation is quite superfluous in this case," Jake just grinned.

"Yes, Ma'rm," was his opening statement, then, unusually for Jake he shut up.

"You appear to be the eyes and ears of this place," Freya told him. So you know all about the CID enquiries. "Could be right, ma'am," Jake replied. "Not that I'm asking you to do my job but I would appreciate your vision of the progress that we would like to see in these enquiries," she asked him.

Freya watched him closely after she asked for his opinion. The flattery had worked, Jake visibly relaxed in the chair as he decided that this 'highfalutin' girl needed a man to lean on and decided that Mr Thomas was not man enough, so naturally, she came to him – of course, she would!

With an abnormally long suck at his teeth, Jake pondered the question and told her everything that she already knew but the one point he made which would later come to pass was that there appeared to be a Russian connection because of the woman and the 'timber boat' and that it would not be long before every spook and their hangers-on would be trying to muscle in and pinch the case from her.

"Watch out for the bastards, ma'am, begging your pardon for language." Jake continued, "When they come a calling don't bother telling your boss, Mr Gaunt. Just refer them to Superintendent Cole he is the man to deal with them. The first sign you will get will be when Special Twigs, sorry, I mean Special Branch get hold of it. From here it will go to London and from there to the spooks. The minute they try to muscle in Mr Cole can smell them out. He'll see you OK." Jake took a deep breath and concluded with the observation that, "Old King Cole might hate your guts ma'am but you're part of his division and he will defend you against all comers."

Freya looked surprised at the suggestion of involving Cole in any aspect of her department's work.

Jake then said. "As you have put your faith in me ma'am, I will return the compliment," he said with a burst of condensation "by watching your back and no one will enter your office while you're not here and before the smelly nasty hits the fan I will warn you first."

"That's all reassuring Jake, thank you," Freya told him "It's after your Going Home time Jake, thank you for staying late." Jake got up to leave, hesitated than almost like a little boy asking for a sweetmeat enquired "Just a couple of questions ma'am if you please," before she could answer either yes or no Jake asked, "Is your real name Douglas Gore Hamilton, three surnames?" He continued, "And rumour has it that you are."

Jake stopped then changed the question to "Are you?" and again he did not complete the question. Jake began again on a different tack, "How did you get a plum job like this what with you being so young, ma'am?"

"Let's put it this way," she told the now hovering Jake. "As I am sure your intelligence services will have told you yes, I did go to university and secured a 'first' in Philosophy, Politics and Economics under a Police funded scheme. In order to ensure that they had their money's worth, they have put me where I am with my hard work being acknowledged, Jake. I did not spend my time on my back to get these jobs. "No, ma'am, I didn't mean that I…." With that stuttering halt, Jake took hold of the door handle.

"I haven't finished yet," Freya told him. "Relating to my surnames, yes, my surname is Douglas Gore Hamilton the only change I have made is to do away with the hyphens. I am quite certain that you know all of this Jake and the reason for these names is that over the centuries marriage contracts among a certain class of Scottish people contained clauses, usually relating to the source of money, to include the addition of surnames through marriage.

If you are hoping to find out where I come into this, then Jake I am afraid that you are going to be unlucky. And as for the other information that you were frightened to ask, don't bother. He will not tell you anything as neither will I. Oh! And bye-the-way I have four Christian names as well, all from my ancestors. Good night Jake and thank you again."

Jake, despite his very recent 'put-down by 'ma'am', left the office a well-pleased man that this new whiz of a girl recognised a fine brain when she saw one. To a certain point, he was correct, but from Freya position, the meeting had removed the possibility of any difficulty from the admin and other Division staff during her stay at the 'D' division.

As she got up out of her chair she, in her mind, went through the work of her department paying particular attention to two somehow related anonymous dead males.

She was thinking about the offer that Bill Gaunt had made her and realised that if her enquiries did not go to plan or yet another body materialised she would have to swallow her pride and go begging to Mr Gaunt for more staff support.

Looking at the clock on the wall she noted that it was now past 7 o'clock and it was time to go home. She had hardly taken a step towards the door when the phone shrilled into life. Should she answer it? Or should she ignore it?

Deciding that her long working day was not yet over she picked up the receiver and began to tell whoever that she was Detective… when she was interrupted in full flow by a voice she knew all too well telling her, 'I've been thinking about my offer from earlier and I have decided to send you a complete squad with a clerk."

"Thank you, sir," she replied to Detective Chief Superintendent Bill Gaunt.

Mr Gaunt continued, "I have been looking up your jobs in hand and I see that your people have enquiries into three burglary's, two suspected commercial frauds, six assaults, one child abuse, eight thefts with two of them involving tens of thousands of pounds, other low-level crime and now two murders. As your murders, frauds and weighty thefts which involve very valuable machinery progress, no matter how smart you might be you will not cope and give each crime the detailed attention each deserves.

Are you sending me a murder squad sir," Freya asked him.

"No," he replied, "These people will take the weight off of your people for the difficult cases that you have and the squad will be under the command of a detective chief inspector but as well as your murders you will have overall command. All you have to do now is find accommodation for them. See Fred Cole and he will arrange something. Good night," and with that, the phone line went dead.

"Thank you, sir," went through her head as she finally shut her office door, looked into the general CID office and wished her 2:00 to 10:00 shift staff 'Good night' and escaped from the station on the third day of her tenure.

As Freya climbed out of her car on the fourth day at 'D' division, the thought of what her two bodies would produce by way of the identifying evidence coupled by her reception from Superintendent Cole when he discovered that she needed a new office for her new arrivals.

As she walked into the station foyer she was greeted by the control room sergeant with "Morning, ma'am, there's a gentleman waiting for you in the waiting room," then directed her across the foyer to the misted glass door of the waiting room. Inside who should be there but the same forensic chap who told her of his mistake with corpse one and the discovery of the telephone number on the inside of his belt.

He was delighted when safely ensconced in Freya's office he told her that on corpse number two he had examined the belt, this time without spilling any ink on it, and although wet, through a microscope he found the same presumed telephone number as found on corpse number one. Because of likely 'comebacks' from the circumstances that he had discovered the number on the first corpse he would omit the fact that he had found the same number on the belt of the second corpse. Freya decided that he had a dry wit when she asked him why he had not telephoned the information to her?

He replied, "Walls have ears but telephones have bigger ears and bigger mouths at the end of 'em." Under the circumstances of that statement, Freya's mind went straight to Jake for a very good reason.

In answer to him asking that the source of the information would be kept confidential Freya replied honestly, "As I do not even know your name how can I quote you? Be assured that I will have a good story should anyone enquire as to the source of this information." The man just smiled and seemed to slide out of the door.

As DI Wilkins came in followed by his senior detective sergeant Freya met them at the door and said to Ron "Get your best team together and bring them to my office for a chat, a serious chat." Ron replied "What team? My blokes are fully occupied yesterday I borrowed those constables from their enquiries. We can't keep them off their jobs."

"Last evening I had a call from the boss who without me asking told me that he was sending me a team because of these double murders." Before she could complete her sentence her DI almost exploded as he told her, "It doesn't say much for us, ma'am, if Mr Gaunt is replacing us with his own team; frankly ma'am, I am surprised that you agreed to it.

He is undermining your competence as well as us. I don't like this at all and I am sorry to say it ma'am, but this wouldn't have happened if Harry Broadweir was still in charge here. He would have played bloody hell with the boss. Thinking about it the boss would never have even tried it on with Harry." Ron concluded his justified outburst with the rather obvious statement, "I've had my say, ma'am, thank you."

"My dear Ron," began Freya, "Your indignation is justified but on this occasion perhaps it might, for your blood pressure if nothing else, to have waited until I had finished what I will now tell you."

"As I was saying Mr Gaunt is sending us his team, listen carefully Ron, to take over our present enquiries.

All the live enquiries will be handed over today because by tomorrow we or rather you Ron will have assembled a murder squad. If you have any constables left over they can stay on their particular job for the time being. Now go and liaise with the HQ mob, they appear to be arriving now, they might treat you with disdain as they would normally be running the show. There Ron, contrary to you presuming that Mr Gaunt was thinking that we could not cope, he is confident that we will solve this one, or to be precise, two murders.

Please be back here within the hour or on the other hand wherever Mr Cole decides to put us, carry on."

With a little trepidation, Freya made her way to the office of Superintendent Cole, knocked on the open door and promptly collided with Jake as he was leaving the office. As he gave way to her she noticed the rather exaggerated wink.

"Yes?" came the by a now-familiar voice, sounding unusually calm. She walked in just as Mr Cole and Mr Thomas lighted their Capstan Full Strength cigarette and pipe respectively. The smoke formed in layers above their heads just in line with her head. "Ah," began Cole, "I had a phone call last night from Bill Gaunt to ask for a suitable incident room for your murder enquiries. Tommo, harrumph," he coughed and corrected the Tommo to "Mr Thomas. "Will select a suitable place."

Unable to resist the sarcastic tone and words he concluded his hitherto quite moderate conversation with the suggestion that "I do of course hope that our miserable accommodation will be suitable for your no doubt important Jolly." 'Why did a dedicated soldier borrow a nautical expression for idleness and or fun," thought Freya as she replied, "Thank you, sir. I wasn't expecting the Ritz!"

Considering that it was only about five minutes after 9:00 a.m. Mr Thomas stood up so slowly as if he had failed to find his bedroom last night and beckoned to Freya.

As they walked along the alleyway Mr Thomas whispered," You've got to thank Jake for this billet, Fred was putting you upstairs next to the parade room, it's a box about twelve by twelve with no phone lines installed. He told Jake to put you up there and to quote Jake he said, "That's a load of balls Fred, you couldn't put a cat up there. I'll put them down in the bunker."

By now they had passed the clerk's office with Jake leaning over the filing cabinet near the door enjoying a long suck on his teeth and went down the, for a Police station, very posh staircase. Down they went lower and lower At the end of the top staircase Mr Thomas explained a doorway to Freya as the quiet entry point for 'The silent one' to come and go with absolute privacy.

Down again they went until Mr Thomas led her through a very heavy door and finding the light switch, into maze of rooms. Some fitted with location boards on the walls, some furnished with diorama appearing to display the county etc in most of the rooms were three phones with the colours of black, red and of all colours, green.

Mr Thomas turned to her and said "Welcome to the bunker. This was an atomic war control room built in the late forties for all the emergency services, except the military. You have everything here, space, phone lines, heat, conference room, showers, kitchen, bunks, both the air and water is filtered the bonus comes with comfy chairs and in your case luxury desks but the hi-poli will make do with steel chairs and desks with tables.

There are only four keys to this place, one for you and 'The silent one' has the other. At HQ, Bill Gaunt and the deputy chief constable will have one. In short, do not lose it or let it lie around. No sergeant or inspector has a key but I suspect that Jake has one squirrelled away. They are unique keys and I would suggest that this place is continuously manned or," adding with a little smile on his lips, "womaned."

"If the use of this place is only used for this enquiry what did you do when you had other murders on this patch?" Freya asked, "Tommo."

"Most murders and very serious crimes here were dealt with at 'Central' and the dedicated Serious crime Squad did all their work there.

I have not been told but I have the distinct feeling that apart from the fact that we appear to have associated double murders here plus the fact that you are here plus the fact that Bill Gaunt is very subtly teaching his specialised squads that he is not too pleased to find his men who he trusted, to be honest have let him down with the seized property from crime sticking firmly to their crooked fingers." Mr Thomas finished with the observation "You have a lot on your shoulders, don't cock it up. God only knows why but you appear to have Jake firmly on your side and a useful buffer between you and Fred. Lucky girl."

"Thank you, Mr Thomas, I will go, and without sarcasm, thank Mr Cole for this very useful space then promptly move in. Are these phones live?" Freya enquired.

"Try one and find out," Mr Thomas suggested, "If they don't get control to phone the GPO to promptly resurrect the lines."

Chief Inspector Thomas tossed her the key "This is the key to your kingdom or queendom. I'll see you upstairs."

All three phones worked with one not going through the station control room switchboard Freya decided that she would unplug all the red phone lines except hers as that now made it exclusive and eager ears on the switchboard could not spread gossip.

Locking the heavy door she almost skipped up the two flights of stairs noting as she went that the posh stairs only went to the floor that 'The silent one' used. Below that it was an all-steel one with canvas covers for the handrails, rank certainly has its benefits.

As she emerged from the depths so she was met by angry voices from the foyer there to be faced by the 'Men from the press' who were arguing with Jake and the control room sergeant. Freya simply walked behind them and went into the office of Superintendent Cole still in his chair and on his second Capstan Full Strength of the working morning. As she told Mr Thomas she would thank Mr Cole for her new accommodation, she did. Without looking at her, he simply nodded as she went into the corridor she saw replacements from 'Central' milling around inside and outside of the CID suite.

'Oh, God, she thought as the officer in charge of this squad approached her. Freya held out her hand to Detective Chief Inspector Sidney Johns which he promptly ignored before angrily saying in front of his men and women, "In all my service, I and my squad have never been so humiliated as to be sent here to handle all your rubbish while you try to do our work which I can tell you here and now you will fail and we will end up clearing up your murder."

She was quite stunned by this outburst from a man that she had known for a long time and worked under until six months ago. She asked him," Sid, what has got into you? Before she could go further he interrupted her with, "I am detective chief inspector, 'Sir' to you and don't even think of telling my men what they can and can't do and as your superior officer I will decide what they do. Understand?" He finished his tirade as both Detective Inspector Ronald Wilkins and Constable Jake Richards arrived, Johns rather roughly pushed Freya aside.

Ron Wilkins pushed his face right into the face of Johns and in so doing caused the extremely angry DCI to jump backwards and trip, purely by chance of course, over someone's rather large feet that were fortunate for Johns as he fell into the strong arms of none other than Jake who by accident, of course, allowed the detective chief inspector to hit the parquet floor with a hefty thump.

"I want to see you in my office now," with a finger pointing at Johns, Mr Cole left no doubt for Johns as to his next destination. There were various ranks of detectives milling about both local and the temporary ones plus all the spectators from a rather frightened Mrs Briggs to the Tour inspector, sergeant and miscellaneous constables. None of them had ever heard such an ill-tempered, abusive and ill-mannered spat.

While a young attractive chief detective was not to everyone's liking there was no doubt that after she was so verbally abused by this man, little in stature and little in mind, to a man and woman they rallied their sentiments behind Freya. To be sure this incident would be a talking point not just locally but throughout the Force area.

Standing at his office door Mr Cole, in a very temperate tone of voice told Freya to come into his office. Cole led the way followed by Johns, Freya, Ron Wilkins and surprise, surprise, Jake. This complement discovered that it was quite a squeeze to all get in, even Mr Thomas was required to pull his normally outstretched legs in at the knees. Because of the way that they entered the office Johns was alongside Cole's desk. "You," Mr Cole quietly said to Johns, "will stand here," pointing to the front of his desk. Which then entailed Mr Thomas jamming himself into the corner by the wardrobe.

Finally, all was settled and then it began, very quiet and restrained as Superintendent Cole looked up at Johns before him and said. "I have served both His Majesty and the present Queen as a soldier from the rank of Private to Warrant officer one. As in all the services including the Police Forces, there is a code of conduct, much of it unwritten and amongst this code is that anyone in authority over another or of equal ranks will treat those above them and those below them with common courtesy particularly in front of those of inferior rank or place.

Have you served in the armed forces or merchant navy Mr Johns?" Johns shook his head and Mr Cole continued, still in a mild manner although both Jake, Ron and Tommo knew that this gentle breeze of one-sided conversation would not last for long.

Mr Cole continued "I was quite satisfied from your earlier conduct that you probably were a butchers boy before you came to this force and have not quite grasped the practical requirements and the common courtesies of authority.

Now that you are here perhaps it's the time for you to reappraise what is expected of you as a senior officer, particularly under my command."

Johns kept thrusting his head forward during the lecture from Mr Cole in a vain attempt to interrupt the flow of damning words which quite naturally Johns did not take to. On the other hand, Jake was amazed to say the very least with the vocabulary used by Fred. Words used in a context such as reappraise, common courtesies and the likes and most impressive of all his local broad accent seemed to have a day off as his words were crafted and spoken in neutral tones. Even Mr Thomas appeared to approve as he nodded calmly in the corner.

When Mr Cole had completed the first part of his 'Little chat', Johns, with beads of sweat breaking out on his forehead and upper lip, almost shouted at Superintendent Cole.

"What's he doing here?" pointing to Jake followed by "I'm not staying here listening to your claptrap, you have no authority over me.

You are just Uniform and I am a senior officer of CID and I am leaving and taking the matter of a constable being at this travesty of a meeting right to the top."

Outside of the office door there was a mad scramble away from the scene at the thought of the door opening and finding inspectors, constables, civilian clerks and two in house CID men, in full view would not have been a welcome sight. That being said, most of the occupants of the office would have been disappointed to find no one 'Earwiggin' at the door.

"Stand still and face me." At these words, Johns stopped trying to get past Freya in an effort to get to the door, a futile endeavour that a wiser individual would not have attempted.

"I said face me," Mr Cole repeated as he leaned over his desk using the blotter as a base for his clenched fists to support his frame. Gone was the neutral tone of voice and accent. A person used to Mr Cole and his ways would have taken heed of the throbbing vein in his forehead and perhaps taken a step or two back. In the cramped office, it was, unfortunately for Johns, not possible to retreat from the now puce face about twelve inches from his person!

"You dare to question my authority in dealing with you? You are a despicable object in that you publicly and unjustly upbraided a fellow senior officer and now you dare to question my authority to call you to account. This is my Division. An ant does not fart on my patch without my authority and although you are lower than an ant you will accept that I can do anything I wish at any time as long as you are unfortunately here including a charge of misconduct if I choose to so do."

Jake still standing guard over the rear of his master mulled through his mind as to the source of the 'If I choose so to do'. As Johns was brushing the spittle of Mr Cole from his natty brown suit, Jakes mind was still, as always, thinking ahead promptly bent down and surreptitiously wrote in the notepad on the desk, "Tell him that I will supervise his men and his work."

"The only authority that can censure me." Johns announced.

"Is Detective Superintendent Gaunt and the chief constable, certainly not you," and with a broad flurry of his hands Johns included all present and standing on his toes completed his statement with "This rabble." With that, he again attempted to get to the door only to be met by Freya being in his way. He attempted to bypass her to the door which resulted in her hitting the door which again caused a second heart-stopping moment for the eavesdropping men and women in the alleyway outside of the door.

For reasons not quite clear, Cole as if by magic lost the throbbing vein in his temple and said in temperate tones to Johns "You seem to think that I do not have authority over your conduct, do you?"

Johns attempted reply was temporarily suspended whilst he removed his handkerchief from his pocket, in so doing he gave Chief Inspector/Acting Superintendent Thomas a sharp and seemingly painful poke on his anatomy. Further delay was caused whilst he mopped his 'fevered' brow and face.

Finally, Johns had the floor as he replied to the question Cole had asked him, "No, you have no authority to do that and I will make a written complaint to Mr Gaunt about you holding this senior officers meeting with a constable present who has no material reason to be here."

To the ever-increasing amazement of everyone except DCI Johns, Cole simply pushed the phone towards Johns, dialled a number and handed the receiver to him and said. "It will be answered by Bill Gaunt, not his secretary, it is my private number to him. I have the same arrangement with the 'chief'.

His words were halted by Johns talking, presumably to his chief superintendent. It was obvious that Cole had called his bluff as poor Johns poured his heart out to his boss including his major complaint that Cole had humiliated him in front of a constable. Whatever the reply was from Mr Gaunt, Johns was rather deflated as he replaced the receiver and for the want of a better phrase looked like a 'broken man'.

"DI Wilkins will instruct you as to the duties your men will perform and that performance will be overseen by my constable who will report either to DCI Douglas Gore Hamilton or if she is too busy, directly to me. You are dismissed."

The sound of the quieter words in the office made the noise of the mad scramble to get away from the office door very obvious as Freya opened the door to allow enough room for DCI Johns to make a very humble exit.

"Stay here miss and you too Ron, hop it Jake and keep an eye on them, and in particular, Johns will be out to get me if he can but, if he attempts it, I will screw the little bastard to the floor."

As the dust settled in the office of Mr Cole and reluctantly Jake vacated his post at the back of Cole, Superintendent Cole settled back in his chair, Mr Thomas re-arranged his legs and pulled his chair away from the wardrobe, and a quiet pause allowed Thomas to refill his pipe and light up as Mr Cole opened his desk drawer and avail himself of a Capstan Full Strength and got his light from the match used by Mr Thomas.

In turn, both drew heavily on their different forms of tobacco with a cough and a prodigious clearing of the throat by Mr Cole signalled the resumption of conversation. "Right," Cole proclaimed, that's that little matter dealt with for now anyhow. Because I supported you to the hilt miss, don't think that I have turned soft on you.

No matter what I think of any of my men I will always protect them against anyone, unless they are in my view dishonest. Anyone that I can't trust to do their job keep their noses clean and dismiss any thoughts of sticky fingers will get a one-way ticket to a courthouse or the Labour Exchange." Looking at Freya he continued, "Your mate Fergusson has the right idea, although I hate to say so, with his 'flimsies'. Brilliant idea, even for him.

I understand that you have given Ron the job of selecting your squad but in view of Bill Gaunt offloading his rubbish on us I need you to at least keep the fraud and serious assault officers in the house as I know that Johns deadbeats will bugger up the jobs and we can't allow that. I want the fraud and serious assault cases charged. Keep our best men on that.

I seem to remember that a while ago we sent three CID constables for secondment to the Regional Crime Squad. I will ask for their immediate return. That OK, Ron?" A negative reply was not anticipated or likely to be given.

Turning to Freya, Superintendent Cole said, "Miss, the next question is when you have your squad, which I expect to hear that you will have formed by this evening with the three others joining you soon. Will you need any of my men?"

Freya replied, "Thank you for your support, sir; it was very much appreciated. At present, I don't know how far this investigation will take us so I can't answer your question directly but should we get into difficulties I would appreciate your support with manpower if needed.

"Right," said the superintendent, "Get to it."

As Ron and Freya turned to leave the office Mr Cole said to Ron Wilkins, "Want a word, Ron." The detective inspector turned around again and Mr Cole indicated for his door to be closed. The door was closed with a decided thud by Freya as she left the office, Ron was standing with his hand outstretched with no door handle to grasp. The thud of the door tended to indicate the opinion of Freya at having Ron being requested to remain in the office.

"Do you think she is capable of dealing with double murder, Ron?" Mr Cole asked the detective inspector. Ron replied "by reputation she is an exceptionally gifted detective and leader sir. I haven't worked with her before but I do trust the opinion of Detective Chief Superintendent Gaunt and in three days she has settled in well under very difficult circumstances."

"I'm sure she is a smart arse," the superintendent said, "but she is too young and she's a woman. What in the hell does she know about life and the scum of the land that we deal with?"

"More than you might think, sir," replied Ron, "she isn't just a pretty face."

From the corner came the observation, "Damned fine figure too," was the considered opinion of Mr Thomas, his only, and to him, the most relevant and important contribution to the discussion.

Ron took a deep breath as he emerged from Cole's office and the smoke inside. Back in the CID section, he went to Freya's office noting that Johns was sitting with his men in the general office looking very sulky.

"Has he finished pulling me to pieces?" Freya asked Ron Wilkins.

With a mischievous grin, Ron asked her, "Did who pull you to pieces, ma'am?" There was no answer just a glowering look from his boss. "In answer to your question ma'am, I doubt if he has finished pulling you to pieces but the good news is that if challenged he will fight your corner and the bad news is that he did not discuss the colour of your underwear. All in all, ma'am, a so-far successful day," Ron concluded with a broad smile.

The smile was not reciprocated as she told him to find his squad and get to the basement ops room with all their equipment as she had just found the pathologists reports on her desk and as yet had not the time to read them but would get Jake to arrange for her desk to be taken to the ops room and start again.

As she walked into the clerk's office to see Jake so like a genie he appeared behind her to announce, "I have managed to get all your furniture downstairs with the exception of your desk, I'll get the men to hump it down next.

All the bits on the top we will put into a message basket separately. "Oh! And by the way," he continued, "the press has been sniffing around it appears that the press office at HQ directed them to you so I deflected it with a no comment but told them that a press release will be made later today or tomorrow. The cheeky bugger then told me that as it's Good Friday they wouldn't be publishing anyway so don't bother."

Freya thanked him for moving the furniture and taking the press call and added. "If you have looked at the top of my desk, it couldn't have been now as I have just left the office means that you were in there after being in Mr Cole's office. What did you read on my desk constable?"

He looked straight at her and replied, "Check that they have analysed the debris on the underside of the van. There's no mention of it being checked, ma'am."

She looked at Jake for a long stare and said. "Thank you, Jake; you do your job and I will struggle to do mine. They have not made me an acting detective chief inspector because of my brown eyes Jake, but thank you all the same for your interest even if the advice on this occasion is superfluous."

As Freya turned away Jake said "By the way, ma'am, Detective Chief Inspector Johns is complaining that we have pinched most of his desks and chairs and asked what his men are supposed to sit on to do their work? I suggested that they might indent for the ones they left behind at HQ. He didn't look too happy. I don't think today is going to be his sort of day somehow."

"Find Inspector Wilkins if you please," Freya told Jake. "And tell him to make sure that there are enough desks downstairs for our people doing the fraud and serious assault jobs. I don't want them polluted by 'that other mob'."

When her desk was finally in its appointed place Freya literally 'got her feet under the table' and made her call to the press to tell them that there were two suspicious deaths at the docks on Monday and enquiries were in hand to find the reasons for the deaths and the identities of the deceased people.

The only question the press asked was, "Are they men or women?"

When she told him that they were men, the reporter appeared to lose interest and surprisingly, in view of what Jake had said there was no mention about there being no newspapers because tomorrow would be Good Friday as it was a late Easter that year.

Freya sorted out the jumble of items from the top of her desk and finally found the interim reports on the bodies of both of the deceased from the forensics, pathologist and the scene of the crime team. The man in the white van was much the same as before but the report on the drowned man was very interesting in that the wound under his left arm appeared to be caused by a narrow sharp instrument probably about four inches long of a diameter equating to a size 00 knitting needle which avoided the ribs and pierced the left ventricle of the heart but not necessarily the singular cause of death.

The lungs of the corpse contained water consistent with polluted river water as would be found in a dock indicating that the person was still capable of breathing when the body was submerged.

Further tests would be carried out on the organs of the body.

From the forensic team came the information that the man in the van had Lovat green fibres under his fingernails. These fibres had been found to be the same fibres that came from the Lovat green coat the body in the locks was wearing when removed from the lock. Identified as Body Number two.

Other than the fingerprints of the body from the lock, no evidence—sound prints could be found on the vehicle containing the bound body identified as Body Number One.

The tape bindings on Body one had human and dog hair adhering to them. Some of the hair was provisionally identified as belonging to Body two. To date no further matching was possible but the dog hair most probably belonged to a black retriever. A veterinary scientist confirmed that finding and had signed a statement to that effect.

Thinking things through, she leaned back in her chair and then went to the door of her new office and shouted, "conference in five minutes. Please pass the word." Five minutes later the team assembled in the 'conference room' probably it was last used in about 1948. At the desk sat Freya, Ron Wilkins breathing heavily as he returned from copying the reports and Detective Sergeant Bill Jobbins.

Freya drew a deep breath and began speaking to her new squad. "Right, ladies and gentlemen I have not yet met most of you so it follows that you have not met and formed an opinion of me. You all will know about me and I do hope that you all realise that I never give up, no matter what occurs and I expect no less from each of you. I understand from your inspector that most of you have dealt with serious crimes including murder before. I expect those people in this category will support their colleagues with less experience in this field. This brings us to our present position.

I have only been down here for a few minutes, in time to read the preliminary reports on two bodies found under suspicious circumstances. The reports are to be circulated between you to save me from reading them out. You have ten minutes to read and digest the reports which Mr Wilkins has copied for you.

Eventually, everyone was looking at those at the table and Freya began her talk laying out the known facts and out laying out the likely course of the investigation. She began:

"We have two bodies connected by a white van with one of the bodies being the driver of the van and one believed to be in the rear of the van trussed up and death caused by asphyxia caused by the bindings.

Also, a passenger in the van was a woman believed to be a Russian National, a crew member on the Russian registered vessel Ordjonykitso. As you have read in the reports the body in the van has green fibres under his fingernails that are identical to the fibres on the jacket of the van driver also some of the hairs adhering to the bindings on the trussed-up body are a match with the van driver.

A reasonable interpretation so far is that the van driver bound up the body in the van after an altercation with that person. The van driver claimed to be the Russian ships agent presumably the reason why he had the Russian woman as a passenger. We now know that he was not an agent for the ship and at this moment the connection between the two bodies and the mystery woman is the Russian ship.

The vehicle licensed name of the driver of the van is Maurice Van White driving a white Morris Commercial van. Why the Licensing people allowed such obvious rubbish to be registered is quite beyond me. We have no identification for the body in the van, no scars, no tattoo, no anything.

At this point, her voice began giving out and Bill Jobbins went to the kitchen to get her a mug of water, the budget for the basement kitchen plainly did not extend to drinking glasses. Before CID eventually vacated the basement there was a ready supply of one-pint glasses.

After her throat was lubricated, Freya resumed her talk.

She began again by summing up what other evidence they possessed. "We have photographs of the face of the bodies for distribution to all Forces and alert them to any reports of missing persons. If this avenue of enquiry fails to get a positive response then we will let the press have the photographs. The other avenue available is a common telephone number between both bodies which we will pursue as of the end of this little get-together."

With that, Freya looked at her wristwatch and leaned down to Ron Wilkins and whispered something.

Freya looked at the team and asked, "Which of you is Mr Dicks?" A hand was raised from a tall man with a mane of fair hair. "It's me, ma'am," he answered.

Freya again looked at her watch and said "It is now ten past three. The courts won't open until next Tuesday as tomorrow is Good Friday and Monday is a bank holiday we need to get a move on. Mr Dicks, will you please get up to the court and get a limited warrant from a magistrate to authorise the GPO to identify the premises and name of the number holder of this number?" As she handed the phone number from the belts of the bodies to D/constable Jeff Dick; when she had finished Mr Wilkins then appointed the men and women to their individual or joint tasks.

Firstly to identify the bodies and draw up a timeline beginning with the woman with the steel teeth when first seen by the staff sergeant and a witness statement from Dick Young the Immigration officer about his involvement with 'steel teeth' and at this point a non-statement background, e.g., gossip about her, his opinions of her role aboard the Russian ship and his general opinion of any matters relating to her and the Russian ship prior to the bodies being found.

Everyone was just getting up to go about their duties when Freya stopped the exodus with "Just a moment." All the eyes were on her with anticipation of a bit of juicy intelligence but what they had instead with the request or rather order as she continued with, "I want this office manned twenty-four hours a day. Work the shifts out amongst yourselves, draw up a roster and leave a copy here please."

DC Judith Manby and her 'winger' DCA (Tony) Carpenter were assigned to this task with the suggestion from Ron Wilkins that they should first question Staff Sergeant Fergusson who may have been the last person known to have connections with the deceased van driver.

His words of advice in respect of questioning the staff sergeant were, "Don't ask him direct questions at first because he will deliberately lead you up the wrong path to simply test your abilities. Ask him his opinion of the whole scene and then pick specific questions to ask but only from what he has told you. Don't interview him with the attitude that he is simply a uniformed staff sergeant.

If you do, he will make a meal of you. He was a very successful detective sergeant but for some unknown reason he opted to return to uniform as one of only four staff sergeants and now he is the only one left probably because Chief Superintendent Bates wants him as a foil to a certain superintendent.

From the moment you go to his office he will be all smiles and pleasant chat, don't be fooled, all the time he will be testing you and he will tell the boss or me if you have passed his test. If it is her that he tells she will be very happy, she justifiably puts her faith in his judgement and if it's me that he tells I will not doubt his judgement.

Of all your interviewees in this case you will not have a trickier character to deal with. Off you go and find Mr Fergusson before he disappears for a long weekend." Judith Manby then asked her inspector, "How come he can have a long weekend sir, other than Chief Superintendent Bates, no one else has the complete Easter off?"

The main reason is to upset Superintendent Cole who, although not here in person, will still be 'on call' for half of the weekend. The second reason is that as a staff sergeant he makes out the duty rosters for uniformed ranks. Need I say more? Anyway, you've seen him about the station even if you have not come into contact with him so get to it quickly."

The reality of the interview with the staff sergeant did not quite go to plan as the two detective's, verbally speaking, fell over themselves in the first minutes of the meeting. Fergusson smiled in a sympathetic manner at their attempts to engage him in casual conversation before the hoped-for 'thrusting questions'. He stopped them in their rather stuttering conversation and in an avuncular tone of voice he said. "Whoa, there. Has Ron been busy telling you how to specifically interview me? I suspect that he has and following that advice, although no doubt well-intentioned and if you Miss, will please excuse the term, he has buggered up your pitch my dears. We will start again with me prompting you on how to interview someone, who from your point of view probably knows more than you about your job.

As your interviewee, you must in your questions treat me as just a usual citizen. Although you are experienced detectives, my advantage over you is simply because of my age and the knowledge of interviewing awkward sods like me." Fergusson's little bit of kind flattery set them at their ease.

Eventually, they left the staff sergeant with a very competent list of questions and comprehensive answers. As they descended into the bowels of the building they compared notes about the staff sergeant. "I don't think that I have really taken note of him before," Tony Carpenter told Judith, I've been here a couple of years and obviously had nothing to do with him and now I've met him I do vaguely remember seeing him. He doesn't throw himself about much."

"Oh, I have seen him several times, I've not spoken to him before, he sometimes looks so severe that unless you had to you would not get in his way," Judith told her colleague. As they reached the basement she stopped in her tracks and said "Two things stand out about that interview. The first was that signet ring, it was seeing that which reminded me of the other occasions I have seen him and the other was the line of flattery he threw us to mitigate his superior knowledge of our job."

"What's so special about that ring?" Tony asked Judith. She replied, "It is big and if you looked carefully when his right hand was on the desk, the ring has a large heraldic shield countersunk into it."

As they stood at the door, with an exasperated tone of voice Judith carefully explained that "His name is spelt with two 'esses' not the usual one and probably the crest in the ring belongs to his family or Clan."

"Yeh, alright," was the indifferent reply from Tony as they went through the door.

Waiting for them in his office was DI Wilkins. They knocked and he smiled up at them and asked "How did you get on with him?"

Laying out the papers in front of their inspector they made no reply to his question. It was seemingly a long time before he had fully digested the information on the page and commented,"

"Yes, fine, not a bad choice of questions and illuminating replies. Would this be a case of the same handwriting both the questions and answers?" Instead of directly answering his question brave Judith asked. "Sir, have you had a 'phone call from the staff sergeant about us?"

"Yes," the detective inspector replied. He deliberately left a very long pause. "Well, sir," Judith asked. "What did he say about us?"

Another long pause ensued before Mr Wilkins replied "He didn't have much to say about your performance but he did bawl at me for sending two unprepared gladiators into the Fergusson arena of professional death with totally false advice on how to deal with him. Satisfied?"

"Yes, sir; thank you, sir," two voices as one intoned the response. Without drawing a breath Judith, ever the adventurous one, asked "Did we pass his test, Sir?"

"You passed my test in that you went into his office and came out again without crying, the crying relates to both of you, that is an excellent start to this ever-evolving investigation," Detective Inspector Wilkins told them.

Mr Wilkins continued, "Now get it written up and see what holes you can find. Then check it against the original unofficial report that the staff sergeant made about his side of the incident. If there's any discrepancy note it and investigate why the reports don't tally, then you can go home and unless ma'am rings you tomorrow you can have a day off. Finally, before you go Tony get two desks ready for the DCs joining us from RCS on Monday. I'm here on Saturday and Sunday. The DCI will be here tomorrow and Monday."

With that, Mr Wilkins left the new, 'Fort Crime' dreading the climb up the stairs to civilisation eventually he got to the foyer and passed Chief Inspector Thomas heading for the top of the stairs."

"Going home Ron?" the chief inspector asked. "Yes, and not before time either. Been a bit of a day what with that Johns performance then getting our gear out of the office down to the bunker."

Ron indicated the stairs using both his thumb and his head before continuing, "then setting up the office down there, selecting my team and starting the process of liaising with other forces to try and find out who the stiffs are. I doubt if anything much will happen over the weekend. What are you doing this weekend?" he asked Mr Thomas.

"The boss will not be here, as usual; Fred is on call over the evening and night-time, and I will be here, well perhaps not quite all the time except for Sunday when I'm off. Night, Ron," said Mr Thomas and Ron replied "Night, Sir."

As he turned to leave the station, Mr Thomas asked him, "Ron is Missy still down there?" The ever-distant reply from the doorway was to the affirmative over the sound of the traffic passing the opening door.

Freya was writing down the names of her previously unknown team when she looked up to see Tommo looking at her through the glass.

He put his thumb up to her and she reciprocated the gesture, and he walked around to her door and settled himself into a chair. "You still look remarkably fresh considering just what a day it's been for you, and for that matter me." Mr Thomas told her. "What do you mean by that remark? Who are you talking about, you or me?" she asked. Looking at him closely she said; "Although, on reflection, I don't suppose that it would be you looking so fresh with that ten hours growth of stubble. What's been wrong with your day sir?" She enquired.

"Fred Cole to be exact," he began. "He's been a pure pain in the…" Mr Thomas hesitated as he revised the word that he was about to say. Then having altered the word for one with the same meaning, continued. "Pain in the backside. I normally act as the moderator for both his temper and his language towards others but, today, it more or less beat all other days in that the spat with that preening prima donna Johns ushered in a continuous line of arguments, rows and overwhelming scenes of temper. You are certainly better off down here," he concluded. Took a breath then began again.

"Firstly he saw 'staff' walking by his office, that is a red rag to a bull if ever there is one. Then the Johns episode that you were involved in; that was followed by a 'phone call from Bill Gaunt suggesting that if Fred wanted anyone to keep an eye on Johns and his team perhaps it might be wiser to have someone of a more senior rank should things come to a head with the chief constable getting involved."

Fred thanked Bill for his concern and then said, "Should the 'Boss' get involved he would be pleased to put him in his place. Only God and the Queen would tell him what to do and then he would still carefully consider their request to change his mind before eventually and reluctantly obeying them."

"Exactly why is the staff sergeant such a problem for Superintendent Cole?" Freya asked Mr Thomas. Tommo thought for perhaps a longer period than was strictly necessary then replied; "I think the animosity between the two happened some years ago when 'staff' was a constable and probably caught Fred with his trousers down, not literally perhaps, but serious enough to earn the continuing fear of," he gave a little laugh then composed himself and continued, "being exposed for whatever the 'staff' has on him.

They have two common traits, one being that they have a measure of contempt for certain people of ranks above them and both have a large measure of contempt for this limp wrist, touchy-feely new police service. They both want a police force with the mindset of 'flog and hang 'em high'. An attitude that is not in keeping with our Police command college thinking and teaching in the early sixth decade of the twentieth century." He looked at her raised eyebrow and said "Well, you did ask!"

Mr Thomas then lit his pipe, realised what he had done in someone's office without seeking permission and apologised for his rudeness and asked the permission of Freya to continue producing copious amounts of smoke towards the ceiling. She said. "Not at all, carry on, the smell reminds me of my father's study at home, he has a pipe and my mother banishes him there when he wants to smoke indoors.

He is happy to go there it means that he can have a 'snifter' without mother knowing and of course avoid all of the visitors to mother from the Lord only knows just how many committees she is chairman of.

My home is akin to a busy railway station with mother as the station master." She then continued, "On reflection, the only person who objects to Father's 'filthy habit' is the housekeeper who gets moans from the lady who cleans his study. Although I saw the woman's husband smoking cigarettes almost continually in the gardens."

Freya then realising that Mr Thomas had not yet finished his sorry tale apologised to him for interrupting his 'Flow' to which he replied, "It's my fault for lighting up. It ruined my train of thought or moans if you prefer."

He took another puff and continued his story." We had just got over that crisis when a call came in of a suspicious death at the Uplands. Johns was back in Fred's room like a rat up a drainpipe the blighter demanded better accommodation for him and his team if they were to carry out his duties as you with 'That constable' had taken all the best furniture and even the CID office clerk leaving him and his team 'sitting on their thumbs' and wanting to know what Fred was going to do about it?

I could see that the very presence of Johns was making Fred simmer and when Johns then said "Well?' The simmering kettle simply boiled over and Fred went into the sort of rage that he had last Monday when you arrived. He shouted, banging his fist so hard on the desk which as usual brought an audience around his doorway.

I won't repeat the exact words used, but they were worse than you had by a mile. Fred had all the usual signs of displeasure clearly visible, his pulsating vein in his brow, his neck visibly expanding over his collar as he thumped his desk. He wasn't just red as usual, he was purple and his lips lost all colour.

From the language he used at Johns to the various titles he attributed to his parentage, his place of origin and his present precarious position involving 'his chums' awaiting the cells with sticky fingers from 'A' division.

Fred does have a certain type of humour when he concluded the tirade with, "Don't worry sonny, I'm sure that they will keep a nice warm cell blanket for you."

"Now get the frigging hell out of here now and always, as the very sight of such a heap of slime as you, either in or around my office, station and Division makes me want to vomit—get out."

Tommo finished his tale with, "The stupid 'B', instead of getting out then said in a plaintive little drawl, "You're not going to help me then?" Fred, by now in an almost normal tone concluded the episode by assuring Johns that the only help that he would get would be a size ten boot up your arse down my station steps."

"So that was your day of days, wasn't it? Did Mr Cole really use the words 'Frigging' and 'Slime?" she asked Mr Thomas. He smirked and enquired, "What do you think?"

In reply to Freya's original question, Mr Thomas told her, "No, it wasn't over yet, Fred lit up and life returned to its usual pace of terror along Mafia road when the half-opened door was pushed fully open and that toe-rag from Special Branch came in.

He only got three steps inside the door and Fred's backside began to hover over his chair when he politely asked the chap, "What are you?"

The chap answered, "I'm special branch."

Still in moderate tones, Fred said to him, "I'm not asking you who you are; I'm asking what you are?"

To which the rather confused fellow replied, "I'm a special branch detective constable."

Fred still in reasonable tones said, "If you are a special branch detective constable what are you?"

The chap replied, "A police officer."

All of this time the constable had one foot still in the corridor. Ah' said Fred. "At last we have finally got through to a smart efficient courteous, polite policeman who practises all the social niceties of his position in society and this police force do we?' With that sarcastically said, the poor little dear, without challenge allowed himself to be drawn into Fred's web.

There was silence for a few seconds until the silly boy pulled his leg still in the corridor into the office. Once again Fred started off slowly as if instructing a child. 'Is it not a social requirement, not to mention a necessity in my Division to;' at this point, Mr Thomas' face became quite animated, as he continued, the voice of Fred became alarmingly growling, 'knock on the door of any personal office and…" the voice became even louder, "particularly when it is my door.

Get out, you miserable excuse for a policeman and if you must speak to me you knock on the door and wait until I tell you to enter and when you face me you address me as Sir if I ask you a question you will answer with the final word being Sir. You will emphasise the 'S' in the word sir in order that the 'S' cannot be misinterpreted as a 'C'.

"Do you, even with the simple brain that you so obviously carry in your cranium clearly understand me?" the thoroughly confused chap just nodded.

Fred looked at me and said in disbelief, "What have I just told this chump?" Turning to the chap in the doorway he bawled, you do not just nod at me; you say 'Yes, Sir', and believe me, son, you had better believe it and act on it. Now get out and let's try again, shall we?

The chap removed himself from the doorway once the almost permanent audience made enough room for his body. As he closed the door, I heard Jake urge him to 'just open the door, don't bother knocking'.

Fortunately, the fellow did not listen to mischief-maker Jake and knocked on the door. 'Enter came the order from Fred'. In came the special branch chap and said 'Sir' twice, which at first I thought was we-we taking but then realised it was just nerves.

'Yes' came from Fred followed by 'Well, what do you want?'

The chap replied, "My detective chief inspector has requested that I collect all the relevant paperwork, photographs and lab reports for the double murders you are investigating, Sir."

That request threw Fred a bit, your who and what does he want? say again he asked." The chap repeated what he had just said but corrected Fred in that 'He' was in fact a 'She'. Fred sat and digested the request then said "You must see Acting Detective Chief Inspector Douglas Gore Hamilton, she is the senior officer on the case.

Why does your boss want these papers?" The chap rather naively replied 'We have an interest in the case sir as well as those in London."

"Tell your mistress, my son, that you will not get any papers from this division whether or not the head of my CID says so, and she most certainly will not do so."

The silly boy insisted again on the paperwork and Fred took off. "Get out. You claim to be special Branch?"

'Yes, sir' came from the boy.

"You can go and tell your lady boss that as far as I'm concerned both you and the rest of your tribe should be called 'Special Twig', that's about as much good you and your paper shuffling mates are, only good for the compost bin." Probably forgetting that he had already said so, he again told Twig to 'Get out'.

This time Twig was pleased to obey and scarpered very promptly.

"Is that all you had to worry about?" Freya asked him. She continued with more of a smirk rather than a smile on her lips. "I bet that it was so hard to sit there through all this for the best part of eight hours without saying a word. Did you go for refreshments?"

Mr Thomas replied," Don't be facetious, you are young enough to be my daughter." Do you have any daughters Mr Thomas?" she asked him.

"No," came the reply, "Just two sons."

Why do you ask?" he enquired.

"I'm working out if it's a good idea to use my feminine wiles on you as you have no experience of younger women. Such an underhand plot might suit my purposes in my pursuit of power over my male superiors, of course not you but, you being more of a conduit to awkward so and so's such as 'Old King Cole," she told him.

"I am looking after your back already without any of your female wiles. But you know that you crafty minx," he replied.

"As I have just told you about my sons I now feel free to ask about your relationship with our 'staff'." Thomas told her.

Freya told him that she would tell him a bit on the condition that it went no further and particularly to Staff Sergeant Fergusson, but that she would have no questions asked.

She began. "I have known Hamish since our University days although he is a few years older than me, he was in his final year as I was beginning my first. We did not join this mob together but we were always in touch.

We went to Kings Weston on our CID course together but I was seconded to the Regional Crime Squad and our relationship took a hit. We both went our professional ways with me keeping an eye on him and he was doing the same with me. We always meet once a year on a certain date and have a very good day or two and the following morning we leave each other until either circumstance throw us together such as now, or our meeting date comes around. I have a feeling that a few days ago I told you some of this. That is all that you need to know."

"I should have known better than to ask. You have deliberately given me a mystery now with more answers needed now than before. I called you a 'Crafty minx a minute or so ago, charming and as beautiful as you are you have deliberately led an old decrepit man right up the garden path, shame on you," he told her.

She let out that melodious tinkling laugh and told Mr Thomas. "There, I have taken your mind off your horrible day with Mr Cole, I have restored your soul and sent you home thinking about something else besides this place and what's for dinner tonight. Good night dear, your wife will be asking where you have been until 6:30. I would wager that you will not tell her that you have been ensconced in a bunker along with a young woman, young enough to be your daughter?" she told him.

"Not bloody likely," were his final words as he headed for the door.

As Mr Thomas left so Freya's detective constable tasked with getting a limited warrant to secure the address and name of the person with the telephone numbers on the belts came in looking rather glum.

He knocked on her door went in and she could see his angst and invited him to sit down in the chair vacated by Mr Thomas. The detective sat then promptly stood up. "What's wrong?" Freya asked him. "This seat is boiling, ma'am," he replied. She told him that Mr Thomas was in the chair and came in rather hot under the collar. She hadn't realised that his nether regions were also that warm.

"What do you have for me?" she asked the detective. He replied, "Nothing ma'am, the GPO would not accept a warrant they demanded a Court Order from a judge of some sort."

"If I was given to swearing, I would do so now," she said, "May I do it for you, ma'am?" enquired the daring detective.

"I think that it is best that we say it in our mind, what I am thinking right now no lady should say, or a gentleman might say in front of a lady. Don't you agree?"

"Yes, ma'am," The detective agreed thinking more of his promotion prospects being dented if he upset, ma'am."

"Right," said Freya.

"Plan 'B' eh? "What is plan 'B', ma'am?" her man asked.

She reached for her calendar and studied it on her desk, then said, "There is a chance that I could give a sworn affidavit to a judge tomorrow and have a ruling and order by Monday."

She thought a bit and then said, "Yes, I am here tomorrow and again on Monday and can serve it on the GPO on Tuesday and if they move their backside we might have a result by Wednesday. Agree?"

"Yes, ma'am," was the undoubted words of reply.

Go home now, you have had a long day she told DC Dicks."

"Thank you, ma'am," he replied and he was gone almost with the speed of a lightning strike.

Chapter 4
Ma'am Spreads the Net Ever Wider

Freya cleared up her desk locked it and turned to collect her coat when she stopped, thought for a few seconds then reversed her recent actions and when her desk drawer opened she took out her incident diary and made an entry for tomorrow. It read, 'check that forensic have analysed the underside of the white van and if they have, what evidence has been found? If not why not?'

She then went through her office exiting routine reasonably sure that the various sergeants and Jake would not have a key to her office in her basement bunker. She looked around the various rooms and eventually came across the first of the nightwatchmen who on this occasion happened to be a woman detective constable. The poor girl probably thought that ma'am had gone home when constable Dicks left several minutes ago.

She was mistaken as ma'am suddenly appeared whilst the girl was reclining in a chair with only the back legs on the ground and reading the Women's Own.

The four legs audibly hit the ground as the frantic attempt to hide the magazine proved to be a desire rather than an accomplishment.

The best that the detective constable could manage was 'ma'am' accompanied with a very flushed complexion.

Freya asked, "Are you part of the 'Night Watchman' pool?"

"Yes, ma'am," was a prolonged rendition of two words. "Are you doing eight or twelve-hour shifts?" Freya asked her. By now the girl had recovered her composure and said "We are doing eight-hour shifts. I do until ten then the ten to six-person relieves me and they are replaced by the six to two relief, ma'am."

"Who decided on these hours?" Freya asked. "Mr Wilkins told us to work it out amongst ourselves mindful of the fact that unless something happened this would be a very long weekend, ma'am."

"As there will only 'phone calls for you to receive or make I think that should I be in your position I would have chosen twelve-hour stints with four of you covering the four days.

More time doing next to nothing here and more time in one stretch at home. But, it is your choice." Freya told her and then added.

"I think perhaps it might improve your career prospects for you to make sure that people like me have left the building before you pick up magazines. It is a good method of self-preservation to keep people such as me off your back with no effort on your part and perhaps you should revise your Judges Rules and study the Bible of Moriarty as women's magazines do not usually help in offering guidance in the application of the rules and police practise of the law which I hope you will be needing in the near future. "Good night," was her earnest wish for the girl. "ma'am," was the response.

As she walked to the stairs she thought 'I bet that girl wishes me in hell and considers me to be a mark one bitch. What she doesn't consider is that I have taught her a lesson in police life but also in any other trade. By the time that she had reached the foyer she began to wonder how anyone so naive could have got into CID.

Under normal circumstances, the girl should have learned all the 'Wrinkles' of being a constable shortly after leaving Police school particularly if her mentor was worth his salt.

As she walked into the car park her thoughts left the station and all matters pertaining to it – unless the 'phone rang with the words.

"Sorry to bother you, ma'am, but…"

All too soon Good Friday arrived and at 5:30 Freya entered her office and eventually settled in her chair and waited for the night watchman to appear. No night watchman appeared so she went through the rooms and no sign of another body could be found. She went into the gent's lavatory and called out, there was no response. Of a normally good nature but still well aware of human failings, her irritation and temper were becoming apparent.

At her desk, she rang the outside number of the control room and the 'phone was answered promptly by a voice which she vaguely recognised. She noticed that normally the person answering the phone would state their name and rank then ask the caller 'Can I help you?'

She put the 'phone down and shot up the two flights of stairs, across the foyer to the control room counter and behind the switchboard was someone in civilian clothes. She promptly returned to her office and phoned the forensic laboratory. Eventually, a rather bored voice informed her that the lab was not open until 9 o'clock as it was a Bank holiday.

Whilst she was sat working out just what she would tell Ron Wilkins about his choice of people for the murder squad the 'phone rang in the general office from the outside line avoiding the station switchboard. She went and answered it and identified herself to find that that on the other end it was the duty inspector from the adjacent police force to tell her that a few minutes earlier a civilian clerk at their central station had looked at the mug-shot that her team had circulated of the man in the back of the van.

The man believed that the photograph was of his former neighbour with the, to Freya, fascinating names of Harrison Hacker, about forty-five to fifty years of age and was when the police 'civvy' worker knew him, Hacker was a civil servant at the Home Office.

Freya asked, "Does your man know where he lives now?" The inspector replied to the negative but their man thought that it was somewhere on or near Salisbury Plain. She then asked how long his man had been the neighbour of Harrison Hacker. The reply came as ten or eleven years.

She then asked the inspector if he could look up the station copy of the 1951 census and see where a person with that distinctive name lived if it was in their patch.

The inspector dashed her hopes of a speedy identification when he told her that the census records were at HQ and the offices would not be open until next Tuesday.

"Are you on duty on Tuesday?" she asked the inspector. After a brief interval while the inspector must have studied his roster he replied that he was on six to two and would have access to the records at about nine and would let her know if the name was on their patch and where. However, in the meantime, he would get his local constable to ask the locals that he might find amenable to a policeman asking questions if any of them knew a Harrison Hacker and where he now lived. Should he find out he would give her or her control room a call?

After she had given him her new outside 'phone number, she thanked the inspector for his cooperation. The call then ended and Freya left the general office for the sanctuary of her office, sat down and chewed over the possible identification of Body number one. Although her missing 'Night watchman' had not yet made an appearance her mood was beginning to mellow with Harrison Hacker being in the 'Frame'.

One challenge hopefully solved, now back to the telephone numbers and what name and location the numbers could give the murder team. The application yesterday for the result from a limited court warrant for information that had worked in the past for her was not acceptable on this occasion for the GPO telephones. Today was a Friday, Good Friday, was there likely to be a High Court judge willing to dish out a Court order to the GPO?

She decided that this question should be answered by Chief Superintendent William Gaunt or his deputy, whichever was on duty. She rang the Central CID office and asked the duty officer who was in charge and was told that it was Mr Gaunt. Freya then requested either to speak to him or could he please ring her and gave her a new outside line number. As she put the 'phone receiver down she noticed a shape slip in and out of the view of her window.

She went out into the general office to witness a young constable diligently studying his pocketbook with pen poised ready to make a quite fictitious entry as to his whereabouts during his tour. "Good morning," she said to the 'Book Worm' "Has it been a quiet night she enquired?" He made a great effort to drag himself away from his critical writing and replied,

"Yes, ma'am, very quiet."

"How would you know that?" she asked him and continued, "no 'phone calls at all?" These questions really flummoxed the detective. "No, ma'am, it was all quiet." Freya then took a chance in asking, "Why did you not answer the 'phone when I rang in?" Not expecting such a question the young man squirmed under the gaze of her very dark brown eyes and after what seemed to be an eternity said, "I must have been in the lavatory, ma'am."

She then knew that she had him on the ropes and took another chance with a 'White' lie,

"I understand, in fact I know, that you were in the control room when your duties were to be awake and alert down here to take 'phone messages and inform those 'On call' the nature of that call, weren't you?"

A whispered 'yes, ma'am' confirmed what she thought. His admission to a dereliction of duty sealed his fate and big boots, a tall hat and a less than comfortable pavement awaited him at the convenience of Freya.

She took a chance at upsetting her boss and rang him before 9 o'clock. In only two rings, he answered with the bold statement of 'Gaunt'.

Apologising for the early call at his home she outlined the difficulty that she was having in getting the GPO to release the name and address of the person living at the telephone numbers found on the belts of the two bodies that she was dealing with.

Bill Gaunt told her that she must have known that any weekend was a difficult time to get hold of any of the judiciary but he would see if he could pull some strings and if successful either she or Ron Wilkins would have to appear before the judge to argue their case for a Court order and as there was no immediate danger to life or property it was unlikely an order would be granted until Tuesday but that he would try for her.

"Have you finished with me now?" he asked Freya. "Yes, thank you, sir," she replied.

"Well, I haven't finished with you yet," Mr Gaunt told her which really put the 'Breeze up' her.

Before she could put in a word, Mr Gaunt asked her just what in the hell was going on with Detective Chief Inspector Johns? He told her that the 'Fellow' had been bombarding him and his staff with 'phone calls about conditions in her station, her conduct with that of Ron Wilkins and above all Superintendent Cole who had humiliated him several times.

Mr Gaunt continued, "Johns went on about Ron Wilkins keeping all the serious crime to your men and leaving him the rubbish. The taking all the furniture from your CID office and leaving him with nothing, being held in obvious contempt by the entire staff in your station and Divisional HQ. "I would like to replace him," Bill told her, "not his team, but I don't appear to have anyone available."

"Is it as bad as he makes out?" he asked Freya.

"All I can say, sir," she replied "is that he is the author of his own difficulties. He came down here with the obvious intention of making trouble in particular about me and my position as head of CID."

Mr Gaunt replied, "Yes, I expected that but not all the fuss that I had to put up with and after all, he has been there only one day.

That having been said, I don't want Fred or you making unnecessary trouble with him and that includes that Jake. Jake might think that he has this entire force in the palm of his hand but he ain't got me. I believe in fair play and I'm not complaining about Fred's involvement but he can go a bit too far."

Without taking a decent breath, Bill Gaunt continued; "Last evening I had a moan from the chief inspector of Special Branch about Fred. It would appear that Fred told your station special branch bloke that he could take a running jump at himself if he thought that he could have any documents pertaining to a current enquiry before that enquiry was completed. Has the chap been to see you?"

"No, sir," she replied," But I have been told that Special Branch has 'an interest' in my case."

"Yes," he replied, "Do you know why?" Freya told him that she had no idea why 'Paper shufflers' would have an interest in her case. "Because of the Russian ship and her with the 'Iron gob'. Watch the buggers or they will try to hand your case to the Mets and I'm quite sure that Fred will not stand for that, not on any account.

If it comes to that neither will I. That's the lot; for now, I'm going down for my breakfast. When I have eaten and it's past nine I will make a few 'phone calls but don't hold your breath." Mr Gaunt advised. "Thank you, sir; I'll wait for your call," she told him."

When it was past nine, Freya was in a bit of a dilemma, did she ring the forensic laboratory and perhaps get held up with them or wait until Mr Gaunt phoned back 'after 9:00'? She came down on the side of her boss.

In the meantime, she went over all the points of interest to her case so far collected. One such matter of great interest to her was the human and dog hair on the adhesive tape which bound up body number one. When she could find out if the name Harrison Hacker was correct and that he was a Civil Servant and if that was his occupation, which ministry or department did he work for and why was he not reported as a missing person?

While deep in thought the telephone ringing brought her back to the present with a jolt. Picking up the receiver she said, "Yes, Sir."

"How did you know it was me?" asked Bill Gaunt.

"Instinct, sir, and I was told as a slip of a probationer that if I answered the 'phone with my rank, collar tab and name I could be held to account for any make-believe accusation whereas if I said 'Yes, sir' the only people I would be likely to offend would be a woman and as our sex doesn't count and no one would know who I was!"

Bill replied "The only person who would claim nowadays that your sex didn't count would be the likes of the pre-historic Fred Cole, bless his cotton socks. Right, down to business. I tried an Assize court judge and he couldn't or wouldn't do it, he is probably busy on the Golf course. I have rounded up a County court judge and he will not do it until Tuesday. Get Ron to the County court at 10:30 with all his facts and figures and Judge Baker will give him an order then as a civil matter rather than a criminal case. It might be easier for them to digest and us to get the details we want."

"Thank you, sir, for your efforts, and I do apologise for disturbing you on a weekend morning," Freya told him.

"Ta-Ta," was his final word.

Freya then rang the Forensic Laboratory and again they stalled on her question relating to the findings from the detritus under the white van. She was exasperated by the delays in giving her their findings.

She asked for' her belt' officer and was told that he wasn't on duty but they would see if he was at home and ask him to contact her but they doubted if he would be the officer dealing with such a mundane matter.

As she rang off she decided that long Bank Holidays were not such a good idea in her trade.

With nothing on the boil so to speak, she made up her diary and yet again went through the events and minutiae of the case to see if there were any holes in her direction of enquiry. She came to the conclusion that the line of the inquiries was heading in the right direction but simply needed to bring to a conclusion that at the minute was a rather distant hope.

It did appear that somehow the Russians were involved and she would certainly get no help from them. On the contrary, they would either ignore any approach by her or feed her totally false information. She had not dealt with any cases dealing with international jurisdiction and if this Russian link was positive, she certainly was not looking forward to it.

Bored out of her mind she looked through all the paperwork that she could find including the fraud and assault cases still being dealt with by her team. Both appeared to be very complex but Ron Wilkins had assured her that the detective sergeants and constables on these cases were excellent at their jobs and he was supervising them and would be responsible for any 'cock-ups'.

At lunchtime, her 'phone rang and on the other end of the line was her 'Friend' from forensics. As he was ringing from home he could not have access to any results from the tests on the underside of the white van but if she would care to wait until Tuesday he would get hold of the chap who carried out the examination and get him to give her the information that she wanted.

However, if he was called back from his long weekend before Tuesday he would look up the results, if any, and let her know. She thanked him and told him that if she was not there get whoever answered the 'phone to inform either her or Ron Wilkins of the result and forward a paper report ASAP.

As she put the phone down, she decided that this weekend was lost, completely lost. Freya decided that she would stay at the station until the two to ten 'nightwatchman' appeared and if nothing had moved by then she would go home and sit by the phone.

There were no calls that afternoon, evening or night and on the Saturday morning she couldn't make her mind up at first whether she would go in or not as nothing appeared to be likely to happen.

After her breakfast, she had another thought and decided that as she was the 'On call' senior officer for the CID she should make an appearance. She duly arrived and found that her six to two woman was at her post and as Freya had made a noisy entry to the general office she gave the girl time to stuff her magazine up her skirt and inside her waistband, as she would have done in similar boring circumstances.

"Good morning," Freya said to the same girl that she had remonstrated with the day before for catching her with her feet up and reading a magazine. Not necessarily for reading but for being caught. A good crime investigator always covers their back, a lesson seemingly learned by the girl thanks to ma'am deliberately making a noisy entry.

"Morning, ma'am," the girl replied very slowly standing up. The girl's ascent to the upright reminded Freya of the days of paper petticoats when she visited Wells Cathedral for evensong. A man, presumably their father, brought his two teenage girls to the service and as they sat in the chairs in front of her so, particularly in the echoing vastness of the cathedral, the noise from them sitting down on their obviously paper petticoats caused a few heads to turn towards them. From her seat, Freya suspected that both girls would have very flushed cheeks.

To her, the rest of the service was a challenge for the young women to avoid any unnecessary rustling from their petticoats as they repeatedly had to stand up and sit down several times.

The gentle standing up and sitting down for her two fellows congregates at Wells to minimise any rustling of paper was now being replicated by her detective constable in a determined effort not to allow any stray rustling of her magazine to alert ma'am to what was stuffed up her skirt.

"Please bring me the logbook for me to peruse," she asked the constable, "in my office if you please," she added.

The constable went slowly but slightly hunched to pick up the book and then approached the opened office door with Freya standing in the doorway with her hand outstretched for the book. As the woman handed the book to her chief inspector so her magazine decided that despite the all-embracing waistband, to allow gravity to take its natural course.

In that instant of descent, no hand could have stopped the magazine from hitting the floor as the owner watched in horror as it struck the floor and then slide only to be stopped by the closing office door. On this occasion, Freya decided that she would choose not to see the magazine in the hope that her constable would finally see that idling her time by reading the magazine on duty was not a 'crime'. The 'crime' was to be caught reading it and should the woman reach officer rank she too would practise the delicate art of discretion.

As Freya sat at her desk and opened the logbook her mind wandered to her first sergeant when she was a probationer and the way that he dealt with transgressions by his constables. One particular constable had been warned by the sergeant not to take his small Japanese transistor in his pocket when on patrol.

On this particular occasion, she was in the sergeant's patrol car or to be precise, van. As they approached the 'point' where the constable should be before the sergeant gave him his new or perhaps continuing patrol.

The constable, without a mentor, was at his 'point' and the sergeant leaned out of the vehicle window and said to the constable. "What have you got in your greatcoat pocket son?" The constable denied having anything in his pocket. The sergeant then told him to produce whatever that he had in his pocket.

The constable very shamefacedly produced a shiny small transistor radio. The sergeant held out his hand and the constable gave him the radio. The sergeant looked at it very closely and told the owner "What a lovely bit of Japanese technology it was." The very silly constable was stupid enough to tell the sergeant that 'Was' in the past tense where the present tense should be 'Is', the constable told the sergeant that he should have said 'Japanese technology it 'Is'.

The sergeant then told him that this was the second time that he had caught him with the transistor on duty and had warned him. With that, the sergeant with the radio still in his hand dropped it on the road, reversed the van and drove forward and crushed the radio, probably flat. The constable appeared to be near fainting.

"Oh, dear, what a Butterfingers I am," said the sergeant. "I don't know just what tense you would like me to use sonny Jim," was the sergeant's conclusion of the conversation. No doubt the probationer finally got the message. Those in authority always win, particularly if you repeatedly twist their tails. A good lesson for her in those formative years and never forgotten.

With the logbook imparting nothing of any relevance since she had last read it, she returned it to her constable and said to her, "I am new here so I don't know any of you very well. How did you become a detective? What made you want to be a detective and have you been on the initial detective course?"

The woman answered that she began her career in the 'A' division and became involved in a woman trafficking crime as a uniformed constable.

After the case was successfully prosecuted her then detective sergeant offered her the chance in CID on a trial period as a plainclothes constable. If she did well in plainclothes she would be offered a place in the regular Criminal Investigation Department but not on 'A' division and that's why she came to the 'D' division before trying to get selected for the Initial Detective course which Mr Broadweir said he would support concluding with, "Before you took his place, ma'am."

Freya then asked her, "Were you still on probation when you went to plainclothes?"

"Yes, ma'am," was the woman's reply, "Why did you ask me that, ma'am?" Freya, remembering her course when she was without warning 'poached' by the Regional Crime Squad and never looked back. she replied to the question with,

"Despite your achievements I am very conscious that you have not fully embraced the necessary guile or to be more plain, the required professionally acceptable deceit towards your superiors by an ordinary police officer never mind a detective.

You should not have allowed me to catch you with your feet up reading a magazine and I was aware of another lapse this morning. I do not intend to sound like your mother, I am only a few years older than you but, now that you have told me about your success in prosecuting the 'Trafficking ring I do wonder why you have not fully embraced the ethos of investigative policing? I do appreciate that this hiatus in the investigating of double murder is for you stuck here very boring and if it is any consolation I too am bored ridged.

If necessary get yourself a piece of paper and doodle or write a poem, a story or what a so and so your superior officer is, anything to look busy and have your Police Bible alongside you just in case Acting Detective Chief

Inspector Freya Douglas Gore Hamilton comes calling." With a rather straight look at her detective constable, she began another story.

"A very dear friend of mine told me the story of when he was a young constable and he regularly had to walk past the inspector's office. Every time that he went past the open door the inspector would not just call out his tab number, no not him. He would shout at the top of his ill-tempered voice, "2963, why are you again idling your time. Get some work done, you idle bastard."

This would happen three or four times a day. The only breaks would be if the inspector was at his refreshment or out of the station. My friend was almost the butt of the jokes with many shouts in the mess room of 2963, "What are you doing here? Idle bastard." Now be mindful that this constable had been a mariner with a far superior background and education than the inspector, yet after a while, the continual oppression was wearing him down.

One day an elderly sergeant, as crafty as it was possible to be, the authorities were pleased that he was a policeman rather than a confirmed rogue, they would never have caught him in a month of Sundays'.

This sergeant caught the arm of my friend and propelled him to his office door. The scene was apparently not dissimilar to a Charles Dickens conspiracy from Oliver Twist. The slightly bent elderly sergeant with a crooked finger beckoned the tall well-built distinguished-looking friend of mine to his office. Behind a closed door, the sergeant offered my friend a sound bit of practical advice which could be construed as 'professional deceit'.

Freya continued, "The sergeant took my friend's right hand and placed a piece of A4 paper folded once in his hand. He then straightened my friend's right arm with the paper clearly visible.

The sergeant then told PC 2963 to walk past the inspector's open door when he had gone past wait for ten minutes and transfer the paper to his left hand, still clearly visible and walk past the open office door again and maintain the system no matter even if he was only going to the lavatory.

My friend, with no small amount of apprehension, did as the sergeant instructed and he walked past the inspector's door without a peep of sound. He again walked past it on his return and again, not a sound.

My friend thanked the sergeant for the advice that appeared to work. The sergeant said of the inspector 'He was a sergeant major in the Artillery and before he came to us he was an instructor at Sandhurst. All they know is to shout and bawl and look immaculate. The truth is that most of the officers and senior NCOs don't know their arse from their elbow and shouting covers up their shortcomings.

It is not at all difficult to get the better of them if you understand just what drives them. You have now got the better of him. He will now boast how he shouted you into submission and that you are no longer idling your time. The thought that you are still 'Idling' with a blank piece of paper has not and will not enter his cast iron head.

The sergeant continued to tell my friend, "I have spent my thirty years of service pitting my limited intelligence against their presumed superior knowledge and intelligence. To date, I have won every round and I lead a comfortable life and next year, if I decide to, I will retire with a nice pension and no ulcers unlike most of the 'white shirts'."

Freya continued, "My friend who at some stage you will probably come across, became a master in the art of understanding the rather low mentality of many of the sergeants and officers. Efficient these people may have been in their work hence their promotion but the arts of management and staff control were lost on most and like the inspector, when unable to cope would then resort to shouting or belittling their inferiors to try and make their rather childish points.

Today Miss you have had an almost full experience of both sides of the argument, think of all the events involving me and my reactions to your failings yesterday and today and make a plan of how you are to develop guile necessary for coping today and protecting yourself and your pension in the future."

Through the long lecture, the woman had sat quietly and seemed to be interested in that elderly sergeant's story. She then asked Freya "Who taught you professional deceit, ma'am?"

Freya replied with the hint of a blush, "My dear friend." She then looked at her watch and said, "After this long lecture you may go home and digest what I have said and in some cases perhaps implied and I will carry on here until the two to ten person comes in then once they have settled in I will go home too."

"Thank you, ma'am, you're very kind," the woman told her.

She replied, "Oh no, I'm not kind, just practical. Goodbye."

When Freya was alone she unlocked her desk and laid her journal on her desk opening it for Thursday with the programme of investigation that she had laid out then and updating it as necessary.

She read;

A) Staff Sergeant Fergusson witnessed a woman with steel teeth at the docks.
Checked with Richard Young Immigration Officer. The woman known as the crew of Russian ship in the dock with name declared as Irina Kristovitch. (Mr Young is of opinion that Russian is not her first language).

B) White van is stopped entering the dock. Inside is the same woman as at A). The driver claimed to be ships agent for Russian ship taking a woman back to ship before the vessels imminent sailing for the Baltic. The driver was later identified as a body in the locks (number two body) identified by the staff sergeant. Photo circulated. To date no response. Positively NOT a ship's agent. Claimed by Dock guards to visit Russian & East German ships.

C) Three days later complaints of a white van obstructing cargo working. Van opened and bound, gagged and blindfolded male body found in the rear (Body Number one). Van identified as the vehicle containing Woman as at (A) and body number two by the staff sergeant. Allegedly entering dock as ships agent.

D) No identity for either body. Body one had a preliminary post mortem. Believed cause of death, slow asphyxiation owing to compression of chest owing to bindings. Prominent long term mole to the left cheek. Fibres under fingernails from the jacket on body two. Tenuous name for body one, Harrison Hacker, a civil servant from a place near Salisbury Plain. Identified by this name from a photo by civilian police worker there.

E) Body two. Preliminary inspection and post mortem. Stab wound under the left arm from possibly long thin weapon probably similar to size 00 knitting needle. Little water in the lungs from an alleged drowning. No identifying marks.

F) Ongoing enquiries: Checking belt phone number (Tuesday)
Checking samples from under van. (Tuesday if not before)
Circulating photo-fit of Iron Gob and her name. (Tuesday)
Why no response yet from a photo of body two (Check with Ron on Monday or Tuesday)

G) Enquire why there were no clear prints or even smudged ones in the van other than those of body two? Wiped? Taken a lot of trouble, why?

Why kill body one? Why bind him up? Why in a dockyard in a van? Was the body to be disposed of from the van? If so where and why? Why kill body two in the dock? Were means of identification, e.g. a wallet removed from the body before disposal in locks. Because he was involved in the death of body one in some way?

H) Common factors with body one and two. Same phone number on the inside of their belts. Forensics to check again on hairs and fibres on the adhesives binding body one. Why no reports of missing persons?

The Russian ship and Iron Gob have a crucial role in explaining events and the reason for those events.

An obvious connection so far is 'spying' or other nefarious activities. Why is special branch 'taking an interest' in the job and not only wanting but demanding the paperwork for the case? (Further demands by DCI Special branch. Mr Cole and Mr Gaunt to deal with on Tuesday. Poor Special 'Twigs')

With her head down writing in her journal, Freya thought that a woolly hat with a bobble went past her internal window.

When she looked up wondering what she had seen and in truth not believing her eyes, a tap came on her door. She looked at the door and could see Mrs Briggs holding a dainty cup of tea. Freya opened the door and Mrs Briggs said "I'm sorry to disturb you Miss but I thought that you would like some tea. They told me that you'm down yer.

Freya just stood there as if in a trance. She collected herself and told Mrs Briggs to come in and have a chair just in time to take the by now half of a dainty cup of tea from the Tea Lady's shaking hand. Extracting her thumb from the tea in the saucer she asked Mrs Briggs.

"What are you doing here on a Saturday morning? You wouldn't normally be here today and although I do appreciate it, you should certainly not have come down two flights of stairs with one hand holding china crockery, should you?"

The diminutive Mrs Briggs explained that "That Jake told I that yesterday was good Friday and I wouldn't be wanted yer. Because none of them would be yer, they don't think that there be still someone still working yer. It upset me a bit Miss so I thought that I would come in today.

I asked if you be yer an' they said you was down yer So I came down but I 'ad to come down with the cup in me 'and as me trolley couldn't get down yer, miss."

She took a drink of the by now cold tea and told Mrs Briggs that it was "Most refreshing," and repeated her warning to Mrs Briggs not to come down those stairs. She continued.

"I do so appreciate your cup of tea Mrs Briggs, but in future, if you are so kind to make a cup of tea for me, tell the control officer to ring me here or still better ask one of the officers up there to bring me the tea; otherwise, I will come up and collect it from your trolley."

"I be so pleased that you be yer Miss. You be a cut above the others but mind 'e it might surprise 'e to 'ear that Mr Cole be very kind to I. 'e likes 'is tea in that pint pot, no milk three spoons a sugar and as strong as tar," Mrs Briggs gave a little cackle for a laugh as her few remaining teeth had a view of the outside world.

She continued, "Mr Thomas be very kind too. 'e sometimes gives I a lift to town and 'e goes into the Bank for I and sorts me money out."

"Sorts your money out?" Freya asked. "Oh yes Miss, 'e knows 'ow to do it." Freya then asked her, "Is Mr Briggs still alive?"

"No, miss," replied Mrs Briggs, "We got married in 1939 and that night' e went away to fight in France and 'e never come 'ome again. It fair broke me 'eart Miss."

The look on that weather beaten elderly face as she told her the truly distressing story almost brought Freya to tears and Mrs Briggs must have noticed and she then said to Freya.

"I be sorry Miss to upset you but you did ask, don't take on, it's gone, nothing will change it. It were a long time ago. 'E were a reservist so 'e 'ad to go. When Mr Cole found out about my 'enry 'e said that I should 'ave a pension and 'e and Mr Fergusson got I one. 'E were so kind, nothin' were too much trouble. I knows that I should 'ave done summat about it when I were young but I were so upset, I just couldn't. Me dad were killed in the Great War and mum 'ad a terrible time bringing us up, at least I didn't 'ave any kids to worry about." The silence between the two women only seemed to emphasise the gulf of age, social circumstances, education and wealth between the two.

After a very long pause Freya then asked Mrs Briggs, "How did Mr Fergusson help you. I did not think that he and Mr Cole got on very well?"

"That's right, miss," Mrs Briggs replied. She then said to Freya, "Mr Cole 'elped I out many years ago then about two years ago they stopped me pension. Mr Cole knew all sorts of high up people in the army and got me the pension and 'ad it backdated so I 'ad lots of money an' I went to the bank and they flummoxed I, I didn't know what they was talkin' about and they said to get a lawyer sort of chap to deal with my money.

I asked Mr Thomas what I should do an 'e said that if I wanted to 'e and Mr Sir Bates would deal with my money and the bank. They took me to a lawyer chap an'. Mrs Briggs then let out a tension relieving chuckle and continued, "they told 'im that 'e would be working fer them and me an' 'e wouldn't get any money fer it. The look on 'is face were a picture I can tell 'e, miss."

Another bout of cackling laughter as she continued, "This bloke produced a lot of paper fer me to read, but..." in a very quiet voice added, "I can't read Miss, I be ashamed, but I just can't. Anyhow it got sorted out an' Mr Thomas looks after it for me with Mr Cole and this lawyer bloke."

"Freya asked again, "How did Sergeant Fergusson get involved, particularly with Mr Cole?"

Mrs Briggs then told her, as best that she could, the complicated events that occurred a couple of years ago,

"Mr Fergusson found I with a letter, he's a lovely man, an' I gave 'im a letter. He read it and then asked I all about the pension from the army an' told me that this letter were from some ministry or other an' that Mr Cole 'ad seen to it for I and then all about the money and Mr Thomas."

Mrs Briggs then went through all the ups and downs of her pension, the reason that she had not received one before and the limitations of her inability to be able to read or write.

Mr Fergusson went to Mr Cole with the letter and let both him and Mr Thomas read it and although at that point Mr Fergusson had not told her that the letter was to tell her that the pension was stopped and that as a matter of charity they would not claim back all the money that they had given her plus the back pension.

She was told by the staff sergeant that her pension had been stopped because of an administrative mistake when Mr Cole got her the pension but that he would take it further with Mr Cole.

The reason that it was stopped was because Mr Cole dealt with the 'High ups' in the army and they arranged it.

Now all that sort of thing had been through a new ministry replacing the War Ministry and they did not believe that Mrs Briggs was married to Henry Briggs. She had never seen her marriage certificate and apparently the friends of Mr Cole in the army never bothered with such things, the word of Mr Cole was never doubted. If Cole said that she was married to Henry, that was an undisputed fact for his friends in the army.

Mr Cole and Mr Fergusson did 'Summat or other' and got her a new marriage certificate which showed that she was married by a special license to Henry.

Even after this the ministry of whatever then, of all things, doubted that it was a marriage in law as records showed that Henry returned to his unit during the evening and the marriage was not therefore consummated and Mrs Briggs was not the widow of Henry Briggs. Staff Sergeant Fergusson knew a lot of important people up in 'Lunnon' and got the pension returned to her and a letter of apology. "'e be a lovely man Miss." Mrs Briggs told Freya. "Who is so lovely Mrs Briggs?" She asked.

"Mr Fergusson, miss," Mrs Briggs replied, than continued, "I know that 'e an' Mr Cole do argue and row but they both 'elped I an' they didn't 'ave to. I knows that Mr Fergusson looks a bit bad tempered at times, but 'es got a 'eart of gold, Miss. 'E will 'elp you at any time an' no trouble."

"I must get on, miss," Mrs Briggs told Freya, "I expect that youm very busy and don't need I tellin' you me stories but, before you told I that you was friends with Mr Fergusson. You 'ang on to 'im Miss, 'e be a good un an' clever."

As the very elderly 'Char' lady left her office Freya noticed that she had the 'Dainty cup and saucer' in her hand as she headed for the double flight of stairs and called to her to stop and allow Freya to carry the china up to her trolley in the station foyer.

The final words of that conversation was from Mrs Briggs, "Youm so kind Miss, I 'ope that youm stays yer with Mr Fergusson."

Freya returned to her office and sat thinking about the story of Mrs Briggs. Yet again she felt her eyes welling up, which for a supposedly hardened detective chief inspector was quite unknown.

People in the beginning of the sixth decade of the century thought that they were hard done by with strikes, demonstrations, youthful disregard for common decency and limited civil unrest.

She asked herself if the modern generation with all the advantages that did not exist in nineteen eighteen could be accommodated with the stoicism and relative good humour as displayed by Mrs Briggs. The bigger question was, could, with all her advantages of birth, education and career cope with the circumstances embracing Mrs Briggs. Freya decided that she would not cope, she would be bitter and resentful, particularly of her class were she in the shoes of Mrs Briggs.

The hitherto mundane Saturday morning was a truly inspiring and thought changing time all because an elderly, outside of work, friendless person, had come into work simply for company and her kind gesture in thinking of others, namely Freya with a 'Dainty cup and saucer' of tea had a profound effect on Miss Douglas Gore Hamilton who in future, without names, lecture about to her conceited, mollycoddled spoilt new CID constables.

If they were capable of absorbing the moral of the account, this would be an achievement that could shape their thinking for the better as they climbed the greasy pole to positions of influence in the police forces of the future.

Both Superintendent Cole and Staff Sergeant Fergusson were of the 'Flog and Hang them' mentality, Mrs Briggs story told a very different side to their character. When someone was in need they buried, for a while, their differences to help someone with problems.

All in all Freya decided that although it was a tearful morning it was life enhancing for her and in the future others; if they were prepared to listen to the story of an old lady far removed from the life of relative luxury that they were all now leading.

That she still had not finished the points of her double murder in her journal no longer concerned her. She found that after the visit by Mrs Briggs she could not put her whole mind to the matters in question and was best left until the afternoon.

When she felt a little more sure of herself she decided to go to her old office upstairs now inhabited by Detective Chief Inspector Johns, and check on her men still involved with existing enquiries.

As she entered the CID office Mr Johns two 'Night watchmen' busy playing Cribbage looked up and promptly put the Crib board and cards under papers on the desk. They stood up then in unison bade Freya "Good morning, ma'am." She returned the greeting and deciding that nothing useful could be gained by remonstrating with them, went to her office and using her key let herself in.

The looks on the faces of the two detectives as she let herself into the office of their boss was quite a picture. Probably the fact that she still had a key for the office was quite a revelation to them and something to tell Mr Johns about when he returned on the following Tuesday.

She unlocked the filing cabinet and dug out the papers of the three fraud cases under investigation. Settling herself in the chair she glanced through the papers signed off by her predecessor Harry Broadweir. Harry was ahead of the game in deciding by the previous Monday that two should go initially to the magistrates court before being sent to the Assize court when it next sat, probably at the Michaelmas Assize.

The other one which he had noted in the margin positively lacked the necessary proof intent or the indisputable evidence of any discernible success.

From her brief appraisal of the papers she disagreed with Harry's conclusion. She decided that although the commissioning of the fraud appeared to have failed, there was a reasonable case for pursuing the necessary intent behind the commissioning of the fraud. She then scribbled her opinion on the papers and her reasoning.

This venture into normal CID work had taken the Mrs Briggs episode from her mind and she then locked everything away and noting a change of faces in the general CID office realised that her own 'two to ten' relief would be looking for the person that they were due to relieve in the bunker.

She shot down the stairs in time to find the relief busy looking for whoever he was relieving and she then told him that she was the person that he would relieve.

She noted that the detective constable was the same one that she had caught lying to her concerning his whereabouts yesterday.

She went into her office and re-opened her journal and read again what she had written about her own cases.

It was obvious to her that both her bodies needed further scientific evidence concerning both the positive cause of death and anything connecting them with practises which would cause 'An interest' by Special Branch and in particular the Harrison Hacker and employment in a 'Ministry', which ministry?

She then went out in to the bunker general office and wrote again that 'phone calls relating to the case should be referred immediately to her or Detective Inspector Wilkins.

She had thought that Mr Gaunt might have got in touch again relating to a court order for the 'phone numbers but she was certainly not going to ring him again during a long weekend.

Since the story of Mrs Briggs had so upset her she could not concentrate, even with the reading of the fraud case notes it had needed all her will power to prevail at tackling the task. Up the two flights of stairs she went almost gasping for fresh air outside of the station.

When she arrived at her home in the city she rang her parents' home in Somerset where she knew the housekeeper would be in charge as her parents would be at their small farm and vineyard on the banks of the river Dart in South Devon.

Freya told Mrs James that she would be arriving early evening to stay until early evening on Sunday and would appreciate cook rustling up something and lunch on Sunday.

Her great-grandfather from Aberdeen had made the family fortune in farms and food packaging, firstly canning and then when freezing was established as a viable of preserving meat, building and owning Freezer works in both New Zealand and Australia then sending the frozen produce to Britain in his own sailing ships fitted with freezing engines to keep the cargo deep frozen for the three or so months that it sometimes took to sail from the Antipodes to Britain.

His success was assured when he introduced meat from 'The Colonies' to the Royals just as succulent as that produced in Britain. The high honours soon followed.

With the advent of steam ships with freezer engines, he created a renowned steam shipping line to carry both his and others produce between great Britain and the Antipodes. Since the late seventeenth century the Court had been the maternal family home. With great-grandfather marrying into the family, he had the court renamed Awatea Court in honour of New Zealand. Being a proud Aberdonian living in England, he insisted on the family Scottish names being retained, hence Freya's numerous names.

After her grandfather took over the running of the family business her great-grandfather, by then a widower, returned to end his days in New Zealand in the 'Scottish' province of Otago.

At 6 o'clock Freya returned to 'D' division to go to the bunker to recover her handbag which she 'forgot' when she left just after 2 o'clock that afternoon. Much to her delight her 'Night watchman' constable was in his position and surprise, surprise, he was diligently reading the Police Gazette.

Unfortunately for the young gentleman he had it upside down and he apparently only realised his mistake when his acting detective chief inspector took hold of the 'Gazette' from his hands, slowly, so very slowly turned it the right way around. The constable allowed his hands to fall by his side as the abject face echoed his mental process and the overbearing silence from ma'am.

Freya went to her office and typed on a piece of A4 paper. 'When you get to Australia your Gazette will be easily readable. It will be the right way up. When you have a moment to leave your post, which I'm sure that you will do very reluctantly, or better still, ring upstairs for the duty inspector and ask him how the staff sergeant deals with constables reading the Gazette upside down?'

Signed.

Freya Douglas Gore Hamilton ADCI.

Locking her office door with her handbag on her arm she went to her detective constable and handed him the typed sheet and said.

"This must be a bad day for you. Had I not forgotten my handbag, your life would have been that so much better. Think about it young man." As she went up the stairs the thought came to her that she had called her constable 'Young Man' yet again, he was probably only a couple of years younger than her.

At the top of the stairs she went into the control room and knocked on the door of the duty inspector went in and told him the circumstances of her visit late on a Saturday afternoon and asked him to ensure that her man was confined to the bunker except for a visit to him to ask how the staff sergeant dealt with repeating police miscreants.

The inspector laughed and replied "With pleasure, and I will point out to him just how cold, wet and miserable it is on the pavement, particularly with police boots leaking and a wet cape weighing a ton at least. If he is so thick that he doesn't take the hint then you don't need him and neither do I. Leave it with me, ma'am."

As she turned to leave the office the inspector said, "Thank you for livening my otherwise boring Saturday afternoon. I will alert the constables to keep an eye out for him, they will love screwing a detective, if you will pardon the expression, ma'am, and the implied slur on your staff."

With a smile that could bring men to her feet, Freya replied, "Not at all inspector, I was a uniformed constable once. Goodbye."

By 8 o'clock, she had brought her Bristol to a halt at the mews of her home. She then walked to the front door where she was met by Mrs James who welcomed her and took her inside her home. Inside she told Mrs James that she would be attending the church adjacent to the Manor for Mattins and after lunch she might return north depending on her mood at the time, whichever it was she would not require dinner, just a snack.

Freya was not sure if Mrs James approved of ditching dinner for a 'snack' but she expected that cook would not be unhappy.

The late Easter day dawned very bright and still as her curtains were opened and a cup of tea deposited on her bedside cabinet. Freya sat up in bed, yawned, stretched and turned towards her cup of tea. As she touched the china her mind went back to Mrs Briggs and she was so relieved to find herself not in the atmosphere of the city but here in the countryside on a most beautiful late Spring day.

She decided laying there in the lap of luxury just what a totally different worlds inhabited by Mrs Briggs and herself. No tea in bed, no one to cook your meals, no one to have conversation with, always penny-pinching and very elderly.

Her thoughts wandered to the question of, if she offered Mrs Briggs the opportunity of a holiday at mothers home at Manor Farm in Devon, would she accept it? Probably not and would it not only be insensitive but cruel to take her to a place such as that when she would have to return to the comparative squalor of her accommodation? Probably not. What about her embarrassment, a terrible price for an elderly lady to pay if she was conscious of social etiquette, her clothes and manner of speech.

She decided that it might be more comfortable to offer Mrs Briggs a week or so at a good sea-side hotel but there again would she feel isolated? Freya then concentrated on the act of getting up and ready for breakfast.

Freya came down to breakfast in a summery design of frock predominately blue and enjoyed a full English, a meal that she only had here at home with cooks specially crisp bacon and beautifully fried eggs. After breakfast she told Mrs James that she was going to church for the Easter morning service and Eucharist and learned that Mrs James and her husband, the head gardener, would also be there.

As she left Awatea Court she walked across the gravelled drive, the south lawn and then into the path through the Avenue of newly budding Beech trees with the Spring sunshine making shadows through the newly greening branches.

Freya had added a white jacket with white gloves to contrast with her frock, blue court shoes and blue handbag. She eventually came to the gate in the Estate wall leading to the immaculate lawn fortunately not containing any graves and the often appalling headstones.

The Court through her Father was the patron of the church and the village school. They paid the stipend of the Rector and his curate, the cost of maintaining the fabric of both the church, rectory and school and in the nineteenth century had paid for the church to be enlarged with some vast improvements to the interior and the tower with the eight bells in the ringing chamber.

Although when she left the Court Freya could hear the wonderful sound of the bells, as she approached the gate into the churchyard the sound of the Easter bells was almost deafening.

She looked at her watch as she passed through the gate to make sure that it was no earlier than five minutes to eleven. It was considered to be a poor show of church etiquette for the 'Gentry' of the village to arrive before the congregation was seated. One by one the bells fell silent and the Sanctus bell then began the five minute tolling before the service began.

As she walked up to the porch where the rector and his curate with their wives were waiting to greet her. No doubt Mrs James had alerted them to her visit. The two ladies did a brief 'bob' as the very elderly Rector Smythe welcomed her into 'Gods House' with the curate shaking her hand.

Freya then walked to the 'Court' pew the first pew on the right and acknowledged the nodding and bobbing from the estate workers in the pew behind the only cushioned pew in the church!

She made a deep curtsey to the altar then sat down, removed her gloves then knelt on the hassock with her hands together in prayer. With Mrs Briggs in her mind, she asked for guidance from the Almighty what she should do for the old lady.

Freya felt the pew cushion move and the front of the pew itself move a fraction. She knew that someone was alongside her and instinctively knew who it was likely to be. She peeped out between her fingers and saw the sunlight through the huge rose east window reflecting from a large gold signet ring. She knew that her suspicions were correct and remained in her praying position as he joined her in prayer.

Freya got up from the hassock and sat back as Hamish followed her. As his hand was on the cushion to pull himself back onto the pew so she covered it with her hand and gave a gentle squeeze. They looked at each other and briefly smiled as Rector Smythe, standing in the doorway of the remarkably beautiful chancel screen, welcomed his congregation to the 'Easter day service on this beautiful Easter day morn'.

"The Lord is risen, Alleluia."

He then told the people, "We will now join together to sing Hymn 125; Ye choirs of new Jerusalem."

As the congregation thumbed through their 'Hymns, Ancient & Modern' for Hymn 125 so the mighty organ burst forth with the musical rendition of the first line before returning to the beginning as the congregation and choir stood up and did full justice to both the tune and words of the hymn.

The mezzo soprano voice of Freya coupled with the tenor of Hamish certainly set a new standard of melody for the congregation and the choir master. Even those in the Rectory pew, not the best of Christians to please, appeared to be in awe of powerful melody from those in the Court pew.

Amongst the people in the Court workers pew the words of the hymn was sometimes lost in the mouthed, nodded and raised questioning eyebrows towards the pew containing Freya and Hamish. The women being both delighted and nosy at seeing their beautiful young mistress with a distinguished looking man and the men simply wondering 'who in the hell is he?' "Please be seated," brought them all out of their speculation as Rector Smythe began his Easter ritual.

Eventually, the Sidesmen stood either side of the chancel as the rector and his curate began the ritual of Holy Communion and eventually invited the congregation to "Take the body and blood of their Saviour," in the Eucharist then quoted the preface for Easter Day 'But chiefly we are bound to praise thee for the glorious Resurrection of thy son…'

Freya and Hamish led the people through the chancel towards the altar rail and as he was about to guide her to the right side of the rail she nudged him straight to the centre of the rail and knelt on the altar steps with Hamish alongside her. As she knelt there she looked up above the altar at a beautiful scene that she'd observed since she was a very small child, the Spring sunshine coming through the huge east window lighting up and almost giving life to Jesus and the saints depicted in the richly coloured stained glass.

Hamish expected the issuing of the bread and wine to begin on the right hand of the rail but surprisingly to him the priest came straight to Freya placing the biscuit in her cupped hands intoning the words 'Take, eat, this is my body, which is given for you: He then repeated the ritual and words to Hamish. The priest then gave the 'Bread' to his server and placed his hands on the heads of Freya and Hamish and quietly said, "God's blessing on you his children."

At this point, Hamish should have been concentrating on Godly and righteous thoughts, instead he was smiling as he looked at the dilapidated, badly weather worn shoes peeping out from under the cassock of Mr Smythe. As his rector continued along the line of communicants, the curate gave the chalice of wine to Freya with the words, 'Drink ye all of this; for this is my blood of the New Testament'. As with the bread before, the curate then did the same to Hamish.

He was pleased to note that the curates shoes were in a satisfactory condition as he then allowed his thoughts to turn to a higher plane.

They prayed before getting to their feet with Freya curtsying to the altar as Hamish bowed his head. They then returned to their pew after coming under much scrutiny as they walked past the line of waiting communicates.

As they knelt in the pew Hamish was facing the brass plaque with the names of those from the village who did not return after the conflicts of the Great War and the second World War.

Amongst the names were those who died during the first conflict and the same name, probably their son during the second conflict. Although it should not have been a surprise to Hamish the names of two women of the merchant navy were included in the list of those killed during the period 1939 and 1945 in the service of their nation.

Although the social and class divide was clearly demonstrated before and during the service, again two names from the First war and one from the second conflict were engraved in the plaque which was a clear demonstration that there is no class system or distinction in death. The names were a James G.R. Douglas Hamilton of 1914 and an Angus James Douglas Gore Hamilton of 1939-1945.

With the final Blessing and a moment of quiet prayer Hamish led Freya out of the pew, she again curtsied to the altar then he stood back to walk behind her just as the occupants of the opposite front pew came into the aisle. Freya stopped as the wife of the man did a brief 'Bob' to her. The man shook hands with Freya and said, "A beautiful morning Miss Douglas Gore Hamilton."

She smiled at him, while Hamish noted the less than pleasant glare from the man's wife. Freya replied "Indeed it is Mr Kerr, indeed it is."

From the expression on his face it was very apparent that he was both confused and irritated that Freya made no effort to introduce him to this Mr Kerr. As they led the rest of the congregation to the porch door so the man nodded at Hamish and said, "Kerr."

Hamish slightly turned to him and said "Fergusson."

In the porch The clerics and their wives bade 'Goodbye' to Freya, with accompanying 'Bobs' from the ladies and head nodding bows from the rector and his curate. To Hamish, Rector Smythe said, with a goodly amount of emphasis to each word uttered. "Sir, I do sincerely hope that you will honour us with your presence soon."

Without comment, he simply smiled and shook hands with the Reverend Isaiah Smythe, D.D. (Cantab).

Whoever was on the belfry warning bell did a spectacular job with their thumb, timing to perfection the departure of Freya from her church porch. As they stepped from the flagstones of the porch so with a deafening crescendo of beautiful sound the eight bells rang out using the method Grandsire Triples.

The sound was of such magnitude that Hamish could feel the vibrations underfoot. As they stepped out so she put her arm through that of Hamish as they headed the congregation along the path. As the sound of the bells were so loud Freya could be assured that no word could pass between the following women about her and her 'mystery' gentleman. She was wrong, it was not the women but a very loud male that gave voice to his opinion that "You'd think it was their wedding." Looking straight ahead, in unison they both grinned broadly with their thoughts, theirs alone.

At the junction of the path with the gate marked, 'Awatea Court' in the wall they stopped and faced each other. He took her hand from his arm and lifted it and kissed it. As he did so Freya kissed him on the cheek then using her glove wiped her lipstick from his face. No one even attempted to walk past them, they just stood still and watched as she went into the avenue of Beech trees and he continued into the Glebe lands to find his car.

During the hour and a half that they had spent together not a single word had passed between them.

As Hamish reached the Lych Gate he looked back over the heads of the people following him to see the estate workers still standing at the gate to the court with a woman standing facing them with her arms outstretched, no doubt ensuring the courtesy was observed of not closely following their mistress to the court.

Easter Monday dawned bright and dry as Freya stepped out to drive to the police station and her CID bunker.

There she found her 'Night watchman' awake and reasonably alert as he had the kettle or rather a Burco urn on the boil for ma'am's tea. A guaranteed way to impress.

Here was a person who had learned the arts of maintaining harmony in any CID office in the land.

In her office there was only one message from Ron Wilkins with said, "This is the slowest investigation ever. Nothing here, nothing there. Been through the facts several times and if it was not Easter we could have half solved this one. See you tomorrow. Ron."

Freya opened her journal and read what she had written about the case and points to be considered and as a very long shot wrote. Go through Interpol with a Photofit of 'iron gob' just to see if any member force has come across her outside of the United Kingdom. In brackets she wrote (Ron, see Staff Sergeant Fergusson for photofit)

She was still racking her brain trying to think of what she may have forgotten when her ' phone rang. On the other end was Inspector Jones of Somstrym Police.

He was pleased to tell her that his men had traced the present address of the late Harrison Hacker and that it was on 'The Plain' near 'nowhere' and along a dirt track.

His chap had not attempted to visit the place but just have a good look around and while driving past the entrance to the dirt track saw a man and woman driving into the track.

Inspector Jones, in a very conspiratorial voice told Freya, "The officer took note of the number plate details and when he returned they ran a check and discovered that the registered owner was 'HM Government, the war office'. What do you think of that?" He asked Freya.

In a similar but female voice to his hushed tones she replied, "I am not too surprised, down here Special Branch have been poking their noses into the case and the involvement with a Russian ship has set their backsides on fire.

As the presumed disinterested wife of the late Harrison Hacker, she has not reported him missing." Mr Jones interrupted her to agree and say, "No, if she had reported him as a missing person it would be flagging up here and to put it simply, it ain't."

Freya asked Mr Jones what shift he was on? He told her that he was now off Tour until he picked up day tour on Tuesday. Between the two of them they arranged for her to send two detectives to meet up with him at their HQ and she asked for Mr Jones to provide a male and female uniformed officer to accompany her detectives to the dwelling and to meet up at their station at, subject to traffic, at 9:00 a.m.

"Why do you want a woman officer from me?" Mr Jones asked Freya.

She replied "Just in case when we tell her that her husband is dead she throws a wobbler but, call me naive if you want but I doubt that the information will be much of a surprise to her. My team coming over will be under the charge of Detective Sergeant Jobbins, "

After the usual niceties their conversation ended. She then looked through her journal and found Bill Jobbins number and told him what had happened and gave him the information of his liaising with Inspector Jones on the morrow.

She sat back in her chair and debated in her mind the breakthrough that Mr Jones and his civilian worker had achieved and just what could follow in that part of her case. This then brought her onto the matter of the GPO and the bureaucratic need for, of all things a court order from a judge of some sort.

What about her chum of the forensic team and the final positive results from the post mortems on the bodies giving the absolute cause of death good enough for indisputable court evidence?

While musing on these details and the staff that she would have available to her tomorrow, she had a vision of her boss, Detective Chief Superintendent William Gaunt, Q.P.M. Should she tell him of the situation? Or should she wait until tomorrow? To interrupt his Bank Holiday weekend once more might be asking for trouble. On the other hand, he hadn't come back to her relating to finding a cooperative Judge.

Freya pondered the pro's and con's for quite a while before deciding that she could cope with his wrath for doing something rather than his wrath for not informing him of developments and decided that she would ring him.

"Good morning, Sir," was the introductory words from Freya to Mr Gaunt, "Thi...." He interrupted her with, "I would recognise your voice amongst the Angels. How are things going?"

She then told Mr Gaunt of her conversation with Inspector Jones and what she intended to do tomorrow morning.

"Firstly," he replied, "I would take the registration of the motor car to the War Office issue very seriously and tell your chaps to tread carefully and take a search warrant, issued by a magistrate from that police area with them."

"Why a search warrant?" she asked him.

His reply, although half expected, surprised her by the sombre tone with which he told her "If this woman has not reported her presumed husband missing, she is hiding something. If when your men get there and she refuses to listen to their 'Harrowing' story in her house and keeps them on the door step, produce the warrant and get inside quickly.

The 'Chief' was contacted by the Home office yesterday. Yes, I know, it defies belief that the Home office was open on a Bank Holiday but it was and the long and short of it is that the War office and the internal intelligence services are putting pressure on the Home Office for us to drop the case and hand the paperwork to them.

The 'Chief' has handed this situation over to me, I have been in touch with Simon Bates and he has put the dirty work on you, me and also on to Fred Cole as the sub commander of 'D' Division.

The internal intelligence crowd are sending a chap to see us tomorrow. This might be trouble, particularly if or rather when Fred Cole gets involved. Although Fred is not directly involved in CID matters the responsibility for this job is to be shared with me."

Freya asked her boss," What is your opinion Sir?"

Mr Gaunt replied, "I'm up for a fight, but I fear that we might have lost this one already. When you get these MI5, Internal Intelligence and the War office fools with the craven complicity of the Home Office against my team, a positive outcome for us is remarkably unlikely. Having said that, with Fred Cole on our side, nothing is impossible."

She thought for a while and said to Mr Gaunt, "In the brief few days that I have known Superintendent Cole he did not strike me as a particularly able negotiator in matters requiring a subtle yet successful outcome, Sir."

"In your assessment of Fred, you are quite right," Mr Gaunt agreed. "But, I have known Fred most of my service days and the fact is that he can outsmart the supposedly smart simply by looking at situations from the lowest common denominator then scaling up to the highest common factor which his adversaries think that they command.

Failing that, his Regimental Sergeant Major side comes into play. He will do alright, I'd rather have him on my side than in the pockets of the opposition, particularly with men from the ministry of Eaton misfits. Be mindful that Fred is the secretary of your local working Men's Club. He mixes, considering his occupation, with every working man which will inevitably mean some rogues. He gives them no favours and they expect none.

They know that he is a man's man and accept that on some occasions he will enjoy his Guinness alone at the end of the bar. That's the beauty of his character, he can mix with anyone from Colonel to a Private soldier with, often inarticulate ease."

She then, with some trepidation, asked Mr Gaunt, "Will you be able to find a compliant judge to deal with the GPO by tomorrow Sir?"

"Done," was his reply and GPO dealt with. I have a name and address, are you ready?"

Freya replied, "Yes, Sir, I'm ready with pen poised," Mr Gaunt's reply began not with the name but warning her not to be a 'Smartie Pants'.

"You only need to say Yes, Sir, I'm not particularly interested in whether you use a pen, pencil or for that matter, a 'Poised' bloody finger."

"Sir," was the one-word reply from her.

"Name; Kurt Rosenberg. Address: Number seventeen. 1st Avenue, Sunny Patch, Gorse Lane, Bayrowbridge. Has your pen, pencil or bloodied finger taken all that down?" Mr Gaunt asked.

"Yes, Sir," she replied then added, "Not exactly an Anglo Saxon name is it? I take it that he was of German descent.

I seem to remember that when the fellow was spoken to at the docks he spoke English with a foreign accent. The origins of this name could be the reason why. Is the address that you have just given me happen to be on our patch Sir?"

Mr Gaunt replied with a surprising fact for her to digest. He told her; "Yes, it is in our patch or to be more particular within the Force boundary. I have done a check for you to discover that the place is on a wooded hillside in a remote location with only a couple of farms for company.

I have spoken to the local constable and gave him a near heart attack when on a Bank Holiday Monday the Force CID commander was on the end of the 'phone. In the absence of any of his superiors he had to answer it, poor devil. Anyway, this constable gave me some very useful and at this point, confidential information which is between you, me and that constable.

Firstly under no circumstances you will go to or attempt to go to that address mob-handed. Only with my authorisation will you or any others have any dealings with that address including covert surveillance being mindful of the ripples that this case is already having further up the line."

Freya was quite astounded by the facts and the tone of commanding voice used by Mr Gaunt as he laid out the 'Do Nots' something that he had never done with her before. Perhaps the interest from Whitehall was jangling his nerves.

She asked her Boss, "Other than we now know who body number two is, presumably, and where he lived, what is so important with this address sir?"

Mr Gaunt replied "It is a very upmarket nudist colony with a guard or person on the gate at all times. If our deceased friend is or was a spy or whatever, what an excellent place to hide. By the very nature of the nudist psyche, secrecy is their middle name.

As Mr Gaunt was speaking, Freya allowed a knowing smirk to cross her lips. Being German our 'Adolph' would be quite at home in such a place. I think that is a touch of brilliance whatever the blighter was up to.

My constable tells me that the place is made up of wooden lodges with all facilities, some owned and some rented for holiday lets. Recreation rooms, indoor and outdoor pools, a huge arena, and a large children's playground. Smart get up by all accounts or to be precise, according to my inquisitive constable."

Freya smiled as she asked Mr Gaunt, "That's a fascinating account Sir. How does the constable know so much about it?"

There was a long pause before Mr Gaunt replied "Some while ago a special messenger was sent from Whitehall with a message for a minister who had his weekend home there.

This messenger went to the place and he was stopped at the gate and told that unless he was a member or temporary member of the 'Association' he was not allowed in. He explained what he was and to who he had to hand the message. No Go. The guard would give no indication whether or not such a person was there and would not give the person, if he was there at all, a message that a messenger was at the gate.

The long and short of it was the messenger went to the nearest police station, a semi-detached house in the village and found my knowledgeable constable and after telephone calls between London and the lowly semi then between London and the subdivision chief inspector, it was decided by a distinctly windy chief inspector that the constable, 'Who knew the area' would be the man to deliver the message.

It was by good fortune that the colony site guard knew the constable and the constable knew quite a bit about the guard which the guard would be loath to have broadcast. They came to an arrangement for the constable to go in the place in civvies after dark.

The messenger had left our constable a sheaf of paperwork to be signed by our naked minister before he handed over the package. According to the constable at about 9:30 as it was almost dark he went in and, found the number of the shack, lodge or whatever and knocked on the door. It was answered by a woman in a 'sort of see through' wrap around.

She appeared to be as surprised as he was to see her and stuttered over his words. The minister then appeared in a dressing gown and a very snooty voice demanded 'What does this fellow want?' Our constable said what he wanted but that he would need identification before he handed the package over and all of the sheaf of papers signed as well as his pocketbook.

My constable told me that the very mention of a pocketbook was like a shot of lightening up his backside. My man then identified himself and he was almost dragged inside of the place. By now the woman also had a dressing gown on and the minister, without reading any of them signed the documents while my man made out his pocketbook. The minister closely studied what had been written in the pocketbook and satisfied himself that his place of residence was not identified, signed, timed and dated.

Chapter 5
Plot Deepens as Ma'am Visits Woodbine Cottage

That was the end of that incident but it gave the constable the chance to look around in the dusk and he was well satisfied with his work and the bottle of Brandy, and a whole box of now rare Havana cigars, then wasted, for his silence on the matter. He was a non-smoker!"

"Apparently," Mr Gaunt continued, "The constable was never asked about the incident, he simply sent the Ministry documents to the clerk at the subdivision HQ for return to London and I am the only person that he has mentioned the incident to. How about that? I have told him that my interest is very confidential and must not be divulged even if his superiors question him. I think that this is enough for now."

Freya then asked Mr Gaunt." What is your opinion relating to the matter of this Harrison Hacker and his presumed wife?"

He replied "Were I you I would not wait until tomorrow, I'd get up there today particularly if our friends in London are nosing about. If you wait you might lose evidence or even the woman herself. In fact, if I were you I would go there after you put the 'phone down."

"Thank you, sir, while you were talking I have already thought of going myself. The only problem is that the inspector that I am dealing with is off today," she told him.

As was expected from Mr Gaunt, his final words on the matter were. "If you want me just call, if not I will see you tomorrow with Fred Cole."

She knew that Mr Gaunt was right, 'strike while the iron is hot'. The only reason that the matter was delayed was that Inspector Jones was off until tomorrow.

She then rang the number for Inspector Jones knowing that he was not on duty today but in the hope that his relief would cooperate.

She ended up with the duty chief inspector who interrupted her story to tell her that Alf Jones was in fact on duty and was outside in civilian clothes 'doing something with CID' and that he would tell him that he was wanted by Freya. Within seconds, Alf Jones was on the 'phone and she said to him "I thought you were off duty today."

"I was," he replied, "but I was having a private and as we discussed, a confidential conversation with my chum in CID and he offered me a couple of chaps but it could only be for today when no one was about. By tomorrow there would be too many top brasses about for him to do anything unless he made it 'A job' then it would no longer be secret and his Special Branch twigs would be alerted.

I came in early this morning and got my two detective chaps to go in the 'Found Property' room and find suitable clothes to look like 'Twitchers', y'know, bird watchers. They did a super job, and one had a deerstalker hat and the other a 'Yokel' walking stick with binoculars and a camera. They looked perfect.

Off we set and parked up in a spinney about a quarter-mile from the lane and as we got near the track leading to the house who should be coming down the track but our War office car with the man and woman in there. As I heard the motor I went headlong into a ditch and cut my leg on some barbed wire.

I heard the car stop and muffled sound of conversation and I thought Oh, God they have been rumbled but this pair of detectives were a class above the rest and I should have known better than to doubt their ability to think, be inventive, act fast and succeed."

At this point, he stopped for the opportunity to laugh as he then recounted that, "As the car approached them they flagged it down and the driver wound down the car window and my man asked him if they had seen a Buzzard in the area as they were trying to photograph the bird. The man answered no but the other 'Dick' with the camera got in three photographs without causing any suspicion, these are being developed as we speak. After the chap had driven away they went to the house or rather run-down cottage and photographed it from all angles. Winning line don't you think?"

She was truly in awe of Inspector Jones and his two 'Dicks' and said.

"That is brilliant, really brilliant, thank you and your detectives. Are you remaining on duty today?" she asked him.

"Yes," he told her. Then added, "Why?"

Freya then asked him if he would be able to get a search warrant in the next hour or so as it was Bank Holiday Monday and that if he could she intended to come up with her inspector and if he would be kind enough to come to the house/cottage in uniform and a uniformed policewoman as the news was broken to Mrs Hacker that her 'Husband' was dead.

The warrant was to be used if she did not show the usual widow response or let them inside.

"I have got a friendly woman magistrate but I need a reason for the issuing of the warrant, what reason would you like me to give her?" Inspector Jones enquired.

Freya replied, "Murder and State security, will that do?"

"Consider it done," he told her and asked, "when are you coming here?"

Once I have collected my detective inspector or the sergeant I will be up with you she told him, then asked "Where shall I meet you?"

Here at HQ. You would never find the lane or track in a month of Sunday's. See you in a bit."

Freya then rang Ron Wilkins and he agreed to go with her on his off duty day if she would give him an 'Hour' to finish the door he was painting, change and get to the station. She then rang Bill Jobbins to tell him the story and to 'Stand Down' for the time being.

Within the 'Hour', they were in the Bristol racing along the new part of the M4 to meet up with Alf Jones and his 'Troops'

As they pulled into the car park, the car appeared to be the centre of attention to the staff of the Central Police Station. As they left the car so a tall uniformed inspector with slightly greying hair and a younger, quite attractive woman police sergeant approached them. This inspector was Alf Jones. There were introductions all around and Mr Jones gave the new Warrant to Freya and admired her car with the comment the inequalities of police life.

Here she was with a limousine and all he had was a cut leg. "No justice," were his words of regret for his misfortune in not being a rich acting detective chief inspector!

Mr Jones led them to two unmarked cars and off they set across the Plain until they arrived at the lane. At Freya's suggestion as they stopped they parked one of the cars across the entrance to the drive and squashed into the other car for the journey to the dwelling. As they approached Woodbine Cottage so the War Office car came into sight parked by the door.

Only Freya and the police sergeant got out of the car and approached the door. There was such a long pause between them banging the door and a response that she was on the verge of getting the others to force the door when it was opened by a woman, probably in the early thirties of medium height and build with, in the opinion of Freya, over long fair hair dressed in a very stylish red dress.

"Yes?" asked the woman. The accent given to the single word question determined that the English language was probably not her native tongue.

Freya introduced the sergeant and then herself and asked if they might "Come inside," as they might have some distressing news for her.

The woman replied, "No."

Freya then asked her if she was Mrs Hacker?

There was a long pause before she replied that she was Hacker. Freya then asked her if her husband was Mr Harrison Hacker? There was yet again a long pause before she replied that he was.

Freya then said to her that she really thought that they should go inside to talk.

This suggestion was met by a very determined, "No."

Freya then asked her when she had last seen her husband? The reply was, "A week ago." Freya then went on to ask where her husband had gone during the week that he was away and when she would expect him home again?

The woman shrugged her shoulders and replied "Why should I tell you anything?" Then turned towards the door. The police sergeant promptly moved herself to stand slightly behind the woman preventing her from getting inside the door to close it.

"Mrs Hacker, this is your final opportunity to cooperate with us or I shall be obliged to use my authority to compel you to comply with my wishes. Do you clearly understand?" Freya asked her.

The woman did not reply and simply gave both women a very sullen look but still kept herself in the doorway, as much as the sergeant would allow.

Freya then produced from her case the photograph of Harrison Hacker from his mortuary photo.

Handing the print to the woman she asked her if that person was her husband?

The woman simply nodded.

"I think that it is past the time for this stalemate Mrs Hacker, you will invite us into your home, now," Freya told her with a decided emphasis on the 'Now'.

Without moving her stance, the woman told Freya that she could not tell her anything that she did not already know.

This statement was the red light to Freya, she produced the warrant and said, "This doc." With that, the woman slammed into the sergeant as she made a determined effort to get into the doorway and in so doing knocked the breath out of the sergeant.

Freya then used physical force for the first time since as a probationer constable she had been called to a hospital where a woman was running amok. She put Mrs Hacker in the armlock position with a knee in the middle of her back and simply for all her worth, leaned back and Mrs Hacker screamed, "Tristan, help me." and collapsed in a heap with Freya under her still holding on for dear life.

Suddenly a voice said, "Let go of her ma'am; I've got her," as Freya released her grip she went on 'All fours' then got up in time to see a figure disappearing into the woods to her right.

With Alf Jones holding the woman and his sergeant getting her breath back, Freya asked, "Who was that running?" Alf replied that as he went to the aid of her so he saw a man running from the back of the cottage. "Don't worry, we've got his car and his photo and we can't search the woods at this very moment."

"In we go," Freya told everyone and with Alf leading the way with the woman carefully locked in his arm they entered the cottage which looked slightly better inside rather than the almost dilapidated condition outside.

Alf sat the woman down as Freya composed herself and looked over at the belligerent look on the face of the assaulted police sergeant.

The sergeant looked at her and asked, "When you have finished with her, ma'am, I am going to 'do' her for assault if that is OK by you?"

Freya told her that we will wait and see, and at that point, Ron Wilkins joined them looking rather dishevelled. In answer to Freya's enquiry as to his usual sartorial elegance being rather 'Under the Salt', he told her that he had taken off after the chap in the woods but had lost him in the dense undergrowth and could he please put a claim in for torn trousers? Hearing this, Inspector Alf Jones said, "What about my trousers and my leg from this morning," and turning to Ron Wilkins said, "I bet my scar is bigger than yours."

This banter took some of the tension off of the proceedings and Freya asked Mr Jones to let the woman free from his grasp. This he did as he sat the woman in the chair and Freya then said to her.

"Earlier you told me that I could tell you nothing that you did not already know. What exactly did you mean by that?"

The woman did not answer. So Freya decided that the 'Gloves should come off' and said to the woman, "Your husband is dead, he was probably murdered." There was absolutely not a flicker of emotion on the woman's face.

She then asked her if she had anything to say or questions to ask. Still, the woman remained silent.

"You will come and identify the body at our mortuary but firstly I want to see your wedding certificate. She then asked where she could find it. Still, no response from the woman.

Freya then told the woman, "I have a search warrant for these premises and the curtilage. As you will not cooperate with me I will now exercise the right that this warrant grants me. Do you understand?"

The woman made no effort to speak or otherwise acknowledge what she had been told. Freya was quite pleased with this response as she had just noticed that the name or number of the dwelling relating to the warrant was left blank negating the lawful authority of the document.

She asked Ron to guard the woman while she took Alf Jones into another room to quietly tell him that the name of the premises to which the warrant related was not specified on the document.

Alf took the warrant from her and wrote, 'Woodbine Cottage' in the blank space and said, "Sorry, I missed that one. Well, it is a Bank Holiday!"

Mr Jones then asked her what she was now planning to do as the woman was not cooperating in any way, and at present, they were getting nowhere. He then went on to ask her about the war office car and the man seen 'Legging' it to the woods.

"Can I use your chaps to help search this place?" Freya asked him.

Taking a biblical instruction as his reply Mr Jones said, "Ask and thou shalt receive." She looked at him with a smirk and asked, "Judging by your quotes Alf perhaps you overdid the church visits on Easter Day.

She then explained what she wanted the searchers to look for, and other than Ron Wilkins looking after Mrs Hacker brought the searchers into the adjacent room and said that she wanted them to look out for documents of any nature, particularly any Births, Marriages or Death certificates.

In fact, anything that related to Woodbine Cottage, any occupations, payslips, photographs of Mr and Mrs Hacker and anything with a name of Tristan, contents of medical chests and bathroom cabinets and in particular look out for strong black adhesive tape and any rope or twine and where they find rugs or carpets look underneath for any 'loot' or hiding spaces.

She then ensured that they all had gloves and told them to be methodical in the order that they searched the rooms.

As the men and woman set off on their task Freya asked Inspector Jones if he had any Scene of Crime or Forensic officers immediately available on a Bank Holiday or any bodies to help with the searching? He told her that he would have to use the 'phone in the living room to summon them to the cottage.

"Yes, please," she said to him he then reminded her that the woman was in earshot there guarded by Ron Wilkins.

"It does not matter," Freya told him, "The 'phone conversation might wake her up to the reality of her situation."

When Alf Jones had gone to make the call she took time to look at what had happened since she had arrived at the cottage. Matters had not gone to her mental plan of events but the use of the warrant was a stroke of genius. God bless Detective Chief Superintendent William Gaunt.

Who would have thought that a warrant would be needed when informing a woman that she was now a widow although it was plain that the woman did know that her husband was dead before Freya got there. How could she know? Unless he was dead when he left the cottage?

Preliminary examination of Hackers body gave the cause of death as asphyxia. Was Hacker asphyxiated here or elsewhere? If elsewhere, who would have told Mrs Hacker and why was she so indifferent to the news? The Tristan that she called for perhaps. Were she and he the murderers?

Chief Inspector/Acting Superintendent Stuart Thomas promptly came to Freya's mind and his insistence on examining the underside of the Morris Commercial White van and his telling her that 'Crimes are solved by the samples on undersides of vehicles'. She wrote in her log to ensure before leaving that a sample was taken off the ground by the cottage door and further down the drive.

Inspector Jones returned from his calling for SoC officers which he told her would be here within twenty minutes. Freya asked him to stay with Ron Wilkins and in front of the woman, layout all that the searchers had found in the cottage.

"It might make her buck up her ideas," she told Mr Jones. She continued, "I'm going for a look outside, OK?"

Freya walked out through the back door, stepping around a prone figure of a policeman under the sink with a huge torch which was probably from one of the cars they had arrived in.

Outside of the door, detached from the cottage wall, was a building at right angles to the cottage itself with a larger attached building adjacent to it. Freya opened the door of the attached building to find that it was a wash-house with very old fashioned washing equipment and a brick boiler and a pile of coal to burn underneath it. By the condition of it, not used in decades.

Although Freya did not have latex gloves with her she had a good poke about but could find nothing of interest but made a mental note to get the chap with the large torch to have a look in all the nooks and crannies which were not easy to see into. While she was very tall for a woman she was not quite tall enough to peer into all of the dark places. After poking about her hands were quite filthy with dust, spiders old webs, bits of bird's nests, woodworm powder and the like.

She then left and walked over to the detached building and undoing the Norfolk latch she went into a nowadays unique, museum quality, communal lavatory. There were five seats over buckets with no screens between each seat.

Those wishing to use such facilities in the early twentieth century simply sat or stood in a line doing what came quite naturally.

As the door to the building swung open she noted that a stout piece of string was holding numerous bits of newspaper for use on the nether regions. She flicked through the paper squares until she found one with 'Daily Sketch 15 January 1947' thereon.

Everything was covered in years of grime, dead birds, dead rats mummified by nature, rusted gardening tools, bundles of hessian sacks, more squares of yellow newspaper, some eaten by woodlice and the like.

Strangely Freya noticed that although there were dirty ancient cobwebs in her hair and shoulders her shoes were not unduly dusty or dirty. In the gloom of the lavatory, she noticed that there was much less rubbish in the centre of the floor. The rest of the floor was covered in the detritus of the ages and masses of crisp brown Beech tree leaves from many Autumn storms, yet there were very few in the middle of the floor.

This scene set her mind on other tracks and she retraced her footsteps to the door; she turned and looked at the scene again and saw that the relatively clean floor only extended to lavatory seat number four. The floor at number five was in keeping with the rest of the interior of the building including a bundle of well-eaten sacks or recycled for birds and four-legged mammals to make nests.

She went to the number four seat and peered in, it looked much the same as the rest of the buckets, full of the same mixture of timeless rubbish found only in buildings in the countryside and this building in particular. As she looked down, she noticed that the handle of the bucket, in comparison to the others was rust-less; in fact, the galvanised handle looked almost unused.

In her position, it was quite acceptable for her to delegate the examination of the bucket to someone else. Not being a person to shirk her responsibilities she bravely and with trepidation put her hand into the hole and grasped the bucket handle.

As she touched the handle so several large rats made a run for safety. Freya screamed and jumped back with her short cobweb adorned hair standing on end.

For a second or two she couldn't take a breath and eventually she regained her composure, and her first thought was regret that the Jack Russell's of her father's gamekeeper were not here, they would have made very short work of the rats. Killing rats was the favourite pastime of the 'Ankle nipping' dogs.

She again grasped the handle of the bucket and lifted it out. She then took it to the doorway and the light and found that it had a homemade lid.

Brushing the leaves off the wooden lid she lifted it off to find several oil-skin bags inside. She opened one to find what appeared to be cine film tapes. In another, she found several diaries and in the bottom one documents with what appeared to be Russian or Greek, certainly Cyrillic writing of some sort.

In view of her now dishevelled appearance added to the mental torture of the rat episode, she took her 'Find' into the sitting room of the cottage. Her arrival into the room in such contrast to the immaculate Acting Detective Chief Inspector who had left it barely twenty minutes ago drew looks of horror mixed with a little amusement by those in the room. Even Mrs Hacker looked alarmed, not at Freya's appearance but at the lavatory bucket in her hand.

Not a word passed the lips of the assembled observers but knowing glances did pass around the room. Instead of displaying her bucket of loot, Freya looked at the amassed items found by the searchers and asked each search party, some of whom must have arrived since she left the main building to go on her 'Treasure' hunt.

She noticed that Inspector Jones was not present. She asked Ron Wilkins where Alf was to be told that he was outside dealing with samples of earth and debris with the scene of crime officers and that he was then returning with them to photograph what the searchers had found and where they had found it.

Freya turned to Mrs Hacker and said, "Do you have anything to say about all these items that we have collected which are believed to be of interest to us?"

The sullen woman simply looked at her and shook her head. Freya thought that in the shaking of her head at least the woman acknowledged that she was being spoken to. Who would know what might come next?

What came next and made most of the people in the room jump. The telephone rang. Each person looked at each other waiting for someone to pick up the receiver. Freya picked up the receiver and simply said, "Woodbine cottage." The conversation then became a one-sided event as the policemen and women of various ranks and from two police forces listened to the responses trying to determine who was on the other end of the line.

"Acting Detective Chief Inspector Freya Douglas Gore Hamilton, sir," Freya said to the caller followed by, "I'm very sorry sir- yes, I do know the protocols to be observed in matters such as these- yes – but if you would be so kind as to allow me to explain to you – thank you, sir.

"This foray into your force area began by one of your civilian staff recognising a photograph that we circulated. The officer dealing with the response then, as any officer would do, offered his services in helping me with my murder enquiries.

Because of the swift passage of events and the interest by non-police third parties I was unable to go through the usual channels and your officers very kindly offered their services should I want them today.

We did need the help of your people and I do apologise for not asking your permission." After the caller had taken a further couple of minutes to make his point, she then told the caller, "I don't believe that any murder was committed on your patch so at this stage it is an investigation into a murder committed within my force area.

In the course of the enquiries today, if any crime or suspected crime has been committed within your force boundaries then I would be please to liaise with your teams. As you are on the 'phone sir I will tell you what I intended to write to your chief constable about Inspector Alfred Jones who has gone beyond his remit to help me in the best traditions of cross force area cooperation and that when you read his report you will agree with me and reward him appropriately sir."

The eavesdropper had again to wait a minute or two while they listened to muffled but presumably crosswords from whoever 'Sir' was as she held the receiver away from her ear. She then put the receiver to her ear and said into it. "You not only appear to have strong views about the fact that my team is on your territory but that I am a woman leading them."

She again held the receiver away from her head before continuing speaking to tell the caller, "As I have told you before sir, I will be writing to your chief constable to apologise for any failure on my part to follow the accepted line of communications for inter-force cooperation in matters possibly involving crimes in adjoining police areas."

Another longish pause ensued until Freya told the caller, "Yes, sir, I do happen to know the name and address of your chief constable. It might be of interest to you to know that he and I are well acquainted as he was my chief instructor at Hendon and eventually my commandant at Warwickshire."

After another pause to listen to the caller, the audience then heard Freya say "Your apology is accepted, sir. I'm sure that you did not mean to insult me or my chief constable and again I do apologise.

When I write to Chief Constable Marshall I will of course mention the diplomacy and kindness displayed by you over my inexcusable oversight in not obtaining your permission to operate in your division. I'm so sorry sir but I missed your name, Superintendent who sir?"

A brief pause before Freya spoke again for her final tease of the caller "Oh, you would not like to diminish the accolade that the inspector is due by having your name on the letter.

That is a disappointment Sir, but it is most noble of you not to steal the thunder of one of your officers by having your praises in writing to your chief constable. Goodbye, sir; yes, should I need any assistance I will call on you and rest assured your teams will deal with any crimes identified by my team and committed on your patch. Goodbye."

She put the receiver down and as she looked around, everyone had something else to look at except her.

"OK," Freya said to those busying themselves with nothing, "You heard my side and I am simply going to tell you from my team and the local team that was a superintendent someone or other who was extremely irate that I was operating here without his permission and also the minor detail of me being a poor misguided, soft brained woman.

She continued. "In respect of permission, he was quite right but who just three hours ago would have thought this." She spread her hands over the collected, hoped for evidence, "would be found in a cottage up a lane or dirt track in the middle of nowhere."

Freya turned to Ron Wilkins and saw him writing. He looked up and asked "Where did you get that from?" indicating the bucket. She replied, "An old fashioned bog house or khazi. To a gentleman like you Ron, it's a communal lavatory with five seats alongside each other and a bucket under each. This one did not contain an ancient motion but something that might induce a bowel movement to someone with a guilty mind."

"A shit bucket?" Ron asked her. She replied, "Not so crude Ron, I expected better of you than that expression."

"I can't spell defecation, ma'am; what shall I put?"

Freya gave her Detective inspector a very straight look and said, "Galvanised bucket, one of, for the purpose of, primary collection of human waste from lavatorial premises."

"I ain't got room for all that, ma'am," Ron told her in a broad yokel accent, can I just put turd and wee-wee bucket, ma'am?"

She laughed, the first time that day and said, "write what you want you silly 'B."

Indicating the 'phone Ron asked, "Another Fred Cole?" she replied, "Similar in volume but not as smart, Fred knows when he is on good hiding to nothing and he would never grovel. This object could not see that I was deliberately playing him along with juvenile flattery and the moment that I mentioned my relationship with his boss, his smarmy crawling was pitiful, but I will hand her over to Alf or their CID if this is all we get.

I really want her on bail for deliberately barging the policewoman, but it is too messy for me to deal with it up here and until we go through this lot there is nothing to implicate her she knows that saying nothing is her 'Get out of Jail card' for the moment. Among all this, do we have her passport and what about her marriage certificate?"

Ron consulted his list and finally said, "Yup, we've got both and in answer to your unasked question, yes, she is not British born and yes again, she was born in Germany in that noble city of Bremen in 1935 and had the maiden name of Helga Rosenberg."

Freya realised that Rosenberg was the name Mr Grant gave for possibly the body number two. Ron was looking at her with an exasperated expression and an arched eyebrow.

"Sorry Ron, something crossed my mind, please carry on," Freya told her inspector. He continued, "She married Harrison Hacker in Germany at the British Consulate in 1956.

It would appear that he was a bag carrier for the Foreign office. I have looked at his payslips or as many as have been found and the most recent one shows that he is now, or was a civil servant, grade three in one of the underwater research facilities of the Admiralty. Where do we go from here, ma'am?" he enquired.

Before answering Ron, the face and neck of Alf Jones, followed shortly afterwards by the rest of his body appeared. Forgetting his damaged trousers and 'wound' in his leg, his humour was improving after his superintendent was politely put in his place by Freya.

"Alf," Freya began. "I have been having a think, not a long think and unless you say no, I will take all this paperwork and the samples from the drive and leave Mrs Hacker with you, mindful of course that she has committed a crime by assaulting a police officer. I suspect that if she cooperates with us, this relatively minor infringement of the law might be charitably overlooked as she has just lost her husband."

The woman looked up but made no attempt to speak.

Ron Wilkins pointed to Freya's bucket and with a smirk asked, "As I have shown you mine is it not time that you showed me yours?"

Freya looked straight into his eyes and putting her hand over her heart replied, "Really Inspector Wilkins. I'm a pure maiden and I'm sure that I really don't know just what you can possibly mean, sir," with a prolonged fluttering of her long eyelashes.

She looked at the bucket and said to those in earshot "That reminds me, I've been here for hours and not made use of the 'Facilities." Turning to Mrs Hacker she asked, "Would you like to use the bathroom?"

The woman nodded and Freya called for a policewoman to accompany her making sure that the bathroom had been thoroughly searched. As the woman walked past her Freya asked her if she would like a cup of tea or a coffee. The woman told her that she wanted a cup of coffee as no tea was drunk in the dwelling.

Freya looked towards her stalwarts, Inspector Alf and Detective Inspector Ron and asked "Who's going to play mother?" Both men looked around the room. "What are you looking for?" she asked them.

In almost unison, they answered, "Someone to make the tea," as they spoke a constable hove into view.

Alf Jones addressed him with the question, "Do you know what a Char Wallah is?"

"Yes, sir," came the reply from the constable, "It is the chap in India that makes the tea," and the foolish boy continued, "It is from their name of Char that we use the expression Char to mean tea, Sir."

Incredulity was written over the faces of the three officers as they stared at the naive, ingratiating constable. The silence was finally broken as was the beaming self-satisfied look of the constable when Alf said to him.

"That was truly a wonderful piece of knowledge that you imparted to simpletons like us and now as I believe that all knowledge should be backed up by practical evidence to demonstrate that knowledge."

Pointing towards the kitchen Alf sarcastically said, "In there you will find all the ingredients to make a drink of tea or perhaps coffee. You boil the water, put tea leaves or bags in the pot add the boiled water ensuring that the tea is good and strong. Let it stand then pour into as many cups as you can find except one for the lady of the house who...." Alf could not complete his sentence as a very dishevelled policewoman came into sight with blood on her face and hands.

No one asked the poor girl what happened as they almost fell over themselves in rushing to the bathroom. It was empty but a window along the alleyway was wide open. Alf made a grab for the telephone dialled his station and asked for the dogs to be sent to the cottage immediately and alerted all patrol to look for Mrs Hacker giving a very accurate description of her appearance.

Freya told one of Alf's men to take the policewoman to a hospital as the babbling sounds of various voices made a mockery of the presumption that the British were cool, calm and collected come what may.

Freya walked to the door with the policewoman and the young woman said, "She called me in, ma'am'; she was behind the door with the heavy glass toilet brush holder. I remember trying to grab her arm and she hit my head then pushed me over. I tried to call out but nothing came out. By the time I was on my feet she had run to the window opened it and I made another grab for her and she kicked me in the chest and I fell backwards, Sorry, ma'am." Freya replied "It is entirely my fault, I should have sent two of you. It is my mistake and I'm so sorry."

Freya turned to Ron and signalled for him to quieten the room down. When calm was restored she said. "I accept full responsibility for this fiasco, I should have given the woman two escorts however, considering the number of policemen in the cottage and those outside the woman should have been apprehended either inside or certainly outside. Did anyone see which way she went?"

The answer was a line of blank faces.

She then told Ron to gather all the evidence and put it in Alf's car and have a guard put on it.

"Conference call, after I've made myself comfortable," Freya told them. "What about us?" came a voice from the back of the group. "You can find yourself a tree or bush," she told him. "When can we have a drink, ma'am?"

"I understand that we have a volunteer tea lady," she replied, adding if they can find any or, apparently there is coffee somewhere and make sure the cups are well washed."

Freya was just washing her hands, an easier task than when she came in from the outside multi seated lavatory when she was aware of exciting loud talk outside of the door. She opened the door to find herself confronted by a brown four pint glazed teapot. The person holding the pot was the 'Char Wallah' constable who would be tea maker.

"I eventually found the teapot, ma'am, and look what's inside," the constable told Freya as he proffered the pot to her. She thought to herself, "There's enthusiasm and there's damned enthusiasm but, offering me a teapot at the lavatory door is a bit rich."

"What do I want with the teapot?" She asked the constable. The fellow took off the lid and turned it towards her and she heard the distinct 'Chink' of glass on a glazed surface.

Noting that the constable had his latex gloves on she said to him, "I can't touch it, I've no gloves on, what is in there?"

With something akin to the flourish of Marvo the Magician, the 'Char Wallah' produced a glass phial and said, "There are two others in here, ma'am."

Freya told him to take it with the other items of interest and look through all the pots and pans in the kitchen and if there was no tea, please bring three coffees into the dining room. The constable then told her that there was no milk as well as tea. she replied, "It is of no consequence anything wet and warm will do thank you."

On the way to her conference, she collected Inspector Alf Jones and her detective inspector Ron and they went into the dining room.

The men sat down while Freya stood and said, "It would appear that we or perhaps I, am getting into a mess here. In fact, one devil of a mess. Can I summarise the last, God alone knows, how many hours of seeming chaos?"

The men nodded their acquiescence and she continued.

"We arrived here to find a woman now known or believed to be Mrs Hacker. Although we came here to tell her that her husband was dead she was not surprised and indicated that she already knew. If so, who told her or did she have a hand in his demise?

To concentrate on the woman; she belted a policewoman in the doorway in an attempt to get back in her home and would not answer any questions or speak at all until I offered her the use of the lavatory. In the lavatory she tried to 'brain' her escort and as I have told you the sending of just one escort was a misjudgement on my part and now she has done a 'runner' presumably into the woods."

Freya took a breath as the 'Tea Wallah' brought in three cups of black coffee. "Have you washed the cups?" his inspector enquired. "Yes, sir, and could I please have the cups back, there are only three in the kitchen and the men would also like a drink?"

Freya nodded to him and with a probable sarcastic little bow to her, he left.

She smiled at the non-verbal show of his individual character and continued;

"Add to the mix of a man running from this house or cottage to the woods plus a government-owned car left in the path. Very highly suspicious considering that at this point, we appear to have other parties interested in our enquiries. If we have any men left when we finish this little talk I want a closer look at that car and if necessary have it impounded and wait until someone howls.

Going on, we have searched this place from top to bottom and recovered a lot of useful information but after the search was considered to be completed, the tea boy managed to find loot in the teapot although the woman said in as many words that there was no tea. Was this to prevent us from going to the pot or did they not drink tea here?

During this time I have been subject to verbal abuse by the divisional superintendent, some of it justified and most of it unjustified.

I belatedly realise that I have stood on one big toe too many by not involving the local CID but you, Alf, were a kindly light in the Bank Holiday gloom and I suspect that neither you nor me could have foreseen this morning just how this simple act of informing a woman that she was a widow would turn into this complication of my murder enquiry some forty miles from here and it would appear involving government agencies of one sort or other."

She stopped talking as the lowly constable with the subtle urge to display his character, knocked on the door and asked for the coffee cups to be returned. He was delayed by Freya who, through continuous talking, had omitted to drink her rapidly cooling coffee. She downed it in one gulp and almost choked herself in the effort.

After the choking episode, Freya was about to start again when another knock came on the door and it opened to disclosed two bodies, one turned out to be a dog handler and the one behind him took one look at Freya and said, "Well, I'll be damned, you, it had to be you."

"What are you doing here?" Freya looked at the man and said, "I could say the same about you quite without the 'damning bit'. Strangely enough within the recent past, someone has used a similar expression of surprise at seeing me."

While Freya and her rediscovered friend stood looking at each other Alf Jones went to the dog handler and took him to the bathroom and the window to get a scent of the missing Mrs Hacker.

In the dining room, Freya introduced Detective Inspector Wayne Butt to Ron Wilkins. And told him that they had met when they were at the detective training school at Kings Weston.

The two detectives shook hands and Mr Butt looked at Freya and said, "I have been watching your rapid progress with interest. For a youngster like you, it has been a very rapid rise, I bet that highfalutin surname of yours helps a bit. It always impresses the common herd who pretend to be our masters. I never hear about your dear chum at Kings Weston. Is he still about?"

Freya was in two minds whether to reply and finally said," Yes, he is still about, we normally meet each year if we can and as a matter of fact he is at the divisional HQ where I am temporally stationed." Mr Butt looked at Ron Wilkins and knowingly winked and said to her, "Surely you can't have two DCIs at one HQ."

Freya replied, "He is not in CID anymore, he's the staff sergeant at the station. When I next see him I will pass on your good wishes to…"

"A bloody staff sergeant?" Mr Butt asked before continuing, "Bloody hell he must have upset someone at the top. Is he one of the ' Dicks' at your command HQ, who have been dipping their hands in the till?"

As she was about to reply the door burst open and Alf Jones "Quick come here," he called to the three senior detectives. They all tumbled out as Alf told them "We have found her."

"Thank God for that," Freya said. Alf told her that there was nothing to thank God for as he led them out of the kitchen door towards the lavatory block.

As they approached the door with the dog and handler outside so Inspector Wilkins stopped them and said, "Cyanide, I can smell it. Stop."

The party came to a shuddering stop as Inspector Jones told them that the dog had traced Mrs Hacker to the lavatory. As they approached they called for her to come out. When they went in she was laying against the sacks seemingly still alive. As they went to her the dog let out a loud whine and stopped a few feet from her. She appeared to look at the dog and then slumped into the sacking.

As they went to her the dog was still frozen to the spot and suddenly a very strong chemical smell met them. They then went outside and the dog and its handler stood guard and Alf came to find the three of them.

The rather collective thoughts of the group were put into words as Detective Inspector Butt succinctly, and with some feeling said, "Bloody 'ell, what a ball up this is."

Freya then said to Mr Butt, "I'm so glad that you're here Wayne. As this is your patch, this is now your enquiry.

But, at least on this occasion, it is certainly not murder." She then continued, "Three deaths all apparently linked by a Soviet ship. Oh, boy, have we a complicated job here 'Johnny' Wayne and this death is the least complicated, perhaps."

Ron Wilkins looked at Freya, then indicated towards Detective Inspector Butt and asked her, "Why did you call him Johnny Wayne?"

There in the midst of mayhem, she looked at her detective inspector almost in disbelief at his question. She replied as if talking to a child, "Ron, did you ever watch Cowboy films when you were a youngster or even nowadays?" Ron, still looking puzzled replied, "Of course, I did. Why?"

Freya, with an exaggerated sigh said, "One of the most famous Hollywood stars in Cowboy films was a man called Shirley, heard of him, Ron?" Ron shook his head. "Shirley was the name of a man who was renamed John Wayne," she patiently told Ron, "Because Mr Butt's name is Wayne, perhaps his mother or father or both of them might have liked 'Western' films they named their son Wayne after their favourite 'cowboy' so it follows that's why Wayne is Wayne."

At this point, Ron interrupted her to announce to the world, or at least those standing outside of a historic lavatory, now turned into a charnel-house, "Oh, I get it, yes, John Wayne. Yes, that's very good.

"I've got a suspicious death to investigate here," Wayne told Freya and Ron plus Inspector Jones, the dog handler and his very subdued canine." My Nickname is not a cause for discussion but as you asked and I'm in a generous frame of mind I will tell you who gave me that name and when." Looking at a smiling Freya he told Ron, "Miss Freya Douglas Gore Hamilton at Kings Weston, House. Now let's get on shall we?"

After Detective Inspector Ron Wilkins told them that the very strong smell of Almonds was the tell-tale scent of cyanide and once the vapour smell had cleared they could approach the body but he added, "Don't get near her mouth."

Wayne dismissed the dog handler thanking him for his help in locating Mr Hacker and told the group that there was no reason to call the ambulance service as she was plainly dead and that such a call would involve even more paperwork.

He said that her would simply get the 'Meat wagon' to take the body to the mortuary with two of his men and see what the pathologist could tell him tomorrow. "Now," he said to Freya, "Tell me the back story until she topped herself and why she might have done such a thing, no doubt in a Nazi-inspired act?"

Freya told Ron to get all the items in the living room indexed, packed up and into Alf's car and when he got to the tea-pot see what was in there and after Mrs Hacker killing herself with cyanide make sure that the doubtful contents of the pot was safe and to please find an officer to guard the body and the scene until it was collected.

Freya then asked Wayne Butt if he could get a photographer here to photograph the items that they were taking away and the locations of where found. She told him that she thought that she had asked Alf to get one but she had not seen one about it and before she told him anything she would like to look at the government car at the front.

As she finished speaking she watched Wayne Butt take an instrument from his pocket and begin to give instructions into it. When he had finished speaking she asked him "Is that the new radio?"

"Yes," Wayne replied. "And very useful, haven't you got one?"

"Not yet," she replied they are still evaluating it but what a boon it would have been here today. Why would Inspector Jones not have one?" she asked. Mr Butt replied, "It is only CID that has them and also in some cars but they already had their mobile radio systems which are not compatible with this one. Anyway, let's hear the story joining you up with the late Mrs Hacker."

Freya simply said. "I've had a couple of murders at the docks with false names etc to muddy the waters, please be so kind and ignore the pun, it was intended. The long and short of why I was here today is that we circulated a photo of one of the bodies and a very smart civilian in your lot recognised it as a former neighbour of his named Harrison Hacker.

Very kindly Alf Jones who, by chance, I spoke to when enquiring about the identity of this Hacker agreed to make further enquiries into the recent abode of said Hacker. His men noted a car leaving the premises and the driver was subsequently photographed by two of your very smart 'Dicks'. I intended to be here tomorrow but events moved on and with Alf, we came here today to see a man disappearing into the undergrowth and on to those woods over there.

Mrs Hacker was very sullen and only answered the doorstep questions if she had to and showed no surprise whatsoever at the news of the death of her husband. Fortunately, Alf had got a limited search warrant which when we told her that we would execute it she deliberately winded our, or rather your policewoman.

We, then in theory, 'Nicked' her and searched the place. I offered her the chance to use the lavatory which she accepted then 'Brained' her escort and went through the window and we thought into the woods. Alf called in a dog and the rest is now history.

Because of presumed interference by 'Other Law Enforcement Agencies' I do not want any of this to go beyond your desk until we, and by we I now mean your immediate circle and ourselves are on firm ground. Tomorrow I, with my governors have an interview with a rep from, 'These Other Bodies'. As soon as that is over I will let you know the state of play. What are your chief Inspector and the superintendent like? Do they interfere with your jobs?"

As Freya drew a breath, Wayne told her, "I'm in the fortunate position that both chiefs are only interested in Golf and the club bar. As long as things are going smoothly they would not even bother to either ask questions or most certainly not to read any reports, that's below their dignity. That's for us minions to deal with.

I can keep this suicide under wraps from the press for a few days as long as the mortuary play ball. Anyway, I'll lean on them and in particular their body humpers or attendants. I've got enough on all of them to do their career prospects serious harm, that includes the pathologist as well.

I will need all the paperwork about today and you can make up what you like about how your job led you here to the lady stiff.

When you are free to fill out the proper story to let me then complete my record but don't be too long. I can only keep the lid on this for a while. My sergeant is as tight as a clam as is Alf and his people and no one else will need to know anything about the antecedence of this Hacker woman until you say so. Is that ok?"

Freya replied, "You are a darling, I will let you have a report of the background to this 'do' probably by Wednesday, is that soon enough?"

"That's fine," Wayne replied then added, "Shall we go and look at this car out the front?"

As they went through the house the photographer was busy with an exasperated Inspector Ronald Wilkins unloading the recently loaded items from the car of Alf Jones. Mr Wilkins looked at Mr Butt and Freya then complained, "First load it now take it all out then load it again, get to the station unload it all again then load it into 'My Lady's' Bristol then unload it again and then lock it away and hopefully go home, unless yet another body appears in the meantime.

He paused for breath before adding, "Not a bite to eat all day and one cup of appalling muck called coffee."

"Have you quite finished and you are not the only one who has not eaten since breakfast and who also has had only one cup of appalling muck called coffee?" Freya told him.

As they took their eyes off of the photographer and Ron Wilkins, she let out a howl of dismay and in a truly agitated voice demanded of everyone and no one, "Where's the car?"

The space previously occupied by the government registered car was empty.

After much rowdy debate and Freya asking Ron why he had not noticed it gone when he loaded the police car with the items from the cottage, to which his reply displayed his tiredness, Ron told one and all, "I have done a hundred and one tasks today including this shifting of mostly rubbish from one car to another & back again and I didn't notice it was gone."

She told him that "We are all tired but this is disastrous. Where is the officer guarding the car, in fact, where are all of Alf's men?"

Alf disappeared around the side of the cottage and returned with the constable who was guarding the body of Mrs Hacker.

Indicating Freya, Ron and Wayne, Alf told him "Tell them what happened to the car that you were supposed to be guarding?"

"I was here looking after the car as instructed to by you sir and I was relieved for a pee by constable 6843.

When I came back he told me that most of the men had been collected by the van and taken back to the station as their shift had finished two hours ago.

He then went back inside the house, and within a short while, a car came in and parked alongside the car, and the passenger got out, and the car he'd arrived in drove off. This man had a clipboard with a car key clipped to the top of it. I asked him who he was and he told me that he was from the number two vehicle pool and had been told to collect the car from a Woodbine Cottage and return it to the transport pool.

He then showed me a document with all the instructions on how to get here and he produced an identity pass with his photo on it. The document that he showed me had his name and, at the top it, said, "HM Government." Looking at Alf Jones the constable added, "Before he drove off someone called for me to go to the back of the cottage and I went where you told me to guard the body, sir."

"Thank you, constable," Freya said to him. "You did as you were told to, it is unfortunate but excusable that you didn't get one of us when the driver first appeared and that you were subsequently were called away. Which brings me to the subject of your immediate return to the lavatory in case your 'body' has disappeared too."

As the constable briskly walked back to his post so Alf Jones expressed his tiredness and frustration encapsulated in the single vehemently delivered word, 'bugger'. He then turned to Freya and said.

"This job today appears to be riddled with avoidable mistakes and this was just another one to add to the list. I'm sorry that I forgot to tell you that we lost most of my men by three forty-five as they were by then two hours beyond their shift. They only left me with two, the tea wallah and the car guard. Sorry."

Freya told him that as with Ron and herself, they were all tired not only by the hours worked but by the twists and turns of the events and yes she had also made some mistakes and not ever having come across such an involved and frankly, difficult situation in her CID career at sometimes she felt out of her depth and it was only the support of him and Ron that she had got by to thankfully hand the case over to Wayne.

They all returned to the cottage where Wayne told them that he would have the two constables relieved and have a two-man guard on the cottage until he could sort out matters of next of kin etcetera.

Freya asked him if his chaps could look around for any evidence of a black dog or cat as she had black animal hair on the bindings also a rope as they had found the black tape used to bind body number one but no rope and could their scene of crime man get a good set of Mrs Hackers fingerprints.

Alf said that there was a dog lead behind the kitchen door and a food bowl under the sink but no sign of a dog. Freya went and collected the lead and the bowl in an evidence bag and then they all went outside to the car while Wayne Butt said that he would stay until the 'Meat Wagon' arrived.

No sooner were the words out of Wayne's mouth than the 'Meat Wagon' hove into sight with the attendants dressed in anti-chemical helmets as a further delay ensued while Mrs Hacker was loaded and with one of the two constables being an escort to the body, departed for the mortuary. No thought was given to a protective suit for the unfortunate constable, a disposable human asset perhaps?

Finally, Freya and Ron were driven back to his police station by Alf Jones and on arrival, once again, Ron had the task of unloading then reloading the items of enquiry into her Bristol. As they were standing watching Ron, suddenly Freya said to Alf.

"That photo which your men managed to get of the chap in that car with who we now know as Mrs Hacker, can I take it now?" Alf replied, "You are in luck the SOCO man developed and printed it there and then, knowing their usual speed, this certainly is an event which may never be equalled."

He then disappeared into the station reappearing with an A Four size envelope containing several copies of the photographs. Freya slid them out of the envelope and she was delighted with the detail of both the face of the man and although Alf had told her that the woman might not be too clear, in fact, it was clear enough to identify her and in the long shot the photographer had managed to clearly show the registration number of the car.

Wayne Butt then appeared to ask her, "Apart from the police reports that you are giving me, can you also do a brief summary of events for Mr the coroner. He is a bit of an old woman. I presume that you will not mention any Soviet connection?" Freya then reminded him of her need for the fingerprints from Mrs Hacker.

He assured her that he would send them down tomorrow by messenger. As they were about to leave she said to Wayne, "As one day I will be one, I object to you using the expression 'old woman'. Why not old man?"

"Ruins my story," a shame-faced Wayne told her. They all said their 'Goodbyes' and Freya with Ron began their trek home.

As they left the station Freya announced to Detective Inspector Ronald Wilkins that "Come what may I am stopping at the first pub that I can find that serves food. My stomach needs food and my bladder needs emptying but, not in that order."

The brief reply from Ron was, "I won't argue with food or the lavatory." Then, quite out of the blue he said to Freya, "How come that lot," Indicating with his thumb from whence they had come, "can have personal radio's yet we don't have any and we are much bigger than them?"

Freya simply replied, "Ron, you know the chairman of the Watch Committee, get him to dish out the dosh and you will have your 'phone or radio, whichever. "Costs must be restrained," she told him mimicking the chief constable favourite words.

After satisfying both their stomach's and bladders they were on the road again. Eventually, they reached their station and as Ron went to empty the car boot again, in an act of mercy Freya told him to simply take charge of the bucket and the teapot and she would get a constable to take the rest of the items to their strong room in the bunker.

When this was done and to quote the Harvest Hymn, 'All is safely gathered in' Ron went home to either his angry, or happy wife, happy to see him or angry that on Bank Holiday Monday he had been away from home from ten to eight in the morning until 7:30 p.m. Thus is the life of any policeman, detective or otherwise.

Freya finished supervising and checking the items put into the CID strong room from the list written out by her detective inspector. She then went into her office in the bunker and opened her journal and began writing of the day's events, the successes and failures and outcomes. When she had finished, she rang to find out how the policewoman assaulted by Mrs Hacker was feeling.

She was then given the girls home number and after going through both mother and father she eventually spoke to the policewoman who assured her that she was not too badly hurt but what did hurt was the fact that at the hospital they had cut her hair off to get to the wound. Freya apologised again to her for not sending two people to escort Mrs Hacker and to tell her that Mrs Hacker had not run far then committed suicide.

The policewoman assured Freya that she held no grudge as it was partly her own fault for being assaulted because she was in a house. On the streets, she would have shown more caution dealing with a prisoner. In the woman's home, she showed no such caution and "Got a split scalp for my silliness. It was no fault of yours ma'am and thank you so much for ringing, few would have done the same."

Freya put down the 'phone and made a note to send the girl some flowers via her station and write a letter of commendation to her chief superintendent. Further note. What is the name of her 'super?'

She then checked on her 'Night watchman' bade him 'Goodnight' and left the station.

When she got home she made herself a cup of coffee then had a 'Wee dram' or two before remembering that on Tuesday, tomorrow, she had to meet up with the man from the Ministry as well as the 'hundred and one' other matters including composing a summary of events leading up to today's part fiasco.

Freya pick up her 'phone and after looking up a telephone number and dialled it. "Good evening. A voice answered Who is calling?"

"It's me," came the reply. "Are you free to talk?"

"Go ahead," the man's voice answered.

Freya had been like a cat on hot coals as she made the call, the simple words 'Go ahead' relaxed her rather more than her 'Wee Dram'.

"Thank you for being at the church yesterday; it was a lovely day, Sunshine, the service and you beside me. Now, the reason for this call," she said, "is…" The man interrupted her by saying,

"I presume that you have had a hell of a day and are in need of support or whatever. I can't remember when you last 'phoned me. It was certainly many years ago. Do you want to come here or shall I come to you?"

Freya replied, "You're right, for the first time in my career as chief of CID. I feel that events are beginning to overwhelm me. Today I made some silly mistakes that I would not tolerate in any of my detective sergeants. Please come over here."

"Where are you?" he asked, and continued, "I have no idea where you live in town."

He took down the details and said to her. "That's a rather posh address, I'll be there before ten."

Freya, a little chirpier than the previous evening, was back at her desk just after seven dictating a letter to the chief constable of the Somstrym constabulary acknowledging the meritorious conduct of the policewoman the day before at Woodbine Cottage and the valued services of Inspector Alfred Jones and Detective Inspector Wayne Butt.

That done, she then wrote out the tasks requiring attention on this day of normal work and her eighth day in the post and working on two bodies, with complications.

The matters to be attended to were, not necessarily in order of importance, get pathologists reports to be used by the coroner on both bodies and the conditions of the various organs. Hopefully, get a copy of Wayne Butts report on the fingerprints, hair samples etcetera from the body of Mrs Hacker.

Write out a not too specific summary of events and deaths leading up to and prior to the arrival of Wayne Butt at Woodbine cottage.

'Sort through the items recovered from the cottage with the emphasis on the lavatory bucket and the contents of the teapot. Send the glass phials from the pot for forensic examination and get fingerprints off of the pot as all the handlers wore gloves including the 'Tea Wallah' when he found it. The phials were to be dusted for prints before being dispatched to the laboratory. Get a written and photographic report on any fingerprints, human hairs, fabric, animal hair and debris found on the tape bindings of body number one.

Get an analysis of the debris under the white van and the sample taken from the drive leading to and at Woodbine cottage. Attend the meeting with Superintendent Cole and the 'Man from the ministry' of whatever. In view of both, the surnames name of the body number two according to Chief Superintendent Gaunt and also the maiden name of Mrs Hacker were of the same German origin, Freya decided to use Interpol and see if they could shed any light on either body although she would need the approval of Superintendent Gaunt and for him to make the application for the enquiry.

Freya then looked at her team and realised that with a couple of exceptions she hardly knew the abilities of her women and men and would need to talk to

Ron who would be best placed to deal competently with each item on her list. While deep in thought a knock on her door brought her back from her thoughts. In walked Chief Inspector/Acting Superintendent Stuart Thomas. "Good morning, sir," she greeted 'tommo'.

"Morning," Mr Thomas replied.

"Are you busy?" he enquired.

She replied, "Never too busy for you sir."

He simply said a one-word reply, "Flatterer."

He then told Freya that his visit, other than to simply look at her and feel better about the world in general. At that, she cocked her head to one side and fluttered her eyelashes resting her cheek on the back of one hand. She then told him the door was always open for him if he said such nice things. His visit was to garner her opinion on the meeting of the 'Man from the Ministry' and that neither the chief constable nor the 'Silent One' would attend.

Freya thought for a moment and cheekily told him that she guessed that something was bothering him by his being in the station before two minutes to nine, precisely.

He just smiled as she then told him that her concern was that Special Branch or Special twig as Mr Cole called them within hours of the bodies being found were asking for the papers of the case. She had never encountered such interest by Special Branch in any previous murder case that she had investigated or been party to any murder investigation.

Mr Thomas told her that he had the same concerns as her about the whole episode and in particular that Fred Cole would be in the chair. He said, "Fred is very good at dealing with police matters but dealing with government officials is a different 'cup of tea'.

I just hope that he controls his temper. If he does rant I will try and lead him elsewhere. Bill Gaunt will be with us and just in case you have never witnessed it, Bill can be quite forensic in his questioning and give a totally false impression that he is of all good cheer and an all-round 'good egg'. He is like a terrier with a rat once he sees the slightest chink in an adversaries armour."

Freya replied, "I wish that you hadn't used the expression relating to the rat, it sends cold shivers down my spine. When we have more time I will tell you why." He then told the main reason for this early morning visit. "I will just be a silent partner in the office during the visit but if you get stuck or wanted to interject at any point simply look towards me and other than Bill Gaunt, I will interrupt then you get in and make your point, Ok?"

"Thank you," Freya said, Tommo smiled and said, when today is over I will tell you my job in the Services during and immediately after the war. Bye-bye."

As he left her office so her waiting detective inspector walked in. "What got him out of bed?" Ron asked indicating the departing figure. "Came to offer me any assistance at today's meeting with the 'Man from the ministry' she told him. Ron then asked her who would be present at the meeting and she told him that as far as she knew it would be chaired by Cole with Mr Gaunt, Mr Thomas, herself and as usual Jake in the background.

"Yet another crush in the 'Boot room," Ron replied then added, "What's your desire today ma'am, and please don't say Peace. In this damn station, such a word is likely to summon the devil, usually in the form of the Old King Cole or nowadays that total git, DCI. Johns. Before long he is going to get a mouthful from me. I've forgotten more about detection than he's ever likely to know."

Freya gave him time to recover from his tantrum and asked him, "Are you still a bit tired from yesterday Ron?"

"Yes, and no, would be the answer to that one ma'am," he replied then added. "As you correctly predicted, Mrs Wilkins, although well aware of and having suffered many years from the police widow syndrome set into me last evening about being missing when I was officially off duty on a Bank Holiday and that I had also worked here on Easter Sunday. In some ways, it is a mercy, notwithstanding Old Cole and that Jerk Johns, that I have a sanctuary here."

"Would it help if I dropped by your home and explained how, in all seriousness, I could not have managed without you?"

Detective Inspector Wilkins looked aghast as he said, "God no, ma'am, thank you for the kind offer but when she saw a very attractive young woman and then find out that you were my boss she certainly would form a disconcerting opinion as to why I was working all over Easter. No, no, the very thought makes my bowels turn to liquid, thank you, ma'am."

"Disconcerting to who Ron?" she asked. He replied, "To me ma'am, to me."

"I would hate to be the cause for any upset in your digestive arrangements, Ron," Freya told him and added. "Thank you for the totally unwarranted and unexpected compliment you have just given me. Now to work."

Ron Wilkins still looked baffled, with his disquiet mind busy in his hour of agony he tried to think just what compliment that he had bestowed on his boss. However, all was lost in the turmoil of his domestic conflict.

She brought him back to the reality of the job in hand telling him.

"I have made a list of the more important jobs that need doing today. You know your people and their skills better than I do so I will leave it to you to appoint them to the job best suited to their ability and if I have missed any tasks please add them to the list."

She then handed him the list of jobs and he read them out loud, much to the amusement of his boss.

When Ron had gone through the list he told her that matters such as the report for Wayne Butt, the examination of the lavatory bucket and its contents. Getting Interpol involved through Mr Gaunt were the jobs that she would do and the rest of it was quite straightforward.

Freya then asked him to go to the Strong Room and get the lavatory bucket and its contents and bring it to her office for her to go through and bring some gloves.

No sooner said than done as she watched him coming down the stairs balancing a 'dainty' cup of tea in one hand and the weighty bucket in the other trying not to miss a step.

Finally, he reached the ground as she rescued the 'dainty' cup of tea with quite an amount of the contents in the saucer.

Ron explained, "Mrs Briggs caught me and asked me to bring this tea down to you. Sorry about the tea in the saucer. I will look the other way while you slurp it from the saucer," he told her.

"Little do you know Ronald Wilkins, that as a child I used to escape from my governess and sneak away to the gardener's cottage, and if he was in he would sit one side of the fire, his lovely cuddly wife the other side and me sitting cross-legged on the rag rug and he would tease me by encouraging me to pour hot tea into my saucer and blowing on it to cool down then drinking it.

So there Mr Wilkins you, other than Mr and Mrs Sams, regrettably both now dead, are the only person to know that about me.

Should I hear it from anyone else I will know just where it came from?" Lifting the saucer to her lips as she walked back to her office she deliberately made the loudest slurping sound that she could and quickly took the empty saucer away from her mouth as she saw a leg followed by the body of Detective Sergeant Bill Jobbins come around the corner.

Behind her, Ron whispered in her ear, "Nearly caught you there ma'am." As she reached her office door she turned to him and said, "If nothing else was achieved then at least it made you more cheerful like the Ron I've come to know in the past eight days."

"I've never known anyone who had a governess or a gardener, that answers how you have your cultured accent, ma'am. How do you reckon Mr Fergusson got his posh accent? Was he born with a silver spoon in his mouth as well?"

She answered, "As I've said before to others down here. Why don't you ask Staff Sergeant Fergusson rather than me about his personal matters? Knowing him I rather doubt that he will answer any personal questions and probably bawl you out for enquiring."

Freya suggested that Ron might give D.Sgt Jobbins the job of supervising the pathologist and laboratory matters and getting the results back within a couple of days and dish out the other tasks to whoever he thought the most capable officer for each job without messing it up. As he left her office he said to Freya," I still can't get over Tommo being here before nine. This, ma'am, is the precursor to a very wild and traumatic day."

He raised his hand-rolled his eyes and declared, "The bowler-hatted striped trousered men from the ministry shall come and smite the Parish bumpkin Police before them into a thousand pieces and then grind them to dust under their highly polished black shoes." With a trembling falsetto voice, he concluded his prophecy, "You have been warned, repent ye sinners against abusing the authority of the all-seeing and hearing Civil Service. Repent I say, particularly Old King Cole."

Freya looked at him as he finished his 'star' turn as applause from the women and men of the murder squad rang in his ears. Detective Inspector Ronald Wilkins became very red in the face as he belatedly realised that his presumed private turn act had the very appreciative audience of his staff.

His boss then said, "Welcome back to the Ron we are used to. Yesterday was just that, yesterday.

Freya's telephone then rang and Superintendent Cole was on the line to say, "Morning, miss," she thought, not only Tommo in early but Cole as well. Perhaps Ron's prophesy wasn't so laughable after all as Mr Cole continued, "I have just been told by our Special Twig that not only do we have the bloke we expected for the meeting this morning but the Special Branch commander at the Met will be here with a bloke from the Home Office, a bloke from Internal security, God only knows what that is, I've never heard of such a bunch, we are the only Internal security worth the name."

There was a long pause before he shouted down the phone, "Are you still there Miss?" Freya assured him that she was and was taking in everything that he had said. He then said to her, "Well, grunt or something occasionally. I think that I'm talking to a bloody wall when you don't speak."

She assured him again that she had taken in every word and added that it sounded a big delegation from what could be perceived as the challengers to his authority over the matter of two murders on their patch.

All he said to correct her was "My patch, my patch. No one else's." and promptly rang off.

She sat back absorbing that which she had just been told when the 'phone rang again. It was Mr Cole again to say, "If you hadn't interrupted me I would have told you that with all these bone heads coming the meeting will have to take place in a classroom. I have told Jake to arrange it in the number two room as the new recruits are in number one. Be there at ten, not ten to or ten past, ten, understand?"

"I'll be there sir, never fear," she told him to which he replied, "Watch your lip Missy," and hung up.

Freya smirked and opened the lid of the bucket, looked in then searched through her desk drawer until she found some latex gloves and then picked each item out of the bucket carefully laying them out on the side table to her desk.

Inside of the oilskin pouch was a child's exercise book with Cyrillic writing on both sides of the paper but on the cover was more Cyrillic writing and underneath was written the name, 'Harrison W.J. Hacker B.Sc. (Oxon).

Freya delved again into the pouch and found four small pocket-sized diaries three full of small closely written English and the fourth two thirds full of the same style of writing with the entries seemingly dated from 1957 until April 1963. She was so tempted to start reading them but desisted and again plunged her hand into the bucket.

The next items she pulled out were small plans of 'Something' on what felt like greaseproof paper. There were twenty-three of these items of drawings. The next and final delve brought very small canisters of film to her table.

She sat and thought of what she should do with it and who could she get and trust to interpret it into laymen's terms suitable to use as evidence which could be easily understood by the lowest common denominator of jury members.

For quite a while she sat and pondered on her dilemma and then lifted the phone and dialled the number of Chief Superintendent Gaunt.

When the secretary to Mr Gaunt answered the call she said, "The office of Assistant Chief Constable Gaunt."

Freya was stunned and rather stuttered her words as she asked for Chief Superintendent Gaunt.

"Who shall I say is calling," asked the secretary.

Forgetting her title in the surprise of discovering that Bill Gaunt was the assistant chief constable she told the woman, "I am Freya Douglas Gore Hamilton."

"I am putting you through detective chief inspector," the woman told her. In the brief time before Mr Gaunt answered her call she thought about the secret promotion of Mr Gaunt and in turn her promotion to detective chief inspector by the secretary.

"Yes, madam, what can I do for you?" Mr Gaunt enquired. "I've heard all about your excursion into the wilds of some country lane only to land up with suicide in your custody. Tut-Tut Freya, not a comfortable position to be in. But there, you'll come out of it smelling of roses as usual I don't doubt."

Firstly sir to congratulate you on your promotion and to ask who told you about the fiasco in Somstrym? she enquired.

He replied. "Firstly you and I talked yesterday morning about your body number two and his residence. You told me of your intentions regarding your then presumed Mrs Hacker and I told you to get your chum over there to get a limited search warrant, did I not?"

"Yes, sir," was her reply.

Mr Gaunt continued, "The chief over there was one of my detective sergeant's years ago.

Wayne Butt was under my command with you and happens to be the protégé of my former Sergeant Wragg.

"Frankly Freya, with the very highest of respect, you didn't stand a chance of confidentiality as I knew where you were going so naturally I rang Wragg, although it was Easter Monday and he, in turn, managed to get Butt off of the golf course by early afternoon and sent him to you without telling him that you were running the show. In our, and your professional circle that is how we work and I'm surprised that you didn't realise or in fact use the same system on your squad.

Finally, in answer to your congratulations on my promotion. Thank you, but to let you know that I have been ACC for many months. It has not been announced until this morning simply because some of the Watch Committee didn't want to stump up the money. In truth, the difference is only a couple of hundreds a year. But politics and budget cuts have to be accommodated as I may have told you before. Anyhow, I am still me, the commander of all investigative policing in this force. I will be down for Fred Cole's jamboree in a few minutes and see you there."

"This call sir was to ask you to make time to come to my office while you are down here. In short, I need help and you probably know people who can deal with the material that I have in confidence, and after what you have told me I mean real confidentiality, not the police version," she told him.

There was a chuckle from Mr Gaunt as he told her that he would be down now and not wait until the time of the meeting at 10 o'clock.

When the conversation ended, she leaned back in her chair and in her mind began going through the events in the case and wondering just how Mr Gaunt was going to manage the situation in relation to the Kurt Rosenberg residence in a nudist colony.

She pulled herself together and decided that she would go upstairs and see what she could scrounge for a breakfast snack and have another cup of tea.

When she arrived Mrs Briggs began to flutter around her much like a mother hen and insisted that Freya sat down while she made her some toast and tea.

After being refreshed Freya returned to her bunker to find Mr Gaunt sitting outside of her office talking to several members of her team.

"Hello," he greeted her, "Just giving some of your team a pep talk and holding you up as an example of what can be achieved by diligent, painstaking and intelligent work ethos."

She quietly replied, "After this job is over having that opinion of me might be quite a challenge, sir."

He just smiled and said nothing in reply.

She unlocked her door and ushered him in. He looked at the side table adorned with most of the items taken from Woodbine Cottage and told her "Quite a collection you have there, where is the problem?"

"I have what is obviously espionage material here but I want it all translated in case there is material there that we can use as evidence to the coroner or a criminal trial should we find out who was involved with the death of body one, Mr Hacker, and the murder of body two who you have provisionally identified as Herr Rosenberg," she told him.

Mr Gaunt ran his eye over the items again and asked, "What do you need?" I need a translation from what is possibly Russian into English. I want reels of probably miniature cine film exposed and I have those greaseproof paper mini drawings. I'm not sure what they are but I don't think that they are a direct help to us but they might be a positive avenue of enquiry into the reasons for what appears to be manslaughter and murder and of course now the suicide of Hackers wife.

I can go to outside authorities for this to be done, but at this stage, I don't want 'Other bodies' to know what we have and then blowing our investigation to kingdom come," she told him.

Mr Gaunt told her "If this so-called Russian is Russian, I know a man who knows a man who knows a former lady translator for the United Nations. She would do it and if it's Cyrillic of any sort she could probably make a good fist of translating it for our eyes only.

With the greaseproof drawings, it might be a little difficult if they are complicated but leave that with me for a while. As to your reels of cine film your own scene of crime people could deal with that one but try to use somebody you know.

Get someone from 'Central' rather than these SOCO's embedded here." As he surveyed the items he asked Freya. "What are these?" pointing to the diaries. "They appear to be the personal diaries of someone and are written in tiny letters which it might take ages for me to read. As with the drawings, writings, cine film they were in my lavatory bucket," she told him.

"Do I need rubber gloves?" He asked with a stern solemnity and smirk. Freya replied, "Just to be sure that you don't catch any nasty bugs I will get every last one of them fumigated. I am expendable as are my team Sir, but you, your Assistant Chief Constableship must be preserved at all costs."

"I was making a joke," he told her.

She replied, "So was I sir, indeed, so was I."

As Mr Gaunt walked to the door he stopped, turned and said to Freya, "Those diaries, my secretary or Simon's have little to do and if you like I will get either of them to transcribe them into easily readable print and if they are needed as evidence they will already be typed up." She then asked him, "What if they don't think that is in their job description?"

He replied. "I'm sure that their job description will not be breached in the typing pool, the choice is theirs and I know which they will settle for. You have more important things to concern you than the working welfare of our Elizabeth and Sarah.

They both know which side their bread's buttered on. As our American, alleged, friends are inclined to say, "They are one hell of a smart pair of cookies. Add the diaries to the list for me to take when this meeting is over." ACC Gaunt told Freya.

"Oh, by the way," he told her, "I hear that we shall have several more visitors at the meeting. It should be enlightening but we are the upholders of the law of the land and whoever these people turn out to be in any argument we must push the point that we investigate all crimes whoever in authority might have a peripheral or direct interest.

We have legal power of arrest, they only have very limited power. Have that in the back of your mind in any dispute."

Freya gave her boss a very direct look and said to him. "You know who these people are already don't you?" He smiled and walked to the stairs.

Freya, just settled herself into the chair when a male voice down the 'phone declared, "I am your humble and obedient servant ma'am, what do you wish of me?"

She replied, "He's only just left my office, how could he have got on to you so quickly." The man replied, modern science ma'am, it's called a personal radio, heard of 'em?

"Right ho, smart Alec, Why haven't I got one? She asked. "Cost, it all comes down to cost and rank of course and an acting detective chief inspector is simply a dot on the ladder of 'Who's entitled' to the very costly and operationally advantageous pieces of valuable gear, ma'am."

"I do know who you are Alex Hardwidge, is this call about my cine reels?" Freya asked the senior scenes of crime officer from central operations?"

"OK. You've rumbled me," Inspector Hardwidge told her and continued, "Send them up by messenger and I'll see what I can do. Send up the camera as well, it will make life easier for me and if you have the projector that would be perfect."

Chapter 6
Ma'am Has Her First Victory over the London 'Establishment'

"If I had the projector I would not need your services and I did not think of looking for a cine camera. No excuses but it was one hell of a day. I will not send them up in the bag. I will get one of my team to bring them up. At all costs they must not get lost and must be locked away," Freya told him.

"Yes," Alex told her, "Old Gaunt did tell me that this was top secret to everybody except the chief. I'll look forward to seeing what's on them, any ideas?"

"No," she told him, "But we hope that there might be something on them that we can use as evidence. They might just be holiday scenes, but equally, they might be quite evil knowing where they came from and how they were hidden plus the reels are so miniature. I have a meeting shortly. It's been nice to make your acquaintance again Alex, it must be all nine days since I last spoke to you. Ta for now."

Before she left her office Freya wrote on her scribbling pad, 'Radio's'.

She looked at her watch as she went up the stairs from her bunker and saw that it was fifteen minutes to ten. As she walked across the foyer past the waiting room she heard the sound of voices from the room. when she passed the door it opened and a man came out and asked directions to a lavatory.

Freya directed him to the nearest lavatory then turned and shot down the stairs to her office, fiddling with the keys and eventually finding the right one and made a dive for her desk drawer. From there she took the photograph that Alf Jones had given her of the man driving away from Woodbine Cottage. Carefully locking up again she ran back up the stairs to the clerk's office. She put her head through the stable door and called Jake over.

"Quick, Jake," she told him in a hushed tone of voice, "In the waiting room is a man whose prints I need without him knowing that they've been taken. Do we have a visitors book? Jake confirmed that they did have one. She continued, "That crystal paperweight over there can I use it?" A nod from Jake was taken as a positive. She continued, "As they pass the door could you be ready with that book and have the weight blocking where a name would go. Let him move it and get his prints, is that alright with you?"

Jake walked over with the book, laid it on the door flap collecting the paperweight and rubbing it clean with a less than Persil white handkerchief. "You've just about thought of everything ma'rm except which one is it?"

As he spoke so the target walked past the office door from the lavatory. Furiously thumbing over her shoulder Freya whispered, "Him, him with the 'tash"

"What if he is not the first one out?" Jake asked. "Just grab him and get his dabs on the glass, apologise to the rest and ask them to come back and sign," she told him.

Freya then went to the office of Superintendent Cole to find it empty except for Chief Inspector Thomas. Nodding towards the desk normally occupied by Mr Cole, she asked. "Where is he?"

"Along in the classroom arranging the chairs as if for a courts-martial, He's in his element is our Fred. Particularly now that so many of them have turned up," replied a cool calm Mr Thomas.

She then almost ran to the classroom and burst in on Mr Cole and a constable arranging the chairs for this meeting. "Sir, will you look at this, please," Freya asked the superintendent. Mr Cole instead of looking at the photograph that she was proffering said.

"I shall heap praise on you in a minute or two and I will defend you up to the hilt against any attack or suspicion of an attack. But, don't think that I mean any of what I say about your superb achievements or forensic ability to pursue and solve a crime. I am using you to put these ministry bastards in their place. Oh, sorry about my language but they really are the scum of the Civil Service otherwise they would not be down here. What do you want me for?"

He then took the photograph from Freya as she told him that the man in the waiting room was the same man photographed in a government registered car with Mrs Hacker. While she was explaining who Mrs Hacker was Mr Cole was very carefully studying the photograph. He suddenly almost shouted, "I've got the bastard I think, put some hair on his head and get that toothbrush off his top lip, yes that's him." As he handed her back the photograph his parting words were. "Delay the meeting by about fifteen minutes."

From the classroom, the superintendent rushed into his office, grabbed his car keys, then threw them on the desk and shouted to Jake, "Get me a traffic car now." Jake, rather unwisely asked, "What?"

By now Cole was at the office door to tell Jake that he needed a car at the station now, this instant.

"And when I give you an order you carry it out at once and in future you say 'What, sir?' And in an unknowing reference to the brilliance and pathos of George Bernard Shaw's writing told Jake to "Move your bloody arse."

All the time that the now heated words between Mr Cole and Jake could be heard across the ground floor of the station and by the people in the waiting room. In the office, Tommo shifted from one buttock to the other uncrossed his legs and eventually stood up, picked up Fred's car keys and in no particular hurry straightened his back and walked towards the almost levitating figure of Fred Cole.

A white-capped 'traffic' driver came to the office and enquired with a dose of menace at having his 'Tea break' about to be sacrificed for some 'Tit' or other.

"Oo's buggering up my day now," the no doubt cultured constable enquired of everybody and anybody. "Fred, you will need these if you are going home," said Mr Thomas as he handed Fred his abandoned keys. "Ta, Tommo. I forgot the door keys were on this ring," said the by now puce faced superintendent before turning to the traffic patrol car driver and growled at him as he pointed to the crown emblem on his jacket shoulder and told the surly constable. "The 'Tit' that you are giving up your undeserved tea break for is me with a crown here. Get outside and put blue lights on as I direct you to my home."

With the departure of Mr Cole, Mr Thomas, after a brief conversation with Freya then went to the waiting room to tell them that there would be a slight delay in the meeting and when they complained of the cramped conditions in the waiting room he suggested that they might avail themselves of the extra room provided by the classroom. They filed out led by Freya who asked them to assemble by the clerk's office door. As they stood there she went to her 'man' and led him to the stable door where Jake was waiting with the visitors book and the page held down by the crystal paperweight.

"Will you kindly make the entry in the visitors book, sir?" she asked him." Oh, do I have to?" the man replied to her. She did not reply but stood preventing him from avoiding the stable door.

"Oh, really," he muttered and with a disparaging look as he picked up the pen from the margin he attempted to push the paperweight off the page and only succeeded in tipping it. He made a grab for it and Jake caught it in a handkerchief, probably, in fact certainly the rather less than the white one that he had used not a few minutes before.

The man signed himself in as Major T.R.B. Quinn, RA and gave his address as London W1. Underneath he added, "and four colleagues."

Jake, almost bristled as the man wrote the title of Major and in a most refined voice, Jake enquired, "Perhaps Major T.R.B. Quinn might allow his colleagues to sign themselves in? I suspect that they can write if they come from London W1.

The major gave Jake a withering look and perhaps rather less than wisely said to Jake. "Look here my man, we make the rules around here and I have no intention of taking instructions from a constable such as you." The major then turned to Freya and in a military tone of voice 'commanded her to take them to, "This classroom or whatever."

As the group walked away one of them took the book and pen from Jakes' hands and wrote Commander Wynne. Metropolitan Police Special Branch.

Jake, with a long and noisy suck of his teeth and a knowing smirk at Freya, picked up the visitors book as she led them into the classroom. Without a word being said, they all sat at the table instead of the chairs arranged for them to sit in beyond the table covered in the flag of the police force and writing pads and quality pens at each chair. The pens were counted out from the clerk sergeant, and when they were collected, each and every one would be accounted for or all hell would break loose.

An edict would ensure the return of the errant pens with diabolical punishment for anyone below the rank of superintendent found to have one. It was not unknown for the clerk sergeant after a meeting to be found going through desks, wardrobes and the jackets of superintendent's left draped over a chair back.

The clerk sergeant was fastidious in his stock keeping and this meeting would be no different.

Freya excused herself and found a constable with apparently nothing much to do and took him into the classroom, moved the unoccupied chairs and picked up the table from the seats now containing the ministry men. To say the very least, it was amusing as they picked up the table so the visitors realised that their briefcases were going with it they made a mad scramble to grab their cases. Had the collective looks in their eyes been a strike of lightning, Freya and her constable would have been a pile of ash.

Without a word during the whole time of furniture moving, Freya left the classroom and went to see Jake and he presented her with the crystal weight and said, with some feeling. "That major is riding for a very big fall," she told him, "Jake I might well have the evidence that will make them fall even more painful. You will be avenged to be sure," Jake finished the conversation by telling her. "I used to eat simple-minded little boys like him in Burma and I still can.

With that in came Superintendent Cole with a grimace which in any other person would equate to that of a smile. He looked in the office and said to Jake, "Find me an envelope that will fit this," he then held up what appeared to be a rectangular piece of board. Jake went to take hold of it but Mr Cole told him that he only wanted an envelope. Jake replied, "I was only trying to get the size." Finally, he fished out three different sized envelopes and said, "Take your choice, one of them should fit."

All the while the clerk sergeant was watching closely, no doubt to ensure that no unsigned envelopes were going out than those that were needed for urgent police use.

The superintendent then turned to Freya and said, "You ready?"

"No," she replied, "I am waiting for my inspector and Mr Gaunt." No sooner were the words out of her mouth than Mr Gaunt walked through the main doors and Ron Wilkins entered the foyer from the bunker stairs. After greeting Mr Gaunt and watching him being taken away by Cole to the sound of "I want to see you in my office Bill, are you leading or…."

The rest of the conversation was lost as they entered the office of the superintendent. Freya turned to her inspector and said, "Sorry to lumber you with my jobs but can you get this paperweight dusted for prints, compare them with those taken from the binding tape used on body one, one Hacker, and either positive or negative pass me a note in the meeting. I saw a SOCO chap wandering around in my office now occupied by Johns."

Ron looked at her as she carefully accepted the crystal from Jake and said to his superior, "You crafty bitc..." He stopped himself just in time as she lifted a finger to his face, turned and made her way to the classroom.

Freya followed the superintendent and assistant chief constable into the room to find Mr Thomas already there unusually in this case at the side of and not at the table itself, in his usual very relaxed pose with his pipe going like the Flying Scotsman.

No pleasantries passed between the two parties as Mr Cole sat in the centre with Bill Gaunt to his right, Freya to his left with the out of breath Jake rushing through the door to stand behind his superintendent, notebook in hand.

As Superintendent Cole sat down he carefully laid the enveloped rectangle carefully in front of him, adjusting its position away from his notepad.

Jake closed the door and 'Old King' Cole addressed the visitors. "Good morning, gentlemen. I am Superintendent Cole, the sub commander of this Force area known as 'D' Division. To my right is Assistant Chief Constable Gaunt, commander of the Central Criminal Investigation Department of this Force. To my left is Detective Chief Inspector Freya Douglas Gore Hamilton and that is Acting Superintendent Thomas, keeping a legal eye on our talks this morning. Behind me is my procedural comptroller.

As he finished speaking the door opened and all on the police side of the table except Bill Gaunt immediately stood up. "Oh, do please sit down." The person then went to Bill Gaunt who then stood up and both men warmly shook hands. The man then looked at the visitors and said to them in his soft well-educated vowel enunciating voice. "Good morning, gentlemen. I welcome you to the 'D' Division, I am the area commander and Mr Cole is my very efficient deputy who runs a very tight ship. My name is Bates. Who exactly are you?"

Before anyone could answer, Fred Cole stood up again and said to his superior, "Thank you for coming, sir; will you please take the chair?"

"No, no Mr Cole, You are the best suited to be the chairman. I simply wouldn't impose myself on you," he replied.

He looked at Quinn and when Quinn told him his name it came out of his mouth as "Major T.R.B. Quinn, Royal Artillery attached to the internal intelligence service. Mr Bates shook his hand and bade him welcome. The next person introduced himself as "Wynne, Commander of the Metropolitan Police Special Branch."

Mr Bates looked closely at Wynne and said, "Ah, yes, I do think that our paths may have crossed when you were one of my constables."

"I think not," was the reply which was followed by Mr Bates pondering for a moment before addressing Wynne again and saying, "Yes, yes, that's it, I do remember you, Mr Wynne. Yes, it was such an unfortunate incident but I see that they have forgiven you." He then offered his hand to Wynne. Wynne made no effort to either stand up or shake hands with Mr Bates.

As the chief superintendent moved to the next person it was audible to most, probably including Wynne as Superintendent Cole quietly told the people at the table, "I'll get that bastard. Like his mate, they don't remember me. "And you are sir?" Mr Bates asked the chair-bound next in the line fellow. The man told Mr Bates, "I do not identify myself."

Mr Cole looked aghast and appeared to rise in his chair before changing his mind and slumping down. The other two committed the same discourtesy to Chief Superintendent Bates.

There was a brief period of silence only broken by the breathing of Fred Cole as he appeared to be straining at the mythical leash holding him to his chair.

Mr Bates then told the three nameless individuals. "I'm so sorry to have to tell you gentlemen as we do not know who or what you are and indeed, you may have been collected off of the pavement. I would most regrettably demand that you return from whence you came, namely the pavement.

I bid you all a very good morning." Looking at Jake he said, "Mr Richards, will you be so kind and escort these three persons back to the pavement. Thank you."

With that request to Jake, Chief Superintendent Bates without fuss quietly left the room. The tension was almost palpable as without unnecessary ceremony Jake with his very best plummy accent told the three men, "You heard what my commander said, move your arses." Then with a noticeable change of tone added with no little menace in his gruff voice, he barked, "now."

"Perhaps we have been too hasty," Major Quinn suggested as Fred Cole, no longer able to maintain his most unusual equitable persona shouted at the three men, "Get the hell out of here and if I catch sight of you again you'll be seeing the world through bars, my bars."

"Wait, Wait," the Major declared then added, under protest we will declare our name rank and department."

Jake reluctantly resumed his position behind Mr Cole as the first of the three less than wise monkeys said. Palfrey, Admiralty, the next declared himself as Cox of the Home Office and the third muttered the name of Glover adding Foreign Office.

"Fine," Mr Cole told the meeting, "Names and words mean nothing to me, now produce documentary evidence that you are who you claim to be."

"Why pick on my colleagues?" Quinn asked Mr Cole and added, "You don't know who I am other than what I have told you."

"Oh, yes, Major Quinn, I know just who you are, the only doubt I have is that of you holding the rank of major." Superintendent Cole told him then continued.

"As there is a lady present I will moderate my language but I'm quite sure that you be aware of someone nicknamed by their Sandhurst term mates as defecate trousers or a similar defining title and as for you Commander of the Special Twigs, it was only your membership of a so-called secret brotherhood that your fingers were wiped clean. I've got something on both of you and don't you forget it, understand?

By now the other three had from their pockets and one from his bag produced identification to the satisfaction of Jake. The door quietly opened again and the former Commander Sir Simon Bates, DSO and Bar RNR softly entered and again with the exception of Bill Gaunt the people at the table immediately stood up as Mr Bates told the three previously non-identifiable people, "Ah, I'm so glad that you are still here. Shall we start again, I'm Chief Superintendent Bates, Police Commander hereabouts?"

He went to the three 'Ministry' men and they all stood up as they shook hands with Mr Bates. He told them, "It's so much nicer when we can all get along together don't you think?" Heads were nodded in agreement although minds might have a different view on the matter.

Going to Wynne Mr Bates told him, "I have just been talking to your commissioner, he was under my command as my second Lieutenant during the war. Nice chap, so pleased to see just how well he has got on. We had a word about you.

Unfortunately, he does not know you so I was delighted to fill him in about your time as a constable and later as a detective constable. He noted my comments and was a little surprised that you described yourself as 'The commander of Special Branch' and told me that one of his staff officers would have a little chat with you tomorrow."

Mr Bates ended his talk with Wynne by saying, "It is so fortunate that I happen to know both of you, it might help with your promotion prospects. Turning to Fred Cole, Mr Bates said, "I'm so sorry to interrupt your deliberations again but it pleases me to see all our friends are still here."

With the end of the unsettling conversation with Mr or rather, perhaps Commander Wynne, Mr Cole took command of the meeting by sliding the large envelope across the table towards Major Quinn. Quinn opened the envelope and withdrew a photograph in a frame, turned it over and whatever he saw had a most unsettling effect on his composure.

"Recognise anybody there?" Cole asked him. The major simply looked ashen as Mr Cole went on "Who is standing back row top left?" The silence was followed by a squeaky reply from the major, "Me."

"Yes," said Fred, then asked, "And who is sitting in the middle of the front row in a 'Sam Brown'?" The major in even a quieter voice replied, "You."

"Just in case you might have forgotten cadet Quinn, I was your RSM. You were simply bloody useless and had two left feet and when under pressure left a distinct smell behind. Remember?" Not a word passed Major Quinn's lips as Mr Cole concluded his character assignation of the previously pompous major, much to the delight of 'Common' constable Jake.

Everything appeared to be settling down as the door again opened to allow Detective Inspector Ron Wilkins to enter and pass a slip of paper to Freya who had so far rather enjoyed proceeding as apparently so had Mr Thomas, now refilling his pipe and as usual searching every pocket for a lighter or Lucifer. She opened the paper read the contents and passed it to Jake who read it as he passed it to Fred Cole. Fred read it then said. "Can we now move on to the reason why you people are here?"

It did at first appear that no one wanted to answer Mr Cole which prompted him to tell the visitors "If you have nothing to say, we have work to do so I may as well call this meeting to a close, agree?"

The man from the Admiralty found his voice to say, "No, please don't. This meeting is important to us."

"Well, major," he asked, "do we go on or not?" The major nodded his asset and Mr Cole simply said, "what do you want?"

Mr Palfrey from the Admiralty said, "I understand from Major Quinn that Admiralty papers and confidential information may have..." Before Palfrey could finish Quinn interrupted and said, "It is not 'may have' your security has been breached."

Freya then asked Quinn "How would you know that their security has been breached, if you do, how do you know and what items have been taken, copied or otherwise recorded?"

Quinn told her, "This is a state secret of considerable importance."

"That Mr Quinn," Freya, looking Quinn straight in the eye, said. "Is absolute balderdash. A five-year-old could come up with a more persuasive answer than that."

Major T.R.B. Quinn, RA, did have the decency to blush whilst shaking his head.

Mr Glover from the foreign office told the meeting that their interest was in any foreign power having access to British, Commonwealth or NATO classified information while Mr Cox from the Home office wriggled on the hard classroom chairs as he said," Mr Quinn insisted that my department should be represented as it might be necessary to point out and insist on the legal responsibility that this Police force has to uphold the requirements of the state as required by my ministry.

As Cox finished his sentence so Quinn told Mr Cole that "You will hand over to me all paperwork and other evidence that you have relating to the death of Harrison Hacker and Kurt Rosenberg. If it is required we will prosecute the case. End of conversation."

The words, "End of Conversation' really put the cat amongst the pigeons. A silence followed those words as Cole very slowly looked at each individual in turn then, in an alarmingly subdued voice looked at the Special Branch representative Wynne and asked, "And Mr Wynne, what is your role in this fiasco?"

Wynne made a huge mistake by looking down then almost whispering, "I am here to check that the paperwork and evidence that you surrender to Major Quinn is correct and complete."

With a voice returning to normal but to Freya, Mr Thomas and Mr Gaunt, it was a voice similar to a volcano in that the magma was boiling and ready to erupt Mr Cole asked of them all, "What makes you think that whatever evidence we have of an unexplained death probably coupled to a murder would be given over to unauthorised people such as you, in particular you Wynne and you Quinn, with rhyming names you are quite a double act."

With an ever-rising voice, Cole shouted at them, "The pair of you would even fail to make a Music Hall double act you're are so bloody useless." Turning to the three Ministry men, in a more moderate voice he told them "Anything concerning your departments we will certainly give you access to once the prosecutors decide that it is not required at the Assize courts."

Wynne, with his eyes still looking at his lap, said nothing but Quinn said, "This matter is within the Official Secrets Act. I command you to hand over all the evidence and documents to me and we will decide if it is in the national interest to involve the public through prosecution in a criminal court. And while you are talking about the case going through the due processes of the law, where are your prisoners or suspects?"

Mr Thomas looked at Freya from his carefully thought out vantage point and broadly winked while Fred Cole was drawing a breath for the next onslaught at Major T.R.B. Quinn, RA. Freya looked at the major and said, "Just in case you have forgotten during the past fifteen minutes, I am Freya Douglas Gore Hamilton and the senior investigating officer of these crimes Major Quinn." As she said the title major so a very loud disparaging sounding snort came from the wrinkled nostrils of Mr Cole.

Before he could interrupt her she continued, "You quite pertinently questioned whether we had any prisoners or suspects." At these words, the major nodded and even Wynne took his eyes off of his lap and looked at her.

"Yes, Quinn, we do have suspects and very strong evidence, enough to arrest the suspect but as is peculiar to my investigations, I believe that if I give a suspect enough rope, eventually, without effort on my part, he, or indeed, she will hang themselves."

As she finished her sentence she slid a photograph across the table to Quinn, the photograph of him in the car with Mrs Hacker.

He looked at Freya and with a forced laugh told her, "That means nothing, nothing at all." She took the photograph back and pushed three photographs across the table to Quinn.

He looked at each one then looked up at her and said, "What are these supposed to illustrate?"

Freya then told him to pass them to Wynne and he would probably know what the photographs depicted. Quinn pushed the photographs at Wynne who picked them up one by one. Studied each then said, "Dabs." Quinn looked at him with questioning arched eyebrows. Wynne then said to him, "Fingerprints."

She then reached over the table and reclaimed the photographs as Quinn asked, "What has that got to do with me?" indicating the three items.

"I seem to remember a few minutes ago," she told him, "that you asked if we had any prisoners or suspects. I then passed you a photograph of you in a government registered car with Mrs Hacker in the passenger seat, the same Mrs Hacker who committed suicide after you ran away when we arrived at her cottage.

The other three photographs are of fingerprints taken from the bindings on a body found dead in a van with debris from the cottage under the wheel arches. The other photographs are from the control sample supplied within the past hour.

The fingerprints belong to a person in this room." When everyone's attention was firmly on her, including that of Mr Cole, in a dramatic, heart-stopping denouement better suited to a west end stage production she told Quinn,

"They are your fingerprints, Major Quinn. At the moment you are our strongest suspect. Is it any wonder that you want all the evidence so that you can destroy it and save your neck. You are free to go, the term 'free' is subject to my whim until I decide to reel you in, that is unless you would like to talk to my team now?

At this stage I'm sure in your presumed elevated social position, you will understand that my underlings, your social and professional superiors will deal with people such as you."

The deliberate totally disparaging final comments from Freya plainly discomfited Quinn and he collected his briefcase and rose walking towards the door.

"Mr Quinn," Freya said to him, "Should you be minded to leave this room until I say that you can, I will arrest you. Do I make myself quite clear?" His only reply was "Major actually."

"Oh, and by the way," Freya said to him," Unfortunately for you when you signed the visitors book as well as leaving your fingerprints behind you shed a hair on the book and on his own initiative Mr Cole's A D C gave my SOCO team the hair to compare with the human hair stuck to the bindings securing body one, namely one, Hacker. Unlike your fingerprints, your hair comparison will take a little longer. I think that if and when I do allow you to leave this room and station, you might consult your lawyer.

As she finished talking, Mr Palfrey from the Admiralty said to Mr Cole. "I see no further reason for me to continue this meeting. I have your assurance that within the boundaries of your investigation that you will inform me of any material illegally obtained by Harrison Hacker from the Admiralty and War Office."

Superintendent Cole stood up and replied, "Of course, we will sir, I do apologise for the fact that you had to witness the apparent downfall of this ridiculous man," indicating Quinn. "At Sandhurst, I was the Warrant Officer responsible for a major part of his training. He was useless there and only commissioned by the skin of his teeth and having influential superiors. I do apologise again. Goodbye." With that, he shook hands with Palfrey and Mr Glover from the Foreign Office also got up, shook hands with Mr Cole and left the room.

Mr Thomas looked at Mr Cox from the Home Office and said," Are you leaving too, sir?"

"No," he replied and continued, "I'm not sure that you have the right to continue with this investigation as it has the likelihood of serious espionage implications for the State.

You must hand this investigation over to the Metropolitan police through the Special Branch represented here by Mr Wynne."

Fred Cole, very red in the face with the tell-tale vein in his temple throbbing as it protruded, went to speak as 'Tommo' got in before him and said,

"I'm glad you brought that matter up, Mr Cox. Quite a thorny problem don't you think?"

"No," replied Cox, "a provincial force such as yours are quite out of their depth in dealing with these matters."

Mr Thomas looked towards Cox and in his quiet measured tone said to Cox. "Robert Peel founded the metropolitan police. The cost was borne by the government. This has continued to the present day. Their income comes from general taxation, in short, both you and me and millions of taxpayers.

In the meantime, cities and counties followed London's lead and created their own police forces paid for by the local taxpayers and controlled by Watch Committees of local worthies.

To unify the system the government needed some form of overall control and, as a means to this end, then subsidised the income from local taxpayers through grants to the various Watch Committees. A system now performed by the Home Office.

Providing that they kept an efficient police force upholding the laws passed in parliament the government allowed the individual police forces to operate as individuals with power vested in the various Watch Committees.

This has continued to the present times. Neither the Home office nor the metropolitan police can usurp the authority of a Watch Committee without evidence of wrongdoing or lack of efficiency.

Unless we or any other force chose to call in the metropolitan police they have no authority to be on our patch or involve themselves in pursuit of our criminal cases and charge the local taxpayer for their not always efficient services. We can easily and efficiently deal with cases such as the one that we are discussing here, and at present, the Home Office has no authority to intervene. I do hope that you clearly understand the situation. Perhaps you would care to argue the point, sir?"

There was a notable silence in the classroom, and it was eventually broken by Cox telling Mr Thomas and the remaining people present, "While I am not certain that you are correct, it would be in your interest and good relations with my arm of government to accede to my instruction to hand this case over to Mr Wynne."

"Far be it for a simple provincial assistant chief constable and commander of the criminal investigation departments to butt in on this very technical conversation, but Mr Cox, I think that is right and proper for your benefit that I should identify the semi-recumbent figure of Superintendent Thomas as having been on the staff of the Judge Advocate in Germany at the end of the war. Do I make my point sir?"

Tommo took the point relating to his casual posture and sat up then began fiddling for his tobacco pouch yet again.

"I have to disagree with you," Cox told Mr Gaunt then continued, "And I'm not confident that a person on the staff of the Judge Advocate who might have been the bag carrier is au fait with the regulations and authority of my ministry."

"No," said Mr Gaunt. "But I believe Mr Thomas to be correct. However, shall we just leave it to your commissioner and this area commander who you met earlier, to discuss the matter? As Mr Bates told you the Commissioner was his junior officer during the war so they have a very friendly association. Which should resolve this affair. Do you not agree Mr Cox?"

No word or facial movement from Cox displayed his opinion except that he looked less than pleased as he with Wynne stood up and ignoring the outstretched hand of Superintendent Cole took themselves out of the classroom.

Freya said to the remaining 'visitor' "You have not had a very good morning, have you? You will be pleased to know that as long as you cooperate with me, your day will not get even worse. I do not want to arrest you and then bail you, the paperwork in those cases take up valuable time. Whilst at this time I do not think that you are betraying your country if you wish to have the benefit of freedom you will surrender your passport.

By the time that you return from here your home, or I suspect homes, will be searched by my team in conjunction with whatever police area is concerned. Certainly the Somstrym police and no doubt the Mets as well.

You will not leave here until we have verified your addresses and we will not simply take Internal Intelligence services as your employer. We have access to all departments of government at the discretion of and through our chief constables. Again, before you leave the station that process of identification will be established. Is that quite clearly understood, Major Quinn?"

Without saying a word, he produced a card bearing his photograph with the identification MI5.

Freya turned to Jake and asked him to get Detective Inspector Wilkins. Plainly Ron was either at the door or not far away, within seconds Ron was in the room and looking at a totally deflated Major Quinn.

Freya told Ron. "When he gives you his verified address ring the appropriate force area and ask them to get a warrant for his address and ask for a team to search his home. I believe that he also has an address in London and the same procedure there but send Bill Jobbins on that one, please.

I will deal with everything here. The Major is not under arrest, he is helping us with our enquiries. If he wants to make a statement after he has received legal advice bring him back here." Turning to Quinn she told him "Each day, including the weekends you will make a 'phone call to this police station. If you miss one call you will be arrested. Is that understood?" Quinn simply nodded. Ron Wilkins then escorted him to the bunker.

As everyone was standing up and shuffling papers Freya asked Bill Gaunt if she might have a word before he left. When Cole and Tommo had left she asked Mr Gaunt if he had circulated via Interpol the photofit of 'Iron Gob'? He said that he was about to do it but was waiting for the photographs of Kurt and Mrs Hacker to send off at the same time. She suggested that the photographs might also be sent to Bremen, the birthplace of Mrs Hacker as this might produce quicker results if any than the ponderous Interpol system. He said that it would be done by his secretary, "this afternoon."

As they walked down the corridor from the classroom, Mr Gaunt told her, "That was a clinical style demolition of Quinn along with the superb onslaught by 'King Cole' although at one time you only just interrupted him before he exploded thank God.

Our Fred can be a handful when he gets the wind under his tail, but with that, Wynne and Quinn, his tail was on fire.

He had that Quinn on his fishing hook and Quinn knew that and when you produced the photographs plus prints he was really cooked. By the way, until now I didn't realise that Fred was such a master of English and humour when he remarked on the Quinn and Wynne double act, quite something to remember." As they walked to the foyer he said, "I will go and see the 'silent one' and get him to set up the neutering of the Home Office in this case with his chum the commissioner. Bye."

Freya then looked in the clerk's office and saw Jake sitting sucking his teeth. She thanked him for helping out with the fingerprints and the very smart move with the hair sample. "That was brilliant Jake," she told him then went on to say, "In fact, it was inspired, d'you want to come on my team?"

Jakes reply was brief and to the point as would be expected from him, "Serve under a woman? Not bloody likely, marm."

"I rather expected that Jake, but the offer is still open, 'bloody woman' or not," she told him.

A voice from the depths of the office told her, "He is useless here but he keeps the white collars off my back ma'am and he has more juicy gossip than a meeting of the Women's Institute so, sorry ma'am, he, for better or worse, is indispensable here. What would his dearest chum Superintendent Cole do without him?" The sarcastic voice of the clerk sergeant asked her.

Freya jumped as a familiar voice behind her said, "I heard that sergeant, the cold wet pavement is within a foot of your office wall, sarcasm will surely deposit you onto that pavement. The only person guaranteed a chair in this station is Chief Inspector Thomas, earthquakes would never move him out of my office." A surprisingly cheerful Superintendent Cole told his clerk sergeant.

"And don't think that I can't hear you Fred." came from his office as Chief Inspector Thomas settled into his chair in the superintendent's office. Freya turned away knowing for the first time since she came here that everyone was in a good mood, probably a very rare thing amongst the hierarchy of this station.

When she arrived at her office there was a large brown envelope on her desk. She opened it to find that it was the pathologist's report which told her conclusively that body number two, Kurt Rosenberg had died from the stab wound under the left arm and his organs were in good order and other than minimal water in his lungs he was a fit man. Body number one, that of Harrison Hacker appeared to have suffocated to death but there was a considerable amount of anaesthetics in his organs and it was the pathologist's opinion that a probable overdose of an anaesthetising drug, Amobarbital, was the primary cause of death aided by asphyxia caused by the compression of the lungs. The drug had been injected into the cardioid artery.

Freya sat back and thought to herself that now that she had a positive cause of death for both bodies it was time to take stock of people and events. Both bodies were murdered in the case of body two it was deliberate murder by stabbing. Body one was probably murdered by accident by virtue that to her reasoning the anaesthetic was probably injected in him to keep him quiet otherwise why bind, blindfold and gag him if he was already dead.

Someone must have overdosed him. Body two perhaps as body one had green fibres which were a match with the coat that body two was wearing when recovered from the locks. Therefore, who killed them and most importantly why?

Were the phials and hypodermic syringe in the teapot the instruments of death for Harrison Hacker?

Most probably they were. She then, without positive evidence decided that Harrison Hacker was being kidnapped and taken to the docks to be put alive aboard a ship.

In view of the amount of Cyrillic writing that she found at the cottage, there was a Russian connection. Iron Gob was from a Russian ship that sailed the same evening as the body of Hacker arrived at the docks in the white van. Was that the connection? She deduced that the case had come to a close for the day as she now awaited news of Ron with Quinn and later Bill Jobbins in London.

Her list of outstanding matters included the results of the analyst of the contents of the teapot, the interpretation of the Russian script, the exposure of the film reels, the transcription of the diaries, the interpretation of the drawings on the greaseproof paper and hoped-for results of the Rosenbergs in Germany with an outside chance that Iron Gob might be identified.

As she went out of her office door she looked into the general office and saw five detectives busy with writing in their journals and on pads. As she watched them so she noticed furtive glances in her direction and deduced that they had nothing to do, not even bag carrying so were making out that they were so busy because ma'am was about.

After locking her office up she went to the stairs and was in two minds whether or not she should turn around and find her 'Team' leaning back in their chairs, perhaps with their feet on the desks now that ma'am was gone.

Freya decided that she would not go back which would be an indication that she did not trust them and in the long run would achieve very little except they would consider her a proper bitch which was often the considered opinion of policemen towards their superiors, male or in this new age, female.

Without further ado, she made her way to the canteen kitchen to find Mrs Briggs and another lady busy with the remains of the lunchtime rush. As she walked through the kitchen door so Mrs Briggs caught sight of her and nudged her catering chum. They turned around and both bobbed their heads as if they knew who she was descended from.

"Good afternoon ladies," Freya greeted them then asked if she could have a cup of weak tea. The unnamed lady grabbed a mug and was about to put a teabag in it. At the same time, Mrs Briggs produced tin and a tea strainer. Mrs Briggs saw what the lady had done and in a loud type of whisper told her that mum would have a cup and saucer with leaf tea and handed the woman firstly the pot to make it in then the ingredients and then the teacup and saucer and then told her "She ain't a docker, she be a lady an' in charge of the detectives."

Mrs Briggs then went to a cupboard and fiddling with her capacious ground level apron pocket produced a key and unlocked the door, opening it to display packets of various brands of biscuits and plates with doily's already placed on them.

"My, Mrs Briggs," Freya told her, "You certainly keep a good cupboard of fattening goodies."

Mrs Briggs replied, "You'm got to 'ave summat to put some flesh on 'ee, not Mum that of course, youm need fat of course." Long pause before in her confusion she added "I weren't thinkin', mum. Me and my mouth, I am ashamed, mum."

She was about to laugh it off then; fortunately, at the last second, she realised that Mrs Briggs might think that she was laughing at her and with a serious face put her hand on the arm of Mrs Briggs and said in a genuinely sympathetic tone. "I do understand Mrs Briggs and please think no more of the matter and could I please have one of your delicious chocolate biscuits?"

As if the weight of the world had been lifted from her bent shoulders, Mrs Briggs smiled again and put three biscuits on the plate. Freya thanked her and made her way into the officers dining room.

As she went into the room she could see someone's head above the chair back. She went further and saw that it was the secretary to Mr Bates. They exchanged pleasantries and Freya quietly asked her if she would care for a chocolate biscuit. The secretary took one and she then sat down facing her.

"Thank you for helping out with the 'Goodies'," she told the secretary. "Mrs Briggs thinks that I should put some fat on and attempted to ensure that I did via three biscuits." She continued, "By the way, I now understand that you have been given the job of transcribing the diaries. Please don't think that it was my idea to give you the task of transcribing those diaries they were supposed to go to Mr Gaunt's secretary…" The secretary interrupted her to tell her that she was well aware that it was Mr Bates who thought that his secretary, namely her, had little to do and judging by his cheerful expression when he gave the diaries to her he knew just what she was thinking.

"In the couple that I have completed so far today, it would appear that the writer is mostly referring to his work as it appears to involve technical words and sometimes whole paragraphs but to date nothing to bring a bit of excitement to a girls heart, especially one who has so little to do all day and every working day. Pardon my obvious sarcasm." The secretary told Freya.

Freya told the secretary that she was hoping that the diaries might indicate exactly what the writer was doing and also discover who the writer was and that she did not expect the 'Dear Diary' entry of a teenage girl with her name carefully written in a copper plate script inside the front cover.

For the diaries to make any sense she had to prove who the books were written by. "The moment that I get any indication who the writer is or was and the continuing nature of any subject reoccurring from book to book it might make my job easier."

She then asked the secretary, "You know who I am but although this is only the second time that we've met I don't know your name."

"I'm Sarah Dodds-Younger, my surname is not quite the mouthful that yours is but it's more than long enough."

"Christian names in future?" Freya asked her. "Certainly she replied, but it's Miss Dodds-Younger in front of Mr Bates. He doesn't like familiarity amongst his senior officers and his office staff, namely me."

With their tea break completed, the two women went their separate ways and when she arrived at the bunker Freya saw that Ron Wilkins was in his office. She went over and put her head around the door jam and said.

"That was a quick trip with friend Quinn, I did not expect to see you back until this evening. How did it go?"

Ron replied "Quite well and your new chum, that Wayne Butt was good. He was waiting for us and stood no messing from Quinn. We searched his flat and found nothing other than usual domestic stuff such as bills, receipts etcetera.

One important thing that I did bring back with me was the hairs out of his hairbrush for analysis along with the receipt from an Ironmongers shop for adhesive waterproof tape. Wayne sent his chap to the shop in the town and bought a reel of tape and it looks the same as body one was done up with. I also brought back two passports in two different names with his mug-shot in both and two different addresses, one there and one in London." Ron stopped and pushed the tape and the passports and the hair in the sample bag to Freya,

As he recovered his breath he continued," Dear old Cole was quite right, Quinn is not a major in the Royal Artillery he was a captain in the Royal Army Service Corps, we found his Army discharge papers and he told me that his only relative is his mother. We also looked at his bank statements and there seemed to be nothing untoward but strangely his monthly pay was not deposited by a named authority as could be expected but by a code number. Perhaps that is the code that they use for Spooks."

"Good job, Ron," Freya told him then collecting the items recovered from the former captain's flat. She told her detective inspector that she would get them dealt with by the SOCO team, particularly the hair samples as the evidence from the single hair Jake recovered would probably be thrown out in court. Ron looked at his boss and with a wry smile said, "my thoughts exactly ma'am."

The wry smile was not lost on her as she apologised to him and said. "Point taken Ron, I should not be too schoolmarmish to an experienced senior officer. I am sorry for what I implied. "Apology accepted but please don't imply that your knowledge is so superior to that of Bill Jobbins or me. Matter closed," he concluded the conversation.

As she turned away from Ron she could hear her 'phone ringing. The call was from Detective Sergeant Bill Jobbins in London. He told her.

"I made good time in getting here and the Mets men gave me an escort to Quinn's place. Plainly we were the second lot to get there this afternoon.

His flat was as clean of goods as a new pin. Whoever the 'Cleaners' were they were not as smart as they thought they were. We turned up his chest of drawers and underneath was Sovereigns, Deutschmarks, Dollars and fifty quid notes, don't see many of them. These looked pretty old, two interesting passports and several letters from his mother with an address on the top. One of them related to the death of his dad. The others appeared to be about his various birthdays.

In his bedroom, we think that something had been taken as a drawer was still open and the dust on the top had been disturbed as if something had been taken from the drawer then put on the top. In the wardrobe, most of the pockets in everything including his dressing-gown were still inside out. If it was his mates, the so-called spy's who turned the place over it is not surprising that Burgess and his mate made a success of their exploits.

Unless you say otherwise I am handing the money to the Met Flying Squad for which I will get a receipt. If we do not want the letters from his mother do I bring them with me to give back to him?

I am returning with both passports and I have taken some samples of hair from his hairbrush for the boffins to compare with those on the binding tape. Any further instructions ma'am?" Freya smiled at Ron Wilkins as she said to Bill, "No, thanks, Bill, if the place has already been swept that's about it.

The passports, anything unusual about them? "Yes," he told her, "They are a German one and what could be a Russian, Ukrainian or somewhere that way, both with his mug in them. I am coming home now, God only knows when I shall get back, rush hour is still in full swing and I bet they'll not give me an escort this time."

"Have a night in town in a good Hotel Bill, I will authorise the costs," Freya told him then almost as an afterthought told him "That's if your wife will allow you to stay in the big city of sin Bill."

"Thank you, ma'am," Bill told her adding "I will specifically tell her that you ordered me to stay on the case up here." Her reply was, "If such a lie maintains domestic harmony in the Jobbins household, sobeit, carry on and good night Bill. I'll see you tomorrow."

As she put the 'phone down so Ron told her that he had heard the conversation and enquired if she still doubted the intelligence of her inferiors now that she was about to inherit yet another bag of human hair?

A smile and shake of her head was her reply.

It was now 6:45 and Freya said to Ron, "Yet again, all that I've had since my breakfast has been two of the chocolate biscuits from Mrs Briggs cupboard, apart from starving I'm tired as I'm sure that you must be, we've all had a busy but productive day now is the time to call it a day."

Ron replied, "You must be the anointed one, two choccy biscuits from Mrs B. Unlike you, your chum Wayne took me out to a lovely Alehouse, and on his expenses, we had a slap-up meal. In fact, ma'am, I'm so full I don't think I'll eat anything until lunchtime tomorrow if not even later."

"What are you, Wilkins?" Freya asked him. "Just getting my own back for the ill-disguised slur about my competence concerning the hair sample, ma'am," he told her.

"Quid pro Quo," was her response as she turned the key in her office lock and they went to their homes.

"I do hope that you've had a hearty breakfast today, ma'am," Ron told Freya as they descended the stairs into the C I D bunker.

"Good morning, Ron," she said to him, and this early in the morning all I want is for my first lieutenant to come out with facetious remarks at the start of a working day. In short, Ron, to quote a vulgar remark amongst the great unwashed. Don't be a smart arse."

When the pair had settled in their respective offices and read up on Division activity during the night and, unless it directly involved them really couldn't care less if other matters requiring investigation were in need of immediate attention. Simply send it upstairs to Mr Johns and his team of eager C. I. D men & women.

When they had finished their reading Ron came over to her office and perched on the arm of the 'VIP chair and asked, "What's on today, ma'am?"

Freya had her nose in her journal and took a while before responding to the enquiry from her detective inspector.

"I am, or rather we are waiting for several answers to various questions. Other than finding more about our demoted Major Quinn and his collection of passports we need to follow up the drugs in the Hacker teapot, the translation of the believed to be Russian documents, the analysis of the hairs recovered from Somestrym and as of today some from London, the transcribing of the diaries and think about beginning the in-depth investigation into the functions of Herr Rosenberg, the reason for his death, who caused it and why.

His reason and employment in this country. Hopefully, his unusual address will provide most, if not all the answers. Is that enough for now?" She asked Ron."

"Where is his address?" Ron asked her. She told him that for the moment the answer was between Assistant Chief Constable Gaunt and herself for reasons that she couldn't disclose until he gave his permission.

"Blimey," declared Ron, "When the ACC gets involved into the confidential side of a murder enquiry when only the senior officer knows the full story while her deputy is excluded from information by the reasoning of confidentiality things are getting serious.

Are you allowed to tell me if a third party is involved? "Yes, Ron," Freya told him, "but it might well be that at that point you will not wish to be involved. Be patient, by Friday you might well be invited to take part in an unusual deep cover operation. Happy now?"

"Intrigued," was his one-word reply.

"At 9:00, I will chase up the analysis of your teapot," Ron told his boss then asked, "What happened to those drawings you found? "Via other channels, they have been sent to the Admiralty to see if they relate to any of their projects if not, probably put them on a fire," she told him.

Their conversation was interrupted by the ringing of her telephone and Wayne Butt was on the other end.

"My chaps have been watching Quinn's flat since we left yesterday afternoon and in the evening he went out to the main post box in the centre of town then immediately returned home and all night and nothing happened and he had no visitors or made any 'phone calls.

When his curtains remained closed this morning, I 'phoned his number and had no reply. My chaps then did a banging on the door routine, still, no response so I went there and we did a shoulder to door exercise and lo and behold, he was still at home in a manner of speaking but the slight draught we created gave him the gentle pendulum swing.

The blighter had only gone and topped himself. His flat has a mezzanine floor and he had tied a line around the top of the stairs and jumped.

He was quite lucky in that his feet were just touching the floor. Mindful of neck stretch, he only gave himself about an inch and a half clearance." The silence was broken by Wayne Butt calling down the line, "Hello, hello. Are you there Freya?"

"Yes," came her reply. "I need a bit of time to think Wayne, there are pluses and minuses to this and all I can think of is that I should have charged him yesterday and kept him inside for twenty-four hours, and then he could have killed himself if he felt that way about life. I would have by then have had his statement, my evidence and a clear conscience.

As it is my boss will be a little cross with my decision to let him free, particularly when I had enough evidence to hold him for further enquiries.

I thought that he might lead us to his nefarious chums. Now, on reflection, the term that I used yesterday has come to pass and I shall forever be associated with my unfortunate comment that I wanted to give him enough rope to hang himself. And now the blighter has done just that."

Wayne then told her, "I will deal with his mother and his employer, although by now I suspect that they will be well aware of his fate. When I am satisfied that there is no suspicion of foul play I will hand the body to the coroner with a statement of the circumstances surrounding his demise if that is OK by you?"

"Yes, that's alright, and I will give you a report from our side of the matter to go in with yours," Freya told him.

"By the way Wayne, how did you know that Quinn had no telephone calls last evening and all night?" she enquired. Wayne replied with a chuckle and in dismissive tones said to her, "I thought that as you were the star pupil at Kings Weston and now the Acting Detective Chief Inspector Douglas Gore Hamilton you would know the answer. I can't believe that you are so naive as to even pose the question of 'How'.

The GPO aren't the only people who know all about the engineering of getting a call from one 'phone to another with just a tiny diversion elsewhere. Quite a common experience amongst we detectives. When you are streetwise we might just let you be an associate member of our professional body one day or perhaps another 'Me dearie."

"Thank you, Wayne, for your condescending lecture and I do hope that the Fuzz never catch you. Such a pity to find you walking around the city centre in sackcloth and ashes with a Dr Penfolds bottle in the ripped pocket telling the world and his wife that 'I was a great detective once', I was, was and was but, I'm going to go straight from now on and apply for a job with the GPO telephones," she happily told him.

"I shall run and tell Miss how beastly you are to me and she will give you the slipper," ended the call from Detective Inspector Wayne Butt.

Freya put the receiver down and turned to Ron and asked if he had followed the call? He replied to the affirmative and she then laid back in her chair and asked the ceiling, "Where do we go from here?"

"Don't do anything for a minute," Freya told Ron. Think your thoughts and I will run over things in my mind. I've made so many mistakes in this case already that I sometimes question my competence and letting Quinn go yesterday without a charge was one of them. Oh, hell and eternal damnation to them all," she concluded. Her normally sunny disposition was behind an ever-darkening cloud.

She swung around in her chair to her desk and picked up the 'phone receiver and promptly put it down again.

Ron enquired "What was that sudden burst of activity in aid of? Sudden movements like that quite ruin my delicate train of thought about Major, Oh! sorry, Captain Quinn, late of the RASC and now late of 'Spooks anonymous'.

She smiled at Ron and told him that "I was going to ' phone sir the ACC but changed my mind as I don't have a clear avenue of enquiry now that Quinn is dead. My looking for an eventual charge for the murder of Harrison Hacker is but a pipe dream now that blighter is dead. One positive is that much of the material that we brought back from Woodbine Cottage is of no further use, certainly no mad rush for it unless or until it gives momentum to our next challenge of finding the murderer of Herr Rosenberg."

Before going any further with Ron, she changed her mind yet again and rang her boss, Mr Gaunt only to be told by his secretary that he was not in the office. She then left a message that Quinn was dead and the circumstances of his death. The secretary told her that Mr Gaunt would not be in until the afternoon and that she would pass on the message.

She then went on and dialled the number of Mr Bates and Sarah, put her through to him. She then told him of the developments concerning Quinn and her thoughts on the deployment of her team. Chief Superintendent Bates gave his blessing to her suggestion as long as the proposals were acceptable to the ACC, Detective Chief Superintendent Gaunt.

There was a period of silence after the calls before Freya told Ron that the greaseproof drawings could be simply passed on to the Admiralty and eventually MI5 or just whoever pulled the strings of Harrison Hacker and his wife. She mused that yet again in her mind and now verbally to herself and her detective inspector. The miniature film reels need processing soon, the hair samples, not a priority, the transcription of the diaries could be slowed down as could the Russian or whatever language the documents are in.

The phials from the teapot were not a rush job or likely comparison fingerprints on the syringe as she was certain that the prints would be those of Quinn or Mrs Hacker. However, they could be those of Kurt Rosenberg. As he too is dead, there was no hurry.

Freya, conscious that her posterior was going numb from sitting and musing a little too long suddenly stood up and made Ron jump, he may well have been dozing.

"What's wrong?" he asked her as she towered over his almost prone body.

"Ron," she began, "manpower. We don't need so many bodies on this job now that we are down to a single death. Her detective inspector simply looked at her quite open-mouthed collected his thoughts and said." I've worked with many DCIs over my career and I have never had a single one remotely suggest, even sitting at the Bear and Rugged Staff in a pool of spilt beer and whisky, that they should reduce their team, ma'am."

She did not answer him he simply picked up the internal 'phone but before she dialled a number she asked Ron, "Do you think that Bill Jobbins could run a team on his own with us to back him up if he was on a very serious case? He is very experienced and I think quite capable with access to us if required."

"What exactly are you getting at?" Ron enquired.

She replied, "I will give him our unwanted team to join up with those we left under DCIs Johns mob. As the senior sergeant by a mile Bill Jobbins would lead the rest of CID until Harry Broadweir came back or you took over when I've gone elsewhere."

"I agree that Bill could lead the team but do you think for a moment the 'nobs' at central would allow it?" Ron replied, then posed the further question, "I know that the ACC has you under his wing but I can't see him agreeing to it and certainly everyone else above Bill's rank would never put up with it or give him any help. By the way, should you not ask him first?"

"I've thought of the points you've made and with both you, and here, I don't see any insurmountable difficulty." Freya tried to assure her doubting detective inspector."

With that, she rang a number and Superintendent Cole said with his usual hostile tone, "Cole."

"Good morning, sir, Freya Douglas Gore Hamilton here, would it be convenient if I were to come to see you now?" she asked him.

"Whatdoya want?" was the naturally anticipated affable reply that was the hallmark of his understanding, considerate, sympathetic character!

"I believe that I have a suggestion which you might agree with sir," Freya informed him.

"I'm very busy as usual but I'll see you now," was his best offer.

"What are you going to offer him?" Ron asked her.

"To kill two birds with one stone," Freya told Ron as she ushered him out of her office, locked the door and ran up the stairs.

She walked along to Cole's office bidding Jake 'Good Morning'.

"Mornin, ma'am," and referring to Cole, informed her that "he's on his high horse today, watch out." Thanking Jake for his warning she knocked on the open door and went into the haze of the cigarette smoke of Cole and the quite pleasant odour of the pipe tobacco of Chief Inspector/Acting Superintendent Thomas.

Avoiding the outstretched feet of Mr Thomas, she stood in front of the desk as Mr Cole busied himself with some totally imaginary paperwork in so doing totally ignoring her. She looked at Tommo and he gave her a knowing wink as Cole still rustled paper continued to ignore Freya. The standoff went on past a minute so she simply went and sat in the visitors' chair.

"Whatdoya think you are doing. Who told you that you could sit down?" he asked. She stood up and closed the office door. "I decide if that door is to be closed, now open it," he commanded her.

She ignored the order of Cole and said, "If it takes sitting in a chair and closing a door to get your attention sir, it only reflects on your total lack of courtesy. The exercise of courtesy should be a prerequisite to promotion to high office within any British Police Force. Should you decide to refer my present verbal conduct towards you to higher office that of course is your prerogative, sir."

Cole picked himself up from his chair and in so doing knocked his 'phone over. With his knuckles and straight arms supporting his upper body over the desk, he leaned forward with a highly coloured face and his temple vein throbbing and his eyes almost drilled into Freya's face. Likewise, she pushed her head forward with her normally bright deep brown eyes now turned to black as she returned the stare of Mr Cole.

The impasse was broken by Mr Thomas saying to Freya, "Well, missy, what brings you up here from the depths of your cosy bunker?"

She replied without taking her eyes off of those of Mr Cole, "I came up here to return the compliment that Mr Cole indirectly paid me yesterday. Plainly I'm wasting my time and effort so I will return to my cosy bunker." With that, she broke her gaze from the eyes of Cole, turned and opened the door and slammed it against the doorstop as she made a rather dramatic exit passing.

Jake in the corridor where he gave her a thumbs-up. She knew that Jake would have been listening somewhere.

"Sir the silent one' wants to see you now," Jake told the still standing form of Superintendent Cole still trying to come to terms with a verbal onslaught from the woman in charge of CID and a lower rank than his.

"Chief Superintendent Sir Bates requires your presence now, sir," Jake informed the superintendent in a very 'official' tone of voice.

With that order, Mr Cole appeared to return to this world looking at Mr Thomas for what seemed to be an eternity. "Are you with us Fred?" Chief Inspector Thomas asked him.

Mr Cole nodded and in removing his hand from the desk his hand struck the telephone receiver on the desk. He then picked up the 'phone and receiver and slammed them down on the desk before straightening his shoulders and shooting his shirt cuffs as he made his way past a grinning Jake towards the door of the Chief Superintendents suit.

Above the door was a red, white and green light with the words of the red one reading 'Do not enter' the white light had the word 'Wait' thereon and the green light had the inviting instruction 'Enter'.

Superintendent Cole knocked on the door and the red light illuminated the instruction 'Do not Enter' Fred Cole then proceeded to march up and down the foyer waiting for the light to instruct him to 'Enter' the suit. By the time Cole had made at least four journeys across the foyer much to the cautious annoyance of the control room staff.

Whilst having a senior officer pacing up and down enjoying or otherwise, a full view of what the control room staff were doing or more often not doing, the red light went out but the inviting green light did not burst into life only the white one telling the ever-increasingly anxious superintendent that he should 'Wait'.

With his experience, Mr Cole should have realised that the immediate summons to the office of Mr Bates then the humiliating wait in full view of everyone in and about the foyer, was a bad sign particularly as Chief Superintendent Bates was not given to petty point-scoring by humiliation.

However, there was always a first time for everything. Finally, after probably twenty or so transits of the foyer, the green light was illuminated and as the chief superintendent's secretary left the office and in went the unsuspecting Superintendent.

The leaving of the secretary should have sent a message to anyone with an ounce of gumption that illustratively speaking, blood was about to be shed in the office and to be sure it would not be the blood of Mr Bates.

Eventually, out came Superintendent Cole. Looking neither to his right nor left he marched into his office and shut the door. Within minutes, out of the same office came Mr Thomas and with the green light already illuminating the foyer, knocked on the door to find a welcoming smile from, 'Sir, the silent one's Secretary.

After a briefer time than that spent by Mr Cole in the presence of the chief superintendent, Mr Thomas emerged and made his way down to the bunker. A few minutes later he emerged from the depths with Miss Freya Douglas Gore Hamilton in tow. There was much speculation from the observers in the control room as the reason for the comings and goings of the past forty-five minutes.

As Mr Thomas and Freya entered the office of Superintendent Cole. The control room staff, the duty inspector, the duty and the day tour sergeants assembled, their speculation was to be assuaged by Jake, the station Oracle. With much tooth sucking and triumphant knowing looks with the restrained laughter of one who knows more than they are likely to impart to their listeners.

When Chief Inspector Thomas went to Freya and told her to accompany him to the superintendent's office she asked the obvious question of 'why'. Tommo ignored her question and simply motioned her to follow him.

She knocked on the unusually closed office door and before she could depress the handle the door was opened by Mr Cole. In front of his desk was the comfortable 'Visitors' chair and he indicated for her to sit in the chair. She waited until Mr Thomas had gone behind her to get into his almost still warm chair.

Slowly arranging her skirt Freya sat facing her recent adversary. Not a word was said as both men decided to light up their respective cigarettes and pipe. With one drawing heavily on his cigarette and the other pulling then puffing the flame down onto his tobacco, Superintendent Cole cleared his throat and addressed Freya thus.

"I feel that it was wrong of me to take umbrage at your conduct earlier and I." Cole hesitated with a contorted face as if in some pain and with a distinct lowering of his voice before telling Freya, "I apologise for my rude conduct towards you. What did you want to tell me this morning?"

The silence was almost as painful as that suffered by Mr Cole a few minutes earlier as Freya deliberately kept the suspense of silence going eventually allowing her penetrating gaze to momentarily drop until her brown eyes drilled into Mr Cole again as she told him.

"I accept your plainly difficult decision to make an apology. Although at the meeting yesterday you did not in words support me I did have the impression that if I was attacked by any of our visitors that you would have supported me."

Cole butted in not agreeing with Freya but telling her, "I don't particularly take to you, or if it comes to that, anyone else either, but even if they are wrong or in the wrong I will always support men in my Division from attack by any outsiders. You're no different. Anyhow, no one went for you, did they?"

Quick as a flash she responded with, "No, only my uniformed Superintendent a day later."

Freya, despite the thick cushioned seat of the chair, felt the vibration as Mr Thomas quietly tapped the leg of her chair. Taking the warning she then told Mr Cole, "The reason that I came to you this morning was to enquire if you were now completely at ease with Detective Chief Inspector Johns in your station and running the CID?"

With his eyes bulging but his temple vein not throbbing, Mr Cole replied, "No, I'm bloody well not. So?"

She looked at Mr Thomas then looked back at Mr Cole and told him. "As my enquiries have been wound down relating to the late Major Quinn."

"Whadoya mean, late?" Mr Cole, not very politely enquired.

"Quinn committed suicide during the night," Freya said. The ever sympathetic superintendent, in a flat monotone voice said, "That's about all that snivelling bastard ever got right. Why haven't you told me before?"

She kept up her staring into the eyes of Cole as she told him. "If you had not been so unspeakably rude to me earlier it was Quinn's demise that I was coming to speak to you about." Mr Cole simply looked at her unabashed before managing the question "Well?"

"As Quinn is now dead it is of little importance except for the paperwork that we prove beyond doubt that he had a hand in the death of Harrison Hacker," she told Mr Cole before continuing, "under these circumstances, I feel that I no longer need the squad that I now have.

It was my intention to help you out by returning enough people to make up a full squad from those that I left behind and those that I no longer need and for the time being put them under the command of the most senior of the detective sergeants, in this case, Bill Jobbins, a very competent officer with Ron Wilkins available for important decisions.

This will result in your friend DCI Johns being sent back to central with his team." A silence followed before she said, "Of course, superintendent, this is subject to Assistant Chief Constable Gaunt agreeing with my proposal. I was going to mention it to him this morning but he's out until this afternoon."

Cole was almost out of his chair with eagerness at the idea and said in a loud confident voice. "Bill Gaunt will agree, I'll guarantee that." He sat down again, stretched and reached for his Capstan Full Strength cigarettes and with what passed for a smile said,"

"Yes, miss, I'm sorry for what I said earlier and for a wom…"

He just stopped himself in time as she asked him "Yet another apology due Mr Cole?"

"Know when you are ahead Detective Inspector and be satisfied madam." Was the only further apology Freya was going to get from Mr Cole on this occasion.

Downstairs into her bunker, she went to relate to Ron Wilkins what had transpired between her and Superintendent Cole. When told, Ron's comment was, "Him having to apologise must have been worse for him than the Working Men's Club running out of Guinness."

Until lunchtime, they worked on the makeup of their teams, one for normal CID work and the other as the murder squad. After lunch Freya rang the ACC, Chief Superintendent Gaunt to put her proposals concerning the new makeup of her CID team to him for his approval or rejection and to tell him about the demise of Major Quinn.

Mr Gaunt had so little to say about Quinn that she was quite certain that her boss already knew all about the demise of the 'Major'. She then changed back to her proposals with which Mr Gaunt was quite satisfied with her intentions and told her to put the change into practice as soon as possible adding that Fred Cole had already been in touch and was "Like a cat with two tails by seeing the back of DCI Johns."

Mr Gaunt continued, "Relating to your body number two, Rosenberg. I have looked at the matter of his home with its unique location and the method, considering the brilliant place that he has decided to use as his home, of how we might approach the investigation in such an environment. My thoughts are still with going in gently-gently.

In such a place a mob-handed approach will ruin any attempt at cooperation from the people who would have known him there.

The only possible way to firstly gather information covertly and secondly to be able to search his premises is to have someone working on the inside."

"Who are you thinking of sir and how are you proposing to get them in there?" Freya asked, almost certain that she knew who it would be.

"All almost arranged," Mr Gaunt told her.

"I have told Chief Superintendent Bates of my thoughts on the matter and from now on he will deal with all the various aspects of getting you in there and keeping you there.

"From the way you spoke am I to presume that it is me that you are minded to send into the lion's den, Sir?" Freya, with her 'tongue in her cheek' asked Mr Gaunt.

"You must fight that out with Simon Bates," Mr Gaunt told her before adding, "My view is that you should go there with somebody as your 'husband'. A married couple would not arouse suspicion. However, under the circumstances, it would have to be someone in whom you had absolute trust and confidence but is also capable of covert activities. The candidate would probably have to be single, we don't want any trouble with a mother hen of a wife, do we?"

Considering that Mr Gaunt had, in theory at least, handed the Nudist Colony brief over to Chief Superintendent Bates, Freya, in view of the long and rather involved conversation with Bill Gaunt deducted that her boss was 'Passing the Buck' but pulling all the strings and strumming them to his particular melody.

"I will ask Detective Ron Wilkins if he will accompany me shall I sir?" She asked Mr Gaunt.

"You can ask him but I'm certain that he would not agree. Would you like him to see you in your birthday suit? I'm certain that you would not. Has he any experience in covert work? Does he have a wife? Would he be prepared for you to see him in the nude?

When you are away for a while lounging about in the colony who will deal with the matters of body one which will still be an active investigation insofar as the interpretation of all these documents you have collected still will be needed to be collated into relevant and non-relevant. Wilkins is the man for that task." Mr Gaunt told her adding.

"I'm sure that you would prefer everyone not to know of your new life. I take it that you have not spoken to anyone about our conversation concerning Sunny Patch and our interest therein?

I would insist that you take home and keep at home all documents concerning this part of your investigation."

"Yes, sir," was all that she could say. Her fate was decided whether or not she liked it.

As Freya swung around in her chair Ron came into her office bearing a 'Dainty' cup of tea from Mrs Briggs with two chocolate biscuits in the saucer. With a flourish, Ron bowed and said, "Your Nippy at your service, ma'am," as he handed the cup of tea to her. Freya said, "Thank you, Mr Nippy," then continued, "but as I recall, the Nippy of Lyons Tea house fame were renowned throughout the world for being dressed in a black dress with a starched white apron, white cloth tiara and black stockings with perfectly straight seams. Are your seams straight Ron?"

Ron put the cup of tea on her desk, tossed his head and said in an effeminate voice, "You girls are all the same." As he turned, lifted his leg-pulling up his trouser leg to expose his sock and telling her. "Know-all-dick, my seam is always perfect on my very shapely leg. All the boys admire them, so there!"

As he went through the door Freya called to him. "Ron, would you like a choccy biscuit dearie?"

Like a streak of lightning, he was by her side with hand outstretched. As he firmly grasped the biscuit from her saucer ensuring that she could not now deny it to him he said in the same high pitched voice, "You're only trying to get around a girl and she ain't having any of it, you've upset me, sister, so there."

She was still smiling at the bit of stupidity as she dialled the internal number of Chief Superintendent Bates.

"The office of Chief Superintendent Bates," the voice of Sarah told her. Freya identified herself and asked if she could speak to the chief superintendent. Within seconds, she was put through to Mr Bates, 'Sir the silent one'.

"If you are 'phoning to complain about Mr Cole, the matter is dealt with and if he hasn't already apologised he will or I shall be wanting to know the reason why." Chief Superintendent Bates told her.

She replied by telling him that Mr Cole had apologised with prompting by Mr Thomas and that her purpose in the call was to enquire if he would be available to see her?

In the background, Freya could hear the voice of Sarah before Mr Bates came back on the 'phone to tell her that he was free at 3:30 and that he would look forward to seeing her then.

At the appointed time she knocked on the door. It was answered by Sarah who apologised that Chief Superintendent Bates was involved with an important call from the chief constable. They both sat down and engaged in small talk until Freya asked Sarah. "What happened between Mr Cole and Mr Bates earlier."

"You know well enough that even if I knew what had occurred between them I would not divulge anything," Sarah told Freya and added, "I'm surprised that you of all people would ask such a question of me."

"I believe that I was just testing the water and it is quite pleasant," Freya told her. "What I'm about to discuss with Mr Bates is a very, very delicate matter, and although plainly I do not doubt your integrity, I had to be quite sure."

Sarah smiled at her and said, "It turned out for one senior officer most unfortunate that at the very moment he had an incoming call that he knocked his receiver off and left it on his desk letting the caller know everything that transpired. That is not tittle-tattle I've told you that because both you and I were involved. I very much suspect that whatever you might discuss with Mr Bates will have a mutual interest between the two of us.

My job is vastly more valuable to me than trying to score gossiping points." Sarah told her.

As Sarah finished the sentence Mr Bates opened his office door and called Freya in.

"Well, Miss Douglas Gore Hamilton, what can I do for you, as if I didn't know?" Mr Bates asked with a smile.

"What are you looking for?" He asked her. Freya replied "Making sure that your 'phone receiver was firmly on its cradle sir."

Again, he allowed a shy smile to frame his lips as she told him, "This nudist colony that I'm to infiltrate. When, what, where and why?"

Chief Superintendent Bates looked quite intently into her face and said, "I have only really known you for about three weeks. You are in one branch of policing and I'm in another but I still have a responsibility for your department nonetheless. Under these circumstances, I am taking more than the usual interest in the investigation which you are pursuing.

Chapter 7
Free Holiday with Expenses for Ma'am and Her 'Husband'

The CID commander, ACC Bill Gaunt has told me the story of this particular part of the investigation and that it is his intention that you and another will not use the usual methods to discover the story of this man Kurt Rosenberg and his part in any nefarious activities. Mr Gaunt is convinced that the success of this investigation lies within this nudist colony.

He has done the work in establishing a location for the address without arousing suspicion. In the course of a conversation with him, we discussed how we could get you in there as holidaymakers if the place which apparently rented huts to nudists. At this point, I was able to offer Bill a possible avenue to find out if the place was a holiday place. The answer came that although it is a residential type of place where most people in their own places and mostly use them for holidays and weekend use.

The rules and regulations are many particularly for holiday visitors and such people have to be vouched for by individuals associated with the colony, camp or whatever or by an organisation known as the Central Council for British Naturism which apparently has only recently been formed.

In short, I am now responsible for this part of your enquiry into the death of Rosenberg. I have a person who does know you and who can vouch for your character and that of your 'Husband'.

"Now," Mr Bates continued, "to answer some of your speculative questions. The 'When'. Probably we can rent a hut or lodge by Saturday week. The 'What' I believed that I have already answered. Likewise, the 'Where' has been answered and also the 'Why'.

What further questions do you have for me?" He asked. Freya was not particularly concerned about being publicly naked but who would be her 'Husband' be?"

She asked Sir Simon, "Apart from establishing the relevance of discovering where Rosenberg lived, what useful information could be gleaned from a nudist camp, which as I understand it, are particularly secretive places?"

"Does anyone else live in his hut? What contact did he have with others there? Is there evidence of a criminal group there? Is there anything there or any cause for anyone there to murder him? Information concerning his association with the now believed to be murdered man, Hacker? Any involvement with the security services? How will that do for a start?" Sir Simon asked her.

He then continued, "Go in there Bull Headed and all you will discover that useful people will be hiding away, not from any guilt but from embarrassment and if you find that nothing is amiss, a complaint to the chief constable at the least or the local MP asking questions in parliament. I'm sure that you might imagine the headlines in the newspapers," Mr Bates ended the questions and replied with a noticeably raised eyebrow.

"I'm sorry to raise even more questions, Sir," she told Chief Superintendent Bates, "Who will run this enquiry while I'm away? Will that person or who else will know that I'm in a nudist colony? Who have you lined up to be my 'husband' as between you and the assistant chief constable it would appear that you have thought of everything except my feelings at not only being naked in public but also having to live with a naked male who I probably don't even know?"

"Ah, yes," Mr Bates sighed before telling her. "We have thought of that and it is our intention to have Detective Inspector Wilkins take over your paperwork while you are away and even he will not know where you have gone. I will have him in here and tell him that you have temporarily been seconded to a very secret division of the Home Office. Which by the way is not very far from the truth although you don't know that at this point."

Mr Bates looked at Freya for a reaction but none came so he continued;

"As for your 'husband' frankly, neither Mr Gaunt nor I can really have an answer to that. Whoever it does need to be capable of covert work as Mr Gaunt has told me that you were during your time in the Regional Crime Squad.

Believe it or not, the question of your 'Husband' is the biggest stumbling block for the pair of us, and in reality, only you can solve it. We thought of sending a female officer with you but that may not be convincing enough and we have only one chance at this job and we think that a man and his wife are a vastly superior combination for a nudist colony than two women covertly asking questions."

She asked Mr Bates, "Who do you have in mind for the man with me, there must be somebody on your radar?"

"As you may or may not know, I was in the Navy for many years before coming here. When I began my career at sea radar had not, as we know it today, been invented. By the time that I left radar was an indispensable part of both a warship and first-class merchantmen. Having studied radar screens in the worst of North Atlantic weather and the calm sunny climes of the Pacific Ocean I can't recall ever seeing a nudist. Plainly acting detective chief inspector, your radar is vastly superior to both mine and that of the assistant chief constable. Who is on your radar?"

Freya laughed and told him, "A simple woman that I am I have the instinct of a housewife and I am certain sir that between you and Mr Gaunt you do have a name in the hat or perhaps on your radar screen. Who is it?"

In his soft cultured drawl, he replied, "You are correct but it would not be fair to you for us to impose a chap on you or if it comes to that, you on a chap.

However, Mr Gaunt did have a likely suggestion. I am not wishing to pry into your personal affairs but…"

She held up her hand and said to Mr Bates, "I have a not so sneaky feeling that I know where this conversation is going sir."

He looked at her for a while before replying, "I'm told by Mr Gaunt on very good intelligence that you and my staff sergeant know each other beyond being colleagues in this police force.

It would appear, and we have checked this, you were both at the same Oxford college at about the same time. After the pair of you graduated you then followed him here and eventually studied together at the Kings Weston Detective college. I understand that occasionally you meet although if anyone enquires both you and he deny having met 'for years'. Is any of this incorrect?"

"In general terms sir, that is correct," she told him. "Are you asking him or shall I do it?" Mr Bates enquired. Freya told him that as both he and the ACC presumed, she would be quite comfortable with Staff Sergeant Fergusson with her and when she met up with him she would ask him to be with her in the nudist colony.

"Purely, by chance, you must understand, the staff sergeant is on duty and I will have him meet us here as soon as possible and if he agrees I will start the ball rolling." the Chief Superintendent told her, again with a little smile on his lips.

"There is a remarkable similarity between the staff sergeant and Chief Inspector Thomas," he, quite out of the blue, told her.

He continued, "The similarity is in their character is that Mr Thomas is a very clever man and on that basis alone should be my superior but he has achieved what he considers to be a comfortable rank and probably has a certain disregard for his colleagues of the ranks that he could achieve with no effort on his part. His thinking appears to be along the line that, if you'll pardon the language,

"I'm better off with the buggers I know rather than the buggers that I will get to know further up the greasy pole."

My staff sergeant appears to have much the same attitude. He is at a responsible rank, and nowadays, the only such a person with this rank in this force and he looks at what he considers to be the half-wits above him and plainly does not wish to be associated with them.

In my position, I'm in some sympathy with their attitude and quite understand certainly in the case of Mr Thomas. He does me a great service in keeping Superintendent Cole from too many excesses, not that I am criticising Cole, he keeps the Division on its toes and I only occasionally have to put a gentle hand on the tiller."

He continued, "Your staff sergeant like Mr Thomas is a clever individual and the word 'Individual' I use to describe his character.

Before the staff sergeant harvested most of his personal files from the records, a dismissal offence, by the way, I saw his record at Oxford and his degree and then his record as a detective with us and then when seconded to the Metropolitan Police.

The met record is still there but Oxford is missing as are his schooling records and his career details at sea.

Little does he know until you tell him, I do have his sea-going records from both the company that he worked for and from the old Board of Trade. Both he and Mr Thomas are in for a surprise in the not too distant future when they will have to make a choice."

As Mr Bates completed his sentence a knock came on the door and the secretary ushered in Staff Sergeant Fergusson. He did not look at anyone except Mr Bates," You wanted me, sir?" Fergusson asked his chief superintendent. He acknowledged Freya with the single word, ma'am."

Ah, yes, staff sergeant, do take a seat please, Acting Detective Chief Inspector Douglas Gore Hamilton has something to ask you." Chief Superintendent Bates told him.

Freya looked aghast as the words came from the mouth of Mr Bates, "I think sir that as you thought of the idea that you should introduce Mr Fergusson to your proposals," she told him.

"I believe that you told me that you would ask Mr Ferguson when you next saw him. I simply put the necessary impetus into the meeting. But I will do the dirty work." The chief superintendent told her.

Mr Bates began by telling his staff sergeant that what he was about to tell him was one hundred per cent confidential and instant dismissal would ensue if that total confidence was abused.

He then began by asking if the staff sergeant would be prepared to be naked in a nudist colony.

"Not particularly concerned, sir," was the reply from Hamish.

Chief Superintendent Bates then told his staff sergeant of the background to Freya's investigation which by the nature of the intricacy of the investigation took quite a time. The dialogue was interrupted by Miss Dodds-Younger entering the room with a tray of tea.

When she had left Mr Bates began again by repeating almost word for word that which he told Freya.

When the full story had unfolded Mr Bates asked his staff sergeant if he was willing to take part with Miss Douglas Gore Hamilton. Hamish looked at Freya and she nodded at him. He then told Mr Bates, "That's fine by me sir."

"I will provide you with all the paperwork needed and I have arranged a courier service between you and me on a daily basis at a daily pre-arranged place to frustrate anyone interested in your activities but I'm quite sure that you will very much rely on your own ability to keep out of trouble.

That's it, you can now discuss it not as a senior officer and station sergeant but as equals. Good luck."

That was the end of the interview with 'sir the silent one'.

As Sarah escorted them to the door she handed Freya a folded up piece of paper and whispered, "don't leave this lying about. Tuck it in your bra and don't open it in the station."

Freya complied and with Hamish then went into the foyer neither of them was too sure of that which they had agreed to.

"I'll ring you tonight," Freya said to Hamish as they went their separate ways, he to his office and her down to her bunker.

As she put her foot on the first step, Sarah rushed out from the suite of Mr Bates and asked her to send Inspector Wilkins to see her boss.

On her way down the second staircase, Freya met Ron on his way up and told him to go immediately to see Chief Superintendent Bates. "Why?" was a not surprising response from Ron to which question she answered, "There are a few changes afoot, but don't let on that I've told you and he's in a good mood."

"Never been any different with me, I was at sea in the war as well." With a smile, Ron went unknowingly to take full responsibility for the future of the case when Freya went to the 'Home Office' for an indeterminate time.

As she went into the bunker she could see a man and woman sitting in the general office with a large bag by their feet. The detective that they were talking to stood up and introduced them to Freya and told her that they were from the Central Film Laboratory Forensic Department of the War Office attached to the RAF and had been sent the material by our SOCO forensic team.

Freya took them and their bag into her office and sat them down. "Does this visit have anything to do with miniature film reels?"

The man told her that it was. Freya then asked if, anyone except themselves had seen any of the films and had only one copy been made?

They assured her that other than the two of them had seen the film and in their bag was the only copy of the originals and if she was concerned she should note that they worked under the Official Secrets Act.

"I have no doubt about your integrity," she told them. However, can you assure me that neither anyone from the war office or any other organisation had or could get access to copies of the film?" Freya enquired.

"I can assure you, ma'am," the woman said. "That unless you allow anyone access to these films it will be only the two of us and whoever you choose to see them who will know what the reels contain." The woman continued, "We have provided you with a running index and full instructions on how to operate the reels.

If you will kindly sign this receipt with your full titles of rank and date we will go, it is rather late and we are based in Wiltshire." Freya duly signed although her surname wouldn't fit on the line so it encroached on the 'Title' line which caused her long-winded rank to be truncated to keep the receipt orderly as every government department demands.

As the two film, people went up the stairs so Ron came down with an expressionless face and without acknowledging his boss went into her office and collapsed into a chair.

Freya walked in after him. Ron looked up at her and declared, "As Laurel said to Hardy, "It's a fine mess you've got me into." Spooky. We have two murders, two suicides and still one murder outstanding and all involving various departments of state. Thank you, ma'am, for granting me this opportunity to show my metal at such short notice. Can I have your office and rank please?"

Freya sat down and looked intently into Ron's eyes and asked, "Can't you manage without some damned woman telling you what to do?"

Her detective inspector replied, with some feeling. "I married one woman who thinks that I can't do without her and I've inherited another woman with the same opinion of the man in the working part of her life.

"Yes, ma'am, I can manage but I would have preferred a little more time and not take the reins halfway through a case. What are you doing at the Home Office? I didn't think that you liked them and after the meeting the other day a Cox of the Home Office certainly appeared not to have you on the Christmas card list."

"Dear Ron," she began, "I told 'The silent one' that I had full confidence in your abilities and I didn't want anyone else messing with a case as complex as this, and in fact, none of the likely candidates including your chum Harry Broadweir could replace you. Satisfied now?"

He did not answer but told her that he was coming up the stairs to tell her that the film reels had arrived and wanted to know all about them.

She told him almost word for word what she had been told about the films and asked if he had access to a projector? "Yes," he told her and added that his chums in the SOCO would supply one.

"Can you operate it?" Freya asked him adding, "Only the two of us must view whatever is on the films and it will be behind locked doors."

"Did the boffins tell you what was on the films?" he asked her.

"No," she replied.

"The films were exposed under the Official Secrets Act and the boffins are prohibited from discussing with anyone, even the owners of the material that they uncover, the contents except to their superiors."

Her detective inspector was silent, digesting the sometimes silly machinations of government.

He was brought out of his deep thought by Freya telling him that she was taking the films home with her to ensure that as was often the case in a police station, they didn't go missing and if interesting, lost forever.

As she picked up the bag of film and put her coat on she saw that it was well past seven and as she looked at the clock so Ron reminded her that he had a wife and arriving at home at this time he was likely to find a very cold meal waiting for him and the depth of chill in the food would be echoed in the face of his wife when he went through the door.

As Freya locked her office door her final words to Ron were "There is no room for marriage in CID!" as she spread the fingers of her left hand in his face and bade him "Good night."

Hamish Fergusson, cigar in hand, was looking at the clock when his phone rang and Freya apologised for it being so late and to tell him that it was only when she was undressing for her bath that she found a piece of folded paper on the floor and realised that it was the paper that Sarah Dodds-Younger had given her that afternoon. After reading the paper she decided to have her bath first and then ring him.

"Doesn't say much for me when I come a poor second to a bath," he told her. "You're always first my dearest," she told him and then added, "even on the 'phone I'm quite sure that you would not like me smelling of police stations and grubby ones at that?"

His response was as she expected. "Never knew CID to get dirty or smell of anything but stale beer and sweat. The sweat is certainly not through exertion but fears that someone will call them to account for their grossly inflated expenses claims for jobs that never existed."

"He that hath no sin, cast the first brick," was the response from Freya. "Anyhow, we can't keep hurling insults at each other," she told him then asked. "What did you think of the business this afternoon?"

"Mixed feelings," he replied explaining that, "for the purpose of your investigation at this point, it seems to be a crack-pot idea.

What exactly do you need to know to solve the case that you haven't already found? Except for the murderer of your man in the locks and I doubt if he, she or it, is still hanging about. The best that you can hope for is a tidying up exercise but still no murderer. If espionage is the cause of the deaths, which at this time it appears to be, why are we getting involved? Having had first-hand experience of the rivalry between the spooks and the plods it would not surprise me if this was yet again another case of old Gaunt aided and abetted by Bates trying to put the noses of Special branch, MI5 & 6 out of joint.

As to us being naked, nothing new there but if we are required to sleep in the same bed, that is another very pleasing matter altogether!"

"I don't think that the concern is about our sleeping arrangements. From Mr Bates point of view I think that us being exposed naked in front of strangers, and before you ask, I did intend the pun, which he thinks might put the blockers on his plan," Freya told him.

"Being naked amongst other naked people is not a concern for me. How about you?" He asked Freya. "Same for me," she replied "but I will not have to contend with the possible, shall we say outstanding involuntary male difficulties when seeing naked females will I?" She laughingly asked him.

His reply was, "Self-control is my middle name, if I gave in to temptation you would not still be unsullied would you?"

A long silence ensued before she told him, "Like you, I too exercise even greater self-control than you ever did and this 'Holiday' will be no exception so cool down sailor, your boat hook has not yet found my 'Heaving line' One day my dearest, one day," she teased him, not for the first time by a long mile.

"What about this note Bates secretary gave you," Hamish asked her.

She told him, "All it contains is a time and date and an address which is 214 Monarch Mansions and bring a towel each. The signature is Sarah. J.C. Dodds-Younger." Then adding;

Monarch Mansions is the very poshest address in the city. I wonder what it is all about?"

"Wishing us a fond farewell with a dip in their very exclusive pool I expect," Hamish told her then added the question, "How in the hell could a police secretary, I acknowledge a very senior one, be living there on her salary?" Does she have a very rich husband or something?" Then asking himself as well as Freya said, "If she has a rich old man why is she working?"

"I've no idea but, she is single now. She doesn't have any rings except for a signet ring, the feminine version of yours." Freya pointed out to him and added the question," Are you coming there too?"

"Yup," was his one-word reply.

"Harking back to the beginning of this conversation," he said. "What evidence do you think that you could get from either getting a warrant and doing the place over professionally or this sneaky surveillance type of job?"

She hesitated a while before replying. "If we go in mob-handed to, for the want of a better description, a secret society they will clam up and run for cover. If they know anything worthwhile they are certainly not going to tell us with the chance that they might end up in the witness box to explain why they were in amongst a nudist colony.

If we go in quietly and there is a story to tell to our benefit we will get it and act on it anonymously. There is a slim chance that our vital clue might be in the people there or in his hut itself. Other than our modesty, we have nothing to lose and get a free holiday."

Hamish, with an enforced unseen sly smile, asked her, "Expenses too?" Her pithy reply was brief, accurate and very pertinent, "Not for clothing chum." The silence of any expression from Hamish told her that her arrow had struck the bullseye.

"Who is going to brief us and when?" was his next question. She told him that 'Briefs' were not allowed in a nude place.

"Ha-ha," was his reply. She continued that she did not know but presumed that it would be Chief Superintendent Bates and his contact in the colony. As to the question of when this ' item of underclothing' would be, she had no idea but plainly it would be in the next five days if they were going to the nudist colony on Saturday week she told him.

Staff Sergeant Fergusson was sat in his office the next morning with a large cup of coffee on the desk and his King Edward cigar producing smoke similar to a steam railway engine.

Having just finished his most recent tour roster his mind, as could be expected, was very much concerned with his forthcoming 'Holiday' when, without ceremony, his door flew open and in came Superintendent Cole his countenance in what could loosely be described as a smiling face displaying uneven teeth blackened by almost a lifetime of being wedded to Capstan Full Strength cigarettes. "Ah, Sergeant Fergusson. I have been tasked by the chief superintendent to appoint someone to take over your job as of Friday next, What about that then. Bet you were not expecting that?"

"Tell me Chief Inspector Cole, who are you thinking of replacing me?" The staff sergeant enquired of his now very red-faced superior.

"I'm a bloody superintendent." The words from Cole exploded in Fergusson's face. Cole then added, "And don't you bloody well forget it now or ever."

" And I'm a bloody staff sergeant, D'y'hear, a staff, staff, staff sergeant and don't you bloody well forget it either. Sir." The staff sergeant told the almost apoplectic superintendent. "Oh, and by the way sir, a distance from you will not cause me any memory loss, and in any case, the documentary evidence that I have will refresh any fading memory of our time serving together when I was a constable, sir."

"Good day to you!"

Within a few minutes, the senior Tour sergeant arrived at the staff sergeants office to announce that he was taking over 'Fergusson's jobs' and wanted to know when he could start and get "Off of bloody shift work."

Down in the bunker, Freya was shuffling paperwork when she was detracted by the sight of two of her constables carrying in various bits of equipment. They were followed by Ron holding a loud hailer. She decided that they were in for one of his comedy turns. Anything for a smile or two!

"I've got your projectors," he told her and added with the loud hailer above his head and an American accent announced, "OK, honey, let's roll, scene 1, and- Action baby."

"Thank you, Mr Goldwyn," she told him and asked, "Do you know how to operate this new-fangled movie projector?"

"Course I do baby, I ain't no hick from the sticks. I'm gonna make ya a star sure as goddamned hell I am. Just watch me."

Ron turned around at the sound of applause the source being the Assistant Chief Constable Bill Gaunt and the Chief Superintendent Sir Simon Bates. With not a hint of a smile from either man, the silence was anything but golden for Ron. Suddenly his happy day had turned to ashes as in a very loud voice the ACC asked the chief superintendent if their choice of the person to replace Acting Detective Chief Inspector Freya Douglas Gore Hamilton was really suitable for the post?

"Perhaps playing Peter Sellers detective on the West End stage, sir," Sir Simon told him then added, "Do you think that you have a detective constable who could replace the acting detective chief inspector?"

"As there is no one above the rank of constable capable of taking over from her I will find some layabout." The assistant chief constable told the chief superintendent.

Ron Wilkins was still rooted to the floor as the men advanced on him with a party of detective constables and sergeants looking on, some quite in awe of having two very senior officers in their bunker.

Addressing the statue like Ron, Mr Gaunt told him. "Whilst your attempt at humour may have been commendable to some audiences I'm sure that the chief superintendent will agree that judging by the expression on your face, our comedy turn was vastly superior to yours." Mr Gaunt with a sweep of his hand towards the assembled detectives added, "Our audience appears to be rather larger than yours Detective Inspector Wilkins, so we get the Oscar but we will generously allow you the curtain call."

The previous tension appeared to be dissipating when it was quickly re-established with the comment from the chief superintendent that, "we appear to have a surfeit of idle detectives here, I think most of them could be assigned to uniform duties on the pavements of this Division."

"I do believe that you are correct," replied the assistant chief constable. Perhaps Miss Douglas Gore Hamilton could weed out those to send back to uniform before she leaves us."

That suggestion suddenly caused the former audience to seemingly fade into the concrete walls of the bunker as the 'Sirs' went into Freya's office and shut the door.

They made themselves comfortable and told her that they wanted to go over the various outstanding matters to still be dealt with so that they knew what her successor would be dealing with. She outlined both cases so far and told them that they had both the Russian papers to be translated and the diary of Harrison Hacker to be typed up into a readable script.

For her part, she now had all the forensic evidence namely the contents of the phials in the tea-pot, the evidence from the binding on Hackers body, the debris underneath the wheel arches of the white van. The certified account of the numbers found on the belts of both men.

She was about to view the contents of the microfilms, hence Ron's star turn, both men had a broad smile at that comment.

She also mentioned the strange money belt found on body number two and when questioned about the relevance of the belt to her enquiries she described the half rounded pouches on the belt but could not connect them with any evidence so far collected or any purpose for the belt but it was so unusual and possibly of foreign manufacture that she believed that she should mention it.

The blank expressions on the faces of her two visitors reflected their opinion of the worth of the belt to either death.

"That's about it gentlemen," Freya told them then added. "If nothing else turns up today I will go through the films with Inspector Wilkins assuming that he can get the projector to work."

"Are you still happy with the arrangements for next week?" Sir Simon asked her. "About as happy as one can be, subject to it being good weather," she told them.

The chief superintendent then handed her an A4 brown envelope telling her that it was the brochure for her 'Holiday' in the sun then added that it was not advisable to leave it lying about and asked her if Mr Fergusson was satisfied with the arrangements?

She told them that Mr Fergusson could not understand what evidence could be found by covert activities that could not be obtained by using a warrant.

"I thought that it had already been explained to you, using a warrant might well destroy evidence and in particular the evidence produced through observation, gossip and local knowledge." Mr Gaunt told her.

He then added, "He gets a free holiday with a striking young woman so he has nothing to moan about. Do the job that he's paid to do and surely evidence and even the murderer will come. Case closed and you move upwards and outwards and he moves upwards into a warm chair."

As if the exit was deliberately timed both men got up from their chairs and made for the door. She went to escort them to the stairs but they told her to remain with her 'comedy actor' and get the films done before Friday.

A very contrite Detective Inspector Ronald Wilkins made a rather less than grand entrance into her office and said to her, "Sorry about that, I hope that it didn't drop you in it too deep."

"No," she told him then added, "However, our plan for a re-distribution of at least half of our people was highlighted when the 'powers that be' commented on the number of idle staff we had here. If for no other reason your star turn has dissipated any argument against personnel cuts down here. Well done, Ron. When you take over from me 'Those upstairs' will give you a relatively easy ride."

Visibly Ron's shoulders resumed their upright position as the weight of his star performance was lifted by the sincere words of Freya.

"Rightyho, Mr Goldwyn," she said to him, "now let us get on with the film show."

As she finished speaking there came a knock on the door and Jake was there holding an envelope.

"Please don't stand on ceremony," she told Jake. "You don't knock when you come in here surreptitiously dear Jake."

He handed her a plain brown envelope and told her, "Look at the address, I bet it's from some nutter with duff info or someone who's taken a shine to you, ma'am." The address simply referred to a 'Detective Gore' with a rudimentary address.

"I suspect that you are right Jake," she told him, and to the obvious expression of disappointment on Jakes' face, she did not open the envelope but casually placed it on her blotter. As he didn't seem in a hurry to go, no doubt having some intention of gleaning a bit of gossip from the contents of the envelope Freya thanked him and told him, "You may go now, thank you."

"In the conference room with the gear," Freya told Ron as she picked up the letter and the films and followed the heavy laden Ron through the labyrinth of rooms, still with their Cold War titles alongside the doors.

While Ron set up the equipment she opened the envelope to find that it was almost a letter from beyond the grave inasmuch as the signature on the bottom was that of Major Quinn telling her of his intention to hang himself and the reasons for such drastic action. Freya did not read further but put the one-page letter in her bag and wondered if his former employers knew of the letter. They always seemed to be one step ahead of her. Perhaps this time they might be one or more steps behind her.

"OK, ma'am," Ron told her. "Ready to roll when you are," he told her as she handed him the reels of film and asked him if the door could be locked. He made no reply but went to the door and turned a wheel and a faint grinding noise appeared to satisfy him and he told her that the door was locked but it could be unlocked from the outside which was most unlikely.

They were just settling down for the film show when the same grinding sound came from the door and some seconds later it opened an inch or so and stopped again and a voice from outside announced," Yer's coffee for ma'am from Mrs Briggs but the door won't open any further." Ron went to the wheel and turned it again, put out his arm and collected the coffee and two choccie biscuits and asked the anonymous person, "Nothing for me?" he enquired 'Bugger orf' was the succinct reply to his question. Freya collected her coffee as the door was secured.

While she sipped her coffee so Ron chomped his way through the chocolate biscuits with a noticeable lack of finesse in comparison to the dainty consumption of her coffee so the black and white half images of stars, mathematical signs and other illegible letters and symbols flashed on the wall opposite the projector.

"This is going to be informative he told Freya," she replied, "We don't appear to have Bombardier Billy Wells banging the Rank gong do we?"

With the words hardly out of her mouth so up came pictures of a boy in the uniform of the Hitler youth movement; then it changed to about ten minutes of scenes of bombed-out buildings followed by women in headscarf's and general wartime shots, presumably of Germany. There was then a long period of nothing but black and white flashes.

The next pictures appeared to be of people amongst whom was Honecker, the sometime boss of East Germany. Suddenly the pictures became coloured. Ron decided that the long period of nothing was the boffins splicing one mini tape onto the big reel as the film rolled on it appeared to simply show bombed-out street scenes.

Another long spell of flashes etc before pictures of people in a park appeared then a picture of a monument with a hammer and sickle. This was followed by a face who both of them identified as Kurt Rosenberg as a youth.

This ran into pictures of young people at what appeared to be a camp by a lake with pine trees in the background and it then displayed a scene which had Ron, judging by his reaction in some state of excitement. The scene was of young people stripping off and frolicking in the lake.

At this point, Freya told him to stop the projector. She then told him to rewind and show the scene at the lake again. With no hesitation, he rolled the film again until she told him to stop.

"In that shot was both Kurt Rosenberg and Mrs Hacker aka, Helga Rosenberg both much younger, she in particular." She did some quick counting on her fingers and said, "She's about fifteen or sixteen there."

Freya decided that the film was from about the early fifties before the communists discouraged organised nudity and that would roughly correspond with Helga's birth date according to her passport, which in the early post-war Germany might well have been guess work.

She then told Ron to carry on projecting and as before there were several minutes devoted to the sights of bombed buildings and then pictures of ugly concrete buildings which she presumed were before and after scenes of destruction and rebuilding. This was followed by scenes from the deck of a ship with shots of snow and again shots of naked people rolling in the snow and generally larking about but with no identifiable locations or faces.

Suddenly the film again went into splodges and streaks as the end of the tape ran free from the spool which seemed to frighten Ron. When peace was restored he turned the lights on and Freya said to him.

"That told us nothing and if the second reel is as informative as this one it will have been a total waste of time except to tell us roughly when some of it was produced. No doubt useful for the various spook's agencies but no use for us perusing a murderer. Break for lunch now and back here at 2:00 p.m. and let me out through that door please."

After lunch, Freya and Ron again met in the conference room to run the next reel of film and the difference was that this second reel was in colour. On the presumption that this reel was a continuation of the previous one, Freya was not too hopeful that this reel of the film would be any benefit to her investigation.

The projection onto the wall at first appeared to be much the same as before of military parades in Moscow and East Germany the locations given away by the buildings in Moscow and the road signs in the German language. More holiday scenes with again several scenes of jollities on a beach and beautiful blue sea with the human participants not having any clothes on which caused Ron to comment "God, those women, aren't they hairy everywhere? Could make three plaits out of that lot." Freya thought it best not to answer.

As the film went on so it showed several house parties, shipyards and several ships at sea, all easily identified as East German. There were several shots which appeared to be of Scotland and various Lochs with several 'Old Puffers' and old Admiralty water carriers chugging through the Lochs. Without any change of background scenery were shots of three younger men, namely the late Kurt Rosenberg, the late Major Quinn and the late Harrison Hacker. On this occasion, Ron, no longer concerned with the length of the Fraulein's various bits of body hair, debated with himself about who was working the camera and noted that they were all in hiking gear.

"Do you think that this is Holy Loch?" he asked Freya as the film rolled on to what was obviously a military site and finally an aerodrome before the film went back to family and continental scenes, probably in the Alps but kept going back to the same scene from various angles then returned to what appeared to be wide grassy plains which could have been almost anywhere but could be identified by women in the shots with long dresses and scarf style head covering.

Plainly Eastern European and then came a shot of Major Quinn, now much older than the Loch scene in the earlier shot, cuddling Helga Rosenberg or Hacker. Then they were kissing with what, without sound, looked like some passion. Again Ron broke into the silent movie to ask no one in particular, "Who was operating the bloody camera?"

As before Freya said nothing as the next scene appeared to be the inside of printing works with several Soviet motifs headed pamphlets urging the workers to rise up, all printed in English, French and Italian. There were many shots allowing them time to clearly see the writing on each one.

The next scene was of what appeared to be somewhere in Britain with grassy cliffs and the sea beyond with Helga Hacker and…

"Stop," shouted Freya, "please rewind a couple of frames to the start of the grassy scene."

She asked her 'Cinema technician' to go upstairs and see if the staff sergeant was in and if so get him down to the conference room.

"Should he know that we have the film, ma'am?" Ron asked as he turned the wheel to open the door. "Of course, he can, he is more involved with this than you would know at the moment," she said and finished her words with, "Go."

After what seemed an age he returned with Staff Sergeant Fergusson.

"What's on Fire?" he enquired. Ignoring his sarcastic question Freya said, "Watch the next couple of frames carefully please. Right, projectionist, let's roll."

As the wall came to life with the rolling greensward thereon so the two figures came into view.

"Well, I'm damned," Hamish Fergusson declared, "Iron Gob' in person. "Stop!" Freya commanded Ron. After a little re-winding back and several re-runs, she asked the staff sergeant "How different was she in comparison to when he saw her?

"She is a bit younger perhaps but the dead giveaway are her feet and ankle socks, her bean pole stature and that beret," he told her.

"Could you give evidence in court to that effect?" she asked him.

The staff sergeant gave Freya a withering look and asked her "Do you think that I'm a recruit with his first parking ticket job?"

"Sorry, de…," she began before she started again with "I'm sorry. That question was unnecessary. I simply got carried away." Meanwhile, Ron was studying the pair with a knowing type of smile creasing his face.

The staff sergeant got up and without a word went to the door and made a better job of opening it than Ron might have done. "I didn't hear a thing, ma'am," Ron assured her.

"Those frames with the young Kurt Rosenberg & Helga in, plus the frame of Rosenberg, Quinn and Hacker in Scotland, plus the frame of Iron gob, please cut them out and get our Scene of Crime chums to print them in confidence she told him. His response was "our SOCO can usually do anything both with and in confidence. "Now can we finish this film, there's not much left."

Other than a few shots of a beach with the three known participants and one unknown undressed female of ample proportions on it. What turned out to be the final shots were of the Woodbine Cottage and the Rosenbergs with a German Shepherd dog.

Freya's final comment was that "My backside is numb; please let me out, Ron."

Back in her office, Freya found a note with instructions to ring the assistant chief constable.

Doing as she was told, she rang through to the switchboard, then they connected her to the command switchboard and finally to a secretary, who then put her through to her boss, wishing that she had used his direct line in the first place.

Freya told Mr Gaunt of the processed films and what they depicted and the stills which Ron would have created by the Scene of Crime department.

"Does that find our murderer?" he enquired. "Not directly sir but in a prosecution the eventual photographs, particularly that of 'Iron Gob' could provide evidence of association," she told him.

"Very tenuous," was his reply. He then went on to say that he had received the translation of the Russian papers and in short they laid out the preparation and systems to be used to get, if the decryption was accurate, Harrison Hacker to Russia, convict him of spying then swop him for one of their spy's and he could return here a hero and continue his work for world peace!

She was just about to speak when Mr Gaunt began again telling her that the Interpol results had come back, surprisingly quickly "But with German efficiency, I expect nothing less," he told her. Then continued, "As before I will cover the information with only the specific points, namely that both Mrs Hacker formerly Rosenberg and Kurt Rosenberg were born in or near Bremen but from what records remained after the war the names were co-incidental, they appeared not to be related.

The last entry on their independent files was for Helga Rosenberg, 'In East Germany'. For Kurt Rosenberg, the entry in 1947 was overwritten. 'Last observed in East Berlin in Communist Party meeting of officials'. I can see no direct association with your investigation but our friendly spooks would no doubt be quite pleased. However, like your film, we will keep this information to ourselves for the time being."

Without a pause for breath, Mr Gaunt told her, "In relation to your friend 'Iron Gob', the information is less certain but this is the nearest that the Germans could get to facts or as they say much conjecture. They think that the photofit given by your staff sergeant might, and only might be a woman known to them as Magda Weismuller.

If it is her she was prominent in the post-war communist scene and may be living in the Soviet Union."

Freya then said to him, "I wonder if it is her who is on the crew list of the 'Ordjonykitso' as Irena Kristovitch particularly as from the description that you gave to the Germans they plainly associate the description with this woman Magda Weismuller but all this was a long time ago and memories fade."

"We are dealing with the Germans here," Mr Gaunt reminded her and she knew just what was coming next as Bill Gaunt finished with, "They are so efficient."

"All we are now waiting for is the transcription of the diaries from Simons secretary and unless they turn up something, we have only the address of Rosenberg and the people there to give us any positive clues as to the murderer now that everyone who might be suspect is dead." Mr Gaunt told her. He then continued the conversation by adding, "That blighter Quinn could have left a note telling us all he knew but I expect that the spooks who did over his flat before your chums got there would have disposed of any note if such a thing existed. I wonder if he was bent? Quite possibly, a lot of that mob of his are."

"I'm sure that you are correct, sir," Freya told him while searching frantically for the letter with the strange title and address that Jake had given her with Quinn's presumed signature at the bottom. But knowing that spooks were involved in his death, the letter could possibly have been written and signed by them.

Freya told her boss, "I don't believe that I have ever been the senior officer of a case that began with such promise and now looks like ending with no collar and the only beneficiary being the Secret Service with us doing all the leg work for them, it's all so futile sir," she told her boss in a flat monotone voice.

"Chin up," he told her, "This case has only run for about three weeks, it might have a bit more meat to it yet, but I have to agree with you, it is very trying but it is not only a criminal element working against us but the so-called apparatus of the state as well.

Although, to date, we have given them a bloody nose but taken a few punches in return. There has been a lot of communication between the top people of MI5 and MI6 with the chief constable and Watch Committee chairman. I believe that the Home Secretary is trying to get the Home Office to lean on us to drop any further investigation.

While you might have powerful agencies against you, you have a solid bulwark against them in the chief constable and it may surprise you to know that Simon Bates has some very powerful friends in the corridors of power and he never hesitates to use them when appropriate and this is the appropriate time and he's putting the frighteners on them to back off and as the chief has told me it appears to be working."

"Thanks for the reassurance, sir," Freya told him then asked, "Do you honestly think that it is still necessary for the staff sergeant and me to go to the nudist colony?"

He replied, "What did I tell you not five minutes ago? Yes, it could be our last chance to find anything to help us and the weather looks fine next week so take your sun hat it could protect your head and perhaps your modesty."

He ended his opinion with a giggle, something akin to that of a little schoolboy behind the bike shed surreptitiously turning the pages of the prized booklet Health and Efficiency. Freya was trying to think of something to say and bring the 'phone call to an end when he started to speak again asking "Those phials of anaesthetic and the syringe. Do we know any more about those and the use of them?"

"I was under the impression that I had already told you about them and the pathologists report," she told him. "Perhaps," he replied. "But run through it again." Freya then told him of the finding of the phials and the syringe and the pathologist's preliminary report and then the final report for the court.

The phials all contained Chloroform, Propofol and Amobarbital, and it was an overdose of Amobarbital that killed Hacker probably at the same time as he was trussed up. The syringe was covered in the fingerprints now known to be those of Quinn and unless evidence to the contrary was found, he was the killer.

"I will ring you before you go on your holiday," Mr Gaunt told her and with a cheery 'Goodbye' the long call came to an end.

Looking at her watch Freya saw that it was now 5 o'clock and decided that she would go upstairs and make herself a cup of tea. As she left her office hugging her handbag she saw her detective inspector on the telephone. She mimed drinking a cup of something at which he shook his head and she began the long ascent to the kitchen.

As Freya finally reached the kitchen who should she meet but Mrs Briggs.

She greeted her with the question "Shouldn't you be home by now Mrs Briggs?"

Mrs Briggs then explained that she rarely left the building until the officers and 'Sir Bates' had gone home and explained that although she had asked several people to take a cup of tea down to Freya's office they all said that they were too busy and "That Jake was not nice when I asked 'im an' 'e told I that you 'ad enough runners ter get yer tea. The lady in Sir Bates office came out and asked if anything were wrong. I said no, and that Jake 'ad disappeared very quick.

I told 'er what I wanted and she took your tea and came down with it Miss. Where is the tea? Freya thought.

She thanked Mrs Briggs for not forgetting her and told her that she would deal with Jake when the most suitable occasion occurred. She then went towards the boiling urn and Mrs Briggs looked very offended that her primary purpose in life was being threatened by the usurper from below stairs, "I'll see to that, mum," Mrs Briggs said to her as her four foot ten inches pushed in front of Freya and said, indicating the officer's lounge, "You go in there an' I will bring a nice cup of me special tea ter you."

Freya did as she was told, found a comfortable chair and took the mystery letter from her bag.

"Dear Chief Inspector Gore.

By the time that you read this, I shall have carried out the suggested course of action that you mentioned when you did not detain me at the meeting and said to your colleagues that if you gave me enough rope, I would hang myself and I have. Clever you! I have been a lifelong Socialist following my father and his father. It was decided that one way of destroying the rotten capitalist system was to be on the inside and I joined the Army and as your superintendent said, I was "Bloody useless."

One of my fellows at Sandhurst was in the security services and he suggested that I should apply, and plainly without even checking my background, they took me on and within a couple of years I was assigned to look after my boyhood chum Kurt Rosenberg a dedicated German communist having been trained in espionage in Moscow. In turn, he introduced me to Harrison Hacker a worker for Admiralty and we had success in passing confidential and secrets about warships and their underwater equipment. We were instructed by Moscow for Harrison to go to Moscow to try and make the plans that he had given us, work as sticking to the plans alone was a failure.

He was then to be arrested as a spy and in turn exchanged for a comrade held here as a spy. He could genuinely claim that he was kidnapped. At the last moment, he cried off so we had to drug him into unconsciousness bind him up into a bundle in case the van was searched and send him off on the Russian ship leaving the dock that evening. Unfortunately, it appears that somehow he died in the van and then somebody killed Kurt, probably in retribution for failure. Comrades do not excuse failure particularly when they fail in an important task.

I have failed and expect my just deserts from my comrade agents, and as my darling, Helga has already followed her conscience and paid the price of failure I am doing the same. I have thwarted you and your fascist ideology and in a short time the workers will rise up and destroy the system and it will be soon. Glory to the Union of Soviet Socialist Republics. Quinn, (Major). Late of the Royal Artillery. Ha, Ha!"

As Freya put the letter down she thought that Quinn had some justification for his assertion that the workers would rise up was not so far from the truth with strikes almost every week for even more non-existent money.

On the way back to her office Freya let herself into the clerk's office and used the new photocopier to take four copies of Quinn's letter. Back in her office she placed each copy in an envelope and addressed one to Assistant Chief Constable Gaunt, one to Chief Superintendent Sir Simon Bates one to Detective Inspector Ronald Wilkins. The fourth she put in her drawer and the original she went upstairs and put into her personal safe in the CID office. With thoughts still on a very involved day of surprises, she left the station and made her way home. The only benefit of leaving work late was that the rush hour traffic had long since dissipated and it was almost a pleasure to drive home.

When she reached her home and had half consumed a watered down malt whisky she 'phoned Hamish Fergusson. Eventually, he answered apologising for the delay and explaining that he had just caught some miscreant trying his door handle. He 'collard' him and on searching the fellow he found a set of skeleton keys. He relieved him of the keys and eventually handed the rogue to a constable with the keys. As he was returning he heard the 'phone ringing.

"In the hope that you are in a good humour, I will remind you that we are going out tomorrow evening," she told him. "Who will collect who?" he asked her. "I will collect you but I want to see you first as I have the brochure for this holiday camp to go through. I've had it for a couple of days," she told him. "Fine, I'll see you about eight," Hamish told her and rang off.

Pouring himself a good measure of Appleton Estate Rum he settled down to ponder why anyone would chance to break into his home in daylight particularly with skeleton keys? He thought matters through then cursed himself for handing the keys to the constable.

When Freya arrived, he told her of the recent events, and without moments, hesitation she said, "London, without any doubt."

"My thoughts exactly," he told her adding, "How bloody incompetent could anybody be. Tomorrow I'll go and see him in the local nick and have a quiet, personal, private unsupervised word with him."

"Don't you dare lay a finger on him? He isn't just any prisoner. Threaten him, intimidate him by all means but, don't give him a slapping." Freya insisted.

He said nothing to her in reply.

After Freya's lecture, they sat and studied all the do's and don'ts of life at Sunny patch. Most of the site was given over to privately owned chalets and bungalows with rented chalets from one bed to three beds with all facilities on the site available to visitors. Recreation rooms, a sixteen-hour opening restaurant, ball-room, lounges, cinema and fitness room. The photographs displayed all that there was to experience.

Outdoors they had courts for various games, tennis, miniten, petanque, bowls, netball and the likes. They also had both indoor and outdoor swimming pools and a children's 'Fun' pool. There were also facilities on the site for fishing horse riding, roller skating arena, miniature railway around the four-acre site, archery and rifle range.

The brochure laid out that visitors should not display any form of sexual interest, ask personal questions of fellow residents or visitors, cause a nuisance by disturbing the activities within the site.

Whilst discrete body jewellery was permitted, ostentatious display of body piercing would not be tolerated. In public areas, all guests must sit on a towel where practical.

"Looks pretty good," Freya ventured. "Staying there must cost a fortune." Was his contribution.

After Freya had gone home Hamish decided that on the following day, he was going to visit an old acquaintance and adversary, namely one Chubby Reynolds.

The fellow's proper name was Carlton Reynolds, but with his predilection for picking Chubb locks, 'Chubby' was the underworld preferred identifying the first name for a trustworthy expert, depending on which side of the law a person stood.

The reason for Hamish to pay chubby a visit was to borrow a set of lock picking skeleton keys suitable for both Yale and Chubb type locks in anticipation of possible difficulty with locks when making covert visits to number seventeen, 1st Avenue, Sunny Patch.

The following morning the staff sergeant rang the duty sergeant at his local police station and enquired about the would-be burglar and what statement they wanted from him and when?

There was a pause while the sergeant looked through the detained person's book and then checked the charge book and excusing himself to Hamish told him that he would enquire of the station sergeant if anything had been passed over to him from the night tour?

Another period of extended silence ensued and was finally broken by the voice of a person who identified herself as the duty inspector. Mr Fergusson then identified himself as the staff sergeant for the 'D' Division.

The inspector told Hamish that she had checked the logbooks and his message to the station was recorded and a further message from the constable by radio that he wanted a car to take him and his prisoner to the station. The inspector had been on the two to ten tour last evening and the constable told her that when the car arrived in the station car park another car followed it in.

As they got out with the prisoner, two people approached them with warrant cards identifying them as two detective sergeants of the Metropolitan Police Special Branch. They put their own handcuffs on the prisoner and drove off before the constable could report to her.

She then rang Scotland yard and after being passed from department to department no… Staff Sergeant Fergusson interrupted her to say"

"No one would admit anything."

"You're right," she told him. "I was going to speak to my superintendent about it when he comes in. I've never had such a thing happen in my service, and frankly, I'm bloody mad about it."

Staff Sergeant Fergusson told her that she should not bother to make any further enquiries as there would never be an answer. He said, "I have been dealing with these people for the past few days and I suspect that the security services are at the back of this. Has the constable entered this in his pocketbook?"

The inspector told Hamish that the constable had made an entry in his pocketbook about arresting the prisoner and the subsequent, "for the want of a better word, abduction, of a detained person."

Hamish told her that "Other than getting a written statement from the constable, to be brutally honest, you will never get anywhere.

Presumably, these idiots think that I have papers that they want at my home and were daft enough to try and burgle my place with me in there. That your Mets for you.

Oh! And as a matter of principle, I do not take my work home with me." Hamish told her then added, "If you want me, as I've told you before, you can find me through 'D' Division."

"Oh, yes." The inspector said.

"I've heard all about you staff. You're quite an interesting chap so I hear!"

"Thank you, ma'am," he told her and bade her goodbye.

By the time he arrived at work, he saw Freya's Bristol already in the car park.

Staff Sergeant Fergusson settled into his chair and called for the log and message books only to be told that there was, "Bugger all in them and as he was late in they had already gone along the corridor and were now on their way to 'Sir, the silent one."

He was digesting that bit of information when a gentle knock came on his door and in walked Freya. "The last time that you did this to me it was the beginning of yet another less than pleasing chapter in our intricate relationship ending in God only knows what," he told her.

"So sorry that I've caused you so much bother dearest." She responded and continued, "The reason for this visit is a follow up to my visit last evening and you telling me of the bloke with the keys who you collared. I was thinking of the reasons why anyone would 'do' you and I decided that it must have been a simple-minded idiot to try to get in when there was a good chance that you might be in and in daylight. On the other hand, if our friend was so simple, why would he have skeleton keys. Idiots don't have such things."

She paused as Hamish leaned back in his chair and arranged his elbows and hands in a pyramid somewhat similar to the pose doctors adopt when listening to a long chapter of ills from a patient.

"Get your hands down and don't be so patronising and pontificating," she told him. "When I went to lock my door this morning the Yale key was very stiff to get in. I think between me getting home last evening and this morning someone has had a go at my lock. Your friend perhaps if, as you say, he had been sprung from the station yard earlier?"

Hamish took his time before answering her then asked, "Is the Yale the only lock on your door?"

She told him that in addition to the Yale she also had a special box lock designed and made by Chubby Reynolds that other than Chubby no one would ever get in. Chubby, she explained to Hamish, is a master craftsman and a rouge but a useful one on occasions.

"What a small world it is," he told her, "I am going to see Chubby today," he then explained his reason to visit Mr Reynolds and added that "It does his heart no good when I arrive. He pleads his innocence before I get my foot in the door. Didn't think that you would associate with a gentleman rogue such as Chubby." He smilingly told Freya.

"I know that it will hurt your pride Staff Sergeant Fergusson, but you don't know everything about me including my associates from the darker side of society. I happen to know that you are associated with Chubby. He gave me your name and title as a reference to his skill and honesty and told me that his string of convictions was a case of mistaken identity on every occasion! Beat that Mr Fergusson," she told him.

"I can understand why our friends from London might want to get in your place but, I can't see that they could associate you with me or that I might have anything of interest to them, or if it comes to that, why to make such an amateurish and futile job of screwing our places," Hamish told her.

"I can understand it," she told him. "If you had seen the total, and I beg your pardon for the expression, balls up, that they have made of this whole incident it is little wonder that no secret is safe in this country.

Chapter 8
The Great Unveiling

Just look at their people who are traitors, and that's only the ones who are caught. Thank the Lord that they are Cambridge graduates and not from our Alma Mater."

Freya then told him that she was going through all the paperwork with Ron Wilkins today and clearing her desk in the bunker and until Friday would be in her old office now that Johns was gone back to central.

"Once I have read the books when 'Sir the silent one' has finished with them I'm off to see our mutual friend Chubby and when I've finished with him I am going to take a look around this nudist colony and have a bite out in the countryside," Hamish told her.

"I take it that 'Around' is on the outside and not on the inside?" she asked as she stood up and with the usual swift hip movement creating a swirl of her dress, she was gone only to reappear and wish the staff sergeant, "Bon appetite," and as she had done on previous occasions, disappearing in a swirl of fabric and leaving the odour of very expensive perfume hanging in the air as a well-aimed desk pad followed her into the control room.

"Ee must be in a mood today," a control room voice announced to anyone in earshot. "Bloody certain that I would throw flowers at 'er not a pad. Ee's a miserable bastard if ever there was one an' she's so classy. Can't see what she sees in 'im." Was the carefully thought out opinion of the soon to be put in his place control room constable as a voice from the staff sergeants office told the opinionated constable.

"You are quite a correct officer; I am in a mood today principally caused by mouthy constables who forget their lowly position in the hierarchy hereabouts. And as to the question of what Acting Detective Chief Inspector Freya Douglas Gore Hamilton sees in your staff sergeant. She sees someone two ranks above you who keeps his opinions to himself and figuratively speaking is more than capable of kicking a constable's arse up between his shoulder blades for insubordination. Now move that useless fat arse and get me the message and logbooks from the secretary when your chief superintendent has finished with them."

Hamish Fergusson finally arrived in the village of, or in reality, Hamlet of Flaidown. He then went on to drive past the entrance to Sunny Patch twice before eventually finding his 'Holiday' residence.

As could be expected the entrance was unprepossessing in its appearance but tidy with mown grass banks on either side of a tall solid pair of doors and a smaller pedestrian door with a rather dainty plaque informing visitors to 'Ring'. Alongside the door was a comparatively small hand-carved sign carrying the legend 'Sunny Patch'.

As he made his third pass of the gates he became aware of a car parked in a farm gate not a couple of hundred yards away from Sunny Patch with a man and woman inside and the woman in the driver's seat. Hamish tried his best to quickly memorise the number plate as he pulled over into a very narrow lane and scrabbled to find a piece of paper and a pen or pencil to scribble down the number plate letters and figures.

He had just completed his task when he looked up to see a large Massey-Ferguson tractor ahead of him. Not wishing to have an altercation with the farming folk hereabouts he engaged reverse gear and began to back onto the marginally wider lane when the blast of a motor horn made him stop and pull forward giving an apologetic wave to the very people that he had just seen in the parked car.

Giving another wave to the driver of the now stationary tractor Hamish took off after the car principally to check that the number plate details were correct.

He drove as fast as was possible in the tree-lined lane but when he eventually arrived at the main road there was no sign of the vehicle.

When he was looking for Gorse Lane he saw a pub on his left before the turning for Gorse Lane. Just a little annoyed that he missed the car in the not quite successful James-Bond-style chase, he pulled into the pub car park and just sat waiting for opening time hoping that they served some sort of food.

Hamish allowed his mind to run over many aspects of his life and what, in his opinion, was a cack-handed investigation into a crime in which until now he had mainly been a bystander.

From these thoughts turned to Freya, their relationship, her career and their now quite enforced holiday in a nudist colony in the middle of nowhere and from his point of view, having no likely satisfactory outcome.

Although in years ago he had taken Freya on exotic and both being of Scottish heritage, surprisingly very expensive holidays when their separate career paths had allowed their respective holiday rosters to coincide.

In recent years Freya's meteoric rise through the ranks and their now totally separate career paths had precluded any long worthwhile holidays but they had always kept up their two or three days short breaks to celebrate Freya's birthdays in October.

They would often either spend them at her mother's small vineyard on the banks of the River Dart or if her mother was at the farmhouse they would stay in or around Dartmouth; a town loved by both for different reasons.

Hamish, for his time at Britannia prior to graduating and then going into the Merchant Navy to get more deep-sea time than the Royal Navy of the fifties, could ever hope to offer to an adventurous young man.

Regrettably, resigning of his commission had caused a lasting fracture in this relationship with his parents which did not seem to unduly concern him.

Freya, for spending her long school holidays there before bringing her school friends to spend the days, the sunny ones at least, sailing and socialising with the foreign students marooned at Britannia during the holidays.

Hamish brought himself into the present when he saw a sign in the pub window informing anyone interested that they had accommodation. At that moment Hamish decided that it might be prudent to book a room for the hoped-for only a week at the most in Sunny Patch using the pub as a bolt-hole if things in any way went wrong.

As he studied the pub so a person opened the door, he looked down at his watch and it was midday as he looked up, from behind the pub a couple walked into the open door. The young woman or more likely a teenager walked with a peculiar type of limp. In that instant, he recognised the woman from the car that he had been chasing. They made no effort to look around them as they disappeared into the gloom of the hostelry.

Hamish, grabbing the paper with the details of their number plate decided to go around the back of the pub from the opposite direction to that taken by the couple as it was unlikely that they would see him. Sure enough, there was the car but he had the registration letter back to front. Suddenly he remembered that in the haste to get out of the car he had left the pencil behind in the car, he mouthed the letters to himself on his journey back to his vehicle.

He then went into the pub and saw the couple sitting down with drinks in front of them. "It's a nice day sir, what'll you be having?" the landlord enquired. "A pint of bitter please and do you do meals?" Hamish enquired and the reply was to the affirmative and a menu was quickly slipped over the bar followed by a pint of Georges 'Bitter.' "Shall I put on a meal slate sir?"

As he agreed with that suggestion, Hamish found a table away from the couple as in those few minutes the bar was rapidly filling up with people to the extent that the landlords wife appeared behind the bar.

After quite some time a girl appeared from somewhere, with an apology for the delay in taking the order from Hamish.

When the movement of people allowed Hamish to see the couple, they too were giving an order to another girl. As the woman was given the menu Hamish noticed that her left hand had a glove on it while the right hand was bare. Bodies allowing, Hamish kept looking towards the couple but although they often looked around they did not appear to look in the direction of him.

After finishing their meal the couple went to the bar and paid their due and through the side window Hamish saw them get into their car a very nice Rover and drive off.

By now the bar was reasonably free and Hamish went there to pay his bill and to enquire if they had a room free for the following week. They did and he booked it under the name of Fergus and fortunately had the cash to pay the deposit and nonchalantly asked for a receipt for not only the accommodation but the beer and meal as well. Expenses needed to be claimed, particularly if your name and nature was Fergusson!

Constable Jake Richards of the clerks office had hinted to others that there could be changes in the role played by the senior, to quote his army background, Non Commissioned Officer. In short, Staff Sergeant Fergusson was the most likely to be affected if the station gossip, Jake, was correct and that thought was at the back of his mind when he collected all the receipts at the pub. If he was going from 'D' division Hamish intended to garner every penny possible from the establishment.

After his pleasant meal Hamish turned back towards the city to find 'Chubby' Reynolds.

Perhaps surprising to some of his fellow rogues, Chubby lived in quite an affluent district and as Hamish pulled up at the bottom of the drive so the curtains twitched. Guessing what would happen be when he rang the door bell, Hamish was not surprised when the bell was not answered. With a surprising turn of speed he shot through the side gate to find Chubby legging it over his lawn towards a Summer house.

"Chubby come here." commanded Hamish adding as Chubby slowed "I'll do this place otherwise."

Chubby came to a halt, looked behind him and said "What do you want Sarge?"

Hamish explained his likely challenge and Chubby led him to his 'Workshop' part of the bungalow.

Chubby made a great fuss of fiddling around going through drawers cupboards and with much huffing and puffing pulled out several key type objects wrapped in oil cloth.

"Did you say Yale and Chubb box type pickers?" Chubby asked him. "At this stage I do not know exactly what I want but give me a general set of keys." Hamish told him.

"I ain't giving you anything, you can borrow them but I want 'em back. Why don't you tell me which door you need to open and I'll do it and be gone before you arrive then everybody is 'appy. I've not helped the plod and the plod have not collard me?"

"In all truth, I would let you do it that way to save you from your so-called mates if they found out; but this might be bigger than both of us and could end my career so, sorry Chubby just show me what to do and I'll go and return them in about a week, could be more and could be less. Much less if they don't work," Hamish truthfully told him.

Chuntering all the way through the familiarisation exam of the station sergeant Chubby finally told Hamish that he could use the keys but "You'd never make even a half-wit safe-breaker and God help you if you try to do this in the dark." Chubby opined.

Staff Sergeant Fergusson then took possession of a full set of skeleton and master keys and as he went he said to Chubby Reynolds, "Keep your side gate locked, you never know what rogues might come through it."

"An' a right rogue just came through it," Chubby cheerfully replied. With a grin at Chubby, Hamish looked around him for prying eyes and left.

Back at the station, he handed in the registration details of the car he had seen at Flaidown for the control room to do a PNC check for ownership.

As he went into his office he saw the senior sergeant who would take over his jobs sitting behind his desk looking very pleased with himself. "I've sorted out the rosters and leave rosters for the next month and even if I say it myself, they are bloody perfect Mr Fergusson. You can go off to your cloak and dagger work knowing that all is hunky-dory in your office." The staff sergeant picked up the rosters, carefully read them and then gently laid them out in a line across his desk and asked his replacement to read the rosters that he had so carefully composed.

They were carefully read and the station sergeant then asked his replacement to compare them with the current rosters. "I will be back in a few minutes to hear your self-congratulations all over again."

"Any answer from the Police national computer system," Hamish asked the control room sergeant.

The sergeant slid a paper to Hamish and the name and address of the registered owner was quite a revelation. Kurt Rosenberg, Woodbine Cottage etc.

Hamish put it in his pocket and made his way down to the bunker only to find it totally empty, on returning to civilisation Jake was waiting at the top of the stairs busy sucking his teeth and stopped long enough to tell him, "She's along in her proper office now that bladder head has left with his tribe of pratts. Oh, and don't get too comfy in your chair, someone else will be warming their ass in it shortly."

Very sarcastically the staff sergeant thanked him for both pieces of information the first being a fact and the second simply being conjecture by him. Another suck of teeth before Jake replied, "Mock if you must, but yet again you will be wrong staff sergeant. Don't worry I will be at your leaving do."

A common term for a delicate part of the adult male anatomy was the plural single word used by Staff Sergeant Fergusson at Jake as he made his way towards the CID office and Freya leaving Jake with the nodding head and the knowing smirk indicating that yet again Jake had scored a bullseye.

In her office, Hamish laid the paper on her desk with the details of the car that he had met in Flaidown and then told her the story. She asked him if he thought that he was being tailed? He then told her about his meal and what he had noted about the woman in that she had a strange limp and probably something wrong with her left hand.

"What's the name of this pub?" Freya asked him. He looked blankly at her and confessed that he didn't know. She gave him a very straight look and told him, "Do you really think that you are cut out to be a policeman or is it a case of overwork or perhaps your mind is on your forthcoming nude exercise? Do tell me darling, which exactly is it?"

"Ha, bloody ha," he said, then adding an overemphasised, "Darling."

He made a dive for his wallet and triumphantly produced the wallet and the receipts for the meal and the deposit for the accommodation. The name turned out to be 'The Scolding Wife' with a pictorial depiction of a woman chasing her man with a rolling pin.

"Almost a perfect description of someone I know well," he told her then adding "6:30?"

"I'll be there," Freya reassured him as he left her office.

On the dot of 6:30, the doorbell rang and there stood Freya in a very fetching classic frock and her towel over her arm. Her only comment at this juncture was "I hope that you are going to dress in something better than old trousers and a manky pullover. It's supposed to be summer."

Hamish chose to ignore her words as he told her that she looked "a million dollars."

Freya again produced the brochure for Sunny Patch and they studied it at length and weather permitting decided to try most of the recreation opportunities.

By the time that they had taken in all of these amenities they were quite exhausted with Hamish saying,

"I know that we read most of this last evening but it appears that neither of us took in much. We were simply too tired and it was too late to digest all of the facilities and pretty pictures. He suddenly stopped talking.

He then appeared to spend a few seconds thinking then smiling and as his parsimonious heritage would dictate, for the second time, uttered "I bet whoever is paying for all this will have the department budget severely stretched by the bill for our expenses paid holiday!"

She responded with the very teasing question "When the auditor comes to checking the invoices how will they disguise the heading 'Sunny Patch Nudist complex'?"

"By unsophisticated forgery." were the three words of simple explanation from Hamish.

They then moved back onto the rules and regulations of the place. Amongst the rules that they could remember from the previous evening were some that they had plainly missed. These rules began with the demand that at all times and in all places total nudity will be observed. There will be no unnecessary noise to disturb other owners and visitors. Children should be encouraged to play responsibly and as quietly as could reasonably expect during daylight hours. From 11:00 p.m. to 7:00 a.m., there will be no disturbing sounds.

Any unseemly conduct will result in visitors being expelled without compensation. Body hair may be removed but any styling must be of a discrete, non-controversial nature or a polite request for complete removal will be given.

At all times the social conventions of organised nakedness will be observed. Photographs will be allowed but the subjects directly in view and those by reason of consequential inclusion must give their consent.

"We read most of this yesterday," she told him continuing with, "I can't remember the 'Total nudity, the children playing and the pubic hairstyling business being there. Anyway as I don't have any hair to 'style', it will not matter. If they say that total removal is allowed it must mean that in other places it plainly is not."

"Fortunately," he said, "it's not my problem but I was going to ask you a week ago if you should let it grow a bit." With arched eyebrows, she enquired, "Just how fast do you think hair grows?"

Hamish simply turned his hands upwards and said nothing.

They just began to read further about the supply of bedding, towels, kitchen equipment, payment for electricity and the various sizes of lodges for holiday hire when Freya looked at her watch and told him to get dressed pretty quickly as otherwise, they would be late at Sarah's.

After a quick wash, shave and change into a jacket and trousers Hamish was holding the door for her to exit when she noticed that he didn't have a towel. A mad scramble by the two of them eventually found a recently laundered towel and they set off for Monarch Mansions. As they drove through the city on the midsummer evening Hamish told her of his concerns about being asked to bring a towel and if their original presumption of using a swimming pool was correct why not be asked to bring a pair of trunks?

"I have been thinking about that too," she replied. "In the back of my mind is a possible reason, but at this point, I simply can't imagine Sarah in that situation. We will see," she concluded.

The rest of the journey was completed in silence as they motored through the ever-increasingly affluent parts of town until they reached their destination where they were met by a gatekeeper at the imposing entrance as the huge highly polished brass sign identified itself to the world as Monarch Mansions. "Good Evening Madam and Sir"

"We have an appointment with Miss Dodds Younger Freya told the man. "The car park is to the left, ma'am, but please park near the entrance and you will be escorted to Miss Dodds Younger." Was the final instructions from the gatekeeper as she drove to where a uniformed fellow directed her adjacent to the main, very imposing doors.

As the fellow held the door so another uniformed commissionaire arrived to announce, "If Madam and Sir would care to follow me I will take you to Miss Dodds Younger."

Hamish could only give top marks to the system where the gatekeeper identified who they wanted to see and 'phoned the information ahead of their parking the vehicle in order for the commissionaire to be on hand to take them to Sarah. Smooth, so very smooth.

They were whisked in a lift to what was marked as the Penthouse suite. As they were ascending Hamish thought what a sight it must be for the commissionaire to usher two people to the penthouse suite in posh clothes with towels under their arms. Why had they not thought of a bag?

Out of the lift, it was only five steps they went towards Sarah who would have been tipped off that they were on their way. She greeted both of them with a kiss on the cheek. Not exactly the 'cup of tea' for Hamish but in premises such as these it was de rigueur no doubt.

Sarah thanked 'Mr Gibbons', and she ushered Freya and Hamish into a very impressive double-height entrance hall and went into what appeared to be an anteroom.

Being a woman Freya had noted that although she and Hamish had dressed for the occasion, Susan was dressed in what could be loosely described as a superior quality housecoat.

On the other hand, Hamish, on sighting Sarah in her, to him, dressing gown, apologised for them being too early.

"Oh, you not, may I call you Hamish rather than Staff Sergeant Fergusson?" He nodded his consent and Sarah continued as Freya drew the conclusion that her unspoken opinion of this meeting was correct.

"This visit I like to think of as a nude social occasion as I hope that it will turn out to be. However, there is an ulterior motive as you may have guessed by my asking you to bring a towel." Freya nodded her head while Hamish looked blankly at both women.

It might surprise you to know that I am the link between Mr Gaunt, Sir Simon and the Naturist movement. While Freya simply smiled at this disclosure Hamish now had a marked look of surprise as Sarah continued: "When the name of Sunny Patch came up I knew of it and Mr Bates knew of my participation in that movement and that particular place. He then asked me for my opinion of getting you in there covertly.

Because of my contacts in the movement, I was able to get the two of you a holiday there with me being the referee of your good and healthy conduct. I have introduced you as Mr and Mrs Fergus and without the secretary of my club knowing put you on their books as members. I have also made you support members of CCBN a new organisation which recently took over from the British Sunbathing Association as the national body of Nudists or my preference for the name of naturist. I have your membership cards here and I filched your photographs, with Sir Simon's permission of course, as identification.

In short, except for your naked bodies and a few do's and don'ts you are all there. Questions please?"

Neither Freya nor Hamish said anything at first then he asked, "When we strip off what then?"

Sarah replied, "If you are comfortable I will come and get you and let you mingle with other naturists then have dinner. If you're not comfortable with that you can leave of course. I was just hoping that this evening might ease you into the relaxing world of a non-judgemental alternative lifestyle which like everyone else who has tried it, you will enjoy the sensation of being without clothes, indoors or outdoors."

"Who will we be meeting?" Freya enquired. "They are from several walks of life, families from grandparents to their grandchildren. Two, in fact, are great–grandparents," Sarah explained, then adding "including different nationalities and locals who I have come across in my connections with the organisations and swimming events of this type of recreation. I have selected a wide variety of people for you to meet. They do know that you are my guests and for the first time sampling this particular type of socialising."

Freya then asked, "what are the social conventions expected of us this evening?"

The reply from Sarah was, "While you will look at their bodies just the same as if they had clothes on it is polite when speaking to them to engage only with their eyes. Those towels in your case will have two purposes. The first is to use it as a modesty cover if you are embarrassed and in your case Hamish, if by any chance you get aroused, which a very few men do at first, it saves both you and others from a perhaps socially difficult scene. The other purpose for the towel is to sit on rather than put your buttocks on to the best chintz. I'll leave you now for ten minutes and then come and collect you if you would like to stay."

As Sarah opened the door to leave so a boy and girl of about eleven or twelve years old shot through the door with the boy holding, which in the scuffle looked like a bag of sweets. They seemed to be so engrossed in their chase that they were spread-eagled on the floor before they got to their knees, apologised and made their way out into the hall.

"Sarah told the, to her, novice nudists, "I'm sorry about that but I hope that is a wonderful example of the freedom of our way of life. Two children soon to be teenagers who enjoy being naked with no hang-ups about their bodies whatsoever. By the way, they are twins. Their parents are Asian, Robert and Joy, people that came from Uganda after independence. Lovely people, lovely children. Before I leave you to get undressed, any questions?"

"Just one," Freya said then asked. "Do your guests object to other bare women having their body hair removed?"

"You mean your pubic hair?" Sarah enquired.

"Yes, I don't want to upset anyone or embarrass you," Freya told her. As usual, I had it removed only days before your unexpected invitation. It grows back quickly enough as it is but not within days."

Susan undid her robe displayed her body and simply said, "Snap." She then added, "It is not only us like this. The Joy I've just mentioned and even my mother are the same. Please don't concern yourself.

We are a minority like this but, other than to another girl that you will meet, no one is judged in our movement, certainly not whether they have body hair or not.

It is the case that people like us feel fresh and clean without it and ladies with a bramble bush are, in their opinion and of course correct, are as nature and their menfolk, intended. If we were dressed who would know, or care whether we were depilated or not?"

Sarah gently closed the door behind her. "How many people do you think she has invited to dinner?" Freya asked Hamish as they began to remove their clothes. "More to the point, is she catering for us all? If she is I hope that she used a pinny and on the subject of clothes, now I understand why she had that glorified housecoat on," Hamish concluded.

"Where does one put ones clothes, there ain't no hooks or wardrobes in here?" Hamish, with a perplexed look, enquired.

"Try a chair," Freya answered as he eventually took off his underclothes while she unbuttoned her dress. He then discovered that she had no pants or bra on, "Travelling light?" he asked.

She replied, "I guessed what this evening was going to be."

They stood there and looked at each other, the first time with no clothes on in almost a year. "You've not aged much dear," she assured him.

A silence followed before she sternly asked, "Aren't you going to tell me that I haven't changed either?"

Hamish smiled as she put her hands on her hips looking intently and in fact menacingly. "You have never looked better," he told her before adding with a broad smile, "for your age."

With a quick grab and twist of a delicate section of his loins, on her return, Sarah found the pair in a strange position with Hamish bent over and Freya's arm disappearing into the contorted body.

They straightened up as Sarah said, "Good. I like people to be relaxed when they try this for the first time," Freya, with a very straight face, said.

"I was simply ensuring that in his agony he would now find it impossible to be embarrassed by any manifestation of likely untoward interest in the ladies." He replied, still slightly bent, "Just be grateful that the subject is not men!"

As Sarah led them out of the room with their towels, plainly only going to be used for sitting on, Freya gave Hamish a quick squeeze of his left buttock.

When they walked across the magnificent hall both realised that they both had put their shoes on and mentioned it to Sarah and she told them that there were flip-flops for their use in the room they had left.

Suitably shod they followed Sarah into an equally imposing sitting room where they were met by what appeared at first glance, to be a sea of smiling faces.

She then led them around the room linking names to faces which would, at that time, never be remembered.

Freya was thinking not of the assembled guests but of how could Sarah feed all these people. When the two children that they had met a few minutes were introduced, it was the end of the line and Sarah took Freya to the drinks trolley.

They turned around to see that Hamish was in deep conversation, not with some shapely young thing but an older lady now sitting down with Hamish perched on the arm of the chair, towel in place.

When Freya approached him so he got to his feet and took his drink from her and, for the second time in minutes introduced Daphne to Freya.

Daphne was Sarah's mother he told her and immediately Freya was absorbed in deep conversation with Sarah's mum while Hamish went over to the parents of the children.

As one would do in or out of clothes on such occasions, their conversation was about the weather, the state of the strikebound country and the necessity of strong government action which they agreed was unlikely as this government were simply appeasers with the rates of inflation completely decimating the buying power of the people.

All this time the wife of this new friend of his had not uttered a word. She was very beautiful with perfect teeth and those dark brown almost enticing eyes.

Out of courtesy Hamish turned to her and told her what delightful children she had and enquired how old they were. She told him that they were twelve years old twins and were named David and Julia.

Plainly the face of Hamish gave away his surprise of British names for their children. The father laughed and explained that as the children were blessed with quite pale coloured skin they chose those names to give the children a better chance in life than having Indian names.

"I am so surprised that plainly well-educated people such as you would deny your heritage to your precious children by giving them British names. It's so sad that you should believe that in order to be accepted as equals they need British names," Hamish told them.

"My name is…" The wife attempted to tell Hamish when he interrupted her to say, Joy! I do remember you are Joy." Turning to the husband Hamish said, "Of course, you must be Robert."

"Our parents had the same idea although both our grandparents and parents were of mixed marriages during the Raj so using British names was not unusual to us. Our respective male lines were in the British India civil service." Robert told him.

It was no surprise that when Hamish was seen having a deep and meaningful discussion with a very beautiful lady Freya would join them and with the re-introduction having completed Hamish excused himself and looked for conversational green pastures elsewhere.

A young couple were heading his way as he was desperately trying to remember their names, without any success, when they introduced themselves as Ian and Poppy the conversation was just about to begin when a very deep gong was sounded and Susan announced, "Dinner is served."

As they queued up to go out of the room a waitress in an apron was standing by the door holding a tray which as each guest left their drink glass.

As they approached the door Freya bumped the arm of Hamish and surreptitiously nodded towards the waitress. When they put their glasses on her tray so Hamish noticed a breast peeping out from the bib of the apron. Other than the apron the girl appeared to have no other clothes on.

Neither Freya nor Hamish had witnessed such a scene as they walked in tandem into the dining room. Surprisingly, the room was circular with a huge round heavily laden table in the centre. Each place setting had a seating card and the ritual of towel placing was performed with almost military precision as was the sitting down, a ceremony in itself.

When they parted to sit on either side of Sarah, Freya whispered to Hamish, "What price for King Arthur's table?"

When everyone was seated it became apparent that the seating plan had been carefully thought out. Other than the children, the adults were sat opposite their partners which did separate the conversation and allowed free from partner-censored chatter between diners sitting to the left and right.

Freya had a look at her dining companions, old, young, fat, slim, balding beautiful, plain. All of life in fact and dressed all the same – in nothing. No fashion faux pas here she was glad to note!

To the left of Hamish was Sarah and to his right was a distinguished-looking grey haired lady who reintroduced herself as Rosemary and pointed to her husband opposite sitting next to Freya, giving him the name of Rex.

The chatter around the table was interrupted by the two waitresses going around the table with the menus. Within a few minutes, the orders were taken and as the girls retreated it became apparent that the girls, apart from their aprons were in fact, in the buff.

When comparing notes later in the sitting room Freya and Hamish came to the same conclusion that of all life's surprises, nothing could match the meal, the setting and the quite unique company for its originality.

In the sitting room, they again mingled with the other guests and between them discovered the young couple were twenty-two-year-olds, the age being supported by the taught, wrinkle-free skin and well-toned bodies.

One was the granddaughter of Rosemary, the dining companion of Hamish, the boy was the son of Geoff and Adelaide, Geoff being described as "Something in the city'.

When the boy, Ian, pointed out his parents Freya looked at the boy's father Geoff, all she could picture was a cartoon of pinstriped trousers, a black coat, a bowler hat, rolled umbrella and a briefcase adorning the naked frame a few feet away from her.

Adelaide was, in her body frame what might be called 'substantial'. It was possible to think of her as the president of the Women's Institute or perhaps captain of the ladies bowls team.

In short, a no-nonsense woman. For much of the rest of the evening both Freya and Hamish were studying the guests and imagining them clothed and their probable occupations. The other guests might and probably were thinking 'Who are these two who Susan is making such a fuss about?' A very amusing pastime.

On the rare occasion when Freya and Hamish were together the young couple Ian and Poppy who had just begun to talk when the dinner gong sounded came over and Hamish introduced them to Freya.

In the course of the general conversation, it transpired that they had graduated from University only that week but wouldn't get their ceremony until the Autumn. Both had taken up offers for temporary work at the Home Office.

Freya and Hamish were well and truly caught out giving each other knowing glances. "Is there something wrong?" Polly asked. Both Freya and Hamish almost fell over themselves to deny anything wrong with her place of employment and even went so far as to commend their workplace choice.

Although it was considered very rude in the nudist world to ask any question it was quite proper to show an interest in whatever a fellow nudist chose to tell of themselves then any questions were allowed.

Polly offered the information that she was Sarah's niece and her grandma "is over there," pointing out the lady that Freya had been talking to during drinks earlier.

Polly then disclosed her pride in the fact that "Grandmas father began a naturist club when he returned from India in nineteen twelve. Only professional people could join until after the war when non-professional people were welcomed." She continued, "When my great-grandfather began what in those days was organised nudity they adopted ancient Hindu philosophy of the gymnosophist as the principals that they would adhere to," Polly told them.

"Great-grandpa and grandma's belief was that physical activity, a healthy diet, exposure to sunlight and a smooth body was the panacea for all the evils of the world. When a new generation of nudists came along many of these rules were no longer adhered to and the high ideals more or less abandoned."

"What do you mean by abandoned?" Freya asked Polly. She replied, "It appears that although between the wars many of our persuasion did still believe in sports diet and sunbathing, many simply wanted to sunbathe and live free from clothing and looking not at the body but at the inner person.

Escape the traditional narrow values of society. By 1930s, the movement had many eminent supporters and it was in that period that the philosophy of meditation faded out along with good diets."

As Polly stopped speaking so Sarah appeared and said, "I do hope that Polly is not dominating the conversation?"

"I am just telling them the beginnings of the movement and the role that great-grandma and great-grandpa played in the development of the nude sunbathing organisation that we have today," Polly told her aunt. All of this time Ian had not uttered a word.

Sarah then led Freya towards what was becoming a chatter of women as the ladies were creating a 'Girls' only circle. As Hamish looked around he noted that the menfolk had likewise made a debating circle and from what he could hear the conversation centred around the winter tour of the rugby team and the chances of England beating the all Blacks.

Looking further around he saw Giovanna the waitresses, pouring out drinks so he made his way over to her and collected a straight Barbados rum and pulled up a chair and sat down on his towel and in peace mulled over the past few hours and the characters that he had come across while the babble of male and female voiced filled the room from two different directions.

From the ladies coven, he could hear the shrill tones of Polly dominating the ladies conversation.

He was disturbed from his thoughts and the study of the expensive-looking carpet by a pair of feet appearing in his vision. Looking up he was greeted by the smiling face of Joy looking down on him. "May I join you?" she asked.

"Most certainly you can. I'll get you a chair," he replied as he stood up and reached for a chair and then brought another one. "I only need one," Joy told him.

He replied. "Yes, but when Freya sees me talking to a beautiful lady like you she will be here like a shot as you will have noticed when we talked to each other before the dinner."

"You looked so lonely here on your own that I thought that you might like some company. If you don't please say so. I won't be offended," she told him with arched enquiring eyebrows. "No, please stay." Hamish told her then asked, "Will Robert not object to you talking to me at a distance from the other gatherings.

"If we had clothes on would anyone object to you or me talking to a person of a different sex in mixed company?" She asked and then answered her own question with the word "No."

"I take your point so what shall we talk about as it appears in these circles it's de rigueur not to ask questions but wait for others to tell you what they think you might want to know. This seems to me to limit conversation." Hamish said.

"We can easily overcome that hurdle as there's only two of us so ask away," Joy invited him.

"Why did you leave the ladies, to save a lonely soul or were you fed up with hearing Polly's voice?" Hamish asked.

"Yes, I was a bit tired of not so much her voice but Polly's verbal and dictatorial attitude to certain practises in our movement," Joy told Hamish then continued, "She has this preoccupation about the origins of the movement, her great-grandparents, body image, tonsorial grooming and so on.

Because with Freya there, a new audience for her, Polly is on her high horse again. The rest of us have heard it so often she knows that she is wasting her time but, she wants to be the centre of attention and the subject of what is and what's not acceptable without clothes on including grooming practises does divide opinion in some circles. If we were always dressed the subject would never arise.

Hamish thought for a while then told her, "She is preaching to the converted where Freya is concerned so that's a time-waster. "It is much the same for me," Joy told him, then adding the observation, "As you can see I too am like Freya, Sarah and a couple of others."

"What is your connection with Sarah and why does she make such a fuss, a good and happy fuss I will agree, of you being part of this gathering of carefully selected people?"

Joy asked him then continued, "She told us that you were new to the movement and would be quite embarrassed as this would be your first time in nude company but you seem to be no different to any of us 'Old hands'."

"I thought that it is considered to be bad form to ask questions in a nude gathering," he said.

"Forgive my nosiness but as we appear to have 'clicked' I did not give convention a second thought Joy embarrassingly told him before adding," Please don't tell me, it would make me feel so bad." Don't worry," he told her, "I'll even it up in a minute by asking you questions."

Thinking on his feet was a skill that Hamish learned at Britannia to outwit the Chief petty officer gunnery instructors when they were after him.

"We have a common interest in keeping the offices of state on their toes and in a random conversation Sarah chose to discuss her connection with the nude movement. We showed interest and here we are and I'm glad that we came," Hamish told her and asked, "What about you and Robert, how did you become involved with Sarah?"

"If you know Sarah so well you might as well know that with her fiancée she was a merchant banker and a very good one at that." She began and Hamish duly nodded as if he knew that Susan was a banker. She went on to tell him, "They had a villa in Italy and as Robert was a client of their bank they invited us to have a holiday there.

This was before the children were born, our children, not Sarah's, I mean my children, Sarah has no children. When we arrived there were a lot of people lounging around all naked.

It was a bit of a shock but we had been nudists when we were in Africa so we had no difficulty in fitting in.

A few of the people here today were house guests then. The two waitresses over there were the young children of the housekeeper who worked without clothes with her husband and sister. Their son, Dino is the chef who cooked the meal tonight.

Sarah and Frank had a good life as they owned one third each in the bank with the original founder holding the third share.

Frank went to the south of France to see a very wealthy client and had a motor accident and died. As you can imagine Sarah was beside herself with grief and not only had she lost her fiancée but within days the founder of the bank died and everything was on the shoulders of Sarah.

Unknown to her the founder had a very good offer for the business and it fell to Sarah to dispose of the bank which she did with the help of Robert, he is an expert in matters of high finance and advises the Treasury on fiscal policy. The next time that you get a tax demand blame Robert; he might have proposed it to the Treasury mandarins," she concluded.

Hamish said, "God, what a situation to find herself in. I have noticed that she does not wear any rings and what you have told me is the reason why. If she sold out I suppose that it's no surprise that she could buy this stunning place."

"This was Franks place and she inherited it and as it appears that he had no close relatives she inherited all his money – less tax of course," she explained.

"Blame Robert for the tax," Hamish suggested. A smiling laugh was his reward.

Hamish stood up and asked her what she would like to drink her choice was Grapefruit juice.

Over at the bar, he watched the steady hand of the 'Barmaid' Giovanna pour out a Grapefruit juice then offer him an enquiring rise of the eyebrows to which the answer was, "a Barbados rum thank you.

A voice with the distinctive lilt of the British Caribbean told him, "Trinidad is better." He turned round to be greeted by an outstretched hand and a broad smile. "I'm Nelson and my wife is, and no laughing…"

"Emma by any chance?" Hamish asked him. "You've got it right. The benefit is that it always breaks the ice," Nelson told him.

Returning the courtesy he told Nelson, "I'm Hamish. Very pleased to meet you and… where is your Emma?"

"She'll be here in a minute, she and the girls are undressing. You know women, take all day putting them on and all evening taking them off. Surprisingly to Hamish, Nelson asked for a beer and tonic water for Emma and told Giovanna,

"The girls will get their own. Where's your sister?" Nelson asked Giovanna. "Over there," she indicated the group of women.

"Drawn the short straw again?" Nelson enquired.

"She'll relieve me when it gets quiet," she assured him as he and Hamish headed towards Joy and her daughter now slumped in the chair.

Joy was in a 'Heads down' conversation with Caroline while her brother was with the men looking quite bored with the finer points of Gentleman's poker. As Nelson and Hamish arrived by them, Joy looked up and then stood up and embraced Nelson while her daughter asked "Are the girls here?"

"They're undressing," Nelson told her. Like a shot, she was gone, collected her brother and the pair disappeared into the Hall.

"Is this anybody's chair?" Nelson enquired.

"No, it's yours if you want it," Joy told him.

He replied, "I'll go over and speak to our hostess then be back, OK?"

"What of your children and this type of life?" Hamish asked Joy.

"I would hope that they continue to enjoy it and that when they fly the nest at eighteen or so take this lifestyle with them and as we have inherited this from our parents and grandparents, that they will pass it on to their children. But their future spouses might change all that, unfortunately. We have been very lucky in that so far, despite marriage the generations have enjoyed being publicly naked."

"Talking of eighteen," she said. "By eighteen I was married to Robert and within a year the twins arrived."

"Was Robert suitable as far as your parents were concerned?" Hamish enquired. She replied "We had known each other since childhood because our parents and grandparents belonged to a movement like this. It was simply love as naturally, we knew physically exactly what we were getting, one of the many benefits of being without clothes."

"Changing the record," Hamish told her, "I'm amazed that Freya has not turned up here as I'm busy spending all this time in the company of a very attractive lady."

"There is a simple explanation," she told him. "Being naked, that's the answer. If you were clothed you could bet your last dollar that she would have been over here like a shot. Take away the clothes and duplicity simply doesn't appear to exist. Can you really distrust anybody if the people all around you have no clothes on?"

"I suppose that we have had our bit of peace now," Joy told Hamish, "It's past the time that I should have gone back to the ladies cabal and as I haven't heard Polly for some time, peace might have returned.

"Thanks so much for our extended chat. I've very much enjoyed it and if I don't get the opportunity again this evening, I do hope that we might meet up again. The entertainment will be here in a mo, I hope that you will like them."

"Having this uninterrupted time with you will be my enduring memory of this evening. I too have really enjoyed it. What is the entertainment?" Hamish asked.

"You'll find out soon," she told him then added, "Don't let the sad hair saga spoil the evening until you have a daughter of your own. It's all of no consequence now and perhaps not even then."

As Joy disappeared he looked over towards Freya and saw her talking to Nelsons Emma and he had a smile as he went towards the door which he thought was the lavatory as he had watched several people go through a door. He opened the door and found himself in a corridor with several doors.

He opened one door only to find himself in a glorified broom cupboard, in most dwellings, a single bedroom at least. He moved onto the next door and as he opened it his ears were assaulted with a cacophony of children's falsetto voices.

While his ears caught the sound, his eyes saw the prone form of David with, judging by the appearance, Emma's daughter sitting on his feet, her sister sitting astride his stomach and his sister, Julia holding his hands above his head as the girl on his stomach was plastering his protesting, wriggling face with what appeared to be cream with cake mixed in.

None of them appeared to see Hamish come in and as he quietly closed the door he jumped 'a mile' as he moved backwards and bumped into another body. It was Freya. Without a word, he gently opened the door and she looked in. They then closed the door to what had now turned into a dual purpose to find a lavatory. On approaching another door, a body emerged followed by another. As the door was held open for them they could hear voices. They hesitated to go further when a voice told them, "Come in, there's lots of room for all."

Yet, again in this building, another unexpected scene awaited them. Facing them was a line of four urinals all shaped like different flowers and a lower one for children. At right angles were four cubicles with very small louvred saloon bar swinging doors about eighteen inches tall. All occupied with the other side made up of three open showers. There were two people at the urinals, a man as could be expected and over the child's urinal, with her legs akimbo, Freya saw a woman.

Trying not to show surprise Freya nudged Hamish, nodding to the woman. He went to the urinal furthest from the woman while Freya waited for a cubical. Hamish discovered that being clothes less was certainly a benefit when it was possible to have immediate access to that which was necessary and likewise when one had completed the task.

The man and woman left shortly before he got into what might be termed, full flow. His concentration was broken by two events, firstly Freya whispering to him that "There are no doors," as a woman vacated a cubicle and the arrival of a further three guests, two women and a man who they had met earlier but simply couldn't remember their names.

Quite putting Hamish off of matters in hand, one lady went in the next cubical to Freya and the man went to the urinals and his lady companion made her way towards the child's urinal when another cubicle was vacated. The woman then turned around and went alongside Freya. Hamish joined her at the washbasins where she whispered, "How about that? There were tiny doors after all but they were so small that people just left them open."

Hamish replied, "I thought that my Rum was stronger than I expected." By now the place began to thin out and back in the corridor Freya said, "When I went into the nineteenth-century lavatory at Woodbine Cottage I thought that was unique but this was much the same.

Everyone there and obviously the same here could have a conversation while answering their various needs. Very friendly indeed. By the way, did you know who she was at the low urinal?"

"No." Hamish told her, "You saw a lot more than I did. Who was it?"

"Our dear young revolutionary for woman's equality with men and the unwanted champion of the smooth female form, dearest Polly, the only black spot of this remarkable evening.

As they left Freya whispered, "Whatever next," Hamish replied, "I've just about seen everything now. Not only daffodil, nasturtiums, pansies and lily-shaped urinals but also their strange clients. I suppose if this was a separate lavatory it wouldn't happen. It must be the urinals that tempt some women. Well, well!"

As they emerged from the corridor so they walked into a scene of chair moving. The whole group with the waitresses Givanna and Flo and a huge man, big in every respect who Hamish took to be the chef Dino were forming the chairs into a semi-circle around the Grand Piano. Daphne called to them to sit next to Sarah. Carefully placing their towels on the chairs they joined her with everyone grabbing a chair.

The door to the corridor slammed open as four children came barging through all plastered in the same mixture that Hamish had seen a few minutes earlier.

As they attempted to make a dash for the kitchens so both sets of parents called the children to heel. The pair belonging to Joy and Robert looked a mess with David not only having his face and torso covered but his hair was matted in cake never mind Brylcreem. Julia had some mess on her arms and chest. The two belonging to Nelson and Emma were not so bad, one was almost clean while the 'Plasterer' was covered in various parts, the cream against the colour of their skins probably made it look worse than it was.

When the clean children were returned and their parents seated applause took over conversation as a lady came in and sat at the Grand Piano and another lady came in, stood in front of the piano and after greeting everyone and 'Honoured Guests' looking directly at Freya and Hamish. Then to much applause she began, not singing as the two 'Honoured Guests' anticipated but having a comedy routine of sketches and jokes one of which was very pertinent not only to the nude audience but to her as well.

> "Why can't a naked conjurer do card tricks?"
> "Because they have no sleeves or pockets!"

She rattled off jokes with the speed of a machine gun. Whoever suggested that a woman couldn't tell jokes. Here was the proof that they could, even in the nude without props.

When she had finished she was replaced by a rather large older lady with noticeably pendulous bosoms she was followed by musicians, some naked and some dressed who sat to the sides just behind the pianist.

The mini-orchestra struck up and the pianist joined in with the large lady bringing her contralto vice into the beautiful melodious sounds. Hamish was taken back to his childhood when a visit to part of his family was never complete unless his aunt at the piano had sung 'Bless This House' and thrown in a few hymns for good measure with the 'Old Wooden Cross' being a dirge beloved of her and detested by Hamish and his parents while his uncle sat in his armchair with hands in a pious frame and his head to one side making out that he was entranced.

The only occasion that there was any fun was when his father had plainly gone to sleep. The voice and the music stopped in mid-verse as the awful voice ceased so father opened an eye. The aunt of Hamish promptly accused his father of being asleep and being very rude.

With both eyes fully open, his father told his accuser "I was not asleep dear, I simply closed my eyes in order not to have any distraction from the beauty of your voice!"

His wife nearly suffered apoplexy in a not a completely successful attempt to stifle a laugh. While those visits were purgatory, this visit to Monarch Mansions was beautiful in both music, surroundings, people and experience.

It seemed in no time before the performances came to their conclusion and to much genuine and in the case of Freya and Hamish loving applause, the musicians took their leave via their dressing room.

As the chairs were being returned to their places they met up again with both Joy, Robert, Nelson and Emma. Although Freya had already met Emma, Hamish had not and Nelson did the honours. In those few minutes, Hamish got the impression of a quite young bubbly woman who appeared to make a perfect pair with Nelson. Their two cleaned up children were talking and larking with the two of Joy and Robert.

Freya asked Emma, "Are your two going to school tomorrow?"

"Yes," replied Nelson with a grimace. They will be tired. We couldn't get here for the meal which has made their bedtime later than usual so we're off now. Emma came up and kissed Freya and Hamish and told them that she hoped that the next time they met they would have more time together. A sentiment apparently shared.

As Emma and Nelson did their rounds of 'Goodbyes' so Joy and Robert were doing the same thing.

When they arrived at Freya and Hamish much the same was said as was said to Nelson and Hamish with Joy suggesting to Hamish as she walked away "I'm sure we can broaden our conversation away from the topic of this occasion next time we meet."

"You can be sure of that," he responded.

Many of the guests were leaving and the handshakes and kissing seemed endless, but eventually, just Sarah, Polly, Ian, Daphne and the parents of Polly were left and Freya told Sarah that they would be 'On their way'.

"Oh, I thought that we might have a nightcap before you went home," Sarah told them. As a matter of courtesy, they decided that it would be rude to leave now.

Yet again, the chairs were moved and they all sat down as Givanna and her sister brought various drinks including of all things on such occasions, hot chocolate and slices of the gateaux leftover from dinner, dished out plates and forks. They then pulled up chairs and joined the company.

When everyone had their various drinks Sarah asked Freya and Hamish if they had found the evening to be fun. They agreed that it had been a memorable and very pleasant experience of a different way of life which everyone seemed to enjoy.

"Good, I'm so happy that you have enjoyed it. As should be expected from this lifestyle there should be no demarcation and it should be a pleasure for all whatever or whoever you are."

Hamish asked. "I don't want to appear to be a Methodist or red hot Socialist, but when you talk about no demarcation, do you invite everyday working people to your parties?"

"From dustman to the duke, they all come here and as long as they don't abuse the privilege, like you, they are always welcome," Susan explained.

"Did you put on all of this just for us?" Freya asked.

"No," Sarah replied, "But I did select the people who came this evening to give you a sample of the broad range of the people who are nudists or naturists as many in the movement like to be called nowadays. After the shock of being naked did you eventually feel comfortable in our company?"

"It was a truly wonderful evening," Hamish told her, "but the only thing that did surprise me was the bathroom arrangements with both sexes all together with the unique urinals as well as cubicles and finding that…" Hamish was interrupted by a very nasty coughing fit by Freya as in her moment of pretending agony she reached out and painfully squeezed his thigh stopping him in mid-sentence.

When her 'fit' had moderated, unfortunately for Freya, Sarah asked Hamish to finish what he was saying about the bathroom. With her hand still on his thigh, Freya gave another painful squeeze leaving her fingernail marks on his thigh. Hamish began again telling Sarah, "that it was so good to see how successfully it was so totally inclusive where everyone was free to use their preferred receptacle."

"The next door down is a traditional lavatory," Sarah told them then adding, "if it is too embarrassing to use what I call the 'All-inclusive facilities.'"

By the reaction of Polly, it appeared that the bullet struck home. Sarah said that she was delighted that Hamish appreciated her choice of design and that the idea of all-inclusive toilet arrangements was taken from some that she had used in France and at Sunny Patch.

In France, it was a common drain that could be used by both sexes being astride it. She thought that that part of the inclusive arrangements was not quite the thing for her home or the sensibilities of British naturists.

Much to the relief of Freya the subject was dropped and changed to where and when they were all taking their nude holidays.

Of the few people now there it was quite surprising how many were going to America and the West Indies. Money seemed no barrier to the preferred destinations.

The general conversation followed before Freya looked at her watch and said, "The bewitching hour is long past and after a really lovely evening I do feel that we have overstayed our visit and it is time for us to say goodbye.

There was much protestation that they were leaving too soon and Susan offered them her 'Facilities' to make themselves comfortable before they left.

As they went down the corridor to the lavatory Freya told Hamish, "If no one is in the lavatory I'm going to see if it is possible to use the lower Pansy." They looked behind themselves as they went in. She looked around and no one was in there. "Stand outside the door in case anyone comes," she commanded Hamish.

Having been a policeman for many years he was quite used to keeping a lookout on many occasions for many reasons but this was the first and probably the only time that he would look out in such nervous anticipation of someone coming through the corridor door or for such a purpose.

To Hamish, it seemed an unreasonably long time before Freya emerged to apologise for the extended toilet break. Hamish would have liked to also use the 'Facilities' but the time-lapse before returning might have been embarrassing and Freya instructing him to simply "Tie a knot in it," didn't help his confidence that all would be well until he arrived home.

Fortunately, no one was looking at the door as they entered the sitting room and said their goodbyes involving a kiss from the ladies present with the noticeable exception of Polly who still welded to her chair was generous enough to spare them any further tirades and simply wave her hand as Sarah led them back to their clothes.

"Do you mind if I stay while you get dressed?" Sarah asked them. As courtesy demanded they duly agreed.

Sarah said to them, "When you said that you had enjoyed the evening, was that being polite or was it really the case that you did enjoy it?"

"I can't speak for Hamish," Freya replied, "But for my part, I have really enjoyed the evening These surroundings, the quite wonderful people here, the delicious meal and the excellent entertainment. All in all, a memorable and superb evening that in all truth, I will never forget."

Hamish then said to Sarah, I simply endorse everything Freya has said, it was almost breath-taking and if you'll pardon the very obvious pun, very revealing!" He then told Sarah that "The booking name that you gave at Sunny Patch was the same that I used at the Scolding Wife. It also is one of my many Christian names. How about that for a coincidence?" There was no response to that question but the poor pun did bring peals of laughter from both women.

Sarah said to them, "I must apologise for the inexcusable behaviour of Polly. Were she not my niece, I would not invite her on these evenings but as this family, that's all blood relatives for three generations and their spouses all enjoy the naked lifestyle, without upsetting someone in the family, I can't stop her coming here. Her behaviour does upset my mother but that's the way it is I'm afraid."

"At the risk of upsetting someone very close with a superbright uppercut," Hamish said, "The positive good to come out of Polly's mania over hair was that it drove Joy, such an attractive lady, over to join me for a most pleasant and informative fifteen minutes or so. Thank you, Polly!"

Sure enough, Hamish received a solid thump in the ribs and it wasn't from Sarah!

"May I ask a personal question of both of you," Sarah asked them as in turn, Freya buttoned up her dress and Hamish pulled on his pants, "Of course," replied Freya. "Firstly you've forgotten to put your underclothes on and, I hesitate to say but, after watching you both tonight and how well you have taken to this evening are you a couple by any chance?" Sarah asked.

Freya smiled broadly as she told Sarah, "replying in the order that you asked the questions. I didn't wear any underclothes tonight as I guessed that this might be an occasion when clothes might not be necessary. If that wasn't the case, the fact that I didn't wear a bra would not have noticed as, without boasting, I am blessed with smaller but firm breasts like you.

The second part of your question is a very convoluted one. Since our university days, we have been very close and were taken as a pair there. When I joined the police force we met up again and carried on where we left off. Through separate avenues, we ended up on the same CID course at Kings Weston until I was seconded to the Regional Crime Squad. We have never worked together since.

We used to take holidays together and we always have a day or two together on or near my birthday but the longer holidays have fallen by the wayside. whether we are a 'couple' is a moot point but we do love each other and in all these years, despite now meeting a beautiful woman without clothes. I believe that he has been, as I have been to him, faithful despite many temptations."

Sarah looked at Hamish, "And you?" she asked. He replied, "As my dear under-wear-less friend said, we have a strange life and, please note, separate beds on holiday. That tells you all that is relevant, and by the way, my association with Joy was solely down to the ravings of Polly and that at all times we sat opposite each other and in full view of the lady's husband and about twenty other people. I rest my case."

"I do agree," Sarah said, "Your romance seems to be quite unique in almost every respect and I suspect, although you may not realise it, very deep.

Such love is very precious and not repeated again in either lifetime. Sounding like the old 'Agony Aunt' and not wishing to be morbid, treasure it. None of us knows what might happen in the next instant." Turning to Freya Sarah said,

"Don't worry about Joy, she has a beautiful face, body and mind and generosity in her soul unequalled in anyone else I know. When I again invite you to an evening like this, would you come?"

"He can answer for himself but yes please for me. It has been wonderful but asking a rude question of our hostess, However much did this all cost?" Freya asked Sarah. She replied, "Finding the money is not difficult for me, in fact, it is a pleasure. I have these occasions about every two months. Sometimes it is a film evening when we usually show films the youngest to the oldest can enjoy, musicals, cartoons and so forth.

Other evenings we have nudist films from around the world. I run them through first to make sure that they are suitable for the children to watch other times we have a social evening with a quiz, charades and general dressing up and tomfoolery. Those evenings always go down well. Although we are not a club the people who come here can bring a trusted friend for a trial."

One further question please, Freya asked Sarah, "Where on earth did you get a nude female comedian and naked musicians and even a nude contralto?"

Sarah laughed and replied, "With Frank, I sponsored young musicians and while there were only three youngsters here tonight we invited several along, dressed of course. Even after one recital several of them including the pianist took their clothes off when they came here. And so it has remained.

The singer we recruited on a naturist holiday in the Alps. Every morning we could hear this voice singing away. One morning we got up early and took a look and it was our singer standing on her balcony singing her heart out along with at least two other very much younger women.

We approached her and found out that she originally came from Australia. We invited her to our musical evenings and here she is you saw and heard tonight. Sometimes she brings younger singers, boys and girls. All very nice and tuneful."

"Don't your musicians talk about these nude evenings to everyone?" Hamish asked. Sarah told him "They know which side their bread is buttered on. Oh, no my dear, their lips are sealed about our musical evenings I can assure you.

When I hold expensive evenings such as this one whatever it cost I give the same amount to charity, it assuages my conscience over my extravagance and our pleasures. I don't think that you have said whether you would come here again if invited?" Sarah asked Hamish.

Walking away from Freya he answered, "Yes, I would love to come again." He paused before laughing and saying, "Only if Joy is there as well, naturally." Freya took a swipe at him and missed, so she had another go, missed again and excusing herself to Sarah calling him, "A slimy toad with the morals of an alley cat."

"Relating to Joy and Robert, just to complicate things for you Freya, Robert and Joy have a lodge at Sunny Patch and in the summer they are often there," Sarah cheerfully told Freya then added, "Let's hope that you don't all meet up. But there again, they do not know that you are policemen so if you meet there it should not be a difficulty."

Handing back their flip-flops and cuddling their towels they took their leave of Sarah at the doors to the lift. As they disappeared down the lift shaft

Sarah called down to them, "Mr Fergusson, ten am to see Sir Simon please. Don't be late."

Sat in the Bristol en route to the home of Hamish, not a word was said until they arrived. "Do you have the odd chair I could use for a nap until dawn?" Freya asked him.

"Of course," he replied, "Come on in."

When in the house he asked her, "Cup of something or a snorter?"

"Tea please," she replied. While Hamish was presumed to be in the kitchen she tip-toed up the stairs went to the bedroom and picked up the duvet and then heard the flush go in the downstairs lavatory and waited until she heard him go into the kitchen then shot into the living room, whipped off her frock and cuddled up under the duvet in the big reclining armchair just as he returned not only with her tea but biscuits as well.

Seeing her comfortably ensconced in his chair he asked sarcastically, "Comfortable?"

"Please put the tea on the table and tell me honestly what you thought of last evening?" Freya asked. He did not immediately reply as he went and took tonic water from a cabinet, slowly opening it plainly giving him time to gather his thoughts before answering after being urged by Freya to "Take all day with your valued response.

I would like to have an answer before we are at work in under five hours!" When he eventually did reply he said. "For a chap with my background the occasion, where it was, the mixture of people, the meal and the entertainment was such an alien experience that the truth of the matter is that it was presumably similar to what is described as an 'out of body' experience. What about you?"

"Other than the childish antics of that stupid Polly, for me, it was like watching a film of make-believe and then coming back to earth with a wonderful experience amongst unique people at ease with themselves and others.

Like you, the venue, people, meal and entertainment was a wonderful package of a different way of life where no one made judgements over clothes, occupations or seemingly age and shape. The other things that impressed me were the children and young people mixing happily with the adults. A wonderful evening just for us to become acclimatised to naked people. It was all wonderful dearest and you did not embarrass yourself, even in front of Joy. Congratulations on your willpower. Now let's sleep."

"I never, in my wildest dreams thought that you would be jealous of me talking to another woman, that's quite flattering, thank you," he told Freya.

She replied, "I'm only kidding, who would fancy a bad-tempered, irritable misery such as you, my dearest. Your distinguished jawline, head of hair, imposing height and flat iron stomach don't appear to outweigh your irritating character flaws, dear heart." Then adopting a familiar west country accent she told him as he laid down on the couch. "I love yer ter bits an' no over woman shall 'av ' eee, see me lover!"

The summer sunshine on her face brought the slumber of Freya to an end. On the couch, Hamish was still in the land of nod as she looked at her watch to see that it was a quarter to seven. She got up and went to the kitchen and putting the kettle to boil she turned to see Hamish busy stretching. "Who's going to shower first?" she enquired. "You. I'm sorry that I can't supply you with a flower urinal dear. You will have to use the common lavatory." Hamish replied. "You go and I'll make the tea," he told her.

Eventually, they had a light breakfast and with no lipstick or clothes except her dress to put on Freya was ready to go to work long before Hamish who insisted on clearing up before he left the house.

As he went past his study he grabbed a sheet of writing paper and envelope before locking up.

When he went to get into Freya's Bristol she asked why he wasn't going in his own car. "Because I'm collecting a surveillance car from the pool to use at Sunny Patch as the registration plate can only be traced to the anonymous name of the clerk to the Watch Committee."

"Smart blighter," Freya commended him, then continued. "If I had not stopped over what would you have done with your car?"

"Left it here and caught a bus," he told her.

As they drove off he noted that from the direction that Freya was taking they were not going visa her home.

"Not going to your place?" Hamish asked her. "No," she replied, "I can manage without mascara and lipstick today."

"What about your clothes?" he asked. She replied, "This frock will do. It's not worth going home just to change that," she told him. "But you've got nothing on under it." A very surprised Hamish reminded her. "Unless it gets cold or some sexy chap meets up with me, no one will notice dear. Don't worry. If you had not watched me undress yesterday you wouldn't be any the wiser," she quite reasonably suggested. The rest of the journey was taken in silence.

When they arrived at the station Freya made her way to the original CID office while Hamish went to see Prudow and pick up his surveillance car. The usual performance took place between the two as Prudow was as obstructive as usual and Staff Sergeant Fergusson ensured that Yard Manager Prudow was put in his place, that being, amongst the hierarchy of the division, only second rung above the car washers and polishers.

After the staff sergeant had supervised the refuelling of the dark grey BMW, he took it to the staff car park and made his way into the station. "Mornin 'Staff," echoed around the control room and foyer as he made his way into his office, noting on the way that his name and rank had been taken off the door.

Inside he found his replacement inspector with his nose down in stacks of roster papers. The inspector said, "God, I'm pleased to see you 'Staff', I'm in a right bloody mess with these." Indicating the pile of unfinished rosters. "It's this annual leave," the inspector explained then continued. "Your instructions were to give the school-age children's parents the choice of August and all others in June or September. How do I know which is which?"

With an exasperated expression, Staff Sergeant Fergusson, in a tone of voice that would be used towards a child said. "I have already told you the simple way but plainly you have forgotten. Listen carefully. Find the Christmas present list from last year's party for the children. Jake will have it in the office. All the ages of the children up to sixteen and their father or mothers name and rank will be on there as well.

"Check that the parents are still in this Division and put out a 'Billy-do' inviting them to put down their preferred holiday weeks in August. You then play around with their duties and fill in where they are absent with those not dependent on the timing of school holidays. Understood?" The inspector nodded his acquiescence. Hamish then claimed part of his desk to write a 'Thank you' note to Sarah for her hospitality the previous evening.

The 'phone rang and the inspector picked it up announcing his name and rank then handed the receiver to Mr Fergusson. 'Staff Sergeant Fergusson here'. The caller was Miss Sarah Dodds-Younger to remind him that he had an appointment with Chief Superintendent Bates at 10:00 a.m. Sarah did not actually say those words. She said, "Good morning, staff sergeant, 'Sir the silent one' wishes to see you at 10:00 a.m. Ring my office bell at about five to ten and wait in my office. Bye!"

In the CID office, Freya met up with Detective Inspector Ronald Wilkins and enquired how things were going with him taking over her job as head of 'D' Division CID and managing the still-open case of the two murders. She then enquired about the stills from the microfilms, and had they been delivered? His reply went along the lines of, "I only put them in yesterday so I'm not expecting them back for a day or so."

She then went through the office logbook with Ron identifying all the outstanding cases, who was the officer in charge of each case and at what stage of the investigation was each of the cases.

When they had gone through the bookmarking each stage of every current inquiry on a scale of one to five Ron asked Freya, "When you leave us where am I going with your murder case? Is it simply sit and wait for information to come to me or can I be proactive?"

"I would like to say be proactive," she told him then added, "Unless the diaries that Miss Dodds Younger are transcribing bring anything to light and nothing more positive comes in from the continent I'm afraid Ron that the case remains open for a few more months and then you will do a review and take it from there."

"Are you not coming back?" He enquired. She told him "I was only sent here to take over from Harry Broadweir who would take over running central until the suspended sticky-fingered ' Dicks' are dismissed, jailed or returned to duty. The sticky-fingered ones are now in court, Harry will not be coming back, I'm going back to normal central to work under Harry until he retires. In answer to your question, No, Ron, I will no longer run this department but I will always be available for these murders if you want me."

At five to ten Hamish rang the bell outside the chief's door, no lights came on but Sarah opened the door and took him into her office. They sat down and he handed her the envelope before enquiring what 'Sir the silent one' wanted him for? "I am by nature and my present occupation the soul of a confidential secretary. "The first part of your inferred question is yes and the obvious follow-up question is 'No'.

With that, a light on her desk shone brightly and Sarah rose to her feet and escorted him into the office of Chief Superintendent Bates. Sitting at the side of his desk was the Assistant Chief Constable and commander of the Force CID Chief Superintendent Gaunt.

"Thank you, Miss Dodds Younger, Sir," told Sarah as she quietly closed the door. "Good morning, Staff Sergeant Fergusson. I believe that you know the assistant chief constable." Mr Gaunt then bade Hamish 'Good Morning'.

There was a long pause before Mr Bates said, "As you may well know, in fact, you do know, that you are the only staff sergeant in this police force. You are the only one left standing and I am the crutch that props up your rank.

I know very well that you can be the soul of kindness, courtesy and help to those below you. I am also aware that you a quick-tempered, prickly, sure of your own invincibility and, on occasions, a conceited character as epitomised by those resignation slips that you and only you, used when you were a tour sergeant. I am now going to tell you something that you will not like.

I do not and will not tolerate any insubordination or sullen temper when I tell you your professional fate. After I tell you, you can go to my secretary's office and consider what I have told you before returning here. Understood?"

"Sir," was the one-word reply from Staff Sergeant Fergusson.

"Your rank will be abolished when you return from your 'Jolly' in the countryside," Mr Bates, with a very stern expression on his face explained and then went on to tell Hamish.

"As a kind gesture on the part of Mr Gaunt and me, we are giving you a choice for you to consider what I have told you before; you have your tantrum and then return to us with your answer and resignation is not an option."

"Sir," was again the acknowledgement from Hamish.

"You are an asset to this Force…" Mr Bates began before the staff sergeant interrupted by saying "Even with my litany of faults Sir?"

"Bite the tigers tail Fergusson and you will surely get eaten. You might bend Mr Cole into a figure of eight knots, but think again when you are insubordinate to me. I have warned you a few seconds ago. You will not be warned again. I expected better than that from a man who has gone through Britannia and held rank in the merchant fleet."

"I do apologise, Sir; it was most remiss of me," a well-reprimanded staff sergeant told his commander.

Ignoring the apology Mr Bates continued "As of tomorrow your present rank will not exist. You can revert to a tour sergeant maintaining your present pay scale or as you are suitably qualified, I will promote you to the rank of inspector as of tomorrow. Now go into the office and think through what I have said and remember, resignation is not an option. If you are so minded, do not think that you will get a glowing reference. Any reference will only state that you joined on a given date and resigned on a given date and that your conduct was satisfactory. That should get you a job as a security guard – if you are fortunate, Fergusson."

"You are dismissed until I call you back for your decision." Chief Superintendent Bates instructed his staff sergeant.

As Hamish closed the door and went to the office to mull over his future as a policeman, in the chief superintendent's office Bill Gaunt asked Simon Bates. "What were his Billy-doos?"

Fiddling in his office desk, the chief superintendent produced an A5-sized paper. It read;

> COMPLETE DETAILS AS INDICATED
> NAME……………………………………………………
> RANK & NUMBER……………………………………………
> I wish to resign from AVALONSHIRE CONSTABULARY
> AS OF…………………………………………………………
> (TIME DAY AND DATE)
> I HAVE SURRENDERED MY WARRANT CARD AND
> OTHER ITEMS OF OFFICE TO SERGEANT FERGUSSON.
> SIGNED……………………………………………………
> THE ABOVE SIGNATORY HAS SURRENDERED TO ME
> HIS WARRANT CARD, STAFF, RESTRAINTS and HELMET.
> SIGNED………………………………………… DATE…………
> Hamish J.W.F. Ciaran-Fergusson. Sergeant. D63

"What is this all about?" Mr Gaunt enquired.

"Whenever Sergeant Fergusson had a constable who had committed misdemeanour's or failed to be to the standard that Fergusson required, he would get a choice, sign this and go without further enquiries or be reported to a higher authority, eventually ending up on my or the desks of the other chiefs that Fergusson served under before coming here as my staff sergeant. Fergusson never stepped over the mark with these chits and it filtered out the simple-minded, saved lots of paperwork, time and 'Appeals' before they would have eventually become rogues in uniform and an embarrassing disgrace to the Force." Simon Bates explained.

"Why did you and others put up with this usurping of your authority by a damned tour sergeant?"

Mr Gaunt asked. "He's reliable, knows his job inside and out and above all he's loyal." Mr Bates replied, and then added, "and he keeps Superintendent Cole on his toes and on some occasions curbs the outbursts of Cole. Poor Cole has never got the better of Fergusson and he won't after today. Yet control of Cole is another reason for Fergusson to stay here as an inspector. Speak as I find, I'll be sorry to see him go but you'll find him an asset at headquarters if he will go."

Mr Gaunt looked pensive as he spoke of his concerns after what he had heard about Fergusson from Simon Bates and the insubordination of his staff sergeant to his chief superintendent. "I'm not sure that I want him now Simon," he told his colleague.

"If you had Fergusson with you at the start of the 'Sticky Finger' or thieving detectives mob he would have got rid of them without our Force being held up to ridicule when these men of yours get to court." Mr Bates told him then asked, "Do you want Freya in now?"

"Yup, partner," Mr Gaunt replied in a mock American accent.

As the staff sergeant walked into Sarah's office he saw Freya sitting there. "What are you doing here?" he asked her. "Don't really know she told him. "Sarah came looking for me as Bill Gaunt is in there with 'Sir, the silent one' and they want to see me. Probably for roasting because I'm not getting anywhere with this murder case. What are you in there for?" she asked him. "For a character assassination and to tell me that one way or other I will be leaving here after our holiday." The bell rang and Sarah took Freya into the office of Mr Bates.

When Sarah came back she just began to speak when her foyer bell rang and when the door was opened it was Mrs Briggs with her tea trolley and six dainty cups and coffee cups on a silver salver, no doubt inscribed, with noble sentiments from some distinguished worthy or other but simply on the underside bearing the legend. 'D' Division officers mess, Keep your 'B' hands-off.

With Mrs Briggs fussing around with tea for Freya and Sarah and coffee for the chiefs office and "Coffee fer you, Mr Fergusson?" the dear lady asked.

Eventually, Freya returned with her cup of tea still in her hand. "What happened?" Hamish enquired and before she could answer, asked her "Still in a job?"

She just began to answer when the bell rang and Sarah escorted Hamish into the 'lion's den'.

"Sit down," he was commanded by Mr Gaunt.

"I have been told by Chief Superintendent Bates of your, what one might call, unorthodox methods of dealing with disciplinary matters amongst your men," ACC, Gaunt told him. He continued, "If I have you in my part of the Force your 'Billy-doos' will not happen. Do I make myself clear?" A mystified Staff Sergeant Fergusson simply replied "Sir."

"You will follow my instructions to the letter and be directly answerable to my deputy." the ACC told him, "Do you understand?" he emphasised the word "You."

There was a short pause for the staff sergeant to give the usual 'Sir' as having understood the instruction. Such a 'Sir' did not sound as a sir should do. Instead a question.

"With respect sir, and I do mean respect, what in the hell are you on about?" Hamish asked Assistant Chief Constable William Gaunt, CBE QPM.

"Chief Superintendent Bates has told me that you are very good at your job as a staff sergeant. I have been testing the water with you Fergusson." Mr Gaunt told him then went on to say. "Amongst the things that I have heard about you is that you seem to have a very independent turn of mind and conduct, useful as a staff sergeant no doubt but does not mark you out as a team player and I understand your independents was the cause of you deciding to leave a promising CID career.

I also have been told that you can be what I call 'Uppity' with your superiors. I understand that such conduct may be because of your former maritime career. In my top team, this will not occur. Yet again staff sergeant, do you clearly understand me?"

Hamish responded with the observation, "No, sir, I don't completely understand you. If my likely conduct is such a difficulty for you, why are we having this conversation? You talk of your 'Top team'.

I am a staff sergeant and hardly ever likely to be in your 'Top team'. Plainly my methods of managing and if necessary disciplining my men are not to your liking. Again, why are we having this conversation sir?"

"We are having this conversation to enable me to decide that if I took you on to my team as a detective inspector, you would be able to carry out the unpopular task with your colleagues of being my 'Witch Finder General'. As my staff officer for personnel management within the criminal investigation and special branch department of this police force." Mr Gaunt explained.

"Would you take such a post, a new post, if I offered it to you?" Mr Gaunt enquired.

"I must have missed the 'Situations vacant' advert in the Police Gazette for this position sir as I know that such a prestigious post would have to be advertised to comply with regulations." Hamish declared with his tongue in his cheek.

"In one way I admire your chancing your arm by telling me that I do not follow the rules," Mr Gaunt warned him. "If I did follow the 'Advertisement of senior posts' directive you would not be offered a prestigious position and from a personal point of view, if you 'Cut the mustard' I will not be buggered about by no hoper's applying for a job that I alone know the terms of reference. I'm offering you the job for all your manifold faults.

You have been recommended by your chief superintendent and Detective Chief Inspector Miss Douglas Gore Hamilton. Although I can't remember you there, she assures me that you were with her at Kings Weston when I was the detective inspector.

Whilst on that subject I would make the observation that the 'Harvesting' of personal records seems prevalent in your case as your headquarters file appears only to hold the bare minimum of information about you, and here in 'D' Division the same wilful destruction of your files apparently applies. In both cases other than a class photograph at Kings Weston nothing is known about you there where the detective chief inspector claims you were third in your class. Do you want this job or not?"

"Thank you, sir; I accept the post even without knowing your terms of reference which no doubt will be presented to me in due course." The Staff Sergeant, for the rest of the day, Fergusson told his new boss.

With words that were a balm to the independent soul of Hamish, Mr Gaunt told him. "I make the terms of reference as circumstances dictate and you have the enlightening task of ensuring my decisions are carried out promptly, efficiently and with the minimum of attributable evidence left lying around. When you have flushed out the murderer of your man in the locks you will be based in my office at HQ."

"Sir," Hamish acknowledged his instructions.

"Enjoy your holiday at our expense. Dismiss," was the parting words of the ACC.

Going into Sarah's office Hamish told her that he had just accepted a job where he didn't know what he was supposed to do with an immediate superior that he had never met with a new boss who was not apparently enamoured by the nature of his character.

"You are going to HQ to make sure that there are no more incidents of 'Sticky fingers' among the more senior officers of CID and nip any repeats of recent events in Central CID in the bud," Sarah told him. "Good luck, and have a nice holiday. I will meet you at 10 o'clock at the 'Scolding Wife' car park on Monday. We will work out daily meetings where and when you want them, Bye."

Hamish went towards the CID office. As he went past the general office so a large figure appeared before him. "Told you not to get your arse too comfortable in your chair. Vacating it today, sir?" asked Jake. "Is there anything that you don't know blabbermouth?" Hamish asked him.

"Yes," came the reply from Jake followed by, "what are you and miss triple barrelled name up to? "For me to know and you to find out." Hamish told him and then added, "By the time you find out we shall be long gone, constable. Ta-Ta!"

When he got along to Freya's office she was with Ron Wilkins in deep discussion. She looked up to see Hamish and told him, "I'm very busy, meet me at lunchtime."

"I'll be in the 'Ploughman's over the road," he told her.

Back in his now-former office Hamish rang the force tailor, Humphrey, and said that he would be sending back his tunic for cleaning and the removal of the sergeant's stripes and crown and the fitting of two pips on the shoulders. Humphrey snorted down the 'phone and said. "It's never worth the effort.

"If you are still the same size, I will simply supply you with an inspector's ready-made tunic. You will have to send your sergeants tunic back to me to balance the books. No particular rush," Hamish told him, adding, "I will be in plainclothes for a while until I expect they'll send me back to Division sometime and it could be sometime soon!"

"Leave it with me 'Staff' the tailor said before adding, "I'll bet Old King Cole will be glad to see the back of you, his arse and ankles won't have quite so many bite marks on 'em." Hamish laughingly replied, "And a lot more will be glad to see the back of me I expect."

"Don't worry 'Staff', I hear that those upstairs think you've got a halo, polish it, chum. No one else will." Humphrey assured him.

Before lunchtime, he went over to the pub opposite the station, found a table got some drinks and waited for Freya. Eventually, she came in; they ordered a pasty in the forlorn hope that there might just be a smidgen of meat inside.

What happened to you?" he asked her. "I'm seconded to the Home Office with the rank of Acting Detective Superintendent advising on matters concerning the employment of and the advancement of women in Police Forces when this present investigation is completed or shelved.

What about you?" She asked him. Hamish looked at her for a while before telling her, "Go it girl, you've done well for yourself, congratulations. My rank as staff sergeant is abolished as of tomorrow and my choice was to return to Tour sergeant without loss of pay or go up to inspector. By implication as a shift working inspector. My face probably gave them an indication of my thoughts on that prospect.

Then the Inquisition changed tack. After they pulled my character to pieces and then beat about the bushes, this was your chum, Gaunt. By the way, he finally gave the impression that I am to be his staff officer bag carrier in chief with specific responsibility for the administration of the various Divisional units of CID and their conduct and avoid trouble before they get themselves nicked.

In a roundabout way, he suggested that I was just the man for the job because I am a loner and am indifferent to the opinion of people about me. Although I didn't say so, I felt like telling him that he is quite right about my character and I don't give a bugger about his opinion of me anyway."

Nothing was said as they ate their almost meat-free pasties when Freya asked, "What rank are they giving you for that job? It's normally rated as a detective chief inspector, well done you."

"I simply want to be a common staff sergeant."

"I have never wished to become a 'White shirt'. Apart from 'Sir the silent one' and old Thomas, I've got no small measure of contempt for the whole bloody lot of them at 'D' Division and of course they know that.

Hence the character that Gaunt thinks would be useful in keeping would-be sticky fingers firmly in their own pockets instead of the pockets of somebody else. Oh, and by the way, I am just humble, Detective Inspector 'Billy No Friends' Fergusson."

"My dearest darling," Freya said to him. "The only reason that you may not be liked has a long history beginning with you having left a successful career at sea, then having a 'First' at Oxford and not joining the boozer led culture of CID.

Although, even after all these years, what, for all your achievements you have never realised is that it is not a pure dislike for you, it is simply a case of uncomplicated plain envy. You've had a life at sea which most would sacrifice their mothers for. You've had an education most could never aspire to." She leaned across the table and gently laid her hand on his cheek and said, "Not silly Billy no friends but simply you are a silly Billy."

Hamish took time to digest the fact that Freya thought of him as a 'Silly Billy' and couldn't disagree with her. A bitter pill to swallow.

"Where are you going to stay in London?" he asked her. In daddy's apartment. It's only two streets from the home office," Freya replied.

They were still 'chewing the Fat' when a decidedly black look came across the bar from the landlord. They realised that their drinks were finished and only the crumbs of the pasties remained. As they were deciding to get up so the landlord arrived at their table and said, "If I had to rely on your spending I would go bust Sarg. Another drink?"

By now they were both on their feet and 'Mine Host' simply said, "See what I mean, one drink bleeding wonders. Cheerio Sarg, see you at Christmas!"

"This Alfie is goodbye, I won't be back," Hamish told him. "Moving on or is this an economy drive?" The landlord asked as they pushed through the throng towards the door.

"Both," was the reply from Freya. "I can see who wears the pants with you two," was the final word as they emerged from the smoky crush onto them just as polluted pavement.

"Talking of pants reminds me that if I whistled that frock of yours would walk towards me. You've been wearing it for sixteen hours. It must pong by now," Hamish gallantly told her then added, "When you walked into the pub the sun shone through that frock and for a second or so it looked as if you had nothing on underneath."

Dodging the traffic as they crossed the road Freya told him "I haven't; if you could see 'Everything' it's lucky there's no 6 o'clock shadow to embarrass me." As they entered the station he did not acknowledge her words so she assumed that probably the traffic had taken her words into the ether.

Chapter 9
Holiday Au Naturel

In the station, they went along to Freya's office where she asked him when he was leaving." He told her, "I'm having a chat with you, then see 'Sir, the silent one', go to central with my tunic for Humph and until I pick you up on Saturday at about one for our first holiday in at least three years and perhaps longer, I shall be at home."

"Are you not coming in tomorrow?" Freya asked. "Not bloody likely," Hamish, with pleasure, told her. "My time here is over." They've had enough of me and I of them. After Bates, it's farewell until return to HQ whenever our holiday ends. While on the subject of holidays. We always had holidays together ever since our days at Oxford In the last few years we only got together for a couple of days at Dartmouth on your birthday. Why?"

"It could be that our career paths have diverged or perhaps something happened to us, you never asked me about holidays and I didn't push the idea for whatever reason. Equally, I never asked you, but why not?" Freya asked him. "Like you, I never asked you because you never mentioned it," he told her.

She looked into his face for a while before telling him, "I Rarely swear, it's so common but, what utter bloody fools we have been all this time. Even at my birthdays, neither of us mentioned holidays because we were frightened of being rebuffed. What utter, utter tits we are Hamish Fergusson.

When you came to my church on Easter Day, I didn't need to say anything. It might have ruined the wonderful occasion. Although I have always loved you on that beautiful morning I like to think that the Lord sent you to confirm my love for you and it might sound soppy but it knew no bounds.

It is only with us working in the same building these last few weeks that has reinforced my love for you. I don't want anything to separate us again, not even you down here and me in London."

"You have just enunciated my thoughts and feelings for you," Hamish told her. "Yes, I am a bloody fool but I think that your rapid climb through the ranks plus your very distinguished background and my reticence to display any emotion has not helped my case. After we celebrate your birthday this Autumn we will plan our holiday next year and other matters, to quote 'Agony Aunt' matters of the heart. Agreed."

"Agreed," Freya told him then brought the two of them down to earth with a list of items to take to Sunny Patch. "No food?" Hamish enquired.

"It clearly stated in their brochure that they have a restaurant there, did you not read it?" Freya asked him. "Washing powder?" he asked.

"We will have a bit of washing to do, even if it's only a sweat rag or two," she told him. "Make sure that we have the normal toiletries, sun crème, etc. They supply the bedding and towels so don't bother with that but bring tea, coffee, booze and soap and our trade tools and most importantly the ordinary camera and the covert one.

Oh, and bring a travelling rug and a jumper in case it gets cold in the evenings. Anything else I think of, I'll ' phone you."

Hamish then left her to mull over what they had just talked about when she was brought back to earth by Ron knocking at her door. 'Work still to be done', she thought as she invited him in.

As he walked along the corridor from Freya's office Hamish passed the door of Superintendent Cole's office. "Staff sergeant, a minute of your time," boomed out of his office door.

Hamish knocked on the door, "You want me sir?" he asked.

"Yes, sit down," Cole ordered.

"You and I do not always agree. In fact, you are a bloody menace to me and often have the upper hand and I suspect, in fact I know that you hate the ground that I walk on. The one concession that I do make to you is that other than the chief and Tommo, you have my respect for running your men and your office exactly the same as me.

I wish you well in dealing with those CID bastards, Bill Gaunt and Miss Hamilton excepted of course. You will have your hands full of make-believe characters who watch and ape too many television detectives.

Kick their arse hard and particularly those Special Branch twigs, I detest those failed detectives, Mr Fergusson.

Anyhow, I've had my say. Good luck inspector. With that, Mr Cole bent down opened the bottom drawer of his desk and presented a bottle of 85%

proof Navy Rum to Hamish. "I've been told that this is your tipple, enjoy it from Superintendent Thomas and me."

The very surprised Hamish then said to Superintendent Cole. "Considering our past sir it is very magnanimous of you to settle our differences and for both of you to give me this bottle and rest assured sir that the contents of this bottle will wipe my memory as clean as a whistle.

Tommo was sat in his usual chair puffing happily on his pipe as Hamish held out his hand to him. Mr Thomas got to his feet and shook hands with Hamish saying "I'm genuinely sorry to see you go. I like to think that we have had a very harmonious relationship and that between us we have kept 'Old King Cole' here from the worst of excesses.

Bye-the-way, we didn't get that bottle duty free off of a ship down in the dock." Hamish replied, "The feelings are truly reciprocated sir, and thank you for keeping the lid on things over the years and your unqualified support. Turning to Mr Cole he shook his hand and walked towards the foyer and the office of 'sir the silent one'.

En route he was waylaid by constable Jake, still sucking his teeth. "Well done, sir," he told Hamish and then asked, "As you're leaving you can tell me what it is that you have over Old King Cole."

"Jake, with Mr Bates, I am the only person in uniform here that you have nothing untoward on. You have been digging over my background for years and found damn all to hold over me. I was a mariner Jake, and Pongo's such as you couldn't and never can screw us down. Accept that on this occasion you have been well and truly stuffed. I have nothing over Mr Cole. Goodbye, Mr Richards," Hamish told him and turned away.

Hamish rang the bell of Sarah's office and asked if he could see the 'Silent one'. No sooner asked for than delivered. Sarah's ushered him into the presence of Chief Superintendent Simon Bates. He stood up and ushered Hamish into his sitting room, indicating the armchairs to be seated in.

"I presume that this meeting is to be your farewell to the 'D' Division," Mr Bates said to Hamish.

"Yes, sir, it is and to thank you for all the help, overtly and covertly, that you have given me since I came here. I did appreciate that support on all occasions. I am leaving this afternoon to prepare tomorrow for Saturday.

"Ah, yes, Saturday," Mr Bates mused for a moment. He then continued; "I know that you are all in favour of a full-frontal, the pun was quite deliberate, search of the lodge and be done with it. As by now you will have gathered, with the assistant chief constable, I believe that a covert approach is likely to get positive results and lead us to the murderer. As you are now well aware, all that we have achieved in the investigation of a crime is bodies, suicides which benefit only the so-called security services. Certainly, not us!

I appreciate that you have not been involved in the case up until now and this part of the investigation involves you for the benefit of your friend, Detective Chief Inspector Miss Douglas Gore Hamilton, but with the nature of your character, I have every faith that the two of you will bring back the murderer or the conclusive evidence to catch one or more.

"Thank you for the excellent fashion that you have performed your duties here and for being a perfect foil for Mr Cole.

Perhaps you will join me in a pre-lunch snorter?" Mr Bates asked Hamish.

Not waiting for a reply the chief superintendent pressed his bell, and by magic, Sarah appeared with two glasses of whisky with one glass of rum and what appeared to be three glasses of gin or vodka.

"Please join us Miss Dodds-Younger." And then turning to Hamish, Mr Bates offered him a choice of libation. "Take whisky or the rum whichever you choose. As a refugee from the Highlands, I thought perhaps you might prefer whisky, as a former mariner I thought you could like the rum, or perhaps wardroom gin? Have all three if you wish but if you do get Prudow to arrange for a lift home. They can deliver your car later.

"Thank you, sir; I'll have the rum," Hamish replied.

"Ye Gods, it was offered as a joke," Mr Bates said, "you'd be thrown out of either of the navies that you served in for drinking that lower deck grog. Please join us Miss Dodds-Younger in a toast to the future success of Inspector Fergusson in his career, his adventure and for his sake wish for excellent weather for the duration of his quite unique holiday at our expense!"

As Hamish was about to leave his chief asked him, "Whatever made a person with your background become, of all things a policeman?"

"I might ask exactly the same question of you, sir?"

Hamish said. "I saw a very limited future where I was," Chief Superintendent Bates explained, "so I became a policeman as a little sinecure with a good pension at the end of it."

"I too, sir," Hamish told his chief superintendent adding. "It is quite remarkable how we have much the same passage of careers for much the same reasons."

"With our paths being so similar, except for my service in the terrible war at sea, I am sure that you will inherit my rank in due course. Goodbye, Inspector Fergusson. We will meet again at Head Quarters, 'till then." A shake of the hand and Mr Bates was back in his office and as later was found, with the door not completely closed.

"I will see you at ten on at the pub." Sarah told Hamish, gave him a peck on the cheek as the voice of 'Sir the less than silent one' told Sarah, "Your duties do not extend to kissing my inspectors."

With a nod and a smile, Hamish was out in the foyer.

He then went to his former office, collected his tunic and other bits and pieces walked up to Freya and told her of the drinks with the chief superintendent and the gift from Old King Cole. She looked surprised at the news and really pushed her luck with Hamish when she told him, "They must be glad to see the back of you dear."

He half-turned from her straightening his spine, lifting his leg behind him bending it from the knee and raising his head sharply turning it away from Freya and telling her in a feminine sounding voice "Sometimes ducky we can go off people you know."

With that, he happily went to the foyer acknowledging the control room sergeant who waved him goodbye as Hamish walked down the steps into a new branch of the career tree, a tree that only the day before he had no intention of climbing again.

While Hamish yawned, stretched and scratched in his very comfortable bed, Freya was collecting a large bunch of flowers before going to work with the new Detective Chief Inspector Ronald Wilkins and handing over the last records of the elusive evidence of the unsolved murders.

There was a knock on the door and Sarah was there with the final transcripts of the diaries from Woodbine Cottage. "He agreed with the plan for him to be abducted to Russia then decided to back out and he plainly had time to write the final piece in the diary and hide them before he ended up in a van at the docks," Sarah told them and then said, "Sorry that there is nothing positive for you."

"We can't make up evidence." Freya told her "But thank you for all this extra work."

"Mr Bates wants to see you whenever you are free," Sarah told her adding," Don't leave it until late this afternoon it is Friday, Poets day and all that."

"Poets day?" Freya enquired. Taking Freya's arm she led her out of her office and out of the earshot of Ron.

"Piss off early, tomorrow's Saturday," Sarah whispered, then giving Freya a squeeze on the arm she was off down the corridor to her sanctuary while Freya, with raised eyebrows, stood watching her disappear.

When Freya returned to her office Ron told her that he was now at a dead-end unless Mr Gaunt allowed him to make more enquiries to find out where Kurt Rosenberg lived other than at Woodbine Cottage where he only appeared to be an occasional visitor or perhaps lodger. Freya suggested that as Mr Gaunt seemed not to want any further enquiries unless some positive information came their way it might be better for a quiet life to concentrate on the other 'Run of the mill' cases in progress now.

"Are you going back to Central?" Ron asked her. "No, Ron, I'm seconded to the Home Office," she told him. "Getting into Spook land?" Ron, with a tone of disdain in his voice, asked her. "Not that I know of Ron," she replied. "I have no intention of turning out like that man Cox, the chap we met at that meeting with all the branches of spook world," she explained and continued, "I will be dealing with policing matters."

"Well, Ron, we have only known each other for a few weeks but you have been a wonderful support to me and I thank you so much and as a parting gift, other than an unsolved murder, you no longer have to call me, ma'am.

For a week or so we are now of equal rank." Freya told him. "What rank are you getting?" Ron, with a worried frown, asked her. "At the Home Office my grade would be nothing less than a superintendent," she explained to her former deputy, then adding "To compromise while there I will be an acting superintendent and then presumably reverting to DCI when I return to Central or elsewhere."

Looking at the flowers in her office, he said, "This is so kind of you to give me such a beautiful bunch of flowers as a token of your esteem for this unworthy and unworldly simple man." Freya replied. "Are your fingers worth a bunch of flowers? Because if you dare lay a finger on those flowers I will have no hesitation in cutting them off, all eight of 'em."

Promptly at two Freya rang the office bell to Sarah. She was then ushered into the office of Chief Superintendent Stephen Bates. As with Hamish the day before, he led her into his sitting room and directed her towards the armchair.

While she arranged her dress as she sat down, Mr Bates thanked her for coming to see him and then told her that while he did not wish to lecture

'Young Ladies' about the clothes that they wore when on CID duties, but he gently told Freya, "In your case, I thought that I might suggest that in future you do not arrive at work without what appeared to be a lack of underclothes under your very flimsy dress, particularly for an interview with your very senior officers. Enough said on that subject I think. No apologies, no protests and no explanations. You agree?"

"Yes, sir," Freya said then continued "It is so difficult not to apologise but…" Mr Bates cut her short with, "I have said that the matter is closed. It is."

"You have only been here a short time but quite naturally I have been monitoring your work and in so doing, your department and your use of the available resources. You came here with the endorsement of Mr Gaunt, and I believe that his faith in you is justified.

I apologise that we are sending you to the nudist camp, but with Mr Gaunt, I believe that there may be a clue to the identity of the murderer that can only be found by covert means. If we barge in as your Mr Fergusson would like, it would cause an upset and lose us the goodwill and vital gossip such a secretive place might reveal to the benefit of your investigation.

I am pleased and congratulate you on your promotion and secondment to the Home Office. I don't want to alarm you but I was sent there much the same as you and I found it very frustrating and soul-destroying.

Nothing ever appears to be done, no one could care less about anything but their Civil Service grades, pension, how little they can do, avoiding blame and how soon they can retire without any responsibility for adverse matters published in the daily newspapers. All told, a very rum lot."

"However," Mr Bates told her, "London life can be very pleasant and the most arduous task will be writing up a very detailed report on whatever that you are there to analyse in the certain knowledge that the report will be filed unread and soon forgotten.

Should anyone enquire about the filed report some spokesman or woman will tell whoever that 'the matter is of the utmost importance and they are employing every avenue to bring the matters to light and the minister will have it on his desk as soon as possible for the attention of the prime minister'.

All a load of blarney of course. The answer to all this as far as you are concerned and the purpose of me giving you this litany of disaster is to prepare you mentally in order that you will not feel the same frustration that I felt. To be forewarned is to be forearmed. Mr Gaunt asked me to give you this depressing picture as after he put you forward for this secondment he felt a twinge of guilt.

To be fair to him, he put you forward simply to push you further up the ladder.

A person like you could easily become the first woman chief constable with a push from Bill Gaunt."

"Thank you, sir, for your warning," she told Mr Bates and against his expressed wishes she told him "I simply have to apologise for my apparel yesterday it was my laziness that let me down."

"What let you down," Mr Bates told her, "was not necessarily your laziness but others of your sex not pointing out the shortcomings of the material from which your dress was made. I have made my concerns known to Miss Dodds – Younger, this incident is not to her credit either.

Oh, and yes. I understand that you enjoyed her hospitality on Wednesday. As he stood up he told Freya "She is a most generous hostess to so many quite unique people don't you think?"

"Sir," was her response as he showed her to the door and said, "Good luck for tomorrow." With a shy smile, he added, "Your dress will be quite suitable there, if not in fact, positively overdressed!"

As Freya was walking back to her office she passed the open door of Superintendent Cole's 'mincing machine' otherwise known as an office and could see the crossed ankles and immaculate shoes of Mr Thomas. She knocked on the door and went into the office. As she entered Tommo got to his feet held out his hand. They shook hands and Freya thanked him for his support and friendliness during the short time that she had been there.

"It's been my pleasure, you are like a draught of fresh air here and I'm so glad that your colleagues with 'Sticky fingers' got nabbed meaning that dear old Harry Broadweir was shoved upstairs and that resulting in your coming here."

The newly Gazetted Superintendent Thomas told Freya.

"Naturally, I'm sorry to see you moving on so soon but you will long remain in my memory for two reasons. One is this case that you are still trying to resolve and that so-called dress that you wore yesterday, Miss Freya Douglas Gore Hamilton. You will not be forgotten by many people, none more so than me. Good luck my dear, you deserve it and cheerio."

As Freya turned to leave the office so 'Old King Cole' was standing behind her armed with his usual Capstan Full Strength cigarette. After a quick cough, he said to Freya, "I won't be a hypocrite and tell you just how distraught I am to see you going on somewhere else. Despite what might be seen by you as my dislike of you, that is not the case." Freya raised her eyebrows at Mr Cole as Tommo nudged her backside. Mr Cole continued;

"I agree that we did get off to a bad start which was my fault but that staff sergeant sitting there smirking at me was too much for a man to tolerate and this resulted in you getting both barrels.

While it may not be apparent to you I have given you strong support." Freya interrupted him with "Yes, sir, and when I attempted to thank you for your support you very rudely bawled me out."

"I know miss and Tommo bawled me out not to mention 'The silent one' He threatened me with an interview with the chief constable. I've never known him so mad.

Anyway, Miss, I wish you well. He held out his hand and Freya thought it childish not to accept the hand and shook it telling him. "You are a soldier sir and I accept that women in the army are less than the dust beneath your chariot wheels.

You will never change and it gives you some pleasure not to change but, change will come and if you still have many years of service left a woman might be your boss. I bear you no grudge. Goodbye, Sir, and best wishes. Once her hand was free she made her way to her office to pick up her bits and pieces and say her farewells to Ron.

A gentle knock on her door and a voice asking her, "Tea, mum."

"Yes please, Mrs Briggs," Freya answered.

In shuffled Mrs Briggs with her best china and the obligatory pair of chocolate biscuits and gently placed them on Freya's desk.

Leaning over the side of her chair Freya picked up the bunch of flowers laid them on her desk and reached into her drawer for a box of Terry's 'All Gold' chocolates.

Meantime Mrs Briggs was making her way out of the CID office. Freya called her back and when she was again in Freya's office Mrs Briggs was told by her, "I am leaving here this afternoon, I won't be coming back Mrs Briggs." Mrs Briggs looked very downcast at the news. "Why, mum?" she enquired.

"It's time for me to move on Mrs Briggs and you have looked after me so well I would like you to accept these flowers and these chocolates from me in thanks not only for what you have done for me but for just being here and talking to me. Mrs Briggs, you really are one in a million and it has been my great pleasure to have met you, thank you."

As Freya got out of her chair to kiss Mrs Briggs so the very old lady stumbled and she caught her as tears ran down her face. Mrs Briggs could not speak for her sobbing. Freya sat her in her chair and laid the flowers and chocolates on her tea trolley.

A voice from the doorway heralded the arrival of Mr Thomas. He looked startled to see Mrs Briggs in a state of collapse and Freya trying to get her into a chair.

He immediately helped to sit a sobbing Mrs Briggs into a chair and then asked Freya what had happened.

"I gave her a bouquet and a box of chocolates, she burst into tears and seemed to pass out before you came. She weighs very little but it was awkward for me to catch her then get her to a chair." Freya explained.

"What's going on yer?" heralded the arrival of Superintendent Cole.

The situation was explained to him and he told them to remain there, not that they were likely to go anywhere. Superintendent Cole walked out of the office a few feet and bellowed at a passing constable to find a policewoman and then report to him 'immediately'.

Back in the office he picked up the internal 'phone and dialled a number and asked, "Is Chief Superintendent Bates still in his office?"

The answer was plain 'No'.

"Good," was Mr Cole's reply.

By now Mrs Briggs had Freya, Mr Thomas, Mr Cole, two constables around her. They were then joined by Sarah.

It was eventually decided by Mr Cole that he would drive Mrs Briggs home with the two constables and if necessary leave the policewoman with her until she decided that Mrs Briggs was settled.

Mrs Briggs was now sitting more upright and had stopped crying and was apologising to anyone who would listen for "Causin' such a fuss." Attempting to get to her feet she protested that she had to collect the cups from the offices.

"Please listen to the superintendent and sit still," Sarah told her. "I will collect the cups and wash them up and tidy up ready for you to start again on Monday."

"I got to see to 'em what's working termorrer, sir," Mrs Biggs told one and all.

No one said a word until Mr Cole bellowed along the corridor "Bring the duty chief inspector here now."

That bellow startled Mrs Briggs and a few around her as Jake emerged from his office and enquired in all alleged innocence of anything being wrong with the indifferent question, "Something up?"

"My boot will soon be up your arse if for once in your useless life you do not get me the chief inspector, now." 'Old King Cole' menacingly told the sage of the station.

With the prompt arrival of the chief inspector, Mr Cole told him. "You will promulgate a Standing Order from me to the effect that as of Monday a car will be dispatched to collect Mrs Briggs from her home at 8:00 a.m. Monday to Friday and another will return her to her home as and when she decides to go home."

"Is that wise sir. Cars are sometimes busy at those times." The chief inspector reasoned. "If they are that busy and can justify it to me, either Mr Thomas or I will collect and deliver Mrs Briggs.

And God help you and anyone else who tries to take advantage of our consideration for Mrs Briggs.

Understood?"

"Shall I call a car in now sir?" the CI asked. "No, I'm doing it." Mr Cole said and gave another instruction. "What you can do is get hold of the force Quack and send him to meet me at Mrs Briggs place."

"He doesn't deal with civilians sir and he might be busy." the CI quietly explained.

Observing the ever-increasingly crimson hue of the superintendent's face, Sarah grabbed his arm and whispered "Not here please."

She led him, spluttering, out of the earshot of Mrs Briggs. As they walked out Sarah grabbed the chief inspector and 'volcano Cole' exploded as only he could "You tell that bag of bones called a doctor that he will do as I order or he will be looking at finding a new post. Understood?"

"Sir," came the less than enthusiastic response.

When Fred Cole and Sarah returned Freya told them, "How I wish that I hadn't given her the flowers and upset her."

"Not at all miss, it was a kind and thoughtful gesture so off you go home and forget all about this."

"I'll see her alright." Superintendent Frederick Cole told her as with Mr Thomas on one side and Mr Cole on the other with Sarah following them with the flowers and chocolates, they almost carried Mrs Briggs down the corridor.

Quite a genuinely touching scene to the concerned onlookers witnessed. Although maintaining his self-appointed role of being the 'Flog 'em and Hang em high' to those around him. Without losing his undoubted authority, Old King Cole had shown his caring and compassionate character carefully hidden under the no compromising exterior of his persona, Freya was so pleased to see. Such a change in character caused by circumstances was not, in her personal life, unknown to her.

As Freya picked up the last of her possessions and made her way down the corridor past the office of Mr Cole she realised that she had just witnessed a peculiar example of the complexity of human nature and a lesson for the future. In all probabilities, Mr Cole since boyhood followed by six years of fighting a war had created the sometimes monster called Cole. But under that bullish and brutal character was a normal human being. In many ways, she was pleased that the events took place this afternoon, and as a result, she was leaving 'D' Division in a much happier frame of mind than expected.

When she left the building Ron Wilkins was entering, "Where have you been?" she asked him.

Before he could answer she told him. "Don't bother answering, I can smell it from here,"

"Just celebrating and it's Friday afternoon, ma'am," he told her. "What have you been celebrating?" Freya asked him then enquired further. "Have you celebrated my leaving Ron?"

"No, ma'am," Ron told her then corrected himself telling her. "Silly me, I don't need to call you, ma'am, anymore, ma'am, Freya do I?"

"If it wasn't my leaving that you were celebrating, what was it?" Freya asked him. "My promotion," he replied.

"If it was truly your promotion Ron, then all I can say is that you have a lousy bunch of colleagues. In any worthwhile, male CID promotion celebration that I have known, by now you would have to be carried. Cheerio Ron. Good luck," she told him, got into her car and mentally wished 'D' Division a relieved and heartfelt farewell. She then drove to her home.

"Did you have to ring me so early?" Hamish asked Freya when his telephone rang at ten past nine.

"Just to make sure that you were awake And packed ready for our adventure," she told him.

They then discussed their respective packing arrangements and decided that other than some tea, coffee, long-life milk and chocolate Hobnobs the rest they could get when in the camp as well as their three meals a day. Clothes were not really needed except for footwear, something warm for the evenings and clothes for when they went outside of the colony.

"I'll pick you up about one," he told her. She reminded him to bring some travelling blankets if it was cold in bed although the brochure for Sunny Patch claimed that all bedding etc was provided.

Dead on time he was at her apartment and picking up her luggage and her. She then checked with him that he did have his warrant card, two cameras and Chubby's keys. Having been assured that everything was with them they set off in the BMW for pastures new.

"Stop, stop," Freya shouted at him. He brought the car to a sudden stop, much to the audible horn sounds emitting from the vehicle behind them. As they rocked back in their seats Hamish looked around expecting to see a pedestrian about to walk in front of them or a child on the pavement or some other impediment. As politely as possible and in the calmest possible voice, he enquired.

"Something wrong dear?"

"Yes, Sorry, I've forgotten my rings," Freya told him and then added, "We must go back and get them."

He looked at her hands and could clearly see that she was wearing her rings. When he pointed out that her rings were on her fingers she explained.

"I'm supposed to be Mrs Fergus when we get there. Don't you think even in these allegedly permissive times that someone will smell a rat unless I have a wedding ring on? Turn around please."

Hamish drove on to the nearest junction to make a turn onto the other lane and returned whence they came. When Freya had locked up and they were on their way again in the open road, he took his eyes off the road and looked at her hands.

On the third finger of her left hand, she had an engagement and wedding ring. The sunlight was reflecting off of the jewel in the engagement ring.

"Those rings look quite at home on your finger," he told her.

"They were my great-grandmothers. Keep your eyes on the road and I'll tell you all about them when we stop for lunch," Freya ordered.

They pulled into a wayside inn which was advertising food and ordered their repast and sat down.

Freya then told him, twisting her left hand catching the light on the engagement ring.

"These rings belonged to my maternal great-grandmother. Her husband was an official of the Cape Colony and had both the engagement and wedding ring made in South Africa before he came home to propose to his eventual wife. How romantic was that?

Having them made before he even asked her to marry him. That's real love and devotion. Eventually, they went all over the Empire." Hamish interrupted her with the observation, "And retired happily to Cheltenham."

She replied, "As Mr Cole might have said, 'Smart arse' You're wrong again. It was to Malvern as a matter of fact."

After the meal, they made their way to Sunny Patch. Hamish pointed out the Scolding Wife pub and in particular the sign of the washerwoman chasing her man with a rolling pin. Freya knew the point that Hamish was trying to make and chose to ignore it.

As they arrived at the imposing gates to Sunny Patch, Freya was busily reading the brochure for instructions regarding their arrival. She rang the gate bell and as the brochure said, a man, identified as 'The Steward' opened the big gates for Hamish to drive in.

He then took Freya up a central path between ranks of chalets or lodges. As Hamish watched them he noticed a particularly unusual thing about the buildings which he had last seen in a place called Cairns in Queensland, Australia.

The building was standing on quite tall stilts as if to get ventilation under them or protect them from flooding. As the site was on a hillside, he thought that there would not be much chance of flooding here!

When Freya returned with the steward they disappeared into a gatehouse and when she reappeared she told Hamish to drive around the back of the line of buildings and she would meet him by their chalet.

From the gate, the road formed a 'U' shape running around the back of the two lines of the chalets and lodges. Presumably to allow children and pedestrians to move freely without the danger of vehicles.

Venturing onto the roadway he soon spied Freya waving at him. By the time he arrived the Steward appeared.

Unlocking the back door to chalet number nineteen they all went in and the chap showed them the full equipped kitchen, shower, washbasin and lavatory rooms. The main room had a sofa and two easy chairs with a fold-out table and a fold-out alleged double bed with a wardrobe for clothes and other rubbish.

Opening the front door, it led out onto a veranda with wooden ranch type railings and steps leading to the wide grassy would-be driveway and facing the buildings opposite.

The Steward told them all the rules and regulations and told them that everything that they spent would be on 'Tick' with a settlement when they left, much the same as is in the brochure and pointed out the various facilities at the top of the central driveway, restaurant, sports pavilion, laundry, bar, recreation room, covered and open swimming pool, tennis/miniten court, Petanque lanes, and beyond that the golf course, walks and fishing lake, a former-flooded quarry working.

He then handed them the keys, and payment cards on a wristband. The keys were one for the door and one for the gate. He told them that you could get hold of him at the gatehouse day or night simply by ringing the bell.

As he went out Freya and Hamish looked at each other before he asked "What was the number of Rosenbergs Lodge?" She replied, "number seventeen and it follows that if the numbering in here is the same as a street and beginning at the gate, his place will be next door. How lucky is that?"

"If you are right," he told her which naturally brought the questioning response, "Am I not always right?"

Hamish looked at her in disbelief and said, "Is this the woman who not a couple of hours ago asked me to turn around because she had no rings on?"

"Woman's privilege." Was, as is always the case, the woman's last and uncompromising word.

They decided that they would undress before emptying the car to show any onlookers that they were 'One of them' When all the bits and pieces were brought in they let the so-called double bed down and in the open position was quite away from the floor, and other than the pillows, it was fully made up. "That's a bit narrow for the two of us," Hamish observed. No sooner had he spoken than Freya jumped up into the bed and told him, "Finders keepers," and adopting a broad west country accent she told him.

"Oh, nay, by all the saint's wicked Zir Jasper, Yous bain't sharing me bed. Me mother warned I about wicked men such as thee, nay, nay and I sez, nay aga'n."

Hamish adopted the lounge lizard speech of Leslie Phillips to assure her that, "I am an honourable Knight of the Realm, my dear, I would not lay a hand on such a dainty delightful young lady such as you. I merely want a soft bed to lay my body on and a pillow to lay my head next to a fragrant, delicate, compassionate flower such as you."

"Yous baint 'aving me maiden'ood unless ye promise I that ye'll marry I," Freya told him.

Holding up the first coin that he could quickly find, Hamish with his best silvery tongued twang said to her.

"This shiny three pence is yours my lovely maid to let me into your delicious soft welcoming bed."

Freya then told the wicked Sir Jasper.

"Me mother told I that as me face wouldn't make I a fortune, me 'oles were me best hassets an' no man could 'av they unless they paid 'andsomly. She told I that nunthin less than a shiny gold sovereign could buy me 'oles. That be the price Sir Jasper 'an nothin' less.

Trying not to laugh he told 'Maid' Freya.

"My beloved child, a gold sovereign is a very valuable coin simply to have a soft, warm, inviting bed for the night.

You will just be my warming pan like your dear soft heart to keep the evil cold at bay and all for this shiny three pence piece, a fortune for such as you."

"This month Sir Jasper, all my body be on special hoffer, a Guinea for each bit or a bargain, fer all the lot for a shiny gold sovereign. What'll it be, all or, none Zir?" Freya, with her legs dangling over the side of the bed, enquired of wicked Sir Jasper with the imaginary stovepipe hat and thin waxed moustache curled at the ends.

Hamish, now giggling like a child said to her, "How long does the special offer last?"

"Till the stock be run out an' the shelves be cleared Zir," Freya told him.

"My dearest, dearest child I am a man of honour, I would not rob you of your virginity, that is, of course, if you would accept my first offer, what about it?"

"I ain't got no virginity wat ever that be but, I must call hoff negotiations as I know that you kind would leave I bearing yer brat then you'd disappear leavin' I in the work 'ouse fer ever."

"You poor dear child, you simply do not know just what you are missing and getting a shiny three penny piece as well." a dejected wicked Sir Jasper told her.

Returning to her normal rather cultured tone Freya told 'Sir Jasper Hamish'. "I do know exactly what I am missing, and you may dispose of your miserly three penny piece where no shadows fall, my dearest boy.

In so far as the question remains hanging as to your place of repose. I will now settle the burning question and allow you to sleep beside me." A broad smile lit up his face, soon to be dispelled when Freya, lowering her tone an octave or so, added, "On the floor!"

"What am I supposed to sleep on?" He asked peevishly.

Freya, still making sure that she was safely abed told him, "I would have thought that a presumed highly educated man such as you and a former detective to boot, would have worked out that the sofa has cushions, the two easy chairs also have cushions and as a special concession I will allow you two, yes, two of my four pillows."

"Great, thank you mother hen. I am six feet two inches tall, and those cushions will not stretch that far. And what about a covering for me?" Hamish enquired. Freya patiently explained, "The travelling blanket in the car, dear heart. I would remind you that while we may have been sleeping together for over ten years but always in our separate beds.

Unfortunately for you moaning mini, there simply 'ain't another bed," she concluded.

The happy pair went about their business of settling into their clean, tidy but rather cramped accommodation before taking advantage of the lovely early summer weather and going for a walk to look around the estate and nose into the various buildings, having a cup of coffee for him and a tea for her to refresh themselves and take the opportunity to size up the restaurant.

Hamish was searching for his own flamboyant towel when Freya grabbed him around the eyes. She whispered, "Look at the back wall." as she took her hands off his eyes.

He stared at the blank wall, saw nothing and refocused on the small window by the door. Still, nothing to warrant his eyes being forcefully covered. He went to turn only to be told," Don't turn yet."

Hamish then was given permission to turn around facing the front windows and door. "What was all that for?" he asked Freya.

She replied "Competition."

"Competition from whom, what and why?" He asked only slightly mystified in case it was another saga of the bed starting over something else. Freya noted the quizzical lifting of his left eyebrow and read the unmistakable signs of discord.

"It was Joy," she told him. "Where is she?" he said while pushing towards the door. "No, not in person but very much like Joy. In short, someone to your taste."

"I give in. I have lost the plot of this episode before it has even started, what has Joy to do with anything here except we know that they own a lodge hereabouts." a by now exasperated Hamish told her.

"Will you agree with me that Joy had a sharp, beautiful mind and a beautiful body to go with it and the most attractive face that any man would die for?" Freya asked him.

Hamish, with the thought, that silence might be a good strategy to adopt, simply nodded.

"I suppose that expecting you to simply say 'Yes' would be too much to ask?" Freya asked.

"If I said no you would claim that I was lying. If I said yes, then, with a triumphant lift of the head you would claim, with a frosty demeanour. "I knew that you fancied her Then I would have to suffer another spasm if pique from you, my dear heart," he explained.

"The reason that I mentioned Joy was that even being a woman I could quite see why a half tidy man could easily lust after her." Freya explained, "My reason for blindfolding you was to prevent you with a dribbling tongue hanging out, not to mention bulging eyes lusting after another girl with, the probable exception Joy's brain, has all the attributes of a very attractive package for a sex-starved individual like you."

As was to be anticipated from a former mariner the response from a slightly perplexed Hamish was "What in the bloody hell are you babbling about. I don't do 'lust'. Kindly do me the honour of speaking to me in plain, uncomplicated English. If you have seen something which would be of interest to me, say so and then we can go and get a drink. Though after this past forty minutes a rum will be needed never mind a coffee."

With a wry smile, Freya looked at him, cupped his face in her hands and said, "You poor Chooky- chou, has mother hen ruffled your feathers?

The lodge opposite I'm talking about. While your back was turned the door opened and out came a child, aged about ten I expect. She was followed by a young teenager, sixteen I suppose and then, and yet another 'then', the second girl was followed by her elder sister, about twenty I would think.

This girl is, by the looks of it from here, a genuine blonde with legs that go on forever, a figure to die for, very tall and, viewed from here very beautiful. As a package, all in all, a danger to any girl in my position.

Now, do you see my correlation between this woman and our dear Joy?"

"No," Hamish said. "Beautiful that Joy certainly is, we were only put together because of that stupid little girl going on about matters which are no different to a woman choosing earrings, a necklace or whatever she thinks is pleasant, comfortable and looks in keeping with her, her clothes or in this case her body.

I've never denied how impressed I am with Joy. Falling in love is not something that I take too easily as no doubt you will agree. Why would I trade you in for a new model? Even with clothes on there is no woman in any gathering who has the beauty and magnetism of you.

You seem to tease me about Joy, what if I did the same about the men, young and particularly old who are like moths to the flame of you? I am mindful of the fact that two older men, namely Bates and Gaunt, according to you, noticed that you were sans knickers. They must have looked very closely or perhaps you gave them one of your patented swing of the hips when you left them."

"Have you now finished dear? I would remind you that Mr Bates and perhaps Mr Gaunt as well, despite the warm weather noticed that I was sans bra as well," she told Hamish.

She put her hand through his arm and pulled him to the door as they went on their route of exploration.

As they walked towards the restaurant they passed several people, young, old, fat, slim, tall and short, a good selection of humanity who seemed very cheerful and greeted them almost as if they were long lost friends.

When they arrived at the restaurant it was to find that part of it was a 'Tea House' and the meal section was behind a screen.

All was spotlessly clean and those behind the counter were in short aprons and the waitress and waiters were a mixture of those clothed and unclothed. As with those behind the counter, the naked ones had small aprons on.

They ordered a tea and coffee and made their first purchase using their card as identification and then signed a chit when the drinks and a Chelsea bun each was delivered.

At the next table was an elderly couple, the lady wore a sarong but the man was naked.

Polite exchanges relating to the weather and conversation centred on the fact that Hamish and Freya were new visitors to Sunny Patch took place between the couples. Standing slightly behind Hamish, Freya put her index finger to her lips. Hamish was quite surprised to note that Freya was the recipient of what appeared to be a 'knowing' smile and wink from the man. In no time at all the man who introduced himself as Ted began telling Hamish the history of the place.

Ted and Ivy were young when they joined their parents at a very wild site in the late nineteen twenties. On those far off days, there was no water or electricity anywhere near the site and they lived in tents. Their respective parents had Douglas motorcycles and a sidecar and everything that was needed was packed into the person in the sidecar. As he spoke, Ted's face betrayed his emotion at the happy memory of those pioneering days.

Ted went on to explain how bit by bit they scraped up enough to buy the material for huts. Many of the huts were First World War barrack huts. One barrack hut made four roomy huts for the colony. When the huts were finally erected they put guttering on them then dug out a hole and eventually bricked lined it for a supply of water from the guttering. Bit by bit the site expanded and membership increased with the advent of a regular bus route through the village. In those days everyone, men women and children were expected to work on the site.

With occasional interjections by Ivy, Ted continued his history of Sunny Patch by telling them about the newer well educated people getting involved after nineteen eighteen when they returned from the war.

These people were what nowadays were known as the cream of society. Their skills were in medicine, politics, the law, criminal and civil, architects and many other similar professions.

Ted chuckled when he told of the wife of a newcomer who when told to help get a meal for the men declared that she had never prepared a meal before and was quite excited to get the opportunity.

He said that although most of the newcomers did little work on the site, some even had their accommodation put up by builders when the site was empty but while these people may not have worked with such enthusiasm as the pioneers they provided valuable help with the finances, legal difficulties and all manner of matters needing expert knowledge.

One of the differences between the pre-war and the post-war nudists was that the post-war intake did not, as a matter of course, bring their children to the site. During the 'thirties' the membership was swollen by the arrival of young families with lots of children and it was decided that the site should have a children's play area and developed into a very popular paddling pool.

In early 1943, the site was requisitioned for the use of the American's. Ted told of the disappointment of the members who treated the site as a place of retreat from active service or the daily grind of wartime, particularly in the cities.

He told Freya and Hamish of how the occupation of the site by the American's had improved it to the eventual benefit of the membership.

They took down the original huts and stored the material away. They built proper roads through the site and built a very large septic tank, drained the water tank and used it for some other reason, had mains water and electricity provided and much to the surprise of Hamish, allegedly widened the lane going past the site.

"Where is your hut?" Ted asked them.

"We are number nineteen," Freya told him.

Ted was obviously thinking deeply and too slowly for Ivy. "By the old tank," she declared. Ted collected his thoughts and said, "It's by the old water tank." An argument then sprang up between the veteran nudists, Ivy complaining that his brain was 'befuddled' and when it suited him, his hearing was poor but to compensate, "his mouth is working better than ever!"

By now Freya and Hamish had finished their bun and drinks and thanked Ted and Ivy for their company and Freya said, "It is awfully bad manners but we haven't introduced ourselves, we are Hamish and Freya. We are not too sure how long we shall be here but with this beautiful weather who wants to go home?"

"Are you Scottish?" Ted asked, "You sound posh English to me."

"A little bit of both," Freya told him as they parted with Ivy giving Ted such an elbow to unsteady him a little.

"That was interesting," Hamish told Freya as they walked around the various recreational places at the top of what in Bath would be called a circus of buildings facing some stunning lodges with beautifully manicured lawns and flowering borders.

"Not what I expected in a place like this. There must be a few bobs laid out there," he said pointing to a superb dwelling in the sunshine looking like an advertisement for some delicious country feast of strawberries and cream. Freya, unusually and without reason, made no reply.

As they wandered on so Hamish asked Freya why she had received a 'knowing' look and a wink from Ted when the introductions were made?

"I didn't notice anything so it was a bit of a wasted wink she told him then added; if he makes an indecent proposal I will be sure to accept." That Ivy will eat you my dearest," Hamish assured her.

They went to the very busy, very modern children's play area with every imaginable structure to give boys and girls enjoyment hopefully negating the need for children to respond to the information that the parents and themselves were bound for Sunny Patch with, "Oh. Do we have to, it's so boring."

With that thought in mind, Freya, remembering her years of youthful discovery and rebellion wondered just what would entice the twelve to eighteen-year-old teenagers here, there were lots of them around so something must be an attraction.

Walking back to their hut Freya and Hamish were cheerfully greeted by almost all of the people that they passed. As they were walking past number twenty-one a fully dressed young woman appeared on the veranda and beckoned them over. As they approached it was noticeable that the woman was blushing as she almost whispered to Freya, "Could I please speak to you?"

Hamish, deciding that the woman wanted women's talk and left them and he continued into their hut next door. After the arduous excursion around the site, the strength needed to lift a cup of coffee not to mention the Chelsea bun had worn him out. Kicking off his flip-flops, he collapsed on the sofa exhausted.

"Wake up you idle creature," brought him back to a semi-conscious state as Freya came in and kicked his feet.

She then explained that next door was a young couple new to the nude lifestyle and the girl needed a bit of reassurance about the etiquette of the nude life and other womanly concerns. "I've told them that we will call for them when we go for our evening meal and they can sit with us and to make sure that they take their towels. Is that OK?"

"No," Hamish replied.

"I've said we will be delighted to help them," she told the reclining Hamish.

"And that's that," she rather forcefully stated.

"Why ask me if you've made up my mind for me?" Hamish quite understandably enquired.

"Because I was being polite and I am a woman of a superior rank to you and I'm on duty. It's a privilege of rank." With smug satisfaction, she made her professional position known.

"More like 'Abuse of power' he muttered. Although clearly hearing him, she asked "What was that?"

"Shuddup," was the final word from Hamish on the subject as he turned his prone back towards her.

Blessed silence filled the hut until Hamish heard the shower going. After much sloshing and gurgling Freya emerged drying herself.

"What gown are you going to wear to dinner this evening to impress our guests?" He asked.

"Principally white with a bit of light brown at the top and bottom with two dark bits with pearls and the pearl and diamond tiara. Is that suitable for the State banquet my lord?" Freya asked him before enquiring.

"You must wear your honours and medals as it is a State Banquet we are attending dear. Where exactly are you going to pin them?"

"I will wear by bum freezer from Britannia to hook them on," he replied laughing as he headed for the shower.

Before he got there he stopped and after looking through the open back door, asked the world in general what exactly old Ted was doing in the wild bramble, holly and ivy bushes behind their hut across the driveway at the back of the huts.

As Freya got to the window by the back door so Hamish moved from the window for her to get a view of Ted coming up the steps of their hut.

They opened the door to see a rather bloodied Ted puffing who then told them that "After talking to you about the water tank I thought that I would have a look to see if it was still there. It is with a little almost derelict shed on the top and brambles growing through the windows. The strange thing is that if you went down towards the gate there is a clear path to it and a newish padlock on the door."

Ted, despite his various scratches, looked very pleased with himself.

Freya asked him, "Why are you so cut about? If there was a clear path why didn't you go down to that instead of coming back the same way that you went in through?"

"Because I'm a man," he told her. Before allowing her to agree with him, Ted looked at her left hand and told her that he could not ask in front of Ivy where Hamish had got a ring like that because Ivy would have given him a thumping for being so rude, pointing to her engagement ring.

"Why do you ask?" Freya enquired. Ted, the bloodied, replied, "I was a jeweller by trade and that is a magnificent diamond with a superb setting."

Freya took the ring off her finger and gave it to Ted. He studied it very closely and said," Even without my glass I can see what an excellent job was made in cutting the stone. Is it insured?"

"No," she told him.

He moved very close to her and whispered in her ear, "Even without my glass this ring as it is set is worth nothing less than five to ten thousand pounds." He then repeated the figure again and in as many words told her that the pair were very stupid not to have it insured and to do something on Monday. With that, he went down the steps returning to probably be scolded by Ivy.

"Is it insured?" Hamish asked Freya. "Yes, of course, but if he had asked for how much I would have been stumped for an answer so it was easier to say no and we had a free valuation."

"We?" With raised eyebrows, Hamish asked the question.

"Wishful thinking dearest heart, just wishful thinking. Do you want your back washed?" she asked as he went for his delayed shower. He thanked her and turned his back on her as the water splashed both of them.

All titivated up for their trip to the dining room Hamish asked Freya the names of their guests for the meal. "I've no idea," she told him.

The suggestion that they might be called Fred and Freya was met by silent disdain from the madam detective chief inspector.

Armed with the only pieces of textile that they needed, expensive perfume and the all-important jewellery Freya and Hamish stepped out arm in arm to wait at the steps of next door for Mr and Mrs Anonymous.

The couple appeared with towels strategically placed to avoid embarrassment. The woman had a pretty face and tidy figure while the chap hardly looked old enough to have left school with the parts of his torso not behind his towel displaying not a hint of hair but with youthful firmness and presumed vigour.

Before they all walked up for dinner Freya checked that they had their payment tags and she isolated the woman from her husband as Hamish attempted to make small talk with him, not very successful small talk. Hamish found it very heavy going to get a word out of him except for the fact that it was Tara who had persuaded him to come to a 'nudist place'.

While the girls were busy chattering away there was a sustained silence from the men.

Tara promptly exposed herself from behind the towel as she entered the dining room while her husband still clung on tightly to his towel until Hamish reminded him that he would need to divest himself of the towel in order to put it on the chair seat.

The scene was something that would be seen on a 'Naughty' seaside postcard as the chap tried to hold on to the towel while allowing enough slack to cover the chair. By the time that he realised that such a manoeuvre could not be performed he had quite an audience from the other diners.

Eventually, he gave up the struggle and plonked down on the chair fishing around for the rest of the towel to tuck under his buttocks.

"Freya has told me that you are new to this type of holiday," Hamish told the man. He then continued. "The first time in such a place as this is difficult for many people but the first lesson to learn is not to look and do nothing causing you to be looked at.

If like your wife you had simply placed the towel on the chair, no one would have bothered to look up from their meal. By trying to preserve your modesty in a mostly fruitless effort to keep your towel in two places at once you have drawn the attention of people to you and that has embarrassed you.

By tomorrow you will take to this lifestyle without any qualms, just wait and see."

The chap kept his eyes on Hamish rather than look across the table at a bare Freya.

"I intend to look at your wife and talk to her," Hamish told him adding," You can and must look at and talk to Freya. You will very quickly get accustomed to seeing her naked and before this evening is out you will take no more notice of her breasts than mine, honestly."

As the waitress came to hand out the menu card the man looked across the table to Freya and blurted out, "My name is Howard Jo…" Freya promptly interrupted him and told him that in places with naked people surnames are not at first mentioned. She told him that it was their protection from future embarrassment with unwanted social connotations and the same applies to occupations and addresses. "You can offer the information if you wish to but it is a matter of courtesy never to ask. Although I have already told Tara my husband's name, in case she hasn't told you it is Hamish."

The first part of the meal arrived with Ted and Ivy making their entry and heading towards Freya's table.

"Hello again," Ted announced. Freya then introduced Tara and Howard to Ted and Ivy and with smiles all around Ted and Ivy went to their table while Freya's party got on with their soups, prawn salad, braised pheasant breast and smoked salmon. As they sat back for the plates to be cleared Tara in low tones said to Freya.

"In the instructions for Sunny Patch, it quite categorically said that we were to be naked at all times yet that lady who came over here had a sarong on. Why isn't she told about it?"

Freya told her. "She is an elderly lady and our bodies will not always look like they do today and carrying a child or children will not help. Her body may be an embarrassment to her in her old age so the rules will quite rightly always be bent for them."

After further talk of bodies, the site, families and facilities the mains had arrived, been consumed and cleared away with the dessert course in front of them. To Hamish, certainly in theory, only being a three-day-old nudist, noticed that Howard was beginning to look around him and seemingly relaxing, probably only until he had to stand up. Hamish thought that will be another star performance of mind over matter.

When the meal was over, sure enough, Howard was a little reluctant to stand up. Eventually, he straightened up, collected his towel from the chair but simply couldn't resist the temptation to hide his nether regions as they left the dining room.

They emerged to find that it was a beautiful summer evening. Freya and Tara chatting away like old friends, but Hamish and Howard are mostly mute.

"Oi! wait for us," announced the now familiar voice of Ted. As they caught up with the foursome so the sound of music could be heard from a large building to their right.

Ivy told them that it was the Saturday evening dance and suggested that they went in with the pair of them. Hamish would have preferred to have continued the walk on such an evening but then changed his mind when he thought of walking on with Howard for the next hour in sullen silence.

Going through the doors they found themselves in a remarkably large assembly room with a stage at one end and a well-stocked bar. The musicians were on the stage, people were dancing with others sitting at tables or just on chairs around the sides of the hall.

With the glitter balls suspended from the domed ceiling, it was apparent that dancing or similar activities were regularly held there.

Accepting the invitation of Ivy to join them, the party of six found two vacant tables and pushed them together to accommodate the group.

Hamish offered to get a round of drinks in and asked Howard to help him remember what everyone wanted and bring the drinks back to the table. Howard began to follow Hamish when crafty Hamish told him. "Howard, you will not be able to carry drinks with a towel in your hand will you?"

With much dogging and diving, Howard relinquished his towel and followed Hamish to the bar.

As they breasted the bar, Hamish said to Howard. "I told you when we were having dinner that very soon you would not notice that people and yourself were naked and 'Hey presto' you're there. It doesn't hurt at all does it?"

A stony silence came from a shy Howard.

Freya asked Howard to dance with her. He promptly told her that he didn't dance. "Then now is a golden opportunity," Freya told him. Dragging him onto the dance floor she put her hands on him. It was as if her flesh was alive with electricity as he went to put his hands on her, pulled them away, then tried again resulting in his hands flapping everywhere. With a deft movement, Freya grabbed his flailing hands putting one around her waist and holding on to the other and against all the rules of dance, led him around the room.

Hamish, after joining Tara in her amusement at her husband's attempt to keep his body well away from Freya while avoiding looking where his feet were going which would have meant looking down at her breasts, Hamish and Tara took to the floor.

As they spun around so a continuously blushing Howard spent more time watching them than concerning himself with his performance.

Much to the obvious relief of Howard the band came to the end of the piece and they all returned to the table and settled down for a drink and chit-chat. There came a lull in the conversation and Ivy took hold of Howard's arm and almost pulled him from his chair as he attempted to grasp his towel.

"You won't need that where we are going," she told him and led him away to the bar.

The group, excluding Ivy and Howard, sat out the next dance, not that they could talk very much as the amplified sound from the musicians tended to be rather overwhelming.

As Ivy and Howard returned, the stage was taken over by three young women, two without clothes and the third in a glittering bra and mini-skirt. They gave a very good selection of the current songs of the early nineteen sixties.

Ted stood the next round of drinks and Hamish went to the bar to help carry the glasses to the table. While at the bar Hamish asked Ted. "What do you think is wrong with Howard. Normally it's the female of the pair who is shy about stripping off but here we have a reversal of roles. Tara, if the way that she danced with me is any indicator, has not only taken to the nude life but in these short hours thoroughly enjoyed it."

In reply, Ted told him that when Ivy took hold of Howard and took him to the bar it was for both of them to have a whisky. Apparently, Howard was teetotal until then. "He now has a different view of this lifestyle and before he collapses I hope that he might remember what he was told by Ivy. She is a mother figure to the likes of him particularly in a place like this." Ted said with a smirk of knowing satisfaction.

While Howard did not appear to totally embrace the naked idea. When the third woman on the stage appeared naked with the others on their second appearance he seemed to relax a little.

Eventually, the evening came to a close and they wandered back to their huts in the darkness under a very dark blue velvet sky. With seemingly enjoyable kisses all around, they parted with Hamish telling Howard, "When we went out you were grasping your towel as if your life depended on it, now you have come home without a towel at all, congratulations on joining the movement."

Howard went into a frenzy asking where he might have left his towel. Very cruelly Freya told him that he would have to go to the hall and look for his towel amongst all those bare people still dancing.

Although it was too dark to see the colour of his complexion, there was little doubt in Freya's mind that after a very pale complexion when he believed his towel was lost to a very red one at the thought of recovering his towel amid naked people. Howard spluttered then plaintively asked if anyone would go back with him, "Please?" In the dark, Freya very narrowly missed embarrassing Howard even more, although in his agitated state he probably would not have noticed when her hand lightly brushed his upper thigh and groin as she handed him his beloved towel.

"As of tomorrow Howard I do hope that you will not embarrass Tara by clinging on to this towel. It's for sitting on only. Promise me or I'll keep it with me," Freya warned him.

As Tara turned the light on in their hut it illuminated Howard clutching the towel as a child would its 'Comfort' blanket.

With 'Good nights' all around, Freya and Hamish retired to their abode.

Hamish asked her for the pencil torch. Her question of why was met with the explanation. "I'm going to work and try the keys of Chubby on the back door of number seventeen. There was a stony silence eventually broken by Freya simply asking "Why?"

"Because I am a policeman and I have a job to do," he replied.

"Why now of all times, it's nearly midnight," Freya said with some despair reflecting in her tone of voice.

"I am breaking and entering and as any burglar will tell you a job goes easier when all honest folk are abed.

As your senior officer I am commanding you to come to bed it is late." Freya commanded.

"Having known you for many, many years I know that invitation was a slip of the tongue and on this and many other occasions I am going to disobey you, ma'am," he told her as he slipped into the ever-lengthening shadows of the balmy night.

Once out of number nineteen Chalet – Lodge – Hut, Hamish stood very still for several minutes before silently making his way to the back door of number seventeen successfully avoiding the shaft of street light between the structures. In bare feet, he went up the steps to the back door and again stood absolutely still watching and listening to the murmured conversation of people going to their beds.

He had just started to sort out the box lock skeleton keys of Chubby Reynold when he felt the hair follicles on his back prickle. Like greased lightning, he turned and grabbed the raised arm of Freya.

Neither said a word as he turned back to his task. Taking the pencil torch from his mouth he passed it behind him and poked her in the abdomen. Like a wraith, she slid past him and hiding the light with her body she directed the beam onto the keys.

After about ten minutes Hamish took Freya's hand and turned the torch off. The silent return to their hut was made easier because the street lights had been extinguished. Hopefully, unnoticed they slipped back into their hut.

"That bloody Chubby has sold me a duff set, none of them fitted a common Chubb box lock," he told Freya.

"Worry about it tomorrow," Freya told him in a calming tone of voice "It is tomorrow now." Hamish told her "And I am worried about it."

"As the more plain-speaking of our colleagues might say on such an occasion, 'Oh, bugger off," she told him.

"If that remark is directed at me I would remind you of a conversation that we had earlier concerning the wicked Sir Jasper when someone twice made reference to selling 'Me 'oles', note the plural. Perhaps you might like to reconsider your unfortunate turn of phrase directed at me, ma'am," Hamish informed her.

"Just a slip of the tongue," she told him adding "You just try it sailor and you'll be singing contralto for the rest of your days, I'll neuter you as I would a Tomcat. Now bed."

After another shower, Freya prepared her bed and threw two pillows onto the floor then got back down and began taking the cushions off the chairs as Hamish emerged from the shower.

"Would it be impertinent to politely enquire what you are doing, ma'am?" he asked Freya, knowing very well what it was all about.

"Preparing your bed dearest heart," she told him. And then asked, "Please get the cushions off the sofa and in the hope that you remembered to get it, bring in your travelling blanket. It might get cold during the night."

Eventually, Hamish settled himself on his basic bed with, from his knees down, resting on the floor as the cushions would not stretch far enough for his six foot two inches frame.

"Please don't disturb yourself," Freya told him. "I will gladly get out of my bed to turn the light out."

As she swung herself down carefully avoiding Hamish, she went to the switch and turned it off. As she turned to return to bed she saw the bend of a backside lifting off the floor heading for her bed.

Freya made a grab at the body and purely by chance, of course, grabbed hold of the first part within her reach.

Following the howl of anguish, all attempts at the male invasion of the bed were abandoned as Hamish retired to the floor and she climbed over him to claim her comfortable place of repose.

In the all-pervading darkness and peace of the night a voice descended from the bed towards Hamish on the floor.

"I didn't think much of your covert movements just now, being naked in the dark must have made you stick out like a beacon, not a competent action for a top three in a detective class," Freya told him. Just a silence followed until the sound of an irritating sounding voice asked,

"Did you hear me?"

Another period of silence followed until from the depths of the floor came the deep reassuring tone of an exasperated man who said.

"If you were so bloody smart why did you follow me naked. Tomorrow I will let you into the art of being prepared for any eventuality when doing anything covert. Now go to sleep."

"Why can't you tell me now?" came down from Freya.

Another hanging silence was broken with the situation inflaming statement from the floor.

"Firstly, because I want to go to sleep and secondly because if I answer you, it will encourage you to continue this unwarranted and may I say, typical female, haranguing, commonly used until they get their own way.

I expected better of you than to adopt the culture of the fishwife. Good night."

It plainly took her a while to evaluate what had been said and the reasoned argument behind the words.

"You didn't kiss me good night," Were her last words.

"Fishwife." were the final words from the floor as a pillow hit him. Tucking the pillow under his calves the silence was only broken by the sound of breathing.

Freya woke up to the deafening sound of snoring. She had been sleeping in the same room as Hamish for about the last so many years and had never known him to snore loudly.

She looked at her watch, and it was 6:30. The room was bathed in the summer sunlight and the snoring continued with some slight variation from the normal loud snore to a snuffle then another long line of snores.

Freya turned over to see a sight to behold. Hamish was on his back a pillow under the back of his neck with his head lolling over it. His arms were up alongside his head. She decided that he was not dissimilar to the pose of a sleeping gorilla. His blanket was down the side of him, and she decided that he must have been warm during the night. Her eyes then looked at the rest of him and saw that he was in a condition colloquially known as being in a state of 'Morning Glory' but not having much connection with the convolvulus plant except both eventually rise, one being blue.

As she surveyed the scene Freya decided that were Hamish old enough by a thousand years, he might have been the model for the Cern Abbas Giant. A naughty thought entered her head. She turned and picked up her water glass from the window sill at the side of her bed, the window glass vibrating to the sound of snoring.

Avoiding spilling any water as she turned back over, she leaned over the side of her bed, dipped two fingers in the water and tried to aim for the pride of Hamish. Freya was fascinated by seeing that whenever Hamish exhaled the tip would make a minute jerk.

She had several near misses before having three successful shots on target. At first, the cold water had no effect despite landing on his groin and 'Morning glory', the snoring still continued.

After her successful shots, his hand came down and grasped the 'Morning glory' gave it a squeeze while still snoring, pulled his knees up, adjusted the pillow and still holding on to his pride and joy, turned on his side. The snoring stopped and Freya watched Morning glory wither as his hand let it go, and he then decided to have a good scratch at the cold water on his skin before letting out a large sigh, licking his lips and presumably trying to reach for his blanket. Failure was rewarded with the gentle sound of regular sleep-induced breathing.

Freya settled back in her bed, had a stretch and turned her back on her little bit of fun and fitfully went to sleep and no longer disturbed by raucous snoring.

A prod in her backside brought her to her senses as Hamish told her, "Get up work to be done."

Looking at her wristwatch she saw that the time was half-past eight. She reminded him that it was Sunday morning before asking "What's the rush?"

He replied, "Breakfast before everybody else snaffles the best eggs. Come on get up. Who's having the bathroom first?"

As could be guessed, Freya used a single word to make her intentions known, "You." Then turned back to the wall again to doze for the time that Hamish would take for his shower and shave.

Eventually, the pair were ready for the day and made their way towards the restaurant and cooked breakfast.

They looked at the hut of Tara and Howard to see if they were about. The curtains were still closed which made Freya laugh at the idea that nudists who spent their time with nothing on would bother closing curtains to prevent people similarly naked from looking in. Hamish did point out that perhaps they were engaged in private practises not suitable for a public display.

"With Howard?" Freya asked. "It's the quiet ones who can't control their sexual instincts." Hamish opined. "Poor Howard," With a straight face, she then let out a giggle as she said, "He couldn't raise a laugh never mind much else.

Hamish suddenly stopped and looked back. Freya asked him why he had stopped? "Just to make sure that their hut was still on its stilts," he replied with a matter of fact expressionless face. They turned and hand in hand walked on to their breakfast.

When the main course, having been eaten in silence, was cleared away they began their toast and marmalade.

"What story were you going to tell me last night after I told you that being bare was not the best disguise for a burglar?" Freya asked him.

He then told her of his very early years as a detective.

"This factory was losing phosphor bronze bearings worth a tidy bob and called us in. The factory was surrounded by a six-foot picket fence and I teamed up with a hairy old sergeant called Bill. Needless to tell you he was called…" Freya added the required words, "Old Bill by any chance?"

"If you know so much, you tell the story, smart arse," he told the grinning Freya.

Hamish started again, "We found four of these picket slats were loose and could easily be removed then replaced without any obvious disturbance so Bill stationed two of the squad outside of the fence and both of us on the inside. Suddenly, while getting ourselves ready to nick them once they had gone through the fence three men were walking towards the hole in the fence carrying these very heavy bearings. I must admit, I didn't know what to do. In broad daylight, we were caught in the open right up against the fence about ten feet from the hole.

Old Bill whispered. "Stay absolutely still son, not a movement." Sure enough, they kept coming towards us, often looking behind themselves then seemingly just looking at the hole in the fence.

Sure enough, they didn't see us. Through the fence, they went right into the trap. One fellow turned and ran back again. He appeared to be quite surprised to see us and was polite enough to warn us that 'The coppers are out there' as still clutching his bearing he attempted to run. The weight of the bearing was making his legs bow quite a bit. To prevent the poor chap from ending up with his balls by his knees, Bill arrested him and the chap was so surprised and grateful that we had relieved him of the bearing that he lovingly attached his stomach to Bills elbow. A great show of affection, don't you think?"

"What a load of old tosh," an unimpressed Freya told him.

"I swear that I'm telling you the truth, every word. 'Old Bill' has gone to the great assize court in the sky but I'm telling you the truth and while we are on the subject of observation, particularly by detectives, men and women including you."

She bridled at the suggestion that she wasn't observant. "What do you mean by that remark?" she crossly enquired.

Before Hamish could answer the waitress came to the table and enquired if all was satisfactory. As his coffee was by now cold he ordered another. At which point Freya told him "You take so long talking I'm not surprised that your coffee is cold. So what do you mean by saying that my powers of observation are rubbish?"

Hamish replied, "Back in the mists of time you and I were at a school for detectives, a very good school. You eventually were seconded to the Regional Crime Squad but not before our class were told that we were to undergo a test of our observational skills.

We were locked out of the grand entrance to the mansion while items were arranged inside. We, yes, you and I included, thought that we were so smart in going around the corner and watching them take various bits and pieces into the hall and memorising as many as we could.

Eventually, we, you and me still included, were let into the hall and the instructor, him with the bouffant hairstyle, allowed us fifteen minutes to memorise and as a special favour as we were his 'Favourite' class we could even write down five of the items to help us along.

We went to town writing the five items that we might forget and remembering the others.

When we returned to the classroom, the instructor said not a word about identifying anything. We all sat in silence waiting for the spirit to move the evil instructor.

Eventually, he asked if we had all got our five items written down? Everyone nodded assent and he then told us to rip up the paper that it was written on. He then asked us to write down those items that we memorised, that we did and again when we had finished he told us to rip it up again.

We, the cream of police society sat there like children at kindergarten."

"You win," Freya told him as the new cup of coffee arrived.

She continued, "Yes, yes, alright, I do remember. Not one of us got it right and after all the mental strain that we had gone through that blighter only asked us one question."

"And what was that one question?" Hamish asked. She replied,

"The observation question was, 'What was the colour of the waistcoat of the man who let us into the hall stayed the fifteen minutes in full view of us then let us out again. We all walked no more than a couple of feet away from him and not one of the twelve of us got it."

"Correct," a gloating Hamish said then went on to ask her, "Do you now doubt my account of rogues not seeing us if you, an acting detective superintendent, failed your observation test?"

"Drink your coffee," was her riposte. After taking a mouthful of coffee Hamish started again with, "Last night you criticised me for being naked while burgling the hut. Had I been clothed, particularly in dark clothes any passer-by would have called the police or worse made a citizen's arrest.

As I was naked in the nudist colony why shouldn't I be trying my key in a lock? The first rule of covert operations, be part of the surroundings. It is, my darling, no use trying to covertly observe a docker at work on a grain boat if you're dressed in Saville Row gear. Shall we go?"

As they walked back to their hut Hamish said, "Whether it was because I was sleeping on the floor or not but at some time I had a sensation of water dripping on me. When I woke up I had a feel around and everything was dry. It's strange how you must dream of unconnected and irrelevant things, don't you think?"

With a deadpan face, Freya replied, "Yes, it really is so strange."

As they walked past the hut of Tara and Howard so the pair emerged. Pleasantries were exchanged and many matters were talked about including sleeping. Tara complained about the very narrow bed which in turn led to the pair of them stuck together with perspiration and had very disturbed sleep. They then asked Freya and Hamish if they had the same problem?

"In all honesty," Freya told them, "We have never slept in the same bed so overheating did not disturb our sleep. "However," she told them, "Hamish thought that he felt water on him during the night, perhaps it was sweat or something. Who could possibly know?"

"If you don't sleep together where did Hamish sleep last night?" Tara enquired.

With unconcealed girlish delight, Freya told her new friend, "On the floor."

A disgruntled Hamish suggested that the couple might miss breakfast if they didn't put their best foot forward.

As the couples parted Freya told Hamish, "Tara is a doctor and Howard is of all things a forensic photographic analyst and art conservator whatever that might be. Believe it or not, he's also a serving Royal Air Force officer.

"How do you know that," Hamish asked. "Because she told me so," she answered. "You didn't ask them did you?"

"No," she told him. "She offered the information. I did tell her of the nudist convention relating to both surnames and other identifying matters and not to ask questions. I did, as a matter of courtesy, tell her that we both worked for the Home Office, which, indirectly is true."

Back in the cabin, Freya asked what the plans were for the day. Hamish told her that he was going back to town to buy a camp bed in the cheap-jack store and if things worked out well visit Chubby Reynolds.

"When we were stopped at the gate when we arrived I noticed that while you were in the gatehouse on the back wall of it were lines of keys. If they are the keys to the various huts there must be one for next door. What do you think the chances are of you keeping the steward occupied long enough for me to get in there and take an impression of the seventeen key if it's there?" he asked Freya.

"If we were not in a nudist camp I could show him a bit of breast or a long pale thigh to draw him away from his lodge. The kind of task you are asking me to do is rather difficult as there is nothing to titillate him with. Do you think politics might hold his attention for five minutes or, perhaps raise the question of social care of the sub-Saharan nations?" Freya enquired mischievously.

"Be serious," he told her.

"OK," she declared, "I will draw him away by asking about the history of the place and pointing out things while walking away with him. Assuming of course that Mrs the steward is not around or the gate bell rings."

Hamish told her that it was all a chance worth taking and thinking on their feet and then went into the shower and wet the soap bar to take the impression of the key.

They went their separate ways, Freya down the central avenue and Hamish taking the road at the back of the huts.

He peeked around the corner of the hut nearest to the gatehouse. The entrance gates were open with Freya busy talking to the steward and gesticulating towards the central avenue. A quick glance around the office saw not a sign of Mrs the steward with his back to the wall of keys Hamish then turned at right angles to be able to both see the keys and to detect anyone coming into the hut.

Walking backwards he soon discovered the top line were keys, one to whatever number. Within seconds, he found key seventeen. Without removing it from the hook, he swiftly pressed the key into the soap pressing it with one hand on top of the other to make a clear imprint.

As he left the hut so who should arrive but Mrs the steward. "Can I help you?" she politely asked. "I'm looking for my wife," Hamish told her while doing his best to hold the soap away from her without holding it too firmly and ruining the imprint. He continued "She came to ask your husband about the history of this place. I saw them going up the avenue."

"So that's why he's left the gate is open. He is an old fool but still my old fool. He is so easily turned by a pretty face. Which chalet are you in?" She asked Hamish.

"Number nineteen," he told her.

"You must be Mr Fergus. Yes, Mrs Fergus is very pretty, we'll have to put the gate being left open down to your wife."

Hamish replied, "I will admonish her for distracting your husband. I promise it will not happen again. I don't want her getting the keys to your husband's heart do I?" A wry smile was the only reply to his mention of keys.

Having twisted and turned in order for Mrs the steward not to see his right hand he darted behind the avenue of huts to return to their 'chalet' and see if he had made a good job of impressing the key. On close inspection, it looked good. His next task was to wash the glutinous mess from this hand.

"Got it?" a voice from the doorway enquired. "Perfect," was the reply as Freya entered the hut.

"What are you going to do next?" she asked. "As I told you earlier my plan is to go back to town and see my dear chum Chubby Reynolds and get him to cut a key. While he is doing that," Hamish hesitated in order to milk as much pathos as he could, then continued "I will go and get my camp bed and pillow on which to rest my weary bones and head."

"Why do you have to do it today, it's Sunday, a day of rest for Christians?" Freya asked.

In very pompous tones he told Freya. "I simply want this job to be over and done with. Get in the hut find absolutely nothing and we can all go home, job done. Oh. I am aware that it is a Sunday. Just call me a lapsed Christian until this job is done."

While he was getting dressed Freya disappeared in to see Tara. When she came back she handed him a piece of paper. Hamish read what was listed on the paper then said, "I'm certainly not going to shop for these. Anyway, no chemists or similar shops are open on a Sunday. You don't need things like these. Who's this for?"

"Tara," she replied. "Since being here, among other things, she is aware that a few things about her body urgently need to be dealt with particularly after looking at that Kirsten and me. In the complex of the camp, bed store will be a shop which deals with such things, probably the chemist department of a Supermarket." Hamish shook his head, to which expression of defiance she told him, "Don't be such a Jessie. Just get on with it."

Collecting his bar of soap and Tara's shopping list, Hamish made for the back door only to be brought up in his tracks as Freya told him.

"Some sort of detective you've turned out to be, more like a defective."

"Do stop wittering woman, what are you on about?" A decidedly irritable Hamish asked. She replied. "You claim that there is no reason for you to be here investigating a murder with tenuous links to this place. 'Waste of time' I believe you called it."

She continued, "We are dealing with murder with a connection to espionage which has led us to here. We have been here just under twenty-four hours next to the hut believed to be occupied by a person engaged in spying and Mr, the oh so smart detective, claims that there is nothing here warranting investigation." She, with some satisfaction, told him, then added as they walked towards his car.

"Just look up at that beautiful blue sky." Glancing up Hamish continued his walk to the car.

"Notice anything unusual dearest?" Freya enquired. "No," came the short reply.

"Tell me," she continued, "are those rather large spiders webs or perhaps they just might be radio aerials waving about from number seventeen. Just a tad unusual don't you think Sherlock?"

"Probably just a radio Ham," Hamish countered as he got in the car and with a wave drove off.

Turning back into the hut she could see Tara on the veranda with Howard hovering in the background. Tara told her that they were going up to the church service and enquired if she was going with them.

The answer was yes and off they went greeting and responding to greetings from other residents and visitors while dodging the numerous children playing various games in the grass of the central avenue they arrived at the assembly hall. Freya was amazed to find so many people there, an organ belting out the Toccata and Fugue and a bare priest with just a stole on, standing before what appeared to be a collapsible altar.

As the congregation stood up for the first hymn Freya noticed a group of girls and boys from about three years of age to about twelve or thereabouts. They were to be the choir and even had a lady conductor with her baton.

They were very good choristers and unlike so many, looked happy.

Forgetting that other than the priest and his long narrow stole, everyone else was naked, Freya really enjoyed the service with a sermon that was exactly ten minutes long and made a mental note that if they were still here on the next Sunday she would take Hamish along.

With Howard and Tara, she made her way to the Barbecue pit to have a pork roll and a drop of cider for lunch.

It was the usual performance when Hamish arrived at the home of Chubby. Ringing the doorbell brought no response. Walking around the side of the building Hamish was brought to a halt by a firmly bolted door. Turning around out of the premises Hamish went up the drive of the next-door property and hopped over the wall into the immaculate garden of Chubby to be greeted by Chubby stating the totally accurate fact that, "It's bloody Sunday. "And no, I ain't doin nuffink fer you and where are my keys?"

Hamish walked up to him while apologising to his wife sitting in a deck chair enjoying the hot afternoon sun for disturbing their afternoon.

Hamish went right up to Chubby or at least as far as the corporation of Chubby would allow. Towering over him, he said in hushed tones with only the slightest hint of menace that Sunday was a normal working day for rogues, particularly those who Mr Fergusson knew their every trade secret and their very nasty and vindictive associates.

"As I reminded you on the last occasion Chubby. You will be pleased to assist Mr Fergusson in producing an accurate key from this imprint. This key Chubby is the key to the lock on my tongue. Make it a good key my friend or my tongue might just go wild. As a special gift, I will give you a set of skeleton keys when the jobs are finished."

"Firstly I ain't yer friend an' secondly those are my keys anyway. When do you want this key?"

He asked Hamish. "One hour," was the reply. "When I return kindly make sure that the side gate is open. Thank you, my friend."

Acknowledging Mrs Reynolds as he left, Hamish made his way to the Retail shopping complex. He found a supermarket and as he had been told there was a chemists department. He then shopped for the items on Tara's list and had to find an assistant to direct him to cream, a ladies razor and other items.

Once that task was completed he then went to the modern version of the Army Surplus stores and bought his camp bed, a sleeping bag, a massive torch and battery plus two boiler suits, one-thirty-six- to forty-inch chest and the other thirty-eight- to forty-four-inch chest.

He was about to leave the complex when he suddenly made a detour from the car park to go into a corner grocery store and purchased several packets of chocolate-coated digestive biscuits.

When he returned to Chubby's home he was made a little more welcome than an hour before. Mrs Chubby even had a cup of tea waiting for him.

Sitting around the garden table Chubby suddenly and wordlessly threw a key onto the table. "Thank you," Hamish said, then asked, "Chubby, how difficult is it to pick a padlock?"

Then, with a deep sigh from Chubby, a discussion took place as to the make, size, age of the padlock. "I don't know, I haven't seen the padlock yet, I've only been told that it exists," Hamish told the head-scratching Chubby.

"Lot of bloody use innit?" he quite understandably remarked. "If it's the old fashioned type you can spring them with a narrow nail file. If it is the modern combination I'll write out the numbers for you to open it." Chubby offered.

With that, Chubby walked off to his workshop then returned with several padlocks ancient and modern.

He then gave Hamish a lesson in the picking of the older more common padlocks then produced the innards of a cigarette packet. On the card, he had written a set of numbers and another column of letters and figures. He went into considerable detail about how to bypass whatever sequence was being used on a combination padlock.

When he had finished, the card of the cigarette packet not only had the figures and letters written down but numerous arrows pointing to various codes made up from the numbers and letters.

"Throw in the file pick and I'll give you back your skeletons," Hamish offered him.

The file came sliding across the table to meet up with the newly cut key. On the return track the skeleton keys ended up in Chubby's lap or what remained of it as his stomach covered most of his thighs, Hamish stood up and thanked Mrs Chubby for her hospitality and when she welcomed him back, "Any time."

"Bugger off," Chubby told his wife.

"The next time that I want to see 'e is in a picture in the paper as you is nicked for burglary. Christ, I'll 'ave a laugh. Pin it up and chuck darts at it."

"Do not take the lords name in vain, Chubby," Hamish warned him. "You'll need 'im afore I do." Chubby cheerfully told him. "Them cells is very lonely places. Ask the monks, they lived in 'em and prayed, oh, yes they prayed."

With the laughter of Chubby ringing in his ears as he went to leave, he asked Chubby for the tablet of soap. The reply to his request was, "the wife will like it with all that perfume. Surprised at you using that Sarg, might just give someone the wrong, or perhaps the right opinion of you."

After another visit to the retail park and the supermarket chemist department, the only bit open, to buy soap Hamish headed for Sunny Patch.

On the front porch, he found Freya, Tara and a truly statuesque very fair-haired girl. Freya welcomed him back and introduced him to Kirsten 'from across the avenue'. "I'm just opposite you," Kirsten told him.

Hamish excused himself in order to unload his car and undress. As he undressed he deduced that this Kirsten must be the girl that Freya was on about yesterday. He agreed with Freya, she really was a 'stunner', a sweet and very distinctive smelling stunner at that. After he had unloaded the car he went back to the porch and still wrapped up, handed Tara her shopping and the list.

"I think that everything on the list is there," he told her. Without a blush, Tara thanked him and Freya announced that Kirsten and her sisters would be joining them for dinner at seven.

Kirsten then said. "They are not my sisters, flattering that the presumption may be but, they are my daughters.

Three faces reflected the total surprise that Kirsten could not be the late teenager or early twenties as judging from her figure and skin texture that the two women had assumed.

Saying something to break the stunned silence Hamish told Kirsten, "You must have been a child bride."

She replied, "Very nearly. I could be a grandmother in my mid-thirties but I wouldn't encourage either girl to marry young.

I did and I am lucky with my husband but so many youngsters are not."

Kirsten stood up and she was a good six foot in height. As with Joy, Hamish saw a vision of total beauty and he could sense the eyes of Freya boring into his back. However, Joy also had a 'beautiful' mind to combine with her body. As with Joy and now this Kirsten, Freya was, other than her skin tone and hair colour, their equal in every respect subject to Kirsten having the quality of mind to complement the quality of her body.

"We will meet you in the dining room at seven," Kirsten told them as she turned, went down the steps and headed over to her lodge.

"Well, I'll be damned," Hamish declared. Before he could justify his words Freya interrupted by saying, "You will be damned if you give her a second glance.

I'm warning you now."

As he went to speak again Freya interrupted to tell Tara, "Our friend Joy has a permanent home here and she could be down here now or in the next couple of days. She is a beautiful woman and a few days ago Hamish of the ilk was, for hours, sitting with her.

So engrossed were they in each other that people began to talk. They were nude at the time. If she comes here you will see what I mean, she is really attractive, particularly to my husband. I'm not going to have that episode again with this Kirsten, child bride or not."

"After meeting you and now Kirsten," Tara said, "I'm glad Hamish went shopping for me, I'm off to do a bit of titivating here and there. See you at seven."

"Don't frighten Howard with your bit of titivating," Freya called after her, adding, "He might refuse to be seen with you unless you hide behind a towel." The sound of "More likely than not," came from the doorway of number twenty-one.

With much banging and a crash or two heralded the arrival of Hamish and his camp bed. When put up it occupied the space between Freya's opened bed and the wall and brought the observation from her that, "If I want to get out of bed during the night I will have to step over you and although I have very long legs I will still not be able to reach the floor. What are you going to do about that smart Alec, although, in your case, smart Hamish?"

"Simple solution to that conundrum," he told her. "Let me sleep in your bed and you will not need your long, and may I say, shapely legs to reach the floor, my dear heart."

"Me ma told I never to let a wicked Sir Jasper into me bed unless 'ee 'as crossed my palm with gold, shiny, 'eavy gold. See like?" Freya, in her interpretation of the west-country nineteenth-century dialect told Hamish.

"If the day ever came that I would have to pay for it, I'd slit my throat," he told her and with a dramatic exit he went through the back door to the car to bring in the rest of his purchases.

"What on earth have you brought those for?" Freya asked Hamish as he laid the boiler suits on his now collapsed camp bed.

"Easy and quick to put on," was his reply. Explaining that if they needed to cover their nakedness quickly in pursuit of a rogue they could slip the suit on and if it was dark they could blend into the background.

"Ha, so I was right Mr Clever Dick," Freya told him before adding. "Who presumed to tell me that a white body was invisible in the dark? These suits are an admission that you were wrong but not man enough to admit that you were wrong. Miserable cur."

He said nothing as he busied himself with his new torch and the enormous battery.

After showering, arm in arm they made their way to the dining room in the restaurant where they found Tara and Howard talking to Kirsten and her daughters.

As they all joined in a conversation about the likes and dislikes of living or holidaying in this type of camp, colony or holiday centre, Hamish was busy, with one ear on the conversation, studying both Kirsten and her daughters.

There was no doubting her beauty but Hamish had a nagging doubt that Kirsten was no simple holiday-maker.

She displayed no particular interest in the wonderful weather, the facilities or her enjoyment of the people there. The only real information was that she had been there for several months and her husband 'Worked in the city'.

As Hamish watched the ladies and bashful Howard sit down Ted and Ivy came in. Ivy went to the table and began a conversation with Freya, Tara and Kirsten. Howard was simply looking into space.

"What is it that attracts beautiful women to you?" Ted asked Hamish, then he continued, "The three most attractive ladies here are all sat at your table, other than youth, handsomeness, bearing and that damned great heraldic signet ring what do you have that I am missing?"

"You're not missing anything, Ted," Hamish told him. "You have Ivy, what more could a man ask for in this world or the next?"

"What more could a man ask for?" Ted asked. He then answered his own question. Pointing to Freya, Tara and Kirsten, he said to Hamish, "If the next world is all it's cracked up to be I just ask for those three ladies with me then it would be paradise."

"Or paradise lost, if Ivy finds out that you covet not only one man's Ox, Ass and wife but all three of them," Hamish told him then enquired what he knew about Kirsten?

"She came here several months ago, probably early spring. I've never seen anyone else with her and when she told someone that the girls were her daughters, boy-oh-boy did that set the tongues wagging. I've noticed that the girls haven't been to any school while she's been here. I don't know why, but I always have the feeling that she is hiding something or running from something. In a relationship, I think that she could be quite domineering. Don't ask me why, it's simply a gut feeling."

"The waitress is at your table," Ted told Hamish "And it looks like Ivy has found us a table. Ta-Ta for now."

The meal was very good, and with the company present, it made it a delightful occasion. After trying his best not to be caught staring at Kirsten, even Howard was just peeking out of his self-inflicted shell.

After dinner was finished the group went for a stroll around the top of Sunny Patch and when they went past the volleyball court the ladies agreed that on Monday they would meet up for a game with Kirsten's oldest girl making up the four.

Back in their hut, Hamish asked Freya, "What do you think of her?"

"Think of who?"

"Kirsten," he said.

She thought for a moment before saying. "She's a bit of an enigma to me. She has beauty, a figure most women would die for, intelligent conversation but no frivolous humour. From her use of English coupled with her name, I presume that she originates from somewhere around the Baltic. I might find out more when we play volleyball tomorrow."

They then settled into an evening of reading a new magazine called British Naturism which they found in the assembly room. The magazine had articles and letters all about the world of nude living and recreation mainly from clubs, not individuals. After a couple of rums, Hamish was in a mellow mood when he saw that it was quite dark outside. Waking up the sleeping figure of Freya laying across his lap he told her that he was going to try his new key in the lock of the next door hut.

Donning their nice new boiler suits and picking up the key, pencil torch and gloves they ventured out into the stillness of the night with only the very distant sound of a Nightjar's song to disrupt the sound of nothing. Suddenly Freya felt the hand of Hamish push her against the end of their hut. In the shadow, she saw a figure at the back door of number seventeen apparently locking the door. The figure then went down the steps and thankfully walked with a strange twisting gait towards the gates at the end of the avenue.

"A couple of seconds earlier and he would have caught us," whispered Hamish. The two of them then, as quietly as possible, debated if there might be someone else in the hut then decided on the balance of probabilities that if there was anyone else in the hut the figure that they had just seen would not have locked the door.

Very cautiously they made their way up the steps and Hamish then, as quietly and slowly as possible put the key in the door lock, turned it and the lock opened. A gentle opening of the door followed by a few seconds of listening carefully gave him the confidence to go into the hut.

He turned to Freya and told her to keep a lookout for the return of their man. "What in the devil do you think I am doing?" she said, by then, to a vacant space as he had already gone further into the hut.

With her eyes darting into the hut and then looking around her through the darkness, all she could properly see was the pinhead of light from the pencil torch as Hamish poked around in the hut.

Freya physically jumped as a hand touched her shoulder. "Get some sort of bag quickly," Hamish instructed.

As quickly and quietly as she could Freya returned to their hut and scrabbled to find a couple of bags. Both contained their arrival clothes, without undue ceremony she dumped them on the floor and quietly returned to Hamish with the bags.

Disappearing into the hut again, he began to make quite a bit of noise as he filled both bags up and again appeared at the door, this time without startling her. He directed her hand down to a bag handle, put something against the wall of the hut and then gently and quietly locked the door.

He then picked up the other bag and whatever he had propped up against the wall and followed Freya rather more quickly than anticipated by missing his step and depositing himself on the ground.

Apart from a bruised derrière as he slipped down the steps, he picked himself up and quietly made his way behind his accomplice into their hut.

With the door closed, Hamish let out a most pent up anguished howl as he dropped the bag and gripped his buttocks. "What's wrong?" a concerned Freya asked. "I fell down the 'B' steps." Still chuntering he dropped his boiler suit and bent over enquiring from Freya,

"What does my bum look like?"

"Slightly red but much the same as usual," she answered now with a disinterested tone in her voice.

Hamish, living up to the female's opinion of men as being lifelong children, sulkily told her that he was in agony and that he was sure that his injury was much more serious than she had made it out to be.

"Don't be such a big cissy," Freya told him as she went around closing the curtains before saying, "Back to work staff sergeant. We will now have a debriefing." Stepping out of the boiler suit now around his ankles Hamish, still clasping his buttocks picked up one of the bags and poured the contents on the floor.

"Inventory please," he asked Freya.

"I haven't got any paper," she told him. He went to the wardrobe, fished in his pockets and turned around waving his pocketbook and a pen and told Freya. "No self-respecting temporary acting unpaid detective inspector would ever find himself without the means to record anything from riding a bike without lights to mass murder. Unless of course, you happened to be an acting detective superintendent!"

"Any acting detective superintendent worth their salt would have minions called temporary acting unpaid detective inspectors to furnish their every need," Freya told him as she grabbed the pocketbook from his hands.

Hamish went to the large objects which turned out to be two paintings, one of a Georgian lady in her finery and one of a seascape, from the style he guessed of Victorian vintage. They then moved on to twenty pamphlets carrying subversive propaganda, Ten passport covers all franked with different country's emblems, fifteen completed passports excluding photographs, five passport interiors, numerous notes of various currency from several nations, three pre-war reinforced boxes as used by opticians containing coloured and clear glass pieces. One bottle of printing ink, two franking dies, stitching thread and two ledgers with what appeared to be Russian writing with the numbers of radio wavebands in a column and a black reinforced cloth belt with semi-circular or half-moon pockets.

After an hour, with several stops to consider the items and many stops for Freya's writer's cramp to recover, the job was done except for getting the items tidily in the bags with the exception of the paintings.

"Post mortem time," she, stretching and pulling her fingers, told her burglar.

He described what he saw and found beginning with a small printing press inside the door with a stitching machine and numerous spools of thread and a franking press with dies. Behind the press were many of what has now turned out to be paintings. To the side of them was a filing cabinet where he got all the passport bits and pieces and the currency.

In the bottom drawer, he found the pamphlets and the two ledgers. He went under an array of radio receivers and transmitters and found the boxes of glass hidden in a cavity in the wall under the radio gear.

Hamish stopped talking, went to the wardrobe and brought back his bottle of rum, picked up two glasses, one from the side of Freya's bed, emptied the remains of her night-time water, poured a good three fingers in each glass. Gave one to her and took a large slug of grog from his glass, pulled a face, shook himself and sat by her on the floor looking their 'Loot'.

Freya took a sniff at her glass, wrinkled her nose then reminded him that she had not consumed rum since their student days when she thought it so clever to drink an unpopular but potent drink.

She took a draught and as could be expected, coughed and gagged after the rum passed her tonsils.

Clearing away the tears she asked Hamish, "What now?"

"You're the boss, you tell me?"

"Paint me the picture from opening the door until you closed it."

He told her, "It was very dark, something like the inside of a cow. Immediately inside was the printing press with a stitcher alongside and the paintings, perhaps a dozen or so behind them. To the side of them was a die franking press and then the file cabinet. Just ahead of that on the opposite wall was the array of radio gear, headphones and other unidentified bits and bobs.

Inside of the filing cabinet, I found all the paper and card items and logbooks."

She interrupted him to ask if the cabinet was locked and if it was how did he get into it?

Hamish grinned at her and took another drink of rum before answering her.

"For an acting detective superintendent, you are remarkably naive. In many stations, in many double-locked strong rooms containing banks of locked filing cabinets in many personnel departments, it has been my privilege to bye-pass locks and harvest my records.

Common to most cabinets, even without the assistance of Chubby Reynolds I have, over my career opened many a drawer, harvested or extracted whatever relates to me which for various reasons I do not wish my name to be connected with.

Particularly that which someone else has written about me, somewhat similar to marriage, it could be for better or quite often, for worse!

I pretended that the cabinet in there contained something about me and almost without touching, it sprung open. I was about to wave my hands and say 'Abracadabra' but it wasn't necessary."

Freya, still sitting on the floor with her glass in her hand told him, "There is a very close connection with what comes out of your mouth with that which comes out of the back of a bull. Have you left anything in there?"

Hamish, adopting the pose and hurt of outrage told her, "No, I cleaned every last bit of evidence and washed the place out, made the bed, put a posy on the table and made a mental note to reprimand the acting detective superintendent for trying to teach her grandfather Fergusson how to suck eggs.

"As the more common people might call someone," Freya told him, "I'm a silly bitch."

"The principal for covert thieving is not to make it too obvious that anyone has been about but at least for a day or so they will not find anything missing. Anyway, I do doubt that our limping friend is likely to report a burglary to the local plod. Let's get this lot bagged up, it should fit better as I just threw it in. Tomorrow or now today, take the car with the loot to the Scolding Wife car park and get Sarah to take it to 'Old Gaunt' at headquarters. It will be safer there under lock and key than at my nick." Hamish explained.

"Unless a certain temporary acting unpaid detective inspector Hamish 'Fingers' Fergusson is about," concluded Freya.

After gently placing everything in the bags and as Hamish correctly predicted there was room left for more goods except the paintings.

"Time for bed?" she enquired.

"Yup," he replied and they set about the new procedure for bedtime at number nineteen. Eventually, after getting Freya into her bed, he pulled the curtains back. At the long door curtain, he hesitated and put the material to his face and took a deep 'sniff'. Eventually, he put up his new camp bed and slid sideways into the sleeping bag.

As peace descended it was not long before Hamish told Freya that before she took the 'loot' to Sarah he would hope to meet Ted and take the coloured glass for him to look at. "Why?" came the question down from the bed.

"That glass could be some sort of gemstone," came up the answer from the camp bed."

"Why would a forger have gems?" came down from the bed. Followed by, "Will he not miss them if he discovers someone has been in his hut?" From the camp bed came," He might well do so, but again, what can he do about it, sweet damn all. So far it's one-nil to us. Good night darling."

"If I'm going to take the goods to Sarah, what are you going to do?" Freya asked.

"Firstly I am going to wake up. That will be followed by the three 'S' necessities of the morning and then go for breakfast. Try and find Ted before you take off to get the glass or whatever to you before you leave then have a good look at this underground water tank."

"Why the interest in the tank?" she asked.

"Gut feeling inspired by Ted saying that the shed on the top is derelict yet it has a new padlock on the door. It is now a quarter to three and although you wouldn't believe it I need my beauty sleep," Hamish, with a make-believe yawn, told Freya. The only reply was the gentle breathing of sleep.

"I'm glad that you're about Ted. I want to pick your professional brain." Hamish told him as, without the ladies, they tucked into a totally unhealthy 'Man's' breakfast.

"I did notice the boxes when you came in. I wondered what might be in them because you carried them as if they were the crown jewels. Are they?" Ted enquired.

"Not sure," Hamish said, "When the coffee arrives I will let you have a look."

Eventually, the waitress took away the very few remains of their breakfast, delivered the coffee pot as she turned away Hamish smiled at the back view of the girl.

"What's so funny about her back?" Ted asked.

"Nothing in particular," Hamish replied "except that it is the first time that I've seen a tattooed buttock with a pierced heart and initials."

"It's quite simple my boy," Ted told him. "If she has the tattoo on her bum and falls out with the love of her life her knickers will hide it from the next boyfriend, well it might. In any event, I expect that the initials could be easily, but painfully changed for other ones."

"Never mind girls bums what have you got for me?" Ted asked rubbing his hands.

Hamish opened the first box, Ted peered in and only said, "Come over home with them. I've got my gear there and it's safer."

As they headed for Ted's residence so Ivy emerged as Freya came up the avenue. The ladies went into the restaurant and the men went on to their task.

Hamish asked Ted if this beautiful villa type dwelling was his permanent home?

As they went through the doorway Ted replied. "Yes, it is, and when we compare this with the ripped tiny tents when we first came here it is unbelievable. The original group or their descendants still own the land here but in the nineteen fifties we leased the site to a company and they developed it to what we have here and we lay back and get a nice little income and benefits in kind, discounted meals etcetera. It's a good life. Now to these bits of glass."

Hamish was astounded at the luxury of Ted's home as he followed him into what was plainly a study or perhaps an office. "As they would say in your native tongue, 'Sit ye doon' Ted invited him.

Ted spread the glass out on his desk and used an eyepiece to pick each bit of glass up with tweezers.

As he put them down he separated them. He then collected one line and put them in a leatherette drawstring bag, the others he returned to the box. Hamish then handed him the second box and Ted performed the same process with the contents of the box.

When he had completed the task he opened the drawstring bag and as before divided up the items into the bag or back into the box.

Straightening up he told Hamish. "In that, you have some valuable and not so valuable gemstones. In the boxes is the rubbish but still worth a bob or two. I don't suppose that you are going to tell me the story behind them are you?"

"Not yet Ted, but I promise when the time comes, and that may not be for a year or so I will tell you exactly what has or is happening here. I will put your mind at rest by telling you that it does not concern Sunny Patch as a place and it is no danger to this place or the people here.

Thank you, Ted; I'm going to visit your old water tank today, the newish padlock that you told spoke about fascinates me and I want to see it for myself.

If there is anything else that comes to light, if I can I will tell you, I will. Thank you again, chum."

"Are you some sort of copper?" Ted asked. "At the moment I am working under a person from the Home Office but having a lovely holiday here in this beautiful weather." Hamish told him adding that "This is totally confidential Ted." as they walked towards the door. Ted told Hamish, "I'll not even tell Ivy."

Both men jumped when a voice asked "What won't Ivy know about?" Ivy sat on a steamer chair on the lawn looking at nothing but plainly hearing everything.

"Promise not to tell anyone dear," Ted told Ivy but, "we were admiring a tattoo on a girls bum and we think that she heard us. We wanted to keep it a secret between the two of us in case anything came of it."

"That's rubbish," Ivy quite reasonably stated. "I expect that there is more to that than talking about it, but like all men of any age, you are born stupid. Forget it. Bye Hamish."

"Bye Ivy. Thanks for showing me around, Ted, very much appreciated." Hamish told Ted before becoming the recipient of a very bold wink from Ted as he went down the avenue passing a now well-groomed Tara and the trailing behind was Howard as always, looking a picture of happiness.

"Where have you been?" Freya asked emerging from the bathroom with a toothbrush in her mouth and toothpaste running down her chin. "Saw Ted, that glass is gemstone and bits of coloured glass and he's separated them for us so you can take them with you. It must be about time for you to go."

After wiping the toothpaste from her chin, she asked," What are you going to do while I'm away? I don't want to return and find you in deep conversation or worse with the blonde opposite!"

"I'm going to have a look at this water tank that Ted was on about. Something is stirring in my bowels about that place. Ted went through brambles and so forth to get to it yet he found a reasonably clear path to get there only to find a newish padlock on the door. All very strange."

Eventually, Freya completed her bathroom tasks and they loaded up the car for her to rendezvous with Sarah at the Scolding Wife car park. In the meantime, Hamish dressed in his boiler suit and shoes then, with his large torch hidden as best he could, took off through the brambles, stinging nettles and scrub holly bushes into the dank quiet woodland.

In some places, he had to hold his hands above his head for fear of scratches but he assured himself that if 'Old' Ted could do it a 'young' Hamish should be able to get through this explorer dense green pith helmeted Fawcett type of jungle.

Eventually, he could see the top of the shed on top of the water tank and then found the trampled down vegetation probably from Ted's 'Expedition'.

When he got near to the shed he saw the back of an almost, except, strangely enough, wearing a belt, a long thin naked figure walking down the made-up path towards the gates of Sunny Patch. Did he attempt to follow the person in order to see where he went or to attempt to identify him? He reasoned that there was a good chance that whichever course that he tried to follow could end up with the 'target' catching him following, particularly in a boiler suit. At that moment he wished that he had put a tell-tale marker on the back door of number seventeen to see if the 'Target' was his mystery neighbour.

Turning to the shed he saw that Ted had not exaggerated when he described the shed as having broken windows with ivy growing through both them and the roof. Other than a track across the concrete of the water tank the rest was covered in moss and algae. He arrived at the shed door and noticed that the hinges had been oiled at some time, probably quite a while ago. He then got to the padlock and found that it was not a combination lock but a quite modern ordinary pattern.

Using the instrument from Chubby he quite easily opened the lock.

For the umpteenth time Hamish stopped, listened and looked behind him but other than a very inquisitive Robin, nothing moved under the canopy of trees. Closing the door behind him he was taken back to his nautical days as he faced a davit with a fully rigged twofold purchase shackled to it. In simple terms, a large piece of metal with a curve at the top with a pulley block secured to the davit and the other part of the block with a hook on it.

Hamish lifted the metal manhole cover to the tank and as he was about to turn his torch on he saw a switch. He turned it on and sure enough the light illuminated what it would not be unreasonable to describe as Aladdin's cave about ten feet below him.

He had been so absorbed with the scene before him that his usual caution had been neglected and this was brought home to him when a noise outside the shed set his nerves on edge.

He cautiously moved towards the door only to see a large Tabby cat racing off down the path.

Exhaling his pent up breath he went out to look around and could see little except for a few feathers which had probably come from the eaten or escaped Robin.

Back inside the shed Hamish picked up the manhole cover and took it outside into the all-pervading Ivy, covering it with the tendrils as the thought of someone trapping him in the tank under the metal cover was a fate that any sensible person would avoid.

Very gently he stepped onto the metal ladder secured to the wall and collected his torch in case he was marooned in the tank by someone switching off the light. At this point, he realised that perhaps he should have waited until Freya returned. Being totally stubborn he continued downwards.

At the bottom, he positively identified what he had noted from above.

To one side of the tank was a crucible with pipes leading to it from numerous small gas bottles on the other wall. In one corner was a huge pile of what turned out to be watch parts, the skeletons of jewellery and various small pieces of metal. Over the crucible was a large expandable pipe that went to the roof where it was secured with the top part leaning down inside the tank. He presumed that the pipe would be put through the manhole cover when they were busy smelting.

A closer study of the crucible made him quite certain that it was used for smelting gold.

As he went around he found pattern blocks for round items about three inches diameter with congealed gold on them.

In a corner, he found a heap of what appeared to be gold coins which corresponded with the size of the moulding blocks and several of the mysterious belts which had turned up during the investigation on and off of various human carcasses.

This was enough for Hamish, grabbing a few coins he turned and almost fell over a motor. Although not certain of the part this motor would play in the smelting of gold he deduced that it might be for the fume removing pipe.

After he had filled his pockets with the gold, he thought that for evidence purposes he would take one of the belts, fill it with coins and take that with him.

As he made his way up the ladder he realised the weight of pure gold as his legs ached by the time he finally emerged into the shed.

He went into the undergrowth, recovered the manhole cover, replaced it then realised that he had not turned out the light. Finally, he was ready to leave. When he went to relock the padlock he realised that while Chubby had taught him to unlock it, no mention had been made to returning it to the locked position.

After trying to secure the padlock again and only half succeeding in that at least the lock now looked secure, Hamish as quickly as his very heavy pockets would allow made his way through the undergrowth finally emerging roughly where he began his journey.

As quickly as possible he divested himself of his gold and left it in the wardrobe. Quickly collecting the camera, handcuffs and his warrant card he went next door where he knocked on the door.

"Is Howard in?" he asked Tara. She assured him that he was and called to him. Howard emerged from the back of the hut, a much larger one than they had, Hamish noted.

"I've a favour to ask of you," Hamish said to him. Then continued," I understand that you are in an occupation which might require the signing of The Official Secrets Act. Are you and have you signed it?"

"Yes," Howard, very hesitantly said.

"Good," Hamish told him. "Will you do me a kindness, it will be heavy work?"

"Of course, he will, won't you Howard?" Tara answered for him.

A meek nod was the reply.

"Thank you, and now could I borrow the bags that you brought your clothes in, Freya has ours in the car and I can't wait for her to come back. By the way Howard I need you dressed for this task." adding mischievously, I'm so sorry to make you dress, I know how much you enjoy this naked life."

Tara gave Hamish a little smile as they watched Howard quickly put his pants on while she found two large canvas bags.

When dressed Hamish suggested that he should put shoes on and they ventured out. Hamish led the way through the undergrowth until they reached the water tank.

He then told Howard what he wanted of him as he let them in without the need of lock picking.

Hamish removed the manhole cover and turned on the light to allow Howard to gaze in wonderment at the scene before him Hamish then got out his camera and took several shots of the tank and its contents. He then instructed Howard how to use the pulley's and swing the davit to land the heavy bags.

That done Hamish threw down the bags and went down in the tank taking photographs as he went and then close-ups of each item on the floor. He quickly put the gold coins in the bags lifting each, in turn, to have equal weight in each. Far from being full, the bags were quite heavy as he hooked them one after the other for Howard to haul up and land on the top of the tank. When that was completed he asked for the hook to be lowered again and hooked the crucible on with the belts then climbed out to help Howard land them.

Turning out the light, Hamish returned the cover to the manhole and gave one of the bags to Howard and he carried the other one and the crucible with the belts.

Noting how Howard was struggling with his bag, Hamish told him that they would walk down the clear path towards the gate. His reasoning was that Howard would never get through the undergrowth returning the way that they had come with the heavy bag and it was no longer of any consequence if they were seen carrying bags as he was in a boiler suit and Howard was fully dressed.

After two stops for the changing of hands, and Hamish hiding the very heavy crucible in the undergrowth, they arrived at the back of number nineteen just as Freya pulled up. Hamish thanked Howard for his 'Sterling' work then asked him, "Why have you not asked any questions?"

Howard replied, "I don't know what you are and if I know nothing about you and your work it will not compromise me in the event of an inquiry. I'll see you later." With that, Howard was returned to the bosom of his family or rather Tara minus their bags. Telling Freya to watch the bags he returned to recover the crucible and took it, with both hands, into the hut.

Hamish lifted the bags of coins, one at a time into their hut and sat down for a stiff rum before telling the story to Freya. She in turn told him about her meeting with Sarah. Freya then took a coin out of the bag and said.

"These aren't coins, they are discs of gold there is nothing on them, they are blank.

From the evidence we have so far, it is very apparent that they are stealing items containing gold, stripping out the metal and smelting it into these coins which they carry in the fancy belts to where ever, for either payment or servicing debt or knowing all about them, into the Iron Curtain countries."

"Right," said Hamish, "There are the remains of small ingots with one fragment bearing what looks like Arabic script. I haven't had time to look at every bit of gold but, we have to get this to safety now.

Will you drive out and find a' phone box and ring old Gaunt and ask for a van and escort to meet me at the Scolding Wife car park by, let's say about two this afternoon."

Without saying a word, Freya collected the car keys and drove away. Hamish was about to have another rum then realised that he would be driving so made himself a coffee instead.

Seemingly in no time at all Freya reappeared and told him that it was arranged for a plain van to meet at the pub with two escorting traffic cars parked away from the pub.

"As they might say in other strands of society, we did alright yer, kid," Freya declared in a happy voice.

Almost guaranteed to put a damper on any sign of cheerfulness Hamish, in a truculent voice told her. "It's all very well patting ourselves on the back for solving several types of crimes which probably have never been reported but, as I told our masters last week, this is a fool's errand and we are no further forward in catching our murderer, the sole purpose of the high and mighty in sending us here."

"Did you enjoy the evening at Sarah's?" she asked him.

"Yes," he replied.

"Do you like the life here, excluding work?" she asked.

"Yes," he again replied.

"We are policemen, we solve crimes and arrest criminals wherever they might be, even in a nudist colony. We may not have a murderer this time but by the time we have grilled our limping chum, we may have a breakthrough.

When are we going to nick him?" She asked "If he's about," Hamish answered. "Tonight, but if possible away from here or at least outside of the gates."

"What charges will you bring against him, just in case his 'Brief' is with him." Freya joked.

"Hamish looked daggers at her as he said in reply. "Pecuniary advantage by uttering forged documents, disposing of stolen goods, in possession of stolen goods, printing and publishing seditious material against the State. The illegal handling, evasion of tax and disposal of bullion. That's for a start. I could put a cart and horses through most of these charges for lack of evidence but even the smartest of 'Briefs' 'ain't that smart at night, particularly after they've been at the bottle. Let's feel his collar first then worry about charges.

Firstly, my dearest acting detective superintendent, we have to catch our limping friend. I've been thinking about that limp. It is not a proper limp. More of a twist. When I was a child I had Polio and in my ward were children with TB spines. Like me, they had to be taught to walk again, and watching our friend, it reminded me of some of the children with me. They would swing one leg more than the other which dropped one shoulder and gave them this unusual gait which was not a true limp."

"Thank you, Doctor Fergusson, for your expert opinion but to an ignorant layman such as me, our target has a limp. That's That!" Freya told her 'In house doctor'

As she went towards the door Hamish enquired where she was going. Her reply was "To lunch."

"What about me?" You stay and guard the loot, I'll bring you back a bun," she told him as she disappeared into the sunshine.

As Freya sat down to lunch so Tara came in and joined her at the table. "What did Hamish do to Howard this morning?" she asked.

"Took him on a trek in the jungles of the sunny patch. Is he okay?" Freya enquired.

"He's taken to his bed and has told me that under the Official Act he cannot tell me where he has been or what he's been doing. In these matters, he is a proper swot," Tara laughingly told Freya.

"He's quite right in one way. As you are not Mrs Gossip from the village newsagents all I will tell you is that without his help Hamish could not have managed to recover some very valuable property which probably belongs to many people and I suspect also to the government. In simple terms, to you and me.

As events move on he will turn out to be your little hero. I have your card so if we suddenly disappear I will eventually contact you and tell you all about this story."

"And get our bags back?" Tara asked. "This very afternoon," Freya assured her.

When Freya returned she found Hamish lying in the hammock on the veranda. Indicating number twenty-one hut she asked him just what he had done with Howard and went on to tell him that Howard had taken to his bed. She then went on to enquire what would happen if someone came in the back door and stole the gold?

"Not a chance without me knowing," Hamish told her. "I've put that crucible against the door and moving that would waken the long since deceased."

Swinging his legs out of the hammock, he followed her into the hut when he became aware that he was being followed. In stopping suddenly a firm body came into violent contact with his back. Turning, both he and Freya found Kirsten attempting to get her breath back.

Eventually, Kirsten recovered, straightened up as Hamish, with an excess of courteous concern enquired "Can I be of any help?"

"Oh, pardon me I was," she hesitated as her eyes darted around the hut to eventually be met with an icy stare from Freya. "Yes?" a severe voiced Freya enquired.

"I don't feel too well. I will go back to my chalet." Kirsten said as she turned to leave.

"Before you leave," Freya said, "What exactly do you want sneaking in here without invitation or knocking?"

"I was going to ask. To ask, yes to ask, if you would make up a volleyball foursome," Kirsten, very hesitantly enquired. "No, goodbye," were the last words on the subject by Freya.

"Was she after you?" Freya asked Hamish. "It did seem unusual that not only did she creep in but she was so close behind me that when I stopped she was right in my back. I just had an instinct that someone was behind me. On reflection, she was so close that it could have been her breath that gave her away," he deduced.

"And poor innocent Hamish had a naked, soft, warm, inviting body to, purely by chance, of course, fold itself around his naked body." Freya sarcastically told no one in particular. "I'll bet she thought that you were here alone and targeted handsome Hamish for her nefarious pleasures." Without drawing a breath, Freya continued. "And the reason that she gave for being here, piffle, pure piffle."

He made no comment but had his own views for the unexpected visit. Following his own thoughts; it was a pity that the crucible against the back door would have been directly in the line of sight for Kirsten. He decided that it would be best not to share his thinking with Freya.

Freya went out to the car and brought in their empty Holdalls and cautiously put all the contents of the bags belonging to Tara and Howard into their baggage.

While Freya stayed in the car, Hamish loaded up the gold, money belts and the crucible with the film from his camera and they set off for the rendezvous with the police security van.

As they entered the pub car park they drew alongside the van. Freya went to the two crew and asked for their warrant cards which the men seemed rather surprised at being asked to produce.

After satisfying herself that they were policemen she told them to take the bags into their van.

When inside the gold, piece by piece was put into bank cash bags and locked into two large strong boxes on either side of the vehicle. Freya held out her hand. The two men looked at her with raised eyebrows. "Keys please," she asked. The men asked her how would they open the boxes if she had the keys? "The assistant chief constable has another set of keys. He will be waiting for you." Freya told them. "What's that?" as Hamish gave the officer the crucible to load. "It makes gold. The Alchemist dream," he told the puzzled coppers.

As the van drove off Freya and Hamish followed it onto the main road where two traffic cars were waiting, one in livery the other a grey BMW. The couple watched as they set off with blue lights flashing.

Back in Sunny Patch, Freya had a shower, 'To get the grime of crime off my body' while Hamish rigged up both hammocks.

He had just got himself comfortable when Freya appeared and made several unsuccessful attempts to get in the hammock.

With a deliberately loud sigh, he alighted from his perch and told her "It's my pleasure to get the poor decrepit old lady into her hammock." Then touching his forelock, he held out his hand for his well-deserved gratuity. Freya grabbed the open hand put it to her mouth and dribbled into it saying, "Thank you, Mellors; you are dismissed!"

Hamish looked at the palm of his hand, studied it then without ceremony, promptly wiped it on her upper arm.

He then disappeared into the hut before emerging smoking one of his King Edward cigars. Blowing a half-decent circle of smoke he hoisted himself back into his hammock.

"When we get out of here I will tell you a little secret," Hamish told Freya. "When we get out of here I will tell you a little secret too," She told him then went on to ask in an American drawl, "What next partner?"

"It's quite simple," he told her. "As we have already discussed, collar the bloke if possible tonight, charge him, as we have discussed before. Pack our bags, say our 'Goodbyes' and bugger off home sharply. Any further questions, ma'am?"

"Yes," she said, "I haven't seen you smoking for quite a while. Why now, what's changed? Are you unhappy? Am I getting on your nerves?"

"I simply felt like a smoke, you are not getting on my nerves, except for asking if you're getting on my nerves, nothing has changed and, yes I'm unhappy," he told her and added, "For the reasons that we have discussed before and over which we will never agree, in particular, none of this helps catch the murderer of one, Rosenberg.

Chapter 10
Sinister Episode

I nick the bloke tonight, then what? Back to Division or in my case Head Quarters. Knock out numerous statements avoiding stating that I was a temporary resident in a nudist camp. Licking the envelopes, putting this episode down to experience and waving you off to Lunnon."

"Were you a female darling," she told him, "I would put your frame of mind down to the onset of the menopause. As you are evidently male, perhaps a mid-life crisis? But, there again you 'ain't mid-life, just yet. It's a beautiful afternoon, go to sleep listening to the song of the birds and the happy laughter of the children in the pool. Night-night."

Later they went to the restaurant and had a delicious meal on their own at first. They were then joined by Tara and Howard. As Tara approached the table with her towel folded over her arm and across her stomach she swung the towel away from herself to announce, "How about that for an afternoons work?" Very impressive, now keep up with the regime and welcome to the exclusive club," Freya encouragingly replied. Hamish just smiled. Howard looked everywhere except at his wife!

After a few drinks at the bar with Tara, as by now, Howard had returned to their chalet, Freya and Hamish went for a stroll around the site in the evening sunshine and at one point passed a couple with a baby. They all exchanged pleasantries and Hamish was very surprised to be looking at a mirror image of Freya. He decided that it might be for the best to say nothing as she would make some sarcastic comment about him being attracted again to beautiful women!

Returning to their hut they waited until dark before their night's work began.

"I'm going out now to keep a lookout. Make sure that you are dressed with your warrant card and cuffs on you. It might be better if you get into the boiler suit. The minute that you see me take off get the car outside the gates until I meet you with him." Hamish told Freya.

It was 10:30, and in the twilight, Freya could just make out the shadow of Hamish as he stood against the far side of their hut. Making sure that she had the car keys and the big torch she stood in the darkened doorway.

Three-quarters of an hour later, she saw Hamish leaving his position and she got in the car and without lights on, waited until he had disappeared through the wicket gate before letting herself out through the main gates.

Hamish caught up with the 'Limper' and said, "I'm a police officer, he grabbed his arm and said I'm arresting…"

Freya could just make out two figures by the wicket gate when she heard the sound of two sharp claps. She saw a running figure but could not see Hamish.

Grabbing the torch she rushed to the spot where she had last seen them and in the torchlight made out the figure of Hamish on the ground. She spoke to him and had no response. The light fell on his body and she could see some moisture on his clothing. She touched it and it was warm and plainly blood. She kept speaking to him while she felt for a pulse in his neck. Freya controlled herself as she detected a pulse. As she got up she noticed that he was holding on to something.

As fast as she could run she went in through the wicket gate up to the hut of Tara. Banging on the door she soon had it opened by Howard. "Hamish has been shot I think, please come," she asked.

Like a shot, a naked Tara was at the door with a bag. When Freya told her that Hamish was outside the grounds Tara quickly donned a skirt and blouse and they ran to Hamish.

With the torchlight on Hamish, Tara quickly cut away the boiler suit to expose a bullet wound with blood beginning to soak into more material. Tara, so calm went about her tasks in part controlling the flow of blood and asked if Freya had called an ambulance?

Freya told her that by the time an ambulance got out to them they could have him at the hospital in her car.

Trying their best to get Hamish into the car without hopefully causing no more damage was a challenge in itself. Pulling the front seats forward, they eventually got him onto the back seat only to realise that he was longer than the width of the seat. Gently folding his knees upwards they managed to get the door closed, they then pushed the front seats up against the body of Hamish preventing him from moving.

Freya thanked Tara and said, "Not a word of this to anyone. You will be contacted tomorrow, or rather today by someone from my department. Thanks, bye."

As Freya got herself into the driver's seat, the passenger door opened, and in got Tara explaining, "He is my patient. It is my professional duty to hand him over to surgeons."

Before she had finished speaking they were hurtling through the lanes at a breakneck speed towards the University hospital in the city.

There was very little traffic to hinder their way and Tara asked where were the blue lights coming from that she could see reflected in road signs. "The radiator screen. This is a 'Q' car." Freya told her not explaining what a 'Q' car was.

As they pulled into the A&E ambulance bays Tara was out and into the hospital while an ambulance driver stood in front of the car telling Freya that she couldn't park there as it was reserved for ambulances only. Freya was about to give the little officious man the tongue lashing that she reserved for such 'jobsworths' when she simply put on the blue lights. He jumped back and went on his way without a word.

Tara reappeared with a trolley and three porters. Considering the exhausting efforts of Freya and Tara in getting Hamish into the car, with seemingly little effort they had him on the trolley in no time.

While in A&E a surgeon arrived and within minutes told Freya that Hamish would be taken immediately into theatre and they would find out the limits of tissue damage. He then added that the hospital had to inform the police of the incident. With that, the clerk appeared and went through all the questions concerning Hamish, and after that, she addressed Freya as 'Mrs Fergusson' and without asking, put her down as the next-of-kin. With that, Tara reappeared after disappearing with the surgeon and then directed the clerk in relation to the injuries as had become apparent.

"Do you have any money on you?" Freya asked Tara. With a negative answer, Tara asked who she wanted to ring?

"My boss." Tara was rather taken aback that anyone would want to ring their boss at such a time as this but took Freya to an office with a 'phone and left her there.

Freya could not remember the home number of Mr Gaunt so in desperation she, for the first time in her life rang the three nine number and eventually got to the main switchboard and after identifying herself got the duty inspector. He then transferred her to the central switchboard.

On that line, she again identified herself and asked for the home number of the assistant chief constable, CID.

That request put the cat amongst the pigeons and after much huffing and puffing, referring the request to some poor chief inspector in his bed, Freya was put on a police line to Mr Gaunt. When a plainly sleepy and gruff Gaunt came on the line she told him the story, warts and all.

The upshot was that he told her that he was sending an armed officer to the hospital just in case the rogues attempted to make sure Hamish was dead. The phrase, "Make sure Hamish was dead," apart from putting terror in Freya's mind and tears in her eyes reinforced the surgeon's words, "At this time this is a fifty-fifty case, but chin up Mrs Fergusson."

"What else can I offer you, not as a policewoman but as Freya?" Mr Gaunt asked. She then told him about Doctor Tara and the fact that other than the blue lights of the car, she did not know that the pair of them were police officers but that she would have to get her back to Sunny Patch.

Leave that with me he told her and asked, "who can I get to help you out, a friend, a relative or who?

And what about your place at Sunny Patch, is it secure?" She told Mr Gaunt that it was not secure but that she would go there when the armed officer arrived and clear it out. Collecting her thoughts about the incident she told the ACC she was almost sure that when she first went to Hamish outside of the gates he was holding on to something like a glove. Before dawn could his scene of crime men have a look over the area in case she was right?

"They will be there at the crack of dawn but if possible I would like this to continue as an undercover job and not arouse suspicion. "He again asked about the assailant and anything that she knew of that might identify him?

"Other than his limp or perhaps ungainly walk and any fingerprints in number seventeen, there was no identifying characteristics. She told Mr Gaunt."

His short reply was "Oh, bugger. I'll be in touch."

Trying to compose herself before she returned to Tara she realised that she didn't have a handkerchief so in desperation made full use of the sleeve of her boiler suit. Outside of the door, she saw two men and a nursing sister.

"Dicks," immediately went through her mind.

Tara said, "These are policemen who…?"

"Thank you, we'll deal with this." the older of the two men told Tara.

The two men told Freya that they were police detectives and were investigating a very serious crime, "Which we believe that you are a party to." They then cautioned Freya and directed her to the office which she had just left. The sister enquired if she wanted anyone with her? Tara stepped forward and told the sister that she was Freya's friend and would be with her.

"Oh, no you will not be with her," the older man told Tara then continued, "a doctor that you might be but you have been or are involved in this crime relating to the use of firearms and from now on you will not communicate with Mrs… What is your name?" He asked Freya. She looked at the wedding and engagement ring on her finger and replied, "Freya Fergusson."

The detective then directed his subordinate to take Tara to the waiting room and closed the office door as he pointed to a chair. When Freya was seated he grabbed a chair, swung it around so the seat was facing her and instead of sitting on it, stood behind it then swung his leg over the back onto the seat and stared at Freya.

The silence was broken when Freya told him, "You are supposed to identify yourself, and by your action with that chair, I can only presume that you have watched too many American FBI films. In short, you have already failed to put me at my ease or pose as the sympathetic, understanding cop."

"Who are you to tell me how to do my job? You are making it all the more difficult for yourself and don't forget, you are under caution. Every word you say is recorded."

"I note with considerable professional interest that you are failing in taking contemporaneous notes of this interview and it has only just begun," Freya told the now very wary officer.

She continued, "I will put you out of your misery after you properly identify yourself. You are?"

With eyes sunk into his skull, the officer said, "I am Detective Constable Ward attached to Mistmarch station."

"In my professional life I am Acting Detective Superintendent Freya Douglas Gore Hamilton attached to the Home Office and frankly constable your approach is abhorrent to not only me but to any policeman worth their salt. It was quite unnecessary to caution me as at that time you had not even established who I was or what part I played in the matter. All, and I repeat, all, people are to be presumed innocent until you have evidence, verbal or material to provide a court with that unadulterated evidence.

"Do you clearly understand me, Detective Constable Ward?"

"Yes, ma'am. I've heard of you," he replied not questioning why one moment she was Mrs Fergusson and next, Freya Douglas Gore Hamilton, his superior.

"And now you have met me. You and your chum will erase this whole episode from both your, so far unused pocketbook and your mind. Should you be inclined to tell anyone, even your nearest and dearest of this incident and, in particular me, you will be summarily dismissed. This matter involves national security and as you will well know a jail sentence awaits anyone breaching matters of national security. Be warned; now get out."

As Mr Ward was about to leave he thought that it was time that he played what he thought was his trump hand.

"The station logbook will have recorded the 'phone call from the hospital. How do you erase that, ma'am, it is an offence to try?"

"Nothing will be erased. It will be recorded as 'Mistaken information with good intent' there's the door, make use of it." Ward needed no second telling.

She then went to the waiting room to find Tara in conversation with an elderly gentleman very worried about his wife just admitted with stomach pains.

They compared notes about their experiences with the law and decided that the pair of detectives were simply incompetent. They then moved on to how Tara was going to get back to Sunny Patch and how Freya was going to change out of her boiler suit and get other personal things from number nineteen.

Both had their backs to the door when Freya jumped as a hand was placed on her shoulder. As she looked up she saw the face of Assistant Chief Constable William Gaunt. She tried to get up but his hand tightened on her shoulder keeping her in the chair. With that, she burst into tears and sobbed her heart out.

Tara grabbed Freya's hand and within seconds she was struggling with Tara's hand and the hand of Bill Gaunt.

"Settle back and let it all come out," he told her.

Between sobs, Freya told them, "I just want my bloody sleeve, I've no hanky."

The people in the waiting room were having a good sideshow which no doubt took their minds off their own troubles. Mr Gaunt gave her his pocket-handkerchief and said to Tara.

"I'm sorry but I need to take Freya into a private room. I will shortly make arrangements for you to be taken home. I will be in touch with you soon. In your profession, you know all about confidentiality, and it most certainly is needed now. Thank you for saving the life of one of my men and being such a friend to Freya at this time."

Turning to leave the room she saw Harry Broadweir in the doorway. As they went through he followed their boss into the anti-room and the door was quietly closed as Tara went back to comforting the elderly gentleman.

"When you feel like talking we are ready to listen." Mr Gaunt told her.

Freya wiped her eyes, nose and jaw before telling Harry and Mr Gaunt of the incidents leading to the position that they were now in, much of it she had already told him on the telephone.

She then went on to tell him about the two detectives who had been sent to the hospital, her reaction to them and the fact of the message in the control room logbook from the hospital.

"It's already been dealt with by Harry. The now sealed book will shortly be in our possession as it no longer exists as a logbook. It is now material evidence for a future date. About a hundred years from now I expect."

This fact did bring a little smile to the lips of Freya as she enquired about plans for the immediate future.

When the guard gets here I will get you taken to Sunny Patch. There you will have a sleep then clear everything out. I'm sorry that I can't get anyone to help you but this is still a covert operation and covert from our colleagues as well.

"At daybreak, I will have an authorised couple of men with a van discretely remove all the contents of the hut next to yours. They will have a letter from the Solicitors of Mr Rosenberg authorising the removal of his property and a drain-clearing squad will go in again discretely, to clear the blockage contaminating the water tank Hamish found. They too will remove everything from that tank before discovering that they were in the wrong place should anyone ask. SOCO women will sweep the hut for prints, evidence etcetera before handing Mr Rosenberg's keys back.

It should be completed by noon at the latest. None of the participants will know the circumstances of what they are doing and will not enter details in their pocketbooks.

"You've just about thought of everything in a remarkably short time. Were you already planning this Sir?" Freya asked.

"We didn't visualise this happening," he told her, adding. "I brought Harry onto this team and between us and Simon Bates we sketched out a likely avenue of action once you pair had set out the scene, never expecting this. We hoped that Hamish Fergusson would direct operations from inside Sunny Patch. Now it will have to be you. By midday, it will be all over and unless you want to stay in there you can hand the keys back and go home."

"Who is going to look out for Hamish?" she asked in an alarmed tone of voice then adding. "I have to be here for him, Sir, duty or not!"

"Certainly for the next few hours there will be nothing that you can do for Hamish and for the rest of your service Mrs Fergusson, you will regret that you didn't complete your task to your own standards," Mr Gaunt told her.

He thought for a moment before adding.

"I will stay here until my man appears and get Harry to take you and your doctor friend back to Sunny Patch now. I will have a car delivered outside of Sunny Patch by Harry. He will put the keys addressed to you as Mrs Fergusson through the letterbox at about eleven.

"No, thank you, sir," she replied, "I will drive Tara back and clear out our hut and return here."

Mr Grant told her, "I want you to supervise, at a discrete and unidentifiable distance, the removal men who will be unlikely to recognise you as they will be from another division.

Even so, they will have 'forensics' with them to do the hut and to do the scene of the shooting. It's lovely dry weather and the results should be good.

Changing the subject, who is his next of kin. They should be told immediately in case the worst happens." He saw that Freya was about to burst into tears again and tried to correct himself but only succeeded in digging a larger hole for himself.

She turned away before answering, "I don't know, they are aristocrats of some sort but I know nothing else."

"I'll get personnel to find out after nine or whenever they get to work. Unless of course, he has managed to harvest his record first, a habit of his according to Simon," Mr Gaunt told her.

Freya collected Tara and they drove to Sunny Patch stopping by the bank outside of the gate. Using the big torch Freya swept the scene and saw the glove that she thought that she had seen before. She gingerly picked up the glove to find a hand inside on a piece of plastic. A tremor of revulsion passed through her as she returned to the car and carefully placed it on the back seat.

Tara had watched her pick up the glove and deduced what it was as Freya carried it to the car.

"Prosthetic lower arm and hand?" she asked Freya. "That felt awful," Freya told her, "I'd rather that it was real rather than that." Tara got out of the car and unlocked the gates and in they went.

"I've already got your card," she told Tara, "I'll give you mine before I leave. It will have my maiden name on it but the 'phone number is the same.

In case I don't see you tomorrow, I do hope that you have my undying gratitude for what you have done for me, never mind Hamish." They kissed and each returned to their own hut.

After making herself a cup of coffee, Freya changed from the boiler suit into her dress, still lacking underclothes but, having access to tissues to catch her tears. She then began to load up the car with their possessions and details of what, whom and where everything and everybody was doing whatever.

She found that by putting down the front seat of the car, she could accommodate the camp bed. The thought crossed her mind of if they had both left the place with the bed, where would one of them sit or lay in the car.

A simple thought but it did lighten her mood. By the time she had cleared out most things, the sky was lightening. On the way out of the back door of the hut intending to put her card through the door of Tara's hut, she saw in the distance a white van seemingly forcing its way through the undergrowth of the track towards the water tank.

It was difficult to tell but there was a naked figure behind the van who she presumed was the warden of the place. Old Gaunt didn't allow the grass to grow under his feet she decided.

She posted her card and locked the door before meeting the warden by the gate. She handed him the key, gave him her card and asked that the bar and restaurant bill be sent to the address, explaining again that it was her maiden name on the card and saying that her husband had been called away and she was joining him.

When she returned to the hospital she found Mr Gaunt still there with a person who she believed might be the armed officer and of all people Sarah.

Freya could not contain the tears as she embraced Sarah. Mr Gaunt did not interrupt them as she poured out her heart to Sarah.

Eventually, both ladies stopped talking and Mr Gaunt said to Freya, "I told you to watch over the, or rather our, removal men. As you are here it is plain to see that you will not be there. They are supposed to be there at 7:30, and I suppose that I will have to become a furniture heaver.

I want it all over before the camp or whatever comes to life." He then went over to one of the chairs and picked up a green plastic bag. Returning to Freya he told her that inside was what was left of the boiler suit a pair of handcuffs and a warrant card. "No underclothes though." Then he added,

"But then, perhaps he's taking after you! I had a doctor call here to tell me that the operation is going well and they have brought in a consultant to supervise everything as the house surgeon is having difficulty with the wounds and tiredness. Quite understandable I would think. Wouldn't you?" He asked Freya.

His reply was a withering look from both Freya and Sarah.

As he turned to leave Freya said to Mr Gaunt. "When you are there with your heavy gang and forensic, please ask the forensic to check the front doorknob inside for dabs. If there are any they might be of use."

"That's my girl," he announced before adding, "No matter how difficult the personal moment, the professional shines through. The dabs will be done. Glad to have you back." Earning yet another black look from both ladies.

With that, he left Freya sitting holding hands with Sarah, each with their own thoughts. Eventually, she asked Sarah. "How did you know about Hamish?"

Sir Simon rang me about, well, sometimes when it was dark and told me. We spoke about the situation and I told him that I would be coming here if he gave me the time off. He told me that as of that moment I was a Special Constable by his decree. He asked me to get hold of a Bible which I finally did, it took some hunting for I can tell you.

He told me to hold the Bible and repeat after him. I then did the bits about 'Our Sovereign Lady, The Queen' and here I am sans a uniform."

Freya simply squeezed her hand and there they sat until a domestic appeared and offered them tea or coffee and a choice of biscuit. There was no charge, just the kindness of the lady which Sarah acknowledged with a donation later on.

While eating the biscuit Freya suddenly said that she had hoped to take Mrs Briggs on a holiday to Devon if she would go.

"Whatever brought that on?" Sarah enquired. "The tea and biscuits." She replied continuing, "I'm not too sure that she would be comfortable in a hotel so if no one else was down there I would go to Mothers place on the Dart and take her off on day trips. Now, this has happened, it won't get done."

"Within the month, I am moving her out of that grotty tower block into a nice retirement bungalow that they have built only a short bus ride from the station and easy walking distance of the shops and Post Office. I have told her of what I propose to do, and after much protest, she has agreed now that I have been able to take her there and show her," Sarah told Freya.

Freya then enquired, "Are they council old peoples bungalows?"

"No," replied Sarah, "they are privately built so I bought one off-plan at a good price with Mrs B in mind. When she no longer wants it I will probably sell it but in her declining years I would not like to see her in a council-run old people's home or worse, so this was my way of helping someone in need. Mr Bates has offered to furnish it but only after she has taken whatever furniture she feels comfortable with from her flat."

A silence ensued as both women thought their own thoughts until Sarah asked Freya, "Would you like me to take Mrs B on holiday if she will come?"

Freya thought for a moment then replied, "Yes please, before the summer is over. And as you say 'If she will come'.

"Sir Simon will persuade her, she worships him. I hope that I am not breaking confidence but he pays her rent. At first, he subsidised her wage then he realised that she was being denied council help because of her income. He stopped the subsidy and now pays her rent with a dollop of rent rebate."

"We'll leave it there until you decide when you are able to take her away and I will make sure that other than cook and the 'daily' there are no others there to embarrass Mrs B," Freya told Sarah.

Again, there was a long silence until Sarah persuaded Freya to go home via the home of Hamish and make sure that all was in order. "Good idea," she said. I'll look around to see if there is any reference to his family to let them know in case Personnel haven't done so."

"If you find them are you going to be his friend or simply his colleague?" Sarah asked.

"That depends on the reception I get," she replied as she got up to leave. "You will not leave until I return?" she asked Sarah.

"I will be here when you return. And if anything happens I will let you know. I have your home 'phone number. Now go and sleep." Sarah told her.

Freya then left the hospital and instead of going home, drove directly to her home village and went straight to the village church as Mrs Watts, one of the cleaners was going through the door. Freya hoped that no one else was in there. After a 'Bob' of recognition from Mrs Watts, Freya went into the Lady chapel and after hunting for the matches lighted a candle for Hamish. She then went back to her pew sank to her knees and prayed as she had never prayed before.

She lifted her eyes to the altar and all she saw through the haze of tears was the indistinct vision of the altar and the magnificent East window. Her whole body shook with the almost overwhelming sense of impending loss and the realisation of all the things that she should have told Hamish but which now seemed impossible to express; except through solitude and prayer.

Eventually, she sensed someone was in her pew and such was her state of mind that she thought it might be an apparition of Hamish. She was frightened to look then she felt a hand on her shoulder.

"Bless you, my daughter, the Lord is with you." She recognised the voice of the rector and gingerly took her hands down, and sure enough, it was the minister. He then took hold of her hands.

In answer to his obvious question, she told him of the incident without giving details of why and how. She kept apologising for her tears and he in return told her to let her emotions take over.

"Do you love Hamish?" he asked in a quiet, gentle voice. "Yes," she replied. "More than I ever thought I did; since the events of last night!"

"Have you told him of your love?" he asked.

"No," she replied. "When you return to the hospital even if he is unconscious, tell Hamish that you love him. Whether or not he hears you is immaterial. Your soul will be at rest knowing that you have declared your love for him and your God will understand and the fate of Hamish will be in his hands through the doctors. Your faith will help you whatever the outcome for Hamish.

Although still distressed, Freya left her church with the rector leading her along the path to her car parked in the Glebe lands. "Are your parents at home," he asked.

Freya replied that she did not think so, and under the circumstance, she did not want to see them.

He invited her into the Rectory for a cup of tea. Freya thanked him explaining that she wanted to inform the parents of Hamish once she had gone to his place and found a telephone number and then get some sleep before returning to the hospital.

With his fingers on her forehead, the rector recited a benediction, and they parted with an embrace.

Freya came to as her 'phone was ringing, looking at the clock she saw that it was 1:30. When she answered it, Sarah was on the other end of the line to tell her that Hamish was now out of the theatre and had been moved to intensive care and the consultant would like to see Freya before 3:30 as he was going home.

Freya was busy preparing herself for the meeting when her 'phone went again and a male voice enquired if she was Miss Douglas Gore Hamilton who had left a message with a servant relating to one Hamish Fergusson? Freya asked who the caller was? "I am his Lordships secretary." the voice said and asked. "Is Sir conscious or unconscious?"

Freya was ready for any insubordination from any servant and, in no uncertain terms told the fellow. "I wish to speak to your master, now."

"His Lordship is engaged with matters relating to the Estate and is not to be disturbed." the secretary deigned to tell her.

"Then kindly put me through to a family member," she insisted.

"None are available madam. Will you kindly tell me if Sir is conscious or unconscious," the secretary enquired.

"Hamish is unconscious," Freya told him with her most authoritative voice.

"There is no reason for the family to visit him until he is conscious." The man told Freya. Then, in a very pompous voice commanded Freya.

"You will inform this house at such time as Sir is ready to receive visitors." Without ceremony, he rang off.

In a loud voice to no one but herself Freya loudly and unladylike declared. "Like bloody hell, I will."

At 2:45, she returned to the hospital, and the consultant told her that Hamish was in a bad way but being young and strong there was no reason to doubt that he would make a good recovery but it would probably be many months before he was capable or wanted to resume his usual pattern of life and work.

He went on to tell her that at such time as Hamish regained consciousness he would be very confused and in a great deal of pain. The confusion would only be temporary but the pain would be for quite a while and with drugs could be alleviated to some extent.

"In short Mrs Fergusson, he is a very sick man and should be kept in 'cotton wool' for the next few months," he told Freya then went on to tell her that he had suffered three bullet wounds. Two had exited the body, one through the top of his thigh chipping his hip bone. The other had exited through his back damaging the muscle supporting the spine and in so doing causing minor damage to the lower spine which should not adversely affect his mobility. The third bullet had entered the body through the lower abdomen and had been prevented from exiting the body by the pelvic cradle. In its path part of the bowel had been punctured. We believe that we have successfully repaired the lower colon but time will tell. That bullet had been recovered and would be handed to the police.

There is an embargo on any information being about the patient or any circumstances surrounding the hospitalisation being circulated to the press or public. "You too must observe this embargo and I regret to tell you Mrs Fergusson that if really necessary you must make up a story for his stay in hospital.

"Thank you for all of this information," she told the consultant and added, "I do know the importance of the secrecy surrounding my husband as I am the leader of the team dealing with the matters involving espionage, murder and now the attempted murder of my husband."

Returning to her professional role she asked, "Who will you give the bullet to?"

The consultant replied, "Your chief constable, Mr Gaunt. He imposed the legal embargo on the hospital relating to the divulging of information about the identity of your husband and his injuries."

"Should you have any further questions, please get one of my staff to arrange either a telephone call or a face-to-face meeting. Goodbye, Mrs Fergusson and chin up, we've done our best, just make sure that your husband does his best, for the sake of himself, you and the medical team."

As the consultant and perhaps the surgeon, left the room Freya went into a reflective mood thinking about the past years with Hamish and in particular the last Easter day worshipping in her little village church. That wordless but uplifting occasion was for her the highlight of their undeclared romance and now that his life was, just a couple of hours ago, and perhaps still remains in such serious doubt, will such feelings ever have the opportunity to be expressed.

Freya pulled herself together and went to find Sarah in the anteroom.

In a quiet voice, she told Sarah all that has transpired between her and the family of Hamish and then went on to the conversation with the consultant and the prognosis for Hamish.

Sarah offered her assistance to Freya in dealing with the Fergusson's by telling her; "I know a lot about them and in particular just where their money is and how much. If you want me to intervene I will gladly do so. It never occurred to me that Hamish was a son of the Ciaran-Fergusson's. Does he use his title?"

"Not to my knowledge or for that matter his proper surname," Freya told her. "Until you said so I didn't know he had a title. I knew that he was from a good family but not an aristocratic one. Is he the heir?"

Sarah replied, "No, he is the second son carrying the title of Honourable. He has a sister. For the purposes of my financial dealings that was all that they were required to tell me."

"Oh, and by the way, I do know your family background. Not from any financial dealings but more from my recreational pursuits. Here we have two families with identical backgrounds, birth, money, influence, education and service to the nation but so very different in social attitudes. Enough of them and more about you.

Sleep? Did you manage to get any this morning?"

"What would you think?" Freya asked. "I will only sleep when exhaustion overtakes me.

I have to give a written statement to Bill Gaunt as soon as possible. Quite what I am supposed to write about I'm not too sure. As far as I was concerned there were two gunshots, but the consultant told me that Hamish had three bullets in or through him.

If I have that important fact wrong, how much more is duff. My statement will be; I saw a man in dark clothing with a strange gait emerge through a picket gate from a holiday camp followed by another man. The pair closed and I heard something indecipherable said then two claps as is made by pistol gunfire.

I saw a person fall to the ground. One of the people made off running awkwardly similar to that of a gorilla. One leg leading and one trailing.

I went over the man on the ground who I know to be Acting Detective Inspector Hamish Fergusson. I could feel blood on his clothing. I then summoned the help of a passing lady who is a bachelor of medicine. She performed surgical practices on Mr Fergusson and we put him into a motor car and took him to the city infirmary.

I then called my senior officers and disclosed the events. Assistant Chief Constable,(Crime) William Gaunt QPM then relieved me of my immediate duties in order that I might concentrate on the welfare of Inspector Fergusson and other peripheral matters."

Freya took a deep breath and said. "And that's that."

"I think that it is time that you went home and had some much-needed sleep." Sarah told her.

In turn, Freya said that she should get her sleep and the argument ended with Freya going home and Sarah pulling another chair to hers and putting her feet up and head back.

When Freya came to she was still in her living room and it was dark outside. She quickly made herself a drink, cleaned her teeth, a quick wash and dressed. Grabbing a packet of biscuits she dashed out of the house and drove to the hospital.

Full of apologies she found Sarah still in her two chairs and fast asleep. Gently waking her up and apologising yet again, Freya asked if there was any news?

"I checked at ten and he was still unconscious but everything was in order and as expected and the only problem was when I was challenged by the armed policeman. Unless I was a hospital worker I was not allowed in the ward. I told him that I was the secretary to Chief Superintendent Bates and he then relented but watched me like a hawk. Hamish looked very comfortable and the Sister seemed happy with the situation."

The ladies agreed that they would work twelve-hour shifts until Hamish came to consciousness and Sarah went home after a very long day and night.

Freya then went along to the ward and as the guard went to challenge her she produced her warrant card. Usually, no one reads the warrant card, but on this occasion, the guard did read every dot and comma then looked at the third finger of her left hand. She could almost see the cogs slowly turning in his head as he tried to work out how this Detective Chief Inspector Freya Douglas Gore Hamilton could be the woman before him as Mrs Freya Fergusson, the wife of the man that he was guarding?

"That's my professional name," Freya told him before he could ask. "Ma'am," was his only comment as she entered the ward and saw Hamish with a distinct grey pallor and tubes with wires feeding into him and also monitors of every type and size bleeping, ticking and whirring away.

What could it be? Was it a map of the tributaries of the Mekong? Or was it a pattern of some sort?

Just what was it? Hamish closed his eyes then opened them again and the same scene met him.

He went to move his head and couldn't. He flicked his fingers and he began to feel pain just about everywhere. He flexed his toes, opened his mouth to speak but no sound came. Where was he? Why couldn't he move his head? Why was he in so much pain?

He opened his eyes again and realised that he was looking at a ceiling tile. The plastic dividers gave the idea of ceiling tiles some credence in his befuddled mind.

"Please lift your hand Mr Fergusson or your finger." The same request was repeated before the name 'Fergusson' gave Hamish the clue that someone was referring to him. He again attempted to turn his head in the direction of the voice but nothing seemed to work. Hamish simply closed his eyes and mind.

"Open your eyes, Mr Fergusson. I know that you have had them open. Do that again and move your hand or fingers please," his nurse commanded.

"Mrs Fergusson, Mrs Fergusson, wake up please your husband is awake." Freya could hear the words but at that exact moment could not quite associate the name of Mrs Fergusson with herself.

She opened her eyes to see a nurse standing over her and the realisation came that it was her that the nurse wanted and what the name Fergusson related to. As she went to swing her legs to the floor it became all too apparent that her legs had gone to sleep. The nurse grabbed her as she began to fall.

"Sit down again until the circulation comes back into your legs." The nurse suggested. Sinking back into the chair Freya remembered why she disliked hospital chairs with their rubberised upholstery coatings. In the few seconds that she had been on her feet she realised that her back, bottom and thighs were cold and wet with perspiration.

Holding her hand while Freya stamped her feet the nurse told her that Hamish had regained consciousness and needed something familiar to him to properly make him aware of his situation.

Freya looked into his eyes and Hamish looked back at her but there appeared to be no recognition.

"Speak to him. Any nonsense will do and hold his hand or put your hand on his face. It will help him." the ward sister told her.

She did as she was told and talked of their time at Oxford and the fun that they had and exploits they enjoyed at the expense of the authorities. She then found that the hand she was holding was gently squeezing her hand. Freya thought about trying to kiss his forehead and although very tall, she could not quite reach his head so gave up on that idea and lifted his hand and kissed it.

"Perhaps come in again in an hour Mrs Fergusson. He will be more responsive to you by then. Unless he asks a specific question simply stick to generalisations and please don't tell him of his injuries just yet." The sister told her as she escorted her past the guard. A different guard had taken over the not so onerous duty of, free tea and biscuits with, subject to a friendly nurse being on duty, a hospital meal thrown in.

Exactly one hour later Freya returned to the ward only to find that Hamish had gone to sleep. The nurse told her that when he awoke she or whoever was in the ward would call her.

One and a half hours later Freya was called to the ward to see that Hamish was awake and drinking through a straw. As she approached the bed he recognised her and although not quite exactly lighting up, his pleased expression was clear to see.

They talked of many things until the ward sister gently touched Freya's shoulder and nodded towards the door.

"Rest now and I'll be back soon," she told him.

"Why am I here. What's wrong with me?" He asked.

"I will explain later," she told him. "Sleep now, dear."

Freya rang Sarah and apologised for disturbing her to let her know the events and told her not to come down on that evening as; "If all goes well I will go home and come back here about nine tomorrow.

He is awake, asking questions that at the moment I am not answering and talking sensibly to me. After the first time I went in I thought that he might not know who I was. On my second visit, he certainly knew me and is now asking how he got into hospital. I'll take advice on answering that question. Bye-bye and bless you for all that you have done."

Freya was beginning to flag when yet another guard approached her and told her that she was wanted on the ward.

With some trepidation, she went in to find that they had almost sat Hamish up. He looked very pale and just lay there looking at her. In turn, she simply sat by the bed holding his hand with a tube feeding a cannula in his hand.

She was trying desperately to stay awake when she realised that Hamish was asleep. She gently put his hand inside the bed rails and quietly left the ward. She put her head inside of the sister's office and told them that she was going home and wishing the guard, "Goodnight." Then she drove home.

The pattern of hospital visits then home and back again and answering many 'phone calls went on for several days with Hamish getting stronger each day. Freya still had not told him the reason why he was in the hospital and let him go on believing his opinion that he must have had a heart attack.

On the fourth day, Freya decided that subject to being alone with Hamish, she would tell him why he was in the hospital. In all their conversations Hamish had not mentioned his work or any reference to their task at Sunny Patch.

With a few less tubes and wires into his body, Hamish looked quite well in comparison to four days earlier.

Freya hesitantly began to tell Hamish of their work together. As she spoke so it appeared to restore his memory and the look in his eyes she took to be a sign that his memory was being restored. As she heard footsteps she looked around and realised that behind her were Mr Gaunt and Sir Simon, no doubt the reason for the bright look in the eyes of Hamish.

"Where are the chocolates and grapes?" Hamish, in a clear voice, asked them. "My boy, when you get your backside out of that bed and give Freya a break, you will get your chocolates and grapes." Mr Gaunt told him.

"Silly question that it might be," Mr Bates asked him, "but how do you feel?"

"Considering that I've had a heart attack it hurts all over and I've got more wires and tubes in me than a car engine," Hamish told them.

"You do know that only two people are allowed in here at one time?" Freya enquired.

Mr Gaunt took her arm and led her towards the door enquiring about his health at the moment and also telling her that it was about time that he was told the truth. "When we walked in and the look of recognition was enough for me to tell him of his situation. It is better that he should know, brutal but necessary truth I'm afraid.

As he is under the illusion that he has an illness he feels ill. When he knows that he is not ill but that his hospitalisation is caused by an incident rather than an illness he will rally more quickly. Trust me, I'm a man."

"That fact I never doubted even after you played the Dame at the children's Christmas party," Freya responded then continued.

"I'm not sure that you and Mr Bates going bull-headed at Hamish is the best way to deal with this matter. The staff here told me not to tell him the facts when he came around after the op."

"Within the next day or so, he is going to get a visit from 'Old King Cole' and perhaps Mr Thomas. They will not be diplomatic, well Tommo will be but not Fred. It is better that we bring reality back to Hamish rather than 'Blood and Guts' Cole. I doubt that either you or certainly Hamish would ever believe that Mr Cole would be concerned about the health of his arch-enemy. He genuinely is.

I promoted him to chief sewage operative inside Sunny Patch and Mr Thomas was the chief removal man when they cleared out the chalet next to yours. On that night or rather a morning, I immediately rang Simon Bates and told him of the situation and what we needed to do quickly. It was all arranged on the spot and Mr Cole and Thomas were ready within two hours and no sooner was it requested than done. No one knew the reason why they had to go to sunny Patch or the fact that you were living there. As far as Fred and Stuart and everybody else were concerned you were going in there only at night."

"Why didn't you use your own men?" Freya asked.

"Frankly, my men do not know anything about this job. They were alright as the humpers but they needed supervision and 'D' division knew more about this job, so for supervision, I chose Fred and Stuart," he replied.

"I know the next question that you will ask me will be about the material that we have recovered. The things recovered from the chalet were all the forged items.

As for the paintings, some of which we know were stolen and from where; they are quite valuable. The machinery is a bit primitive but it made superb forgeries. We recovered many thousands of pounds and it is being processed to find out if that is forged as well.

All the radio equipment we have and the table that it was on with the call signs, wavelengths and so on. We left the metalwork on the roof as it would have been too obvious for us to dismantle it.

In the tank, they had quite a time removing a lot of the material. There appeared to be thousands of broach, necklace, ring and bracelet mountings with a lot of wrist and pocket watch parts.

The gold is being assayed now and will probably be in the region of a hundred thousand pounds worth, but what did they use it for or rather where did they use it?"

"You've had a busy time of it," Freya said and then told Mr Gaunt. "When I saw the sewage squad going in I didn't think for a moment that 'Old King Cole' was leading the charge."

"They recovered so much material that other than the driver the team had to walk out as there was no room for them in the van." Mr Gaunt told her then added. "All in all, a successful operation, I'm very pleased," he told her with a smile.

"With the exception of the fact that Hamish is still near death's door," Freya said. "We have no prisoner and no murderer. I'm not pleased sir, not only for our failures but with the exception of getting severely wounded this was exactly as Hamish predicted before we arrived at Sunny Patch. I simply hate it when he's right. In short, if we could trust them, what we have discovered and recovered is a gift to the spooks but of no use to us in arresting common criminals."

"Strange that you should mention that," Mr Gaunt told her "I have been informed by our intelligence people that there has been a notable increase in the surveillance of the activities of this Force by unspecified sources. What are the odds on this being the spooks once again?"

Freya sat in silence until finally, Mr Gaunt told her that he would collect Simon and leave her in peace.

With Sarah, Freya took it in turn to do all day visits which appeared to suit them, their respective superiors and not least Hamish. The only hiccup in the recovery process was when they took Hamish back into the operating theatre to check how successful his repair to the colon had been. It was a success but the new operation set his recovery back a week or so.

Slowly Hamish left his bed behind and attempted to walk. It was not a great success and he then endured weeks of agonising pain as the professionals or as he called them 'Medieval Rack operatives' tried to get him moving. As it turned out it was a long painful process.

Freya decided that now Hamish had been released from his ward bed and, thanks to a mystery donor, was now in a private ward, that it was time for him to read the mail that she collected over the past fortnight on her trips to his house.

"I've brought you your post to deal with," she told him.

A groan was the reply.

"It's no use moaning," she told him. "It's time that you got your brain into gear and letters in brown envelopes usually stir the emotions. Don't you think?"

"Bills, usually bills, you know how to keep an invalid cheerful don't you?" he replied.

Sure enough, there were bills, several of them and a letter from his Father. He read it and handed it to Freya. It read.

"With your mother, I regret that you have been involved in an incident. We do hope that you will be fit again soon and if we are not otherwise engaged perhaps you could find time to visit us and tell us about your life in England. Regards," followed by an indecipherable signature.

Freya read it again and decided not to comment.

Hamish looked at her face which spoke volumes about her opinion of his father.

"Were I dead they would probably claim that they would attend the funeral if not otherwise engaged," Hamish, with a chuckle, concluded.

"You might laugh about it but I think it is quite disgraceful. In fact, the most uneducated and uncultured people in the land would not treat their kith and kin as your parents appear to treat you." Freya, in no uncertain terms, told him.

"And," she began again, "should the opportunity ever present itself I'll be damned if I will not fail to tell them so. Are they all barbarians north of the border?"

Another nose to nose stand ensued until Hamish broke the verbal impasse by reminding Freya.

"Take ye care for I'm a product of 'North of the Border' and, if it comes to that, where did most of your many names come from?"

Not attempting an apology Freya said; "It is because of my Caledonian lineage that I'm allowed to criticise the Scots. As I have offended you, I will confine my remarks to just your parents and one or two more tartan-clad individuals."

"Well, I'm damned," Hamish addressed to no one as he opened a plain brown envelope and removed a ten-pound note and a business card.

The envelope was addressed to Inspector Fergusson at the former station of the 'D' division. It was then redirected to Police Headquarters and from there redirected to his home address. Finally, it was delivered to his wheelchair.

Freya simply sat there with one eyebrow cocked in anticipation of an explanation for the outburst of, "Well, I'm damned."

She waited and waited as Hamish seemingly and deliberately took his time in opening his correspondence and remaining silent.

Eventually, he completed his task. Neatly stacked the envelopes. Folded his hands into each other and looked, unblinking at Freya.

"If you are going to play silly childish games I'm off to the Home Office and I might visit you at weekends if I'm 'Not otherwise engaged' she threatened.

"That tenner and card were from my 'Tailor' at HQ," Hamish informed her then continued. "When he was going through my old station sergeant tunic he found these items in the inside pocket and most honestly returned them to me via, just about, the entire force area.

"So?" came the rather abrupt and less than eloquently phrased question.

Hamish prolonged his reply, in this case not to irritate her but to collect his memory and thoughts and to reason his reply to 'So?'

Eventually, he told her. "This my girl, if we are very, very lucky, might just be the key to the murder of one Kurt Rosenberg. Please pass me the telephone."

Freya quite rightly decided not to push for an explanation just yet. For the first time in nearly three weeks, she saw a brightness in his eyes. Her Hamish was on the mend she hoped.

She gathered from the one-sided conversation that the call was about photographs after Hamish went to great lengths to identify himself and the occasion at the docks when he had met whoever he was talking to. Eventually, the call ended with an agreement that Hamish and the person on the other end of the 'phone would meet in his ward about noon.

Hamish put the receiver back on the hook and with a satisfied smile told Freya." If you sit quietly and don't interrupt I will tell you a saga that might, only might, justify me being the new design for the lid of a pepper pot.

"The Friday before you arrived at 'D' division I stood in for a bone idle inspector who was off rogering someone's wife in duty time. In the course of my patrols at the docks, I came across a character climbing up lamp posts and telegraph poles fixing numerous cameras and cables to these poles in what he described as an experiment in time-lapse photography.

His control panel was all lights and bits and reminded me of the comic, 'The Eagle' and Dan Dare in his spaceship.

His subject would be a Russian ship due to leave the dock at twilight catching her while she was in the locks near the inner gates. If it worked he would use the same system on the outer lock gates for vessels entering the locks en-route to the dock itself.

I asked for his permit to be in the dock area with a camera. He produced his permit and gave me his card which I must have put in my tunic pocket. I had completely forgotten him and if it wasn't for our dear tailor this avenue of investigation might never have opened up."

"This is the most animated that I've seen you in months," Freya told him as she took the business card from his lap. Why are you so confident that this is the key to the job?"

"I'm not that confident," Hamish explained and continued,

"In rough terms, my involvement began with me visiting our chaps at the dock. I was standing by the guard at the gate when I, or rather we, were approached by a long thin woman in ankle socks, a long off white raincoat topped off with a black beret. She smiled at me, and for the first time, I looked. into a mouth of metal. I'm not joking it was as frightening as it was unusual.

It turned out that she was off of a Russian timber boat and that was that. The following day I was in the same position when a white Morris Commercial van came to the gate to enter the dock. Inside of the van was my metallic mouthed friend and the driver was a person we now know to be Kurt Rosenberg posing as the agent for the timber boat. In the back of that van was the trussed-up body of Mr Harrison Hacker.

It might, just might, be possible to get a photograph of that area as the Russian ship sailed and be able to identify who skewered our Kurt. John Crocker, the photographer has not printed all the photographs as he was not satisfied with those that he had already printed. As I expect you heard he is coming here tomorrow with the printed pictures from the cameras covering the inner locks but there may be other unprinted ones that might be useful."

"So far so good my dearest, but why did you not remember all this when we were up to our knees in the quagmire a few weeks ago?" Freya, as sympathetically as possible, enquired.

"From the onset of this 'do' I have not played any part in the case except for a peripheral interest until the grand finale of living in a nudist camp and ending up full of holes. That a photographer would be of interest to you never crossed my mind and if it had I would not have thought of the relevance of it, even less would I have looked for the card," Hamish explained before adding, "God bless honest tailors."

"Frankly old chap, you've failed your basic course of detective training and should we not get a result from these photographs, you're out on your aristocratic Scottish earhole!" Freya exclaimed before asking, "What time is 'Armstrong Jones' calling on us?"

"Not before 10:00," he replied.

"See you then," she said before giving him a peck on the cheek and with the usual hip swirl of her skirt, was gone.

Hamish used his best turn of flattery to the ward sister managed to get a six-foot trestle table brought to his room overnight. After the various requirements of his health conditions had been met he prepared himself for the visit of Mr Crocker.

Freya arrived first with a voice recorder, camera, statement forms, magnifying glass and a receipt book. On asking Hamish how he had managed to get a trestle table put into his room his reply was simply a broad engaging smile and a wink.

"Was she attractive?" Freya asked. The answer came in another broad smile and a wink.

"I suppose that if the bullet had been an inch or so lower your testosterone would have taken the same path as your testicles and we wouldn't have this table. Something to be said for lousy marksmanship." Freya, with a philosophical turn of mind, deduced.

"A gentleman to see you," heralded the arrival of Mr Crocker with his photographs.

After introductions and suitable words of commiserations from John, as he wished to be known. He handed Hamish some photographs from one of the cameras covering the inner locks.

While Hamish and Freya were studying them John explained that what he called his camera traps had not produced the 'Stop-frame' photography that he wanted. But that evening was a test of the system and he had now redefined it to give a seam-free action photographs.

Most of the prints were suffering from what an amateur might call, camera shake. It made pretty patterns but not much else. There were dozens of prints to go through and many did not cover the inner lock gates or the timber boat.

After a cup of coffee, Freya and Hamish began on yet more prints. Now making a pile of those for further investigation and the rejects.

After a couple of hours, it was becoming difficult for eyes to focus properly and Freya asked John if he was positive that these prints were from cameras covering the inner locks. "Oh, yes," he told them and Hamish told him that in the event of them finding any which helped the investigation they would need to be identified by him as the photographer and the time, date and place of the scene.

John agreed to sign every photograph and agreed to go through the rest of the film from the inner locks area and print them.

As John began to collect up the prints Hamish stopped him and asked if they could be left for him to go through them again when his eyes had recovered from the unintentional abstract art that John had produced.

This was agreed and Hamish asked for an assurance that no film was discarded from any of the cameras used that evening. This John was happy to assure Hamish that nothing would be destroyed.

"Are you a professional photographer or an amateur specialising in ships?" Hamish asked him.

"I'm a professional but as I may have mentioned to you at the time, ship photography is more of a hobby rather than a source of income," he told them.

"You will be paid in full for any photographs we need and put on the invoice your total travelling expenses such as those that you have incurred today." Looking at his wristwatch, Hamish added, "And your lunch costs."

As the 'goodbyes' were said Freya asked for three of John's business cards which in a flash of a hand were in her palm.

When he left, the ward orderly appeared with the lunch menu and Freya took herself off to the public restaurant while Hamish wheeled himself from under the table to prepare for his repast.

When he opened his eyes it was to see Freya looking through the photographs. In reply to his question about her success in identifying anyone Freya replied.

"Other than a couple of men in peaked caps, no one else, but the photo is very clear and it shows the back of a ship."

"Stern," replied Hamish.

"What did you say?" she politely enquired.

"Stern," he said, then adding, "the rear end of a ship is called the 'Stern."

"What a smart arse you are sailor boy," she told him. "Stern to you and 'Back' to me. And pulling rank on you, 'Back' it will be!" A snort was his first reply. The second reply was, "A ship has a stern, a cow a rump, a woman a derrière, or two, a train a rear and an alleyway a back. Plainly your education left something to be desired."

"As I have said before and almost certainly will in future, I am the acting detective superintendent, you are a common inspector, so I win and can we please get on with the photographs?" Freya asked.

When the argument, crushed by rank, was completed they set to, each with their own pile of photographs or very artistically created patterns merging vessel, sky, lock gates and quay wall in a kaleidoscopic scene but in black and white.

Eventually, Hamish began making another pile of photos in his lap which over the afternoon extended to quite a number of prints.

Unbeknown to him Freya had been doing the same when viewing came to a halt as the orderly brought in tea and Rich Tea biscuits.

After the first quaff of tea, Hamish told Freya. "I think that I might have some usable prints here but as they are now, they would not stand up as evidence without there being the professional and unchallengeable interpretation."

"You were there at the scene with nautical knowledge of the layout so I'm at a disadvantage in knowing what I'm looking for other than two identifiable people. All I've had so far are the two in peaked caps." Freya explained.

"That chap Howard, you know, the husband of Doc Tara, what did he or she say he did for a living?" He asked Freya.

"If I remember correctly," she said. "He is a something lieutenant in the RAF and is an expert in photographic analysis and interpretation. Why do you ask?"

"If he's any good he might be the bloke to look at these 'iffy' prints and give his opinion," Hamish told her.

"What's wrong with forensics doing it? It's their job and a 'phone call will have them here to collect them this afternoon," she asked.

"With all the strange goings-on during my association with this bloody case, I'm not sure, with the exception of you dear, that I trust anyone to be on our side.

If forensics are not watertight that could scupper this line, our only line of enquiry. Depending on his ability to come here and how long it will take I would prefer him to give me a truly independent opinion that I could use with confidence at the Assizes." Hamish thoughtfully said.

"Do we have any positive photos?" she asked. "Yes," he told her. "I've some definitely clearly showing the ship, the lock gates and quay wall and two figures facing the ship. I have another one with only one person facing the ship and another with the stern of the ship disappearing below the lock wall and a body jumping down to the disappearing vessel followed by one of arms plainly visible above the lock wall."

They separated the various piles of photographs into the useless pile, the possible pile and the quite good but not sequenced pile. Freya went off to get some large envelopes for each pile while Hamish had a nap and a good think

When Freya returned she packed up the photos while Hamish pretended to sleep, wrote a note, gave him a peck on the forehead and left with the three packets of prints.

When he was satisfied that she had gone he pulled himself round to a sitting position and read the note; it read. "Darling. I have taken the photos and from now on I will deal with them and ask if Howard can help us interpret them.

I am going to contact the photographer and chase up the undeveloped spools to get them here for Howard if he comes down. When we were in the hammocks at Sunny Patch you told me that you had something to tell me 'When this is over' What was it? Bye, me. Xxx."

On the following day, Freya arrived to be told that Hamish was again to undergo two operations, one for his hip and one to check on any lasting damage to his spine. Not good news as he already had a second opening up for his colon, now two more.

Apart from her distress at this turn of events, she had just negotiated a suitable convalescent home for him to continue his recovery and it was a room with an annex suitable as an office for him to continue his police work undisturbed.

After Hamish had improved from the first of his two new investigative operations Freya was able to tell him of events surrounding the photographs, the second delivery from John Crocker the photographer and her visit from Howard. Tara couldn't come as she was on duty over the weekend.

Freya went into great detail about the various techniques used by Howard to interpret the photographs and in many cases with success.

With John Crocker, they were able to sequence the prints and there was no doubt that if Hamish could positively identify 'Iron Gob' and Kurt Rosenberg, with one omission they could make a case of murder from the photos they had. The omission was the shot taken as the camera moved on the lamp post.

She explained that Howard had taken that one and two others with him to use another secret method for unscrambling visual effects.

"The disappointment at the moment," Freya explained, "is that, subject to more analysis, the photos showed the woman pulling what appeared to be a screwdriver type of instrument out of the left chest of the man and then a print of what appeared to be the weapon going through the air past the quay wall and towards the lock gates. Followed by what was probably her lower leg pushing the man, or perhaps rolling him over the lock wall and then the easily identifiable one of her jumping on the ship as it went down past the top of the wall of the inner lock gates."

"What is wrong with that sequence?" Hamish asked her.

"Freya replied, I want a shot of her putting the knife into him, by pulling it out she could claim that she was trying to save him after someone else had stabbed him.

"If I am understanding you correctly, you have said that one of the sequenced prints shows her pulling the weapon out of his chest. If that is your belief. Explain how you came to this conclusion?" he asked.

"Because that's the way that I saw it. Plainly you have found something wrong. Get it off your chest or you'll be morose every time I appear." Freya quite accurately predicted.

"I'm not happy with your assertion that the woman is pulling the knife or whatever out of his chest. Is that operation as important as you think as evidence of murder?" Hamish questioned.

"Until Howard comes back with anything different we will use it as I see it and remember all the prints are time coded. Try arguing with that fact in court. Unless otherwise confirmed, 'Iron Gob' is pulling out the screwdriver and that's not good enough for me," Freya, in a 'No messing about' tone told her professional subordinate.

Hamish said nothing for a few seconds before he picked up the photograph and magnifying glass, studied the photograph again before triumphantly declaring,

"Got it, that's it. It's the bloody bracelet. Got the bastard." He then told Freya of the heavy gold bracelet that he had noticed on 'Iron Gobs' wrist.

"If you see where the bracelet is, high on her wrist she is plainly pushing the instrument into him. If she was pulling it out the bracelet would be down almost on her hand. That's her done for."

"Well done, darling," Freya told him adding. "With the other photographs and hopefully Howard's positive interpretation, it's job done but without a chance of an arrest. Damn, damn," she concluded.

"Harking back to the note that I left you a while ago," Freya said. "What was it that you were going to tell me when we left Sunny Patch?"

Hamish smiled and took his time to answer. When he did he told her.

"I was introduced to the naked way of life when I was in New Zealand a few years ago and, on and off I have practised it ever since. Mostly on various suitable beaches. I have never belonged to a club and until I met up with you I enjoyed the company of three ladies in nude sunbathing in New Zealand.

The three ladies were at different times I assure you. I adopted the slogan of a nudist publication of many years ago that 'Sunshine is the first principal of health' and I have enjoyed it ever since but on my own since the days that I was at Oxford with you."

Hamish continued, "I was surprised that you didn't make any protest when I was put onto this case simply because the 'Powers-that-be decided that you would be more comfortable with me at Sunny Patch." Before Freya could interrupt he went on to tell her.

"It was quite a surprise to me when you appeared to take to being nude in front of others without complaint. In fact, you seemed more at home than me. Have we been wasting years of mutual enjoyment?"

"Yes, dearest heart," Freya told him, "I did take to it rather well. I have been a nudist since I was born. My parents, my brother and both sisters are of the same persuasion and surprise, surprise my parents own one of those beautiful bungalows at the top of the Avenue at Sunny Patch. In fact, my sisters were there with us, one with her husband and baby.

I did note the 'Knowing wink and prolonged look from Ted. He and Ivy knew who I was but not what I do, and thankfully said nothing before I could speak to them without you around. My sister saw you, several times. The only problem that I could foresee was if Joy and her family came to their chalet here. Small world, don't you think?"

Hamish smiled at her and said, "I saw a woman who was the spitting image of you with a man and baby on our last evening there. I was going to comment to you about it. Then rather than being accused of undue interest in beautiful undressed women, I would keep my mouth shut."

"That was my sister and we agreed to ignore each other while I was working there. Clever boy." Freya told him.

"While on the subject of Sunny Patch," Freya said, "Tara told me that when you were shot and I went back to clear out the hut, she got up to see Kirsten, the stunning blonde who you denied ever noticing until she was in our hut, packing up her car and leaving while I was clearing out our place."

"I'm not surprised," Hamish told her. "I sussed her as a spook or a rogue after being there less than a day so I'm not that surprised that she took to the hills. Once she realised that the police were about inside Sunny Patch, she was gone in case they began going hut to hut on enquiries.

But fairs fair, she was as you say a stunner and to think that those girls were her children and not her sisters were almost a biblical revelation if ever there was one."

"The only way that I knew that she was a natural blonde was to look at her teenage daughter. Freya explained. "Why would she be a spook or a rogue?"

"When this is all over Hamish told her "I will tell you and in time I may be able to prove it. It's all about a case having a 'Smell' about it. Something for you to look forward to darling."

"Getting back to business." Hamish asked her, "Where are the photographs now?"

She replied, "Old King Cole has them in the master safe with the two keys shared. One with Chief Superintendent Bates and one with him. I had a meeting with Mr Gaunt, Mr Bates, Mr Cole and Harry Broadweir. I briefed them but, with the exception of Fred Cole, they were a bit put out about letting an unknown airman deal with the photos instead of their forensic team.

I explained your reasoning and was soundly told off for firstly allowing my number two to make decisions that should be within my remit and secondly bothering an injured man to make an important decision."

"Typical hierarchical mentality, the official line must be followed even if it leads to nowhere," growled Hamish. He thought for a minute then declared; "Well, bugger them. It's me full of holes, it's me on the ground, it's me that they have used to cover your modesty.

Their systems have failed so far. My system will succeed but will never be acknowledged by yesterday's men. I am surprised and pleased that Cole was with me. I never thought that I would say such a thing, but after a visit from him and now his support; God bless 'Old King Cole' and may his Capstan Full Strength never get the better of him. But they probably will!"

Freya soon took her leave, and Hamish settled down, closed his eyes while his brain went through every aspect of the case, those that he had been involved in and those to which he was only an interested bystander. And so another day throughout the many, passed as did yesterday.

As the days passed he drew nearer to what was hopefully his final operation. His bright spot of the passing days was the visit from Tara down there for a seminar on virus control and elimination.

Regular twice-weekly visits from Sarah and yet another visit from 'Old King Cole' who told him that the work by Howard had been a success and that other than "A bloody stupid red or black judge and a really smart QC despicable bastards that they are, a conviction for murder is assured."

Mr Cole sat back quietly confident that he had pleased Hamish. He then had another thought and said, "Why in the hell couldn't you choose a British woman to skewer the bugger, we'd have her nicked by now instead of in Russia or wherever she is. I expect that Miss Whosit has told you all about it anyway.

Hamish assured Mr Cole that Freya had told him nothing but equally he had never asked her.

"We have now got out an Interpol warrant for murder with her mug on it and the cooperation of the Germans. I didn't approve of this twinning business between our force and theirs.

With my dad in the first lot and me in 1939, we fought the buggers for too long to want to be friends but they have come in useful now." Fred, with the suitable disdainful facial expression, told Hamish.

When Mr Thomas kindly gave Hamish a visit, welcomed though he was, it was noticeable that both Fred Cole with his Capstan Full Strength cigarettes and Stu Thomas with his Golden Virginia pipe tobacco cut short their visits for the mandatory and desperate puff and a draw respectively.

Like them, he too, on occasions, missed a comforting Appleton Estate Rum and a King Edward cigar. The rum was not allowed by the hospital or Freya, but when she pushed him outside she would allow him a cigar if she remembered a match to light it with!

"I've spoken to Sir Simon," Sarah told Freya, "he is quite happy for me to take Mrs Briggs to your mother's vineyard for a week sometime in September if you are still up to it?"

After a quick telephone call, Freya came back to tell her that if she could take Mrs Briggs there the first week of September it would be fine.

To not cause Mrs Briggs any embarrassment, cook would look after her in the house and Sarah at all other times.

Sarah told Freya of the difficulty to get Mrs Briggs to agree to have a break.

Mr Bates gave her an ultimatum 'Go with Miss Dodds-Younger or give up your job here. She told him that she didn't have any clothes to wear so couldn't go.

"I have been hearing that excuse from ladies most of my adult life beginning with my mother and onwards to you," Mr Bates, in a very kindly tone told her.

"But I ain't a lady like yer mother sir." was her response. "Every woman is a lady by the nature of their conduct whatever their clothes, wealth, class and education might be Mrs Briggs. I will see that you have nice clothes and money to go with them.

This is a wonderful opportunity to celebrate your new home with new clothes and a holiday with Miss Sarah. Just take it all and be relaxed and thankful." Mr Bates told her. Determined to have the last word, Mrs Briggs said as she turned to leave the office. "Look at me 'ands, sir, theym a disgrace." She turned towards Chief Superintendent Bates and held out two gnarled, arthritic fingered, yellowed nailed rather grubby looking hands.

"They are not hands to be ashamed of Mrs Briggs." Mr Bates told her. "They are an unwritten reference to a lifetime of hard work and toil. You have a week before you go. Your clothes and hands will be dealt with."

"Do you believe in God Mrs Briggs?" He asked her. "Course I does sir," she replied. "Did his son have fine clothes, did he worry about his hands?" she was asked.

In the most rare of occasions, Chief Superintendent Sir Simon Bates was bested, not by a woman of high birth or high intellect but by an uneducated charwoman.

It was one of those golden moments that Sarah would never forget as Mrs Briggs told her boss. "I weren't there to see 'im sir an' I don't think that 'ee worried about 'is 'ands when they nailed 'im up, sir."

"There you are Mrs Briggs, you can hold your own against anyone," Mr Bates told her and looking at Sarah he said. "Get her hands seen to just before you go away. Goodbye ladies." Was the end of the saga in the office.

During the next five days, Sarah had to keep reassuring Mrs Briggs that she would look after everything. After getting her some outer clothes and noting the size, surreptitiously Sarah bought Mrs Briggs new underwear. She then took her to have both her nails and her hair tided up with a not completely successful visit to the local shoe shop and Sarah took the opportunity to buy Mrs Briggs a suitcase and a make-up box.

On a disappointingly overcast day Sarah collected Mrs Briggs from her new home and after checking that all things that should be turned off were off, then loaded Mrs Briggs and her suitcase into the car and made off for the River Dart.

On arrival, they were met by the housekeeper, her husband and the cook. Although a younger person, cook was in most respects a copy of Mrs Briggs.

Soon they were all settled in. While it was a reasonable assumption that Mrs Briggs might feel out of place it was Sarah who felt awkward.

The three residents took well to Mrs Briggs but they treated Sarah with the embarrassing deference to a mistress from her servant.

Sarah tried to break the social stigma but without success so finally gave in after attempting to dine in the kitchen with the rest of them. The housekeeper insisted that Sarah should be waited upon in the isolation of the dining room.

At breakfast the same performance of reversed snobbery took effect. Sarah deliberately spilt some coffee as an excuse to go to the kitchen and see if Mrs Briggs was comfortable.

As she opened the door she could see that the laughing Mrs Briggs had taken to life in the kitchen like a duck to water.

When asked what she would like to do on the first day of her holiday Mrs Briggs asked if she could stay around the house. The host and hostesses seemed to be very happy at that idea, particularly cook.

On that first day, it seemed that the only fly in the ointment for Mrs Briggs was that no one would let her do anything, even make her bed. By late afternoon cook let her help with preparing the vegetables for dinner and to Mrs Briggs, this was heaven on earth.

On the second day, the weather had improved and Sarah took Mrs Briggs on a car ride to Plymouth and was happy to watch her slowly taking to holiday life. She finally persuaded Mrs Briggs to have her photograph taken looking out to sea. They were sitting taking in the sunshine on the Hoe when, without warning, she asked Sarah. "When will I 'ave ter pay back all the money spent on I an' this 'oliday?"

Sarah was so taken aback by the question that it took her a few seconds to answer. "Mrs Briggs, you do not pay for anything. Everything is taken care of by Sir Simon, Chief Inspector Douglas Gore Hamilton and me."

Mrs Briggs looked closely at Sarah and said, "But you've bought me 'ouse fer I an' all this as well. I gotta pay fer sommut Miss. 'Oo be this Douglas somebody?"

"It's Freya," Sarah explained.

"I'm sorry, miss," Mrs Briggs told Sarah and continued with her handkerchief to her eyes and tears about to fall, "I've never 'ad charity. Thank you, miss. Please take me 'ome."

Sarah explained to Mrs Briggs that she was certainly not having charity. This was simply a gift for all her years of devoted work and Chief Superintendent Bates had gone to so much trouble to arrange this holiday as a gift for her that he would be upset if she didn't enjoy herself.

The mention of Mr Bates changed the attitude of Mrs Briggs. She whispered to Sarah. "I be a silly old woman. I'm sorry Miss." Mrs Briggs then fiddled with the hasp of her new handbag, produced her purse and asked Sarah if she would get them an iced cream.

Sarah was about to tell her that she would pay for the two cones and then caught herself before she refused the money. After discovering that Mrs Briggs did not realise that she had a choice of flavours took the money and went for two vanilla cones.

After lunch for which they agreed to go halves with the payment, Sarah took Mrs Briggs to the Plymouth Gin Distillery for a tour and a sample.

Just as long as there were regular sit-downs all went very well as they strolled through the pre-war parts of Plymouth. In the distillery, Mrs Briggs seemed a little confused as to what a distillery was and when she found out she told Sarah, "Me mother drunk Gin an' she weren't a good woman when she'd 'ad a lot. I ain't never drunk. Do you miss?"

Sarah told Mrs Briggs that she did drink and Plymouth Gin was her preferred drink so this visit was the perfect place to get some bottles.

From her expression, it seemed that Mrs Briggs did not agree.

The following day Sarah took Mrs Briggs to Dartmouth. The weather could have been a little better, but apart from some early drizzle, it was dry. Once again with regular rest stops, they explored all the little alleyways and shops. They had a good morning in and around town with coffee above a bakers shop in the Butterwalk.

Deciding that it was quite a long walk for Mrs Briggs to get to their destination for lunch, Sarah drove to the Upper Ferry and they had lunch in the 'Yachties' hotel there. Mrs Briggs attempted to take the bill from the salver as presented by the waiter.

At a look from Sarah, the waiter changed course and gave it to Sarah. When Mrs Briggs protested Sarah played her trump card and told her that Sir Simon had given the money for all their lunches. There was no further protest.

Sarah drove back around Dartmouth and as they again faced the Upper Ferry Sarah pointed out the Britannia Royal Naval College sitting over the town and told her that it was the place where Staff Sergeant Fergusson had trained to be a sailor. That seemed to impress Mrs Briggs until in the evening she heard her telling cook that she had passed 'Staff Sergeant Fergusson'.

The next day Sarah decided it should be a day of rest for Mrs Briggs. Sarah took the opportunity to have a wander down to the river and simply enjoy herself watching the passing yachts, ferries and small craft passing down to Dartmouth or up to Totnes.

The following day she took Mrs Briggs to Buckfast Abbey and again she reluctantly posed in front of the doors of the Abbey for another photograph before going onto the pottery at Bovey Tracey on the edge of Dartmoor.

The following day Sarah decided that it would be another rest day for Mrs Briggs. She decided to drive to Salcombe where a friend, an author lived. They had a busy, enjoyable day on the water exposed to the sunshine, and for September, soft warm breezes. Not exactly excellent weather for sailing but it was the best place to avoid the crowds in the narrow congested lanes and alleyways. To top off a wonderful day Sarah was able to use her photography skills to take some excellent maritime scenes.

The following day Sarah decided that as Totnes was not that far away she reasoned that it would be only a short car ride to get there, but accepted that Mrs Briggs would not manage the hill so she would confine the visit to the area of Steamer Quay. They arrived there at mid-morning and had coffee before sitting and watching the ferry from Dartmouth berth there.

As the vessel came alongside Sarah took several photographs before the passengers almost poured ashore scattering all over the place. "Mr Larcombe, Mr Larcombe, 'Coo-ee, hello," Then with a surprisingly deep tone Mrs Briggs shouted, "Mr Larcombe it's me yer."

Sarah was busy looking for whoever Mrs Briggs was shouting at when, at some speed for a very old little lady, Mrs Briggs set off after a man and woman walking by the café. As Sarah tried to catch up with her the man and woman stopped and turned and Sarah took no notice when her camera around her neck clicked. "This is me old neighbour Mr Larcombe, an' 'is lady. 'e used ter live in my block of flats." A very out of breath Mrs Briggs hesitatingly explained.

While Sarah made small talk with Mr Larcombe his lady friend did not say a word and mostly kept looking away while both Mrs Briggs and in turn, Sarah tried to engage her in conversation.

When Mrs Briggs wanted to talk about their time together as neighbours it was obvious to Sarah that from their body language and the simple 'Yes' or 'No' replies to Mrs Briggs, they wanted to be off. "Please Miss, will 'e take a photo of us?"

Sarah noted that there was a distinct refusal from the man with the woman nodding her head. Finally, the entreaty from Mrs Briggs wore them down and she stood proudly in front of the pair.

Through the view finder, Sarah aimed for the best shot and pressed the shutter button. Nothing happened. She apologised and tried again. Nothing happened. She realised that the film had not been wound on.

Quite puzzled she tried again and all worked well except the woman averted her face. "Sorry, I'm afraid you were looking down," she told the woman. "We'll try another. Smile and look at me," she asked. Again the woman put her head down and turned her face away.

Mentally Sarah made her mind up that one way or another she would get a decent photo for Mrs Briggs. "Thank you," she said as she still had the camera to her eye and as they all moved to say goodbye Sarah pressed the shutter button.

As the pair walked away Sarah noted two unusual things about them. Mrs Briggs was very flustered when she came back to Sarah and told her that they were not as friendly as they had been when Mr Larcombe lived on the same landing.

The poor old lady was quite upset by their attitude to her so Sarah suggested that they might go on to Newton Abbot and have lunch and if she felt like it, perhaps a bit of shopping. Mrs Briggs still thinking about the meeting with someone she knew so far from home said nothing as they made their way back to the car.

The following day Mrs Briggs asked cook if she could stay with her and it was cheerfully agreed.

Sarah was quite pleased that after yesterday's performance at Totnes Mrs Briggs would be doing something with someone she liked.

Taking the spool of film containing their excursions to Plymouth, Dartmouth and points in between from her camera, Sarah set off for Dartmouth again.

In Dartmouth, she found a film processing shop that would process a film for collection in twenty-four hours. When she handed the spools in she told the assistant that one of the films had several unexposed shots and to ignore them when developing the film. Her concern was totally wasted as the girl told Sarah, "They goes through a machine. It ain't worried what's on 'em or what's not."

After taking her receipt and buying two more films She went for a coffee at the Railway Station Restaurant, a station that had never seen a train in it since it was built. A slight oversight by Mr Brunel.

The following day, a beautiful sunny day, again Mrs Briggs asked if she could stay with cook. As before this was happily agreed to by cook and the housekeeper. They suggested that they would take Mrs Briggs for a picnicking type lunch at the river edge while watching the boats go by.

Sarah took a couple of bits of fruit and made her way back to Dartmouth to collect her photographs.

Back in her car, she went through the photographs then checked that all the negatives corresponded with the photos. Satisfied that they did, she realised that the reason that the shutter would not operate was explained by her arm striking the shutter button when she took off after Mrs Briggs as she in turn rushed off after Mr Larcombe. That print was a perfect portrait of Mr Larcombe and his lady friend.

With a smile of satisfaction that inadvertently she had thwarted the efforts of the woman to hide her face both before and the final shot. However, the first shot was by far the best.

From Dartmouth she made her way along the coastline, on a sunny day such as this, there was no seascape in the world that could compare with this view and that included the Cote de Azure.

After going through Stoke Fleming and Strete she dropped down to sea level at Strete Gate and parked adjacent to Slapton Sands.

Taking the travelling rug, her handbag, sun hat, camera and fruit, Sarah made her way along the shingle beach to where there were many people and their children who she presumed were probably from private schools who not returned from holidays yet. In the curve of the shingle bay were many small craft at anchor, and the people from the various craft were ashore enjoying games. It was a very pleasant feeling to strip off, lay back on the rug, administer the sun lotion and close her eyes allowing the sounds of the surf breaking and high pitched children's voices from far away drifting over her. Peace, perfect contentment!

Eventually, she sat up, adjusted her eyes to the bright scene and found a party of four young girls not far away. She thought it unusual that in the brief time that she had been there so many happy people were around her. She looked at her wristwatch and realised that she must have been in a very deep sleep.

"Excuse me," said one of the four youngsters, "Could you please take a photo of us," and handed Sarah a camera. She moved around them until the sun was at her back then did a circuit of them and with the girl's permission used several shots to capture all of them at their best.

When she had finished her task she handed back their camera and asked one of the girls to take a photograph of her and handed over her own camera. Sarah sat with the cliffs behind her and then she stood up for the next frame. Her photographer along with another girl had almost olive skin and decidedly accented English.

In conversation, Sarah discovered that the girls were foreign students studying agriculture near Newton Abbot. The four had arrived early for their course which did not begin for another fortnight so they were here, there and everywhere enjoying themselves in the meantime.

They wanted to send the photographs home to their parents and asked Sarah where they could be processed without the beach scenes being censored. Sarah rummaged in her handbag and gave them her receipt for the processor that she'd used at Dartmouth and assured them that the beach scenes would not be destroyed.

Later she wondered what their parents would say when nude photos of their daughters arrived on their doormat? Unless of course, they were of the same persuasion as their frolicking daughters.

After her fruit lunch, Sarah began to put sun lotion on her legs, arms and as much of her back as she could reach. One of the girls saw her impossible task and came over to help. It was quite noticeable that with the many people spread out over half a mile of beach just how quiet the beach became over the normal lunch hour.

Eventually, Sarah decided that it was time for her to leave her 'Paradise' and return to Mrs Briggs. The girls were all in the surf and waved at her as she dressed and began the long trek back to her car.

The moment that she returned via a florists shop, she asked permission to use the telephone and rang Freya. When she got through to her, Sarah asked if they could have a meeting the next afternoon when she had returned from the holiday. The time and meeting place agreed, Sarah went off and found cook and Mrs Briggs.

It seemed that everyone had enjoyed themselves with their stay at the river bank and she heard later that Mrs Briggs spent much of the time quietly asleep in her chair. When Sarah asked Mrs Briggs if she had enjoyed herself she was told that cook had helped her take her stockings off so, "No one noticed," but "it was so peaceful that I 'ad trouble in stayin' awake."

After dinner cook arrived with all of Mrs Briggs laundry, washed dried and ironed and they began to repack the case for the return home the following day. It was agreed that it would be an early start the following morning and after a good night's sleep Sarah woke up to a rather overcast day.

They had just finished breakfast when a tall, striking, greying haired lady came into the dining room with the housekeeper in tow.

"Hello everyone. I'm Flora, Freya's mother. I do hope that you have had a good holiday and have enjoyed your stay here. I understand that cook has been looking after you, Mrs Briggs. I do hope that she's not been leading you astray."

Whilst not a pretty sight by any recognising, Mrs Briggs mouth was wide open. She almost fell off her chair as still with her mouth open she stood up and tried her best to do a curtsy only to stumble. Flora caught her in time as Sarah made a dive for her as well.

"Oh, mum, I be so sorry." Her voice caught and tears began to flow. With Flora on one side and Sarah propping her up on the other, Mrs Briggs was near to collapsing as she continued between sobs.

"I be sorry to be such a bother to you all. Thank you fer lettin' me come 'ere. Everybody been so kind and 'specially Mrs Windsor. Thank 'ee, mum."

Looking at cook in the corner Flora said. "Thank you, Mrs Briggs. After your endorsement of the kindness of cook, I supposed that I will have to increase her wages!

I'm so pleased that you have enjoyed it here and perhaps you would care to come again. You have certainly given my staff such pleasure with your company that if I give them the chance, they will insist on you coming again." They then sat a bemused Mrs Briggs back in her chair.

Turning to Sarah, Flora held out her hand and told Sarah, quite truthfully. "Freya has told me much about you and it is delightful to meet you. I think that it is very generous of you to give your time and probably money to make the life of an elderly lady a little easier. Thank you."

"I must say 'thank you' for your kindness in allowing us here," Sarah told Flora. If you'll excuse us I will take Mrs Briggs upstairs to finish packing as we must be away soon as I have a meeting with Freya at two."

"I'll see you off whenever." Mrs Douglas Gore Hamilton told her.

With the help of cook, they managed to get Mrs Briggs ready to leave. Sarah then collected three bunches of flowers from her room and made a silent prayer of thanks to the Almighty that when she bought the flowers she included the housekeeper's husband quite forgetting that he was a man. Now that Flora had turned up the third bunch could go to her. Sarah wrote out the labels for Mrs Briggs to sign.

It was a painfully slow exercise to get her fingers to work. And, in reality, it was Sarah's writing that told the recipients who the flowers were from. For the gentleman, Sarah wrote a cheque and found an envelope in the library.

As they all gathered in the dining room Sarah entered with the flowers and a spare handkerchief.

She held onto Mrs Briggs as she went to each person handing out the flowers. The only mistake was when she offered the gentleman flowers instead of the envelope. As it was corrected, Sarah thought, "How the truth will out."

When they got to Flora Mrs Briggs again attempted a curtsy and bowing her head said, "Me lady."

Flora said nothing but bent down and kissed Mrs Briggs on the cheek. It was quite a contrast. A tall elegant lady with refined chiselled features bending almost double to kiss a diminutive charlady.

As they went towards Sarah's car with Flora still holding Mrs Briggs up, she protested.

"Me lady, you shouldn't, help I." and attempted to disengage her arm.

"Without wishing to be rude, Mrs Briggs," Flora told her, "You are old enough to be my mother. Was she still alive? I would help her and you are no different a human being to her so I help you quite naturally."

After much waving and tears from Mrs Briggs, Sarah drove away and other than a toilet stop reached Mrs Briggs home via shopping for milk, bread, veg and chicken to last her over the coming weekend.

Sarah then went home, unpacked and waited for Freya to arrive.

After talking about the holiday Sarah asked Freya. "How far have you got in finding the chap who shot Hamish?"

Freya told her that there was no change because the reality was that other than the false hand and lower arm there was nothing to go on until they had occasion to detain someone and fingerprints or no arm could be matched, there was little hope of progress.

"In any event," Freya told her, "the case now belonged to Harry Broadweir and Ron Wilkins with her taking on a consultants role.

"How is Hamish getting on?" Sarah asked. "A bit stronger every day," replied Freya. "I hope to bring him home this weekend if all goes well. Once he's at home I hope that we can dispense with the armed guard and settle him in."

"Do you think that you could have him out on day release this afternoon?" Sarah asked.

"Why?"

"Because it might be that I can help you to discover who shot him and if you can get him out I will keep the information until then," she told her.

After she persuaded Freya that she had what might be vital information concerning who shot Hamish. Freya rang Assistant Chief Constable Gaunt and told him that Sarah had important information and possible evidence to detect the person who shot Inspector Fergusson.

"If you want me for a meeting on a Friday afternoon," Mr Gaunt told Freya, "the information had better be extremely good. As Harry Broadweir is the lead in this case I will have him here. Three o'clock sharp and no longer than four," he told her in not an exactly friendly tone of voice.

Freya took Sarah to pick up Hamish from the convalescent home, explained why they were taking him to Mr Gaunt. The guard insisted on going with them as well.

Once in the car with Hamish having the front passenger seat pushed well back Freya said, "This car is advertised as being 'A carriage to convey for four six-foot gentlemen'. It's lucky that Sarah isn't a gentleman, or there wouldn't be room, would there, constable?" The question was followed by total silence.

At HQ, Freya slowly helped Hamish up to Mr Gaunt's office where they found Chief Superintendent Bates also in residence.

After the usual greetings, Sarah was asked, quite understandably, the reason for the meeting.

She then asked Hamish, "Can you identify the man and woman that you saw at lunch at the Scolding Wife?"

"Yes," he answered.

"Was there anything unusual about the pair?" Sarah asked.

Hamish thought for a brief time before saying. "Other than she kept her gloves on while eating. Not much else except that she held onto the chaps arm both in and outside of the pub."

"Was she tall and thin?" was the next question.

"I suppose so. On reflection, yes, she was slender but tall for a woman," he replied then asked, "Why?"

With a flourish, like a conjurer producing a rabbit out of a hat, Sarah handed Hamish a photograph of the pair leaving the ferry at Steamer Quay and asked, "Are those the same people on the gangway?"

Hamish studied the photo and asked Mr Gaunt for a magnifying glass. When it was produced he looked carefully, seemed to think about it and finally said. "Yes, it could well be them."

Buoyed by her success so far, provisional detective Sarah told the assembled company.

"From what I have been told and overheard about this case I have very good reason to believe that the man who shot Hamish was, in fact, a woman, then waving the photo at everyone she triumphantly said; "that woman." After a silence expected in such a statement, Hamish asked, "What makes you so sure?"

She replied, in a manner something similar to that of Perry Mason concluding his cross-examination of a murderer in his best denouement in an American Courthouse.

"Your suspect has a distinctive walk. The woman at Totnes had a distinctive walk. The woman at the Scolding Wife wore black gloves, the woman at Totnes wore black gloves. Whoever shot you left a black-gloved hand and lower prosthetic arm when you were shot!"

Another silence gripped the meeting until Sarah produced the rest of the photographs and told the story of Mrs Briggs, Mr Larcombe and the lady who visited him at his council flat.

Mr Gaunt had to call the meeting to order such was the disturbance around the room. Hamish looked at the rest of the photographs and told everyone that definitely the woman that he saw with the man at the pub were the same people.

He asked Sarah, "How did you get one superb shot at her and with one exception she is avoiding the camera?"

"That dear Hamish was a complete fluke," she replied. "I had photographed them getting off the ferry, wound the film on and cocked the shutter for the next photo when Mrs Briggs took off. As they turned around to look at Mrs Briggs so I rushed to grab her and my arm or hand must have hit the button and we have the shot. I was surprised when I collected the prints to see that one amongst them."

"That's her without a doubt. You are brilliant Sarah, in more ways than one." Hamish said followed by; 'Hear, hears' all around.

"The long and short of it," she told the assembly, "is that without the original generosity of Freya in telling Mrs Briggs that she would take her on holiday which, as a result of events beyond her control, couldn't happen. My being available to take her, and Freya's mother's vineyard home being available, the kindness of allowing me to have time off and the financial input by Chief Superintendent Bates, we still would be looking for an unknown and unidentified gunman rather than gunwoman who we can now identify pictorially."

A general discussion then took place about letting the SOCO have the photographs and negatives to enlarge and distribute and institute the all Ports warning system and Interpol.

"By the way, Harry," ACC Gaunt asked Harry Broadweir, "I don't recall seeing any report from you about the arm and glove that Inspector Fergusson grabbed as he was shot. I'm sure that there was an identity code on the arm we could use. Has it been identified to whoever it was made for Harry?"

Instead of admitting that he had done nothing about it, Harry went all around the houses in his reply invoking the need to identify all the items from the hut and water tank at Sunny Patch without a 'Team' to help him.

"Surely the need to arrest the person who shot a colleague is more immediately important than buggering about with items not in need of identification until a collar is felt." The plainly very annoyed assistant chief constable told Acting Detective Superintendent Broadweir. There was a strained silence as without any words spoken the ignominy of forced retirement, albeit by only a few months before the normal retirement, was there and then imposed on Harry for negligence.

"It is not all your fault Mr Broadweir," Mr Gaunt told the person that a few moments before he had addressed as 'Harry'. "I should have checked up on the matter and I accept the blame that I didn't do so but, a chief superintendent should not have to be supervised under any circumstances."

Turning to Hamish Mr Gaunt said. "I do apologise to you Inspector. This Police Force, through me, has let you down, badly. I'm so sorry.

As of now I will personally deal with the arm and identify the owner, despite having to deal with the ethical secrecy of the NHS."

Addressing Sarah, Mr Gaunt said.

"Thank you for what you have done for this investigation as a civilian. It is nothing less than inspired how you drew the various aspects together of, to you, hearsay. Quite a brilliant deduction. Thank you from all of us." With a smile, a rare commodity during the meeting he continued.

"Should you feel the need to engage in further detection I'm sure that I have a vacancy somewhere." Turning to Chief Superintendent Bates he said, "Your such a lucky man Simon to have a secretary of this calibre."

"As you're all here," Hamish said, the thought occurs to me, Has anyone paid off my reservation at the scolding Wife pub?"

"Yes, I have," Simon Bates told him. When you were shot I put a couple of men in your room for the rest of the week to keep a watch on Sunny Patch. Nothing happened and no questions were asked by the Landlord."

In reply to Bill Gaunt, he said, "I'm lucky to have Mrs Briggs and Miss Dodds Younger but without the connection, the very lucky connection between Mrs Briggs this fellow Larcombe and Sarah's deductive prowess we would still be nowhere. Bully for Mrs Briggs."

The meeting ended with the dejected Harry Broadweir leaving first. As the rest stood up to leave Mr Gaunt said to Freya. "We now have photographs of the murderess, photographs of the would-be murderess and hopefully her prints from the camp and perhaps a name from the arm. We're moving but I want you back from London or to supervise this job from London."

"I've only been doing a couple of days a week for the past weeks at the Home Office so I will fill in for you if you get rid of Harry but who do I get as a team that you didn't give him sir?"

"He had whoever he wanted." Mr Gaunt told her and added, "But dear old Harry wanted to do things himself and as we have just witnessed, overreached himself.

You can pick two people from the central pool, preferably a pair that you have supervised before.

Don't take Harry's office yet, I'll find you another one. Make whatever arrangements you like."

The meeting dispersed with both Freya and Sarah taking Hamish and the guard back to the convalescent home. The moment that they left the guard at the door Sarah told them of her holiday with Mrs Briggs and in some respects what an eye-opener it had been into the life of an elderly less well off, in fact, deprived lady.

She then went on to tell them of her trip to find her friend at Salcombe and all about the four girls that she saw on Slapton and the unexpected meeting with Freya's mother.

Before Freya took her back home Hamish bundled her into his arms and gave Sarah a tender, probably because he was still tender himself, hug and kiss for all that she had done for him whilst on her holiday and then told both ladies.

"So far this entire case has depended not on the expertise of us in prosecuting the investigation, in fact, we have been nothing better than mediocre but on a run of bloody good fortune or luck if you prefer. If we never get beyond where we are now, the whole case has been of failure on our part but with the help of extreme luck, thanks to the Gods at last we might be getting somewhere."

The only response that he had from his ladies for his in-depth and controversial analysis of the case was a thoughtful, carefully considered response comprising of the single word, "Balls."

As the two laughing ladies left his room he responded with the exclamation;

"Some 'Ladies' you pair turned out to be!"

A few days later Hamish received a 'phone call from Freya "I know that this information will be of interest to you. We now have the name of the person with one arm and in a million years you will never guess her name."

Without waiting for a reply, she continued. "Anna Rosenberg and her address not only for this new arm, but for the old one are of all places, Woodbine Cottage. Would you believe it?"

Bill Gaunt used up most of his favours with the minister. He used the same method to find out about friend Larcombe. His name is Roy Larcombe, he is forty and according to his National Insurance number, at present in receipt of unemployment pay. And the Labour Exchange described him as an unemployed chauffeur. His present address is unknown and he hasn't drawn any unemployment money for a couple of months.

Hamish replied, "Yes, I would believe all of it and leaving aside Larcombe, it would not surprise me if she was the daughter of 'Iron Gob'. Both are of an identical build now that a name and place connect them. Well done."

"Thank Bill Gaunt. Freya told him. "I was in his office with the chief constable and their QC when they went to the Health Minister. Say what you want about avuncular Bill, he is brilliant.

He puts on the persona of a bumbling country copper on his bike by the parish pump to lull them into a benign frame of mind.

Then he let rip with both barrels and blasts their prevarications and arguments to pieces, from the minister, through civil servants to heads of NHS and the same for the department of labour. Believe it or not, he even got both their National Insurance numbers!"

"All that we don't have is the three collars," Hamish said, despairingly.

"Things are getting better. Thanks to Sarah, Howard and your photographer friend," Freya told him then said, "Chin up. They are on the All Ports Warning list and Interpol systems. They can't run forever and we'll be there to catch them."

Determined not to allow his pessimism to fail or perhaps to rein in the optimism of Freya, Hamish concluded. "Not if they are anywhere in the Eastern Block."

Freya stood looking down at him with an exasperated expression and told him. "Hamish James William Fergus Ciaran-Fergusson, it is of no surprise to me that you remain unmarried.

What woman would take on such misery-guts as you? I'm off." As she went through the door Hamish had the final words telling the disappearing body. "And it's me who has the damned holes in my hide. Think on girly, think on!" He then shouted at her now disappeared back, "who told you my names?" Your A5 chitties on the desk of 'Sir, the silent one' Freya, laughingly, shouted back at him.

After a further month in the convalescent home, Hamish was allowed to return to his own home, only needing a walking stick to aid his leg.

With the drawing in of the nights so his thoughts turned to Freya's October birthday and their tradition of having one or more days together on such an occasion.

Since his return home, Sarah and Freya had been taking it in turn and turn about to visit him and see that his 'fridge was well stocked, washing to the laundry much to the annoyance of his 'Daily'. Other than the pair of them and her, the only other visitors Hamish had was his physio and, with an outstretched arm clutching a bottle heralded the welcomed arrival of Fred Cole and Stuart Thomas, usually on a Friday afternoon. There would be little doubt that the visits, in constabulary time, would be logged as. "Compassionate attendance on a sick colleague!" Every Friday?

When the three policemen were together the sitting room smelt like the mess decks of a ship, a mixture of pipe, cigarette and cigar tobacco under the "Swinging Lamp." Of Hamish.

As the lamp swung under the forecastle so a nautical or other tales could be told, most of it bunch of lies. The tale had to be completed before the lamp stopped swinging. Failure to do so resulted in the forfeiture of the man's grog ration or in the merchant navy, the beer ration. The only exception to this rule was when Duncan McLeod told of his 'Pay off' being spent, not as one would presume, purely on alcohol but a mixture of booze and the buying of sheep to take home to, of all places, 'Lewis'.

It was such a long, plausible and very funny tale told only in the mournful tones of a Stornoway man that beer was added to his ration on that particular occasion of "Swinging the Lamp."

Although very much appreciating the attention that he had from the ladies, Hamish craved some male company where language and manners were not so important and from his seeming enjoyment of the visits, Superintendent Cole no longer appeared to resent the background, education and silver-spooned privilege of Hamish. As he told a tale of the sea so Fred Cole tried to top it with a tale of his Army days while Stu Thomas threw in his tales of the fall of France and the Nuremberg trials. Matters concerning their present occupations were considered to be well 'Below the salt'. All-in-all, very congenial times.

It was at such a convivial meeting that the non-occupational talk being considered, 'Below the salt' was abandoned when Fred Cole told Hamish that they, they being the chief constable, Mr Gaunt, 'The silent one', Freya, Hamish, Tommo and himself with Sarah as secretary to her three senior officers had been summoned to a meeting in London. This meeting with the so-called

Head of MI5, a Home Office and Foreign Office minister with the deputy commissioner of the Metropolitan police and the commander running the real Met's special branch.

The meeting was headed as a 'De-brief and to regulate working relations between provincial police services and National interests'. It was to be held, of all places, at the Savoy at 3:00 p.m. on 21 October.

Neither Fred nor Stuart knew why they were being summoned to the meeting as they did not get directly involved in the case of Rosenberg, man, woman and presumably daughter v The Crown.

Before they got involved in tales of yesteryear Superintendent Cole made his position very clear by declaring.

"De-brief my arse, they are looking to pin us down to obey their orders. Like bloody hell. If they're looking for a fight they'll get more than one.

If they want a meeting with dainty sandwiches, vol-a bloody vaunts and Earl Grey tea they can forget it when old Cole is in town, at the Savoy or anywhere else."

Fred stopped for breath then continued. "The bloody Savoy, who pays for that?"

"Their budget?" Hamish hesitantly suggested.

"Not bloody likely," Fred said, "Us, yes, us. It's our taxes that pay for the Savoy!"

With his legs outstretched, ankles neatly crossed and contentedly chewing on his pipe Tommo, at his mischievous self, quietly suggested that the venue of the Savoy would keep people in employment, adding "I'm sure that you will agree Fred?"

That tell-tale vein in Fred's forehead was quite prominent as his mouth opened, closed then opened again to state very forcibly. "No, I don't bloody well agree and stop winding me up you pair of buggers. And they're all bloody foreigners there anyway."

Shortly after they had left, Hamish phoned Freya and began to tell her about this new twist to a very convoluted story.

She stopped him in full flow by telling him that she already knew of the meeting and as it was the day after her birthday she was booking up their suite at the Ferryman's hotel at Dartmouth before telling him about everything. They would leave Dartmouth and go straight to the Savoy. She had also booked in at the Savoy to have a couple of days in London after the meeting.

"It's all done and dusted is it?" Hamish asked her. "Please don't say it in those tones," she said and then added, "I'd hoped that my arrangements would be a nice surprise for you. I'm not too sure now."

"Sorry dearest," he told her, adding, "being a temporary cripple makes me very susceptible to the thought of people treating me as they would a child. In short, not being in control of my life."

"That was never my intention. It was to be what I'd hoped would be a really nice surprise, half-ruined by Cole and Thomas and completely ruined by your unattractive response." Freya firmly told him.

"Do I cancel these arrangements or are you going to accept them in good grace or even, very good grace?" The, by now, very annoyed lady enquired.

"Very good grace darling. Thank you from the bottom of my heart for your kindness. I really don't appreciate you as I should." A cringing Hamish told her.

She replied.

"In that case, I will come to you and pack your bags for both places and that will include your evening dress. I've booked a box at Covent Garden for IL Trovatore; it's about time that you told the truth. Never mind telling me 'From the bottom of my heart' when in truth you meant, 'The heart of my bottom!"

With both of them laughing down the phone lines, love and peace were restored.

As October brought on the full Autumn colours it brought on the indifferent weather and much shorter days.

While Freya and Hamish were motoring down to Dartmouth in the Bristol, so down came the Devonshire misty light rain turning to persistent rain as they passed the Dartbridge Inn. When they drove down College Way so the rain turned back to misty drizzle obscuring the enchanting view of the river.

On arrival at the hotel, the porter was hovering in the foyer.

After sitting so long it was quite an effort for Hamish to get out of the car but with the help of the porter and the receptionist, he was soon up the steps and being greeted by the general manager and other staff.

After Freya had supervised the removal of only the luggage needed in Dartmouth, leaving the rest for London, she then gave the keys for the Bristol to the porter enabling him to park the car. She then joined the throng at the desk and engaged in the polite conversation before being taken to their room on the third floor at the end of the hotel looking downriver towards the Castle.

One of the little things that always delighted Hamish was not necessarily the ambience of the hotel or the pleasant soft décor of the dining room or the remarkable food or the quality of staff, but small green plaques affixed to each door.

Instead of a numbered room, the rooms had names linked to maritime histories such as Sir Walter Raleigh, Ferdinand Magellan, Sir Francis Chichester and Admiral Cunningham. Hamish, being a Scottish lad was very much of the small, detailed but nonetheless significant matters mentality, from both money to plaques on hotel room doors. Such small things brought a smile to his lips. 'Little things fit little minds, little pots… etc.!'

After a lunch of Devon crab and local ale with their umbrellas up, they ventured out down the embankment to have a general look around. Hamish experienced that indefinable sensation of a seeming weight lifted off his shoulders and, despite the drizzle and a walking stick, he enjoyed the lightening of his sometimes sombre moods.

In the evening after dinner, they sat in, for want of a better description, the alleyway that passed for a bar. Wet oil skinned yachtsmen brushed past the guests in the bar and once changed into blazers and slacks the conversations were mostly of where they had come from, what they had done and where or what they would do following day. For a very superior hotel where usually everyone sat in isolation, here, from lords to commoners all mixed in and enjoyed themselves even if the ladies posh dresses became a little wet as the oil skinned sailors and would-be sailors brushed by.

The knock on the door brought both of them to their senses. Freya, still trying to wake up stumbled to the door and found a waiter with their tray of tea and the morning papers.

Hamish still appeared to be asleep so she climbed back into her bed and laid there thinking pleasant thoughts of nothing in particular other than about him.

Eventually, he pulled himself up on his pillows and requested that he should be served tea and have access to Freya's bed. Perhaps, rather surprisingly. he was allowed in without comment by Freya. They then sat in silence both looking at the unrivalled view of the river Dart from the upper Ferry down to Dartmouth castle. Even at that time in October, the morning river was quite a bustling water highway.

Eventually, they realised that they had spent rather longer in bed than was anticipated. If they intended to have breakfast they had to get up. The usual race to be in the bathroom first took place with the far more agile Freya claiming the first prize.

Their first complete day in Dartmouth was spent in motoring here and there in South Devon enjoying the uncluttered lanes now that the tourist season was over. For some reason, Freya drove to Blackawton and went to a place called Sheplegh Court, at some time Eisenhower's HQ.

They stopped at a café in amongst the cottages at Torcross. During the conversation, Hamish brought the subject of Sarah into the conversation and asked Freya if she knew how a wealthy former banker or financier ended up as a police secretary?

Freya told him what she knew and replied. "She told me that after her fiancée died she simply wanted to get away from the rigours of financial management and answered an advertisement for secretaries in the police. The salary was and is of no consequence.

She started in the pool and was sent as a relief to 'the silent one'. After a week he asked her to become his PA, and the rest is history."

They motored to Brixham, fishy Brixham, where he showed Freya the pilot boat which brought the channel pilot out to his various ships when they were voyaging up the channel to London or elsewhere. She tried her best to look interested but seemingly failed.

"It was your father's ships that the pilots took up the channel," Hamish told her, adding "Try to look interested. That's where your fortune comes from." "And other places," she added. "You haven't told me that you worked on Father's ships before. Were they good?" she asked.

"One of the top companies in the world to work for," Hamish told her. Freya looked at him in silence for a few seconds just to make sure that he wasn't being sarcastic. Satisfied that he wasn't she told him "I should puff out what I have for a chest in pride, particularly as Fergusson the 'Great' has endorsed the superiority of my father's fleet."

They returned to the warm embrace of the hotel and after dinner again availed themselves of the bar and all it represented.

As it had not been such a wet day other than moisture from the river water, passing oil skinned bodies did not leave angry, dress damaged ladies in their wake. When Freya had retired, Hamish again conducted the seafaring community choir in rousing and sometimes obscene renditions of fo'c's'le head shanties.

Freya woke up to the rather discordant tones of a usually very good tenor voice singing 'Happy birthday to you dear Freya. Happy birthday to you."

As with some difficulty she looked over to the other bed to witness a badly hungover Hamish half out of bed with a totally stupid grin plainly attempting to get his eyes to focus. In the end, he simply slipped out of bed and became a crumpled mess on the floor.

Eventually, getting himself on to all fours he gingerly made his way to her bed.

"Oh, no, you're not," she told him as, with bleary, bloodshot puppy eyes he silently pleaded for an invite into her bed.

"It is warm, comfortable and a sheer pleasure to be in here alone," Freya explained, adding. "I'm quite sure that the same criteria apply to your berth as well." Then concluding with the pithy statement. "In short sailor, sling your hook."

The mumbling by Hamish was interrupted by a knock at the door. Freya jumped out of bed to prevent the waiter from entering the room with the tea and coffee with the obligatory biscuits and in so doing seeing Hamish in a heap on the floor.

After closing the door on the man and then, with a change of mind, going to help puppy-eyed Hamish into her bed on strict but probably, to him, totally non-comprehended rules.

Having poured out the drinks and climbed into the narrow space left to her by the large frame of Hamish, she pushed her pillows against the bed head sat back and looked at him, perhaps asleep with a smile of contentment in his alcohol-induced stupor.

Not necessarily thinking of anything in particular she realised that when she rushed to open the door to collect the tray from the waiter she was in the buff. "Oh! God, I must have been naked yesterday as well," she told a mystified and, still half-dead to the world, Hamish.

Her sudden burst of laughter caused him to wake up to the reality of his position.

In Freya's bed no less, with the warm, comfortable, perfumed atmosphere of total bliss being all around him until he stretched out his hand and touched, warm, comfortable, perfumed flesh.

Although limited with the leeway given by the sheets, Freya produced a mighty strike on the errant hand with the verbal warning, "Try that again and it won't be just your gunshot wounds which will incapacitate you, darling. You've been warned and this is my birthday, not yours. You do not get presents of any kind and none of the kind that you are thinking about right now; on my birthday or for that matter, yours either." As they sat there, him felt hard-done by and her wondering if she had been a little too hard on him. Freya suddenly asked. "What time did you come up?"

"I dunno," was the reply. Not willing to give up the chase she told him.

"I left the bar at about 11:30, and you had just begun to conduct the varied mariners and make-believe mariners in a manly rendition of saucy sea shanties. I'm sure that 'Oh Shenandoah' should not contain the words that I heard when waiting for the lift to come down and it isn't a sea shanty either, O, wise ancient mariner that you claim to be," she concluded with a disarming smirk.

He made no reply and with a slightly unsteady hand drank his cup of coffee then wordlessly handed the empty cup to her for a refill from the percolator. After his second cup, he just managed to get himself out of bed and into his wardrobe. He returned with a slim oblong beautifully wrapped container.

He handed it to Freya and said.

"Happy birthday my darling."

While she was opening the parcel she was thinking to herself 'How did he manage to get out anywhere under his own steam, to buy a present?'

When the paper, ribbon and card was removed it became obvious that it was a beautiful leather-bound jewellery box.

When she opened it she was speechless; inside of the box was a necklace and pendant made from the deep red rubies only found in Ceylon, surrounded by diamonds suspended from a diamond-studded platinum chain. The necklace was complemented with a pair of earrings and a broach similar to the pendant.

While Hamish was busily trying to get his head to work properly, Freya was simply staring at her gift. Finally, finding her voice, she said.

"There are not enough words to describe just how beautiful this is. It is truly wonderful. Thank you so much," she turned the box towards Hamish only to find him breathing deeply and fast asleep.

She turned side on to him and used her knee to thump him in the thigh and as she struck him remembering that she had hit his injured thigh.

If the earth had swallowed her up at that second she would have been delighted. With a howl of pure anguish, Hamish went bar rigid saying nothing but his twisted face betrayed the pain.

The scene in the room was, in a perverse way, not dissimilar to a comedy sketch. Hamish howling, Freya frantic with guilt rushing here and there apologising many times the apologies being interspersed with. "How bad is it? Shall I call a doctor, What can I do?" as he rolled around in bed.

"Please, please," she begged Hamish. "Tell me what I can do for you?"

Laying still he replied, "For an acting police superintendent you really should not panic so.

Then with a wide smile, he told her. "I was pretending to be asleep and I anticipated either a thump in my chest or a knee in my groin so my hand was already down there and that is what you kneed dearest heart. All's well!"

Freya stopped in her tracks, opened her mouth and let forth a stream of language more suited to a dockside stevedore than an acting police superintendent. The nicest adjective that Freya used, called into question the marital status of his parents when he was conceived.

"Is that the language you were taught at your finishing school?" Hamish asked. The reply was a pillow in his face.

After their bath and shower respectively and a singular shave they were dressed to go down for breakfast.

Over the breakfast table, she asked Hamish how he had managed to buy such a beautiful and expensive present for her.

Waiting until he had swallowed his toast. He replied, "First the beauty is thanks to geology and the skill of artisans. The expense is in that I allowed a wealthy woman to get your gift. She brought a selection of three gifts that she thought would be appropriate for me to choose whatever I thought that you would like.

I chose the one you have without knowing the astronomical price. Had I known I would have asked her to swallow her pride and find out what Woolworths had to offer. In fact, I did suggest that particular course of action. I was so surprised when the lady concerned, of high birth, used much the same disgraceful language towards me as you did less than an hour ago.

This lady only invoked the marital status of my mother after she said, amongst many other things that I was a mean Scottish scroat, which I presume is an abbreviation of the scrotum, and a Highland b... to boot."

"Sarah I presume?" Freya asked. His reply was a nod as he began buttering the next piece of toast.

When they finally passed the reception desk on their way to the lift Freya noticed the knowing smile from the receptionist towards Hamish. She thought, 'Yet another one he has collected. What service has she performed for him I wonder?'

Hamish unlocked the door and stood back as Freya walked into the suite. On her bed was a most attractive creation of flowers and an envelope.

"You darling," were her only comments as she opened the envelope to find an embroidered birthday card inside bearing the words, "With all my love on your birthday and thank you for your love and care for me over the past four months."

Freya was in her seventh heaven as they sat holding hands on the sofa looking out of the window at the river scene against the backdrop of the towering wooded hillside on the opposite bank bathed in the spectacular colours of the autumn.

"What do you want to do for your birthday?" he asked her.

"Nothing in particular," she replied, adding, "Perhaps a slow walk along to the Boat Float, go and have a coffee, a walk around the bandstand and stroll back here for lunch and have a quiet sleepy afternoon here before going down to dinner. A drink at the bar and definitely, positively, absolutely and finally no shanty singing. I want a good night's sleep before driving to this meeting at the Savoy."

It was then decided that Freya would easily get them to London by three if they left Dartmouth at eleven. Once they had gone up the A.38 they would join the almost completed M4 and straight through from there to the Strand.

Freya left the suite to take her new present down to reception for it to be put into the hotel safe and get a receipt.

Eventually, they dressed ready for the cool temperature outside with Freya insisting that he should wear his hat. Suitably dressed they ventured out of the hotel with Hamish leaning heavily on his silver-topped Rosewood cane. When it was obtained in the Far East as a young man, little did he ever imagine needing the cane until he was a very old man. Whatever will be, will be!

When by the floating pontoon a man in uniform wished them 'good morning'.

"Good morning to you, master," replied Hamish with a wave of his cane.

"How did you know that he was a master," Freya asked then added, "He only had three unusual bars on his shoulder."

"I didn't know," Hamish told her. "Everyone, even you, is susceptible to flattery. That chap might be the dockmaster or a ferry master or none. He has gone on his way quite happily, if he's a master he is satisfied, if he isn't he will go away with a nice warm glow of achievement recognised by some old dumb tourist on a cane."

They managed to find a dry wooden bench on the south embankment and just sat there each with their own thoughts watching the Kingswear passenger ferries scuttling across the river with far fewer passengers than a month earlier.

When the cold finally made them desert their very enjoyable perch and maritime view they went to the other side of the Boat Float and into the hotel there for a warm-up and a coffee. In earlier times they had booked into this hotel with a room facing the river. It was all very plush but after dark until about two the morning the noise from drunken revellers was unbearable.

Point taken and although they sometimes dined at this their former hotel, the Ferryman's Hotel was far quieter; In fact, almost silent until the vehicle ferry started up at 6:30 with the rhythmic splash of the paddle wheels soon inducing sleep again.

After dinner, Hamish joined Freya in the bar and was instantly engaged in several conversations at the same time by the men of his sea shanty choir from the last evening while it appeared that the various wives and lady friends were busy commiserating with each other over the last evening's performance.

While encouraged to have another melodic evening, Hamish, stood fast against all entreaties to start up the shanties with only the clean ones to be sung until the ladies retired again. His refusal to comply with the chorister's demands earned him a smile of gratitude from the manager's wife behind the bar.

After making sure that she had the complimentary bathrobe ready on their final dawn at the hotel Freya was ready for the visit of the waiter with the coffee and tea. When the knock came she promptly covered up and went to the door. She didn't need to have bothered, it was a waitress replacing the nonplussed waiter from the previous two mornings.

As they sat in Freya's bed looking down the river towards the castle Hamish noticed a merchant ship tied up to the buoys. To his eye, it appeared to be a timber ship. Sometimes timber carrying ships went up to Totnes but in his professional judgement from his years at sea, the ship had too much draught to go upriver even under a high tide.

At breakfast, Freya told Hamish to have an extra egg as it was doubtful if they would get lunch. He went up in the lift while Freya paid the bill at reception and recovered her gift from the safe then, simply for exercise, ran up the stairs.

Hamish, instead of preparing to leave the hotel, was sitting looking at the Daily Telegraph with his other newspaper, the Manchester Guardian across his knees.

"Apart from other things that I can easily find for you to do at this moment. There is a peculiarity that I have been observing about you for years and I have refrained from questioning it until now as on this occasion, it annoys me and on such a lovely break for the two of us, it should not." Freya said.

"The peculiarity?" he asked.

"Why do you buy and read two newspapers, one politically to the left and one politically to the right of centre?" She asked.

"In order to get a balanced view of the unapologetic charlatans running this nation. Satisfied?"

"Yes, when you have checked the drawers, wardrobes and the bedside cabinets and put your shoes on; grandpa!" Freya sternly told him.

With bags packed, Freya rang down for the porter, and in due course, the Bristol was loaded with her flowers sitting on the back seats. They said their farewells to the general manager, reception staff, the porter and Jack, the doorman, a true man of Devon who always seemed to be on duty and was a mine of information and a bit of gossip, depending who he was talking to.

With her arm tucked into his arm, the pair made their way along towards the Boat Float, he leaning on his stick and Freya cheerfully swinging her handbag with her present safely tucked inside.

As they neared the park Hamish looked towards the merchant vessel moored between the buoys and told her that it was a Russian timber 'Boat' easily identified by the Cyrillic script written name the hammer and sickle emblazoned on the funnel and the myriad of radio antenna abaft the bridge.

"Mornin', Sir."

"Ah, and very good morning to you, master," Hamish said looking behind him to see the same fellow that they had spoken to the previous morning.

"Why is the Ruski timber boat here?" Hamish enquired.

"She was brought in on the evening tide last night claiming stress of weather and engine trouble sir. I don't know where she got the 'Stress of weather' from. It was not much of a blow yesterday but she has got a bit of a starboard list on her." the mariner told him.

"Timber boats often have." Hamish opined and continued."

"Will the people up at Noss Mayo repair her?"

"Not unless the crew do it. The Russians and East Germans will go to any lengths to prevent anybody into the accommodation or engine room." The master replied.

Quite ignoring the hand pulling at his arm, Hamish told his new-found chum." Some years ago we were in the Red Sea doing about nineteen knots and overtook an elderly little Russian ship with enough aerials for a fleet, not a poky little rust bucket such as she was. I was on four to eight watch and the radar was showing a fast-moving vessel astern of us. Looking from the wing of the bridge it was the same rust bucket. In the flat calm sea, we were still doing nineteen knots when by ten she was past us.

We eventually caught up with her waiting for a convoy through Suez. No small wonder that they do not want anyone to inspect the engine room. Goodbye, master and thanks," Hamish said and gave away to the tugging on his arm.

"You are of the gender that complains women talk, even to a lamp post if no human is available.

Great pity the complainants weren't here to listen to you, a male wittering on. The poor master having to patiently listen to you!" she told him.

As they turned towards Royal Avenue Gardens, Hamish whispered, "Don't look to your left, keep walking."

As they approached the park he pushed Freya onto a bench and asked her.

"Do you have your warrant on you?"

"Yes, of course," Freya replied. "Why?"

"Walking towards us is Iron Gob with the man and woman that Sarah found.

As fast as you can get over to the 'Nick' in Mayors Avenue and get as many coppers as you can find quickly."

As Freya got up from the bench Hamish told her "Bring handcuffs. They must not get back to the ship at any cost. I will follow them, they seem to be heading up the Embankment."

Freya took off to the nearby police station. Hamish waited until they were ahead of him and pulled himself off the bench and fortunately for him, the trio were simply strolling along towards the Upper ferry.

Freya opened the door of the police station and rang the desk bell. After two more rings, a sergeant appeared and before he could open his mouth she produced her new acting detective superintendent warrant card. The sergeant studied it, studied Freya, looked at the card again then said.

"Yes, ma'am, what can we do for you?" In seconds she told him that she wanted three people arrested for, "Murder, attempted murder and assisting an offender."

This request was met with a sharp intake of breath followed by the slightly incorrect statement by the sergeant that "Your warrant, ma'am, does not cover any part of this county except for two miles if you are in pursuit of an offender."

"You are not correct sergeant but we must hurry so I will officially tell you that I'm laying information before you of indictable crimes and the perpetrators of same on your patch now."

The sergeant, now relieved of the necessity to make a decision as to him Freya's argument made sense and after all, she was a superintendent, albeit a very young and rather attractive one.

"I'll have to ring my inspector, ma'am."

"No time," she told him as a constable emerged through the door. Turning, Freya grabbed him as the sergeant lifted the 'phone receiver. "Have you got handcuffs and your staff?" Freya asked.

The constable stood stock still and when Freya introduced her rank it was plainly obvious that the constable did not believe her. Pulling at his tunic she hauled him out of the station door with the sergeant following and protesting.

As they emerged so were the general public and also the three wanted people walking past the bandstand with Hamish quite close behind them.

With Freya leading the troop, they approached Iron Gob and her mates.

Approaching 'Mr Larcombe' Freya said.

"I'm a police officer and I…"

Not waiting for Freya to finish her official introduction, Iron Gob made a run towards the edge of the Boat float the constable floored her within yards. As she went down so a very slim long silver coloured pointed screwdriver type of instrument skidded across the ground. Mr Larcombe turned to run back when somehow or other, quite by chance, of course, his legs became entangled in the rosewood and silver-topped cane of Hamish and Mr Larcombe found himself without any breath as he hit the ground.

In trying to extricate the cane from Mr Larcomb's legs, most unfortunately, of course, the rather heavy silver top came into contact with the back of Mr Larcomb's head. He decided that with no breath and little if any consciousness it was perhaps better to remain where he was.

When Hamish looked around him there seemed to be a considerable amount of sightseers and the woman from Sunny patch pointing a gun at Freya and the sergeant.

As he took a few steps towards them the woman told everyone to stand back or that she would shoot, presumably at Freya or the sergeant.

Yet again the heavy silver end of the cane came into its own and with an arm breaking swing Hamish brought the top of the cane down onto the woman's wrist and the gun discharged into the ground and very fortunately the bullet ricochet into the air and probably ended up in the Boat Float as her scream echoed along the Butterwalk colonnade.

The woman's scream was just slightly louder than the unfortunate constable as Iron Gob bit into his arm. Using the constable's own staff, Freya clouted the woman on the side of her neck, in law it should have been her shoulder but the ends justified the means as the woman collapsed stunned and the constable painfully discovered the strength of metal teeth.

Freya used the constable's handcuffs to secure Iron Gob as she did so Hamish noticed the heavy gold bracelet on the 'Iron gobs' arm and shouted to Freya. "Get that bracelet at all costs and that silver thing on the ground." Freya still struggling replied, "She can't lose it with the 'cuffs on her."

At the same time, the sergeant attempted to handcuff a suspected broken arm or wrist and a false arm. In the end, he decided that it was not a feasible endeavour and hauled her screaming, protesting and using most unladylike language to the sergeant and onlookers as he hauled her to her feet. Hamish turned around to see what had happened to Mr Lamborne to see that he was still in the same position on the ground with a kindly gentleman taking his ease sitting on Lamborne's back and a kindly lady sitting on his ankles.

These two kindly passers-by identified themselves as a police sergeant and his policewoman wife from the Somerset force on holiday in Dartmouth. Hamish identified himself and the dear people offered to help in any way they could. Hamish looked at his wristwatch and the whole incident had lasted just short of six minutes. The three prisoners were taken to the police station with the aid of the two Somerset officers.

The constable was sent along to the cottage hospital for rabies vaccination and a dressing or stitch to his arm while the Sunny Patch woman was put in a cell to await the arrival of a doctor.

Freya asked to use the telephone and the sergeant claimed it first because he wanted instructions from his inspector at Kingsbridge.

Eventually, all the legal and medical matters were attended to and a 'Hurry up' wagon was sent to take the prisoners to Exeter and even more paperwork and medical inspection.

Freya had made contact with the now Deputy Chief Constable Gaunt and relayed the news, and between them, they dealt with all the matters surrounding the arrests, the soon to be protests by the Russians and all other matters including the reams of paperwork including the very important statements by Freya and Hamish.

Mr Gaunt then told her that he would contact the deputy chief constable of the Devon police and discuss the case and that he would transfer Freya to Sarah so that she could dictate her statement of facts to counter any legal arguments from the lawyers for the three who they would meet with at Exeter.

"It's getting late for us to get to London for this meeting," Freya told her boss and asked, "Could we have an escort please, certainly until we get to the motorway."

"You'll get one all the way to the Savoy. How long before you leave?" Mr Gaunt asked.

"Once you put me over to Sarah, say in thirty minutes time from the Ferryman's hotel, sir," Freya told him.

"I'm picking up, 'Him' upstairs Fred, Tommo and 'The quiet one. We'll be on our way in less than thirty minutes," Mr Gaunt told Freya.

"Not a word of this outside of us please," Freya asked.

"Silence is golden," was the reply.

"I'm ready Sarah told Freya as Freya dictated her 'Holding' statement to her and thanked her for her efforts in obtaining the beautiful birthday jewels.

Good as his word, Mr Gaunt arranged that at every force boundary a car was waiting to 'Blue light' them to London after calling at Exeter as a courtesy to debrief the assistant chief constable on events leading up to and including the arrests and asking for the prisoners access to a solicitor before transferring them to his HQ.

When Freya and Hamish went to the hotel to recover their car a police traffic car was waiting for them.

Before they drove off Freya said to Hamish, "Is your bladder capable of lasting until Exeter? If not, go now." Hamish needed no encouragement as he disappeared into the hotel. On his return, he did his best to avoid Jack the doorman but failed as Jack almost blocked his way with the exciting news that there had been a shooting in the park.

With a very regretful voice, he told Hamish, "There was nobody killed or even injured but somebody thumped the woman with the gun with a walking stick sir but…"

"Sorry Jack, I'm in a hurry. Tell me later please, it sounds exciting." Hamish said as leaning on his cane, he promptly disengage from Jack and joined an irritated Freya in her car as they drove away under police escort.

At Exeter, Freya asked for the Bristol to be filled with fuel while she settled all the matters relating to the prisoners who would shortly arrive from Dartmouth.

Again, the same instruction from Freya to Hamish. "We will not be stopping to make use of any facilities. Make use of the lavatories here.."

Freya went into the inspector's office of the traffic department to settle the top speed limit for the various force traffic department car escort towards London and to sign the chitty for her fuel. The inspector looked at her in astonishment when she produced her pen. "Ma'am, you do not sign anything for fuel down here. Have it with the compliments of the Devon constabulary."

"That is very generous of you, thank you," Freya answered.

As she left the office she heard a voice say, "Blimey, sir; that was generous."

"If she'd been a hairy arsed male superintendent I would have charged him for it." The inspector told whoever the other person was.

"You're just a sucker for a pretty face sir," the voice told the inspector. As she pulled the door closed Freya heard the inspector say, "True, how very, very true my son."

The journey to London went faultlessly, and in the metropolitan area, they were afforded a motorbike and car escort to the Savoy.

As the motorbike and the police car turned out of the Savoy forecourt so they sounded their sirens. The blue lights drew enough attention, the sirens echoed around the forecourt of the building making sure that Freya was the centre of attention.

Nonplussed by the attention Freya fiddled in her handbag and produced the wedding and engagement rings that she had worn at Sunny Patch and slipped them on her finger as the top-hatted doorman opened the door for her to alight in the manner befitting a person escorted by the 'Blues and Twos!

As the other doorman opened the door for Hamish to alight so he put his cane out. "May I assist you sir?" the man asked him.

"If you would be so kind, thank you," Hamish told him.

As he was armed out of the Bristol he thought, "I bet this chap is thinking, 'What's an old man like this doing with a young corker like her' in a car like this?'

As Freya supervised the last of the luggage for the Savoy and handed over her keys so Hamish made off towards a perfumers concession in the forecourt.

In no time he was back at reception when he heard a familiar voice behind him. Looking around he saw Mr Thomas and Mr Cole.

When the greetings were completed, Fred Cole told Hamish in reasonably hushed tones, "Why in the bloody hell am I here? I've, no, idea, why are we here? We've nothing to say and we were only on the periphery of the case anyway. There's nothing to 'De-brief' us about."

Hamish smiled and told him. "Sit back and enjoy the ride sir, it's all on expenses. "I've been telling him that all the way up here," Tommo said. Adding, "He claims that he wanted to be on his allotment this evening. I told him that it would be dark by seven but he's still harping on about it."

"Heard that you have been on the south coast for your birthday," Fred Cole told Hamish.

"Had a good time?" he asked.

"A nice quiet time and indifferent weather sir," Hamish replied thinking that it would be better if he did not tell 'Old King Cole' that it was Freya's birthday not his.

With a sly smile, Mr Thomas asked Hamish. "I did not see it but, I presume the personal escort by the finest of the Metropolitan Police with the impressive display of blue lights and sirens on your arrival achieved the desired effect?"

"What effect sir?" Hamish quite naturally enquired. "How about the undivided attention of the entire staff also I noticed a bloke that I take to be the manager fawning and scraping in front of Acting Detective Superintendent Freya Douglas Gore Hamilton. And I strongly expect that you had a mighty discount in that perfume shop as well.

I think that they all thought that it was the Queen arriving for, as you mariners would say, 'Tea and Tabnabs' all round."

"I've been expecting you in our rooms and here you are gossiping like a fishwife." The three men simply wordlessly looked at Freya. She was dressed in a grey suit with a white blouse and the jewels from Hamish adorning the picture. With her long legs, the trousers enhanced the appearance along with her slim frame allowing the jacket to be a firm and flattering fit. Hamish noted that her rings, having made their point, were now missing.

"If that." said Superintendent Thomas emphasising his point about Freya with exaggerated hand and wrist movements, "doesn't floor them, nothing will. Look around, everybody's looking at you girl, you're a stunner," he declared.

Then turning to his chum Fred he asked "What say you?"

There was a momentary pause in order to put his thoughts into words, the new Chief Superintendent Cole, not a man for flattery or indeed uncalled for praise, coughed, cleared his throat and to the total astonishment of all present who knew him, declared "A mannequin couldn't look any more impressive," Fred Cole surprisingly announced before returning to his accustomed scowl."

Hamish turned to Mr Thomas and whispered, "A battleship about to be launched is described as 'impressive'. I name this ship Freya Douglas Gore Hamilton. May God bless her and all who sail in her."

"I heard every word of that Inspector Fergusson and as sure as night follows day, you will pay for that. You are on duty and I am your superior officer by two ranks at this time and in a most generous frame of mind at this very moment.

I will not put you on a misconduct fizzer, but in terms that you will probably understand, I will explain that; you are sailing very near a shoal Mr Former Mariner."

"Are you the party for Sir Richard Jamesbury?" A man, who by his very demeanour, shouted 'Government clerk' asked any one of the four strong party. "We are," Freya said, then adding, "you lead and we'll follow."

"All except me," Hamish explained. I'm off to the gents."

When the remaining three were led into a delightful room they found a long central table with one side being the host party while at the other side sat the chief constable, Mr Gaunt, Mr Bates and surprise, surprise, Sarah at the far end.

Another surprise was that the chief constable was sitting at the far end of the table and not in the middle as would be expected. That chair was occupied by Mr Gaunt.

Mr Gaunt signalled for Freya to sit next to him.

By the time Hamish came in leading with his cane, the clerk closed the door and the rotund man in the middle position on the other side of the table glared at him. Hamish looked towards the man and could see a vacant chair on his right-hand side.

Hamish signalled to the clerk to attend him. He then gave the clerk a small item in a beautifully crocheted bag and gave him a note bearing the legend. "Please put on the vacant place at the table."

The rotund man looked at the clerk then the item before rising to his feet and saying;

"I am Sir Richard Jamesbury, head of national security and answerable to the prime minister.

My team are Mr Glover of the Foreign Office, Mr Cox of the Home office Commander Symonds of Special Branch. Scotland Yard with Assistant Commissioner Brown."

Not as would be expected, Mr Glover introduced the team with the chief constable not saying a word. While he was talking Freya looked down the table towards Hamish. He was grinning at her and inclined his head towards Chief Superintendent Frederick Cole.

Freya shifted her gaze and could see Mr Cole staring at the enemy as he would cheerfully describe them. His gaze seemed to dart between Glover, Cox and Jamesbury and already the vein in his temple was beginning to throb before hardly a word had been spoken.

Jamesbury told the group that it was very much regretted that relations between a small provincial police force should be such that they wilfully and to his eyes, deliberately obstructed the machinery of state security allowing it to be compromised by a so-called investigation which had achieved nothing but jeopardised an investigation into matters which in turn negated the efforts to protect the nation.

"I do not object to you going about your business, but with my team, I take no delight in telling you that collectively you are a disgrace. As I've mentioned before, you, in your petty ways have completely ruined a large international task to uncover a spy ring under the control of the Eastern bloc.

Although you, Superintendent Cole, did your best to insult the team that urged you to desist in continuing to interfere in our methods to protect the nation some months ago including rubbishing the valuable work of the Special Branch. I put it to you that you contributed in your diatribe to drive Major Quinn to his death.

A truly disgraceful episode. This meeting is called so that we can ensure that such interference does not happen again and this meeting will be a warning to any upstart provincial civil police force that serious consequences will follow if they even attempt to emulate your petty performance. Do I make myself clear?"

Hamish looked up the table at the chief constable and by both his pallor and the plainly obvious sweat on his brow that with every word spoken by

Jamesbury he was watching his anticipated 'K' aka knighthood, disappearing not just down the drain but sinking slowly into the brown waters of the Thames.

As the gaze of Hamish returned towards Jamesbury he became aware of none other than Kirsten from Sunny Patch striding into the room with all eyes on her.

She smiled at Jamesbury and sat in her chair lifting the item on the table before her with a puzzled frown crossing her forehead.

"Ah," said Jamesbury, "This is Mrs Erricksen, my number two here, she will give you chapter and verse the obstruction that she faced when, single-handed, she was engaged in dangerous surveillance work by police constables of your force.

There was a pause in proceedings while she called the clerk over and plainly asked why the crocheted bag was in front of her. Equally plain to see was the clerk whispering in her ear and pointing to Hamish. On the other side of the table, Freya was sending witheringly, ice creating looks, down the table towards Hamish.

Mrs Erricksen told the company that at considerable personal danger, she had discovered the lair of a most dangerous spy ring and was gathering evidence of their activities when her efforts were stymied by interference from people who she, at that time, believed to be criminals.

These people totally destroyed her operation and could have exposed her to very serious consequences including her life.

Chapter 11
Luck and a Double Birthday Bonus for Ma'am

"Since a few minutes ago on entering this room I see sitting opposite me the very people who prevented me from completing my task." Pointing at Freya and Hamish, she asked, "What has this bag got to do with me?"

Freya replied, "I know nothing about it but in good time there is little doubt that I will."

Hamish looked at Kirsten and said. "As your Mr Jamesbury has..."

"I am Sir Richard, not Mister," Jamesbury pompously interrupted Hamish.

Totally ignoring Jamesbury, Hamish continued. "As Jamesbury has implied and clearly said we are a simply an 'Upstart provincial civil police force' of no consequence in the grand plan of our betters such as your boss would like himself to believe."

Never moving his gaze from Kirsten he continued, "My colleague liked to cultivate the totally mistaken idea that I was mesmerised by your beauty and lithe body and that I could see no wrong in you and in fact all I was seeing in you was a sexual attraction which you were pleased to cultivate Mrs Erricksen.

I believe that you thought much the same. You were both wrong. As they say in all the best TV cop shows, I sussed you out within our first day of association. An upstart provincial civil police force that we may well be, but we could teach you a few things about covert operations.

Without the intention of boasting, within a few hours of duty, our most inexperienced uniformed officer could tell you that you do not wear perfume, aftershave or eat garlic while on covert operations.

It was your perfume that allowed me to trace you wherever you went including three uninvited visits to our hut, cabin or chalet or whatever one calls it. Lesson one; Do not hide behind door curtains. Lesson two; do not touch things with perfumed hands. Lesson three; wipe door handles after use, particularly those inside of doors!

During three days or nights you paid visits to the hut cabin or chalet number nineteen and to the water tank, did you not?

In view of the amount of perfume that you must have used in that operation, I have, at great expense, albeit with a large discount because the perfume shop here thought that I was someone of importance, bought you a bottle of your favoured perfume.

Please accept it with my compliments and I will gladly keep a place for you in our next CID Initial Detective Course should you wish to improve your capabilities in a Provincial but as will be disclosed, very and in this case, lucky and highly successful force."

Mrs Erricksen, with haughty disdain, pushed the perfume to one side as Hamish whispered to Mr Thomas, "I'll bet you a fiver that she eventually takes it home."

"Proceeds to charity?" Mr Thomas asked.

"Yes," he replied.

"You're on," Tommo told him.

"I fear that we have been side-tracked," Jamesbury told the assembly. "Do any of you have anything constructive to say about my opening remarks?"

It was quite possible that the chief constable saw his 'K' going even deeper, probably into the mud as Mr Gaunt pointed his finger at Fred Cole.

Mr Cole got to his feet and instead of addressing his remarks towards Jamesbury, he looked towards Sarah. In the silence, she looked up as Mr Cole asked her, "Did you get all of that down, ma'am?"

"Every word, sir," she replied. "Good, here is another very long one coming along. Ready?"

Sarah nodded.

There was little doubt that Mr Gaunt had discussed who would be the lead defence advocate, 'Old King Cole' himself. In turn, Mr Cole was going to make this his never to be forgotten brutal, career and character destroying Swan-song.

In an unusually refined voice and carefully enunciated words the now Chief Superintendent Cole looking directly at Jamesbury said to him.

"It is quite a coincidence that I should be put in such a privileged position within months to address a meeting each chaired by people that I previously knew; more of that later on.

I'm trying to understand quite why Superintendent Thomas, Inspector Fergusson or me were brought to this place to discuss a case in which all three of us only had a peripheral role although, in saying that, Mr Fergusson almost paid for his minor involvement with his life which as I understand it Jamesbury, none of your people put themselves in mortal danger.

You made the claim that I drove your major to his death. I merely pointed out his shortcomings and if it comes to that, I will also eventually do to you Sir Richard Jamesbury, Military Cross.

I recognise some of your people here. At our previous meetings your man from the Foreign Office, nice fellow, had nothing worthwhile to say.

However, your Mr Cox from the Home Office did have something to say but it was of such little significance that I have forgotten his argument. Digging into my failing memory I seem to recall that his contribution related to the control of my force by the Home Office. I think on that occasion he was sent away with a flea in his ear and should he resurrect the same arguments that the same flea will again be in his ear."

Stopping to light a Capstan Full Strength, he looked up towards the chief constable who not only had probably lost his 'K' forever but judging from his contorted face was contemplating following it into the Thames. But there again it might just be indigestion when he thought of the expenses bills including that for expensive perfume, arriving on his desk for the Savoy Luncheon, times five!

"Now to you pair," said Chief Superintendent Cole addressing the Commander of the Special Branch and the assistant commissioner.

"Whoever the chap from Special Branch was I simply pointed out that he and his likes, which included you Commander somebody or other, are a total waste of police resources. You are simply paper shufflers and so-called intelligence conduits between hard-working coppers and the Home Office.

For some, God-only-know, reason, you are idolised by the press and the television scriptwriters and you are in reality 'followers' hanging on the tails of real policemen. So whatever you care to say in justification of your worth; when I've finished your justification will only increase the reasons why you should not exist as a department. As I told you or your man last time. You are simply failed detectives who couldn't make the grade in or out of uniform."

Fixing his eyes on the assistant commissioner Mr Cole said, "On the last occasion a meeting of this nature took place the demand was made that the metropolitan police would put in their people to run any investigations involving Provincial forces and government security departments.

Should such thoughts be occupying your mind at this moment, I would suggest that you forget them and tell your boss the same.

You only involve your resources in my force when and if you are invited. We cooperate with each other when necessary in order to provide a service to the citizens of this nation. You will not serve the citizens by interfering in my force. In short; keep out unless invited. Do you understand?"

The assistant commissioner looked up and told Mr Cole. "I think the force can only be described as 'My' by the chief constable, not a superintendent. "I was in my force before anyone else sat there and if that's the only matter that you are concerned about perhaps you might think it seemly to be somewhere else." Mr Cole very eloquently told him. Silence and a feeling of anxious anticipation of what might be said next were felt around the table.

Mr Gaunt broke the deadlock of silence by inviting Freya to join in the discussion.

She told the meeting that until a month ago she was the senior investigating officer of the case involving the death of Kurt Rosenberg. After the shooting of her colleague and her temporary secondment to the Home Office, Detective Inspector Wilkins was keeping a watching brief of the case on her behalf.

At the mention of the Home Office, Mr Cox sat up and appeared to take notice of Freya, she in turn paid attention to him and said. "Before I continue with my account, there appears to be some confusion relating to the role that the Home Office plays in the operation of what has been described as 'An upstart little provincial civil police force'

Chief Superintendent Cole has covered much of this ground already but I would like to add that the only other function that the Home Office would use in the operation of my, yes, my force would be if there was a need to censure the chief constable or there was a failure in the administration or effectiveness of the force beyond the control of the Watch Committee. As neither of these events has or is likely to happen, to me, there is no purpose in us detaining Mr Cox from his other important duties."

"Mr Cox represents the interests of the Home Office and by definition includes the State in relation to events which involve internal security matters." Declared Jamesbury, putting Freya in her place.

"Thank you for that information, Mr Chairman," Freya with a slight hint of sarcasm, told Jamesbury.

She looked towards Mr Cole and could see the temple vein throbbing increasing and thought to herself perhaps it is a time for 'tea and tabnabs' to let him cool down.

While I would prefer to have my version of events aired now, might I suggest to Mr Chairman that we adjourn for light refreshments?"

"Why?" Jamesbury asked.

"If for no other reason sir, that with my colleague neither of us has enjoyed any drink or food since 8:30 this morning."

"No, carry on," Jamesbury told her.

At that point, Mr Cole boiled over and said to Jamesbury.

"Beg your pardon ladies, but Jamesbury you are a first-class vindictive bastard by any standard." The room erupted into a wall of condemnation of Chief Superintendent Cole He simply stood glaring, at the people on his side of the table instead of those opposite. Very strange indeed!

Mr Gaunt told Mr Cole, "Ease off, Fred; you've put the cat amongst the pigeons. I want to win this one, don't bugger it up."

"Will you apologise to me?" Jamesbury asked.

"Not bloody likely until you accede to the request of Superintendent Douglas Gore Hamilton." was the response from Mr Cole.

Looking towards the almost cowering chief constable, Jamesbury insisted, "Cole should be removed from the meeting."

"If I might be allowed to speak," Freya told the fractious meeting, "To allow tempers to cool perhaps we might adjourn for a cup of tea and a biscuit if nothing else."

"We will ask for the refreshments to be brought in," Kirsten Erricksen told the meeting while Jamesbury spluttering his words attempted to find a sympathetic ear, apparently without much success.

Meanwhile, both Mr Bates and Mr Gaunt took Mr Cole aside and were plainly lecturing him which once again he was not taking kindly to their argument judging by the throbbing of the tell-tale temple vein.

The chief constable was simply sat down and seemingly stared at the wall. Was censure by the Watch committee the inevitable outcome of this so -called 'De-briefing' exercise?

The doors opened and waiters pushed in two trolleys with the refreshments to the quality that was expected at the Savoy.

In one respect it was a relief to see both sides joining in conversations that were probably more productive than all the formal de-briefing meetings could ever be.

Even Freya and Cox of the Home Office appeared to be on reasonable conversational terms. Only the chief constable was still sitting at his seat with an unconsumed cup of tea on the table in front of him.

Jamesbury was standing without finding anyone to talk to. Hamish went over to talk to Fred Cole simply to keep him in the group.

During the recess, Sarah came down the room to speak to Freya and told her that her telephone statement was being typed up for her to sign at the meeting if it could be brought up in time for Ron Wilkins to use when he put the three in front of the magistrate to remand them in custody.

When eventually the meeting reconvened Kirsten Erricksen was in the chair and invited Freya too, "Please continue with your information."

Freya replied, "Thank you, Kirsten, you might not be too happy with what I have to say and certainly Sir Richard will not."

Turning to Jamesbury she said, "I seem to remember less than an hour ago that you referred to my police force as an upstart provincial civil police force, with the distinct implication from the title that you were so plainly pleased to bestow on us, that we were nothing better than a rabble of security guards who not only failed to solve a crime but hindered an efficient, organised team of vastly superior beings in investigating a threat to national security. Is that a correct summary of your words Sir Richard?"

"That is correct," Jamesbury told her, then delightedly added. "You plainly have no leadership at the top and judging from recent developments, oafs in ranks below. The reality that you should all be charged with obstructing the pursuit of crime."

Freya asked him. "Do you think that you could detect and arrest a murderer, particularly in this case? And sir, I know that you're talking a lot of twaddle in your assertion of prosecuting me under this fictitious charge of 'Obstructing the pursuit of crime.'

Perhaps you should join Kirsten in being instructed in the basic theory and practise of policing before talking such nonsense, particularly to an audience of experienced policemen."

Jamesbury replied. "I expected better from you madam. You are no better than that oaf over there." pointing at Fred Cole. There was a sharp intake of breath around the table as Fred Cole went to stand up.

Freya told him. "Please let me finish sir, it will help your argument." Fred, very hesitantly decided to sit down as his buttocks slowly reached the seat. "Thank you, sir," Freya told him before turning back to Jamesbury.

"Now, back to you Sir Richard." Freya, in her finest modulated authoritative voice, said.

"To lower the temperature in this magnificent room I quite reasonably asked for a refreshment break as Inspector Fergusson and I had not eaten or taken a drink since our breakfast.

This was refused and we witnessed a quite disgraceful episode between allegedly cultivated, educated and reasonable people on both sides of this table.

The reason that we could not have refreshment since breakfast was…"

"Oh, get on with it woman," was an interrupting instructing order from Jamesbury.

"Thank you, sir, I do enjoy your interruptions, they simply prolong the story and eventually to your discomfort.

The reason that we could not have refreshments since our breakfast was that by the knowledge and guile of Inspector Fergusson, this 'Little Provincial, and by implication inefficient, force' arrested one Helga Rosenberg for murder, one so far unidentified woman, probably named Rosenberg for the attempted murder of Inspector Fergusson and a male accomplice only known as Larcombe who will initially be charged with assisting an offender.

It is unseemly to crow about our success but shall we say, I do believe Sir Richard, despite your bluster and condescending manner of speech along with the words you used. We are, sir, the 'cock of the walk'. Now perhaps you will be man enough to apologise."

Other than Mr Gaunt, Mr Bates and Sarah, there was a stunned look around the table.

Like a shot out of one of his beloved Howitzers, Fred Cole was on his feet, knuckles on the table, hunched shoulders and the temple vein doing the equivalent of the can-can. Addressing Sir Richard Jamesbury, Military Cross. Mr Cole, in an unusually moderate tone of voice, asked Sir Richard for what act of bravery had he been awarded the Military Cross?

"I served in the Burma campaign and we were caught in a position which compromised our safety and I led my men under heavy fire to safety and then re-engaged and defeated the enemy. I don't see what this has to do with this meeting." Sir Richard opined.

To those who knew him and also to Mr Cox of the Home Office and Mr Glover of the Foreign Office who had witnessed it before with Major Quinn,(Deceased) This moderate tone of voice would soon see Sir Richard humiliated.

Mr Cole allowed a brief smile, that in itself being very unusual unless he was in the Working men's club propping up the far end of the bar.

He then enquired, "Do you have a date and year for this incident?" In his position, although he knew not of the devious ways of Mr Cole in eliciting information to discredit his tale. Jamesbury gave Mr Cole all the information that he required.

"You sir are a bloody liar." a by now almost snarling Fred Cole told Jamesbury. I was there at that very incident and although you have a large paunch nowadays and your face is a good artists impression of the moon, I recognise you and your name. You were a subaltern in the Royal Artillery.

You ran away and left us behind. We lost two men looking for your worthless hide as when you disappeared we thought the Japs had shot you. Pity they didn't. They couldn't have, you weren't there to be shot were you?" Taking a deep breath Fred continued.

"As for your Military Cross, did you get that for re-grouping and defeating the enemy? I didn't set eyes on you from that day until now. The officer who led us back into the jungle was a poor frightened second lieutenant but a bloody sight braver than a gutless, incompetent, lying fraudster such as you.

I strongly suspect that our colonel accepted your story and probably because your fathers fought alongside each other in the first lot or belonged to the same club, then put you up for the MC.

At least seven others who were there on that occasion are still alive and can support my story including the sergeant. I was one of the two corporals, the other one was killed when we advanced again."

No one said a word as Sir Richard Jamesbury MC arose from his chair and just walked out.

Mr Cole looked after the departing Jamesbury and said to no one in particular, "What odds would anyone take on me potting two gutless half-wits from the same service in two consecutive meetings. Coincidence or what?"

No one replied.

After a prolonged silence Mrs Erricksen called the meeting to order and congratulated Freya on her arrests then adding. "We will pursue this case as soon as your prisoners are brought to London.

"Until the criminal cases involving murder and attempted murder are concluded you will not have any connection with the prisoners," Freya told her then adding. "We will not countenance any possible interference which could compromise our case or the carriage of justice.

I regret having to tell you this but other than treason, at this particular time murder is the equal offence with capital punishment the penalty."

While Mrs Erricksen simply stared at Freya a cough came from the end of the table and everyone turned to look at Stuart Thomas in his usual semi-recumbent position at the end of and parallel to the table.

In his quiet, measured manner of speech he said. "The case will probably be brought to the Central Criminal Court for prosecution and it is at that point that further charges relating their activities in this country can be put to them. Just thought that I would mention it."

Mrs Erricksen simply stared at Superintendent Thomas then thanked everyone for their contribution in the hope that in future there might be more harmony between the various law enforcement bodies.

She then enquired; "Any further questions?" Hamish was sorely tempted to ask what might be happening to the 'K' of his chief constable but decided that now might not be the appropriate time or place.

"This meeting is now closed. Thank you, all; goodbye." Kirsten told the people who were already clearing the table of their effects.

"Now that you have arrested the participants can we liaise about our interests and I acknowledge that it is your duty to charge these people but we would like the opportunity to question them and put in additional charges where appropriate?" Kirsten told Freya.

Freya replied, "Once the QCs get their teeth into this case I believe that our charges will take precedence.

When sentenced, your trial, if you don't mind your dirty washing being exposed, could commence but it's all in the air, the experts will no doubt, decide. I, or rather with Hamish, have delivered three prisoners with ample evidence to support our case so from my point of view, other than the court appearance, we are finished with all of this.

Ron Wilkins will tie up the loose ends and that's that. Whenever it suits you from my point of view you can interview them when we have finished with them."

"I will be in touch and bye-the-way, your jewellery is beautiful and well set off by the background of white and grey Kirsten told Freya as with a deft movement she scooped up her perfume and left the room.

"You owe me a fiver," Hamish told Mr Thomas.

In reply, Mr Thomas told him, "For this entertainment, that is a gift." Taking the fiver out of his wallet Tommo cheerfully handed over the money.

Without warning an arm was thrust towards Freya with a card in the hand. It was the hand of Assistant commissioner Brown. Freya took the card looked up and he was gone.

Freya looked at the card, then turned it over to read, 'There's a better place for you up here. Ring me on this number, it cannot be tapped'. A number was followed by the signature 'Sid Brown'.

"Now there's a choice for you girlie." A very familiar voice spoke into Freya's ear, She looked up and turning her head she saw that the speaker was the now Assistant Chief Constable Bates.

He again spoke into her ear and softly said, "It's a difficult choice for some women. Marriage and children versus glittering career." As a simple man, I suggest that you think carefully before saying, "Yes."

Plainly Mr Bates had read the card over her shoulder.

The scene in that room was similar to a nursery with a semi-circle of intent listeners with Freya as the teacher telling them not a fairy story, but how the case was solved, and prisoners were taken.

When she had completed the tale Hamish looked up and said, "Luck and bad luck," then explained.

Bad luck for me that I didn't have a van searched when it entered the dock. Bad luck for the then Detective chief Inspector Freya Douglas Gore Hamilton when she let Major Quinn leave the station. Bad luck when we failed in simple investigative tasks.

Bad luck when our principal suspects could not be properly identified, were foreign nationals from countries without an extradition treaty.

Bad luck when they put two holes and three bullets in my hide.

"However, Luck that owing to the misconduct of an inspector I was on duty at the dock when Iron Gob brought herself to my attention. Luck that I saw her enter the dock in a Morris Commercial white van wearing a large, identifiable gold bangle.

Luck when a photographer was setting up cameras around the locks, luck when by a meeting in an unusual place that we came across a very skilled intelligence officer who could interpret the photographs.

Luck when an eagle-eyed forensic officer found a 'phone number in an unusual place.

Luck when at a pub with the ever truthfully telling name of 'The Scolding Wife'. Someone in the audience laughed at the name saying "How true, how bloody true."

Hamish smiled and continued. "At that pub, I saw a man and woman who luckily attracted my attention as they appeared to have been following me a while earlier. Luck that Miss Dodds-Younger was able to oil wheels to put us in a position to obtain conclusive evidence and to discover the fragrantly true reason for Mrs Erricksen's presence at that location.

Luck that Miss Dodds-Younger kindly decided to take the station char-lady, a very old but loved lady, on only the second holiday of her life.

Luck that this elderly lady identified a man and woman who has now been arrested for attempted murder.

Luck that these two people were in South Devon and in the same place as dear old Mrs Briggs. On a slightly different tack. What will happen if Mrs Briggs is called as a witness. Will they put learned tomes in the box to allow Mrs Briggs to see over the top?"

Again, laughter from the audience.

Continuing his theme Hamish told his audience.

"Luck that Miss Dodds-Younger had her camera with her, even better luck that she inadvertently took the most valuable photograph to support our case and subsequent arrest.

Luck that as all good policemen should have in their 'pocket', I had a good safe breaker I could use.

Luck that we should be in Dartmouth, luck that a passing Russian ship should seek safety at Dartmouth with engine failure.

Luck that Iron Gob, AKA Helga Rosenberg, and her two accomplices should have decided to go ashore or perhaps were ashore.

Luck that we were in the town early because of this meeting."

Pausing for breath and to light up his cigar in recent times a rare pleasure, Hamish returned to the fray saying,

"Luck that in a very small police station there were uniformed officers who only prevaricated for a couple of minutes before accepting our story aided by

Freya's warrant card and the final little bit of luck, personal luck, in that a doctor was on hand when I was shot and that I survived with the constant support of Sarah Dodds-Younger and Acting Detective Superintendent Freya Douglas Gore Hamilton.

This has been a very lucky break for an 'Upstart little provincial civil police force."

"Hear, hear," came from his attentive audience.

Hamish looked up the room and could see his chief constable still sitting on his chair. He walked up to his boss and enquired, "Are you OK, sir?"

"Yes, thank you, Fergusson," he replied before adding. "I am not happy with the manner with which we conducted ourselves today.

Whilst I think that man Jamesbury was a total disgrace, it was not necessary to be as base as he was. While suitable for a barrack-room the conduct of Cole was quite reprehensible.

He could have taken the chairman to one side and said whatever that he felt it was necessary to say. I'm surprised that neither Mr Gaunt nor Sir Simon took Cole to task for his disgraceful conduct, particularly in front of the assistant commissioner."

He thought for a few minutes, then repeated, "Simply disgraceful and it reflects on badly our force." He thought for a further few seconds, then added, "Also, who taught Cole the long words and articulate manner of speech he now uses? This was the first and I hope the last time I hear him address a meeting.

For the reputation of our force in one respect, I'm glad someone has worked on his diction and elocution even at his age."

After yet another longish pause the chief constable said. "I did think that your colleague gave a good account of herself.

Her recent promotions have occurred so quickly thanks to Mr Gaunt, that when I saw the assistant commissioner watching her very closely then later handing her his card, well, I believe that it was him; I realised that he was offering her a post up here and that I could be censured for not putting her through the senior command course yet.

She needs that course now but we are being stymied by this Home Office secondment. Ferret out her thoughts and let me know.

When you come back to your post as my administration officer this sort of delay for all ranks will be eliminated."

Hamish walked away trying to reason out exactly what his chief was trying, in a cack-handed way, to tell him.

Was it for Freya's benefit or was he telling him something which went over his head? The other question baffling Hamish was his words, 'My administration' as in My Administration officer. He was under the impression that he was to be in that position under Mr Gaunt.

Hamish found Freya and Sarah deep in conversation as a waiter walked into the room and spoke to them.

They nodded in unison and in came a person with a folder. Freya opened the folder and appeared to be reading it. Hamish asked Sarah what Freya was reading?

"Her statement," came the reply and she told Hamish that she had taken Freya's statement over the telephone and as the car was waiting to take her and her luggage to London her shorthand was passed to a typist to put into words for it to be taken to London for Freya to sign and return by messenger in order that Ron Wilkins could charge them with the offences and retain them in custody until a magistrates appearance.

After the signing was done the room was empty except for Freya, Sarah and Hamish. Freya told Hamish that Sarah was staying at the Grosvenor Hotel overnight and that she had invited her to join them in her box at Covent Garden and for supper later on with them at Scotts at the top of Leicester Square.

"Would it be a Banana box, a Pineapple box or perhaps an Apple box that you have at Covent Garden?" Hamish mischievously enquired.

"Totally ignore his infantile humour," Freya told Sarah. "We're going for a rest now and we'll pick you up later."

"No, thanks," Sarah said, adding, "I'll meet you there. I do hope Hamish that I'm not playing gooseberry?"

"In view of our common interests I would not think so and Freya claims that I have no romance in me along with the fact that I've never found you prickly in the least. We'll see you later."

In their rooms, Freya and Hamish had a post mortem over the afternoon's events and decided that they had won decisively including the card from the assistant commissioner. He then told her of his conversation with their chief constable and the senior command course.

"I've thought about that during the past year," Freya said. "He's right, other than in our force I couldn't get a job elsewhere at my rank. I wonder what has stirred his soul?"

"Keeping you 'In house' perhaps," Hamish said, before telling her. "I've been told this afternoon that all these promotions this week, Gaunt to deputy chief constable, Bates to the assistant chief constable, Cole to chief superintendent and Thomas to full superintendent is because they will all be retired within the next twelve months and it will leave them all the wealthier with their pensions and lump sums and good vacancies to boot.

Is one of those top vacancies for Miss Freya Douglas Gore Hamilton?"

They ordered some refreshments to be delivered to their room but Hamish was deeply asleep when the trolley arrived.

Later, refreshed, showered and dressed they made their way to the foyer only to be met with clicking fingers and the cry, "Steward, over here if you please, chop-chop my man."

Sitting around a table were Messrs Cole, Thomas, Gaunt and Sir Simon Bates. All waving their hands.

The waiters were looking around to see who was calling them.

"I really thought that a penguin had escaped from the Zoo." Mr Gaunt told the assembly. "No, it's a waiter of some sort, well, he's dressed like a waiter." Was the observation of Stuart Thomas. While from Sir Simon came the cry, "That's my Tiger, my personal steward." Then he clicked his fingers and said. "Pink G&Ts all-round my man and put it on the captains chitty."

The cause of the mirth was Hamish in his evening dress with Freya on his arm in a very pale grey off the shoulder evening dress, long evening gloves and a wrap with her necklace, earrings and broach displayed in all their sparkling glory. "We're off to the Garden for Il Trovatore," Freya told the men. "Can't see Mr La-di-dah Fergusson digging up much at the Garden in his Penguin suit." Old King Cole announced as the other hotel guests in the vicinity looked on with some quite understandable disdain towards the source of the noise and mirth.

"On a serious note," Sir Simon said. "Miss Douglas Gore Hamilton you really are most beautiful, a sight for sore old tired eyes. You are a very lucky man Fergusson. You've scrubbed up quite well yourself!

We hope that you have a wonderful evening." 'Hear-hear' came from the party with Mr Gaunt telling the couple, "Make sure those jewels don't get snatched and do bring us back some prisoners, preferably a spook or two."

"Are you all staying in town?" Freya asked Mr Thomas. He replied "No, we have cars coming up here to pick us up at about eleven and deliver us to our homes.

Freya went to the bar, spoke to the manager, signed a chit, re-joined Hamish and they went out to their cab.

As they went through the door Fred Cole could be heard telling everyone, "The head waiter has forgotten his top hat, yer top hat, his tit-fer. Oy! Fergusson, yer 'at."

Hamish kept on walking with a smile on his lips and a reassuring squeeze from Freya' arm.

On their way to the opera, Hamish asked Freya, "What were you doing at the bar?"

"I signed a chit to give the high and mighty a round of drinks. With the exception of the boss, they've had a good day and we've had a day that we will remember always, exhausting but at the same time exhilarating."

To emphasise her opinion, with her arm tucked through his, she gave his arm another reassuring squeeze.

The evening at the Royal Opera House was all that could be expected, quite magical in fact. When they arrived at Scott's for supper Hamish, despite his earlier nap was decidedly tired and the ladies offered him the opportunity to return to the Savoy while they enjoyed supper.

He made a feeble protest and eventually acquiesced to their suggestion and took the opportunity to walk on his own back to the hotel. The first distance of note that he had walked on his own since the shooting.

Over supper, Freya and Sarah talked of many things with Hamish figuring in most of the subjects.

The subject of the insurance on the gift of the jewels came up and Freya told Sarah that he had insured them in order that she would not know their approximate cost or value. Sarah then told Freya, "Those were not off the shelf. With the others, they were made to his design and he chose the one he preferred, the others went back as stock to the jeweller. Those jewels were made specifically for you and cost a great deal of money. Even I was staggered by the amount that he paid. Staff sergeants pay must be more than I thought or perhaps he won the 'Pools."

Freya smiled and nodded without further comment.

Sarah told a surprised Freya that she was selling up and buying a property in the countryside. She explained that when Sir Simon retired she would also leave the police force and take up gardening and village life with the prospect of giving all her like-minded friends a better venue for them to enjoy their particular pastimes in good weather with all the facilities expected and somewhere the children would have room to explore and be themselves rather than being stuck with their parents as was the case at her evening soirées.

"While on the subject," Sarah told her. "I have missed Hamish coming to our soirées, I know that you and I made up a pair but it isn't the same," she told Freya and continued by asking, "When do you think that he will come again?"

"We have talked about me coming to your evenings while he has been unwell but he is conscious about his scars, particularly as they are in his groin and above," Freya told her, adding. "It will be quite a challenge to get him to join us."

Sarah said, "My next soiree will be a film night in a fortnight, it will be all dark so no one will see his knocks, anyway we don't look at bodies. I will work on him. I want him back with us and I know that Joy so enjoyed her in-depth chat with him and she is looking forward to the next time."

Her reply from Freya was simply a prolonged "Hummmm."

"I know that this is none of my business and of course you do not have to answer my question," Sarah said to Freya, then asked, "After all the recent goings-on and your, in-so-many-words, offer of a top job in the police up here where do you see your life and career going considering your very young age and undoubted success at your job?"

Freya didn't answer immediately and Sarah feared that she was going to ignore the question when Freya lifted her head and began talking.

Like Hamish and I suspect like you, I was born with several silver spoons in my mouth. I have a title and have enjoyed everything that has gone with that and since you told me about the antecedence of Hamish and like him, I have rarely used that advantage in my private or professional life. What I have achieved is by my own efforts and help from sheer good luck and my mentor, Bill Gaunt. This case, the reason for us being here, is very much down to luck as Hamish would have it.

I have less than eight years to consolidate either my very successful career or to find a man to marry me and produce children.

I would hate to end my life a spinster without giving children produced by me all the opportunities that I've enjoyed. Equally, I would be so unhappy to share my inevitable old age with an ancient crock of a husband and no children or grandchildren to enjoy.

It is a dilemma, and in recent years, it has been constantly in the back of my mind.

When I was at Bristol on the Initial Detective Training course we had the first woman superintendent from up here come to give us a lecture.

She plainly was not married so presumably did not have children. She was probably in her fifties and although I didn't think of it at the time, as I have progressed through the ranks, at each of my promotions the vision of that woman looms ever larger and her likely end. Nephews, nieces and Godchildren and in particular their wives and husbands all in her final days fighting for whatever generally worthless bits and pieces of her property they can grab.

All pure imagination perhaps, but real enough to me. Would Solomon in all his wisdom have an answer? Either to procreate, or possibly become the first woman chief constable? One day it will happen, but to who?

Sarah, do I go on to a glittering career or chance having a childless marriage and missing the career of a female lifetime? I'm so sorry that much of what I've said probably relates to you but you did ask and I have poured out my innermost thoughts. A thing that I would not do to anybody else.

I'm sorry and I do understand if you take offence at my lack of sensitivity."

Sarah replied, "Rest assured Freya I do not take offence at your heartfelt feelings. I made my choice many years ago, and to date, I've not regretted it. Should I ever fall in love again I might change my mind. It may surprise you to know that I'm the same age as Hamish so I still have a few years left to produce children, but unlike you, I have never been too keen on children, maybe I'm too selfish but that's Sarah Dodds-Younger for you.

What of you and Hamish?"

Freya ordered another couple of drinks and said. "We met at Oxford, he was in his fourth and graduation year, and I was a fresher. We hit it off there and then and it was a lovely time for both of us. To me, he was a man's man.

A former mariner, tough, reliable, straight speaking and nobody's fool. When he left and joined the police we still had that flame and when I graduated we were together again for a brief period. We then met again at Detective school, and still, the flame shone until I was whisked off to the Regional Crime Squad and we separated, not deliberately but our paths went in different ways.

After a time we began going on holidays together but that eventually died. Hamish settled for uniform after a very distinguished CID career and found his niche as a staff sergeant in the 'D' Division.

We still met up on my birthday each year. Sometimes our paths would cross but not very often. We did in some years have a holiday together. To the best of my knowledge, he had no other women in his life, and for my part, I chose not to be too close to any other men.

When I was sent down to take over 'D' Division CID. I saw Hamish for the first time since my last birthday. He was sat in his office, lord and master of all he surveyed and as he has already said his only involvement, in this case, was purely by chance. On last Easter day, I went to matins on my own except for some of the household in the pew behind me.

I was on my knees in prayer and I sensed that someone was beside me. I peeped through my fingers and it was Hamish on his knees next to me.

We took communion together and strangely alone. It is customary for my family to take communion privately but I have never known the other communicants to wait at the chancel door for us to finish before they knelt at the rail.

We left the church arm in arm seemingly with the world and his wife holding their breath as we left the church porch. We went towards our gate into the estate from the churchyard and he then walked out through the Lychgate.

Not a single word passed between us but there was an unspoken bond, a meeting of emotions that I have never experienced before. A single word, just one word between us would have broken the wonder of that meeting at my own parish church.

If we ever go our separate ways, for me, that magical time will never be repeated or forgotten and I hope and can believe that Hamish may have felt the same.

To most people he is simply a dour, sometimes very bad-tempered self-satisfied Scot. The real Hamish is totally different away from work."

At Sunny Patch we were like an old married couple, knowing each other's feelings but keeping things professional most of the time. There you have it, my story of a thirteen-year-old romance."

Sarah looked around them and told Freya."

"I do believe that the management would appreciate it if we departed this place. They are not exactly putting their coats on, but I do get a certain unspoken word without the frizz of electricity between us as you had with Hamish that we should go."

"Miserable looking and superior acting is the trademark of Hamish," Sarah told Freya as they waited for a cab to be called. "However, as you have said and as I have discovered in the past few months, he has a charm, the type of charm that, to use my mother's words, "Could charm the birds from the trees."

His cultivated indifference to the opinions of others, particularly his superiors is his defence mechanism which is sometimes known as keeping people at arm's length."

The cab arrived and when they were seated Sarah completed their conversation about Hamish with the observation that "He could live without other people and his presumed dourness is the personification of that. He will make a very good father one day." Sarah was dropped at her hotel and Freya headed up the Strand.

When she returned to the hotel she found all the lights on and Hamish still fully clothed even with his dress shoes on, stretched out on her bed.

She gently removed his shoes in his very deep sleep and was relieved to note that he was not snoring. She undressed and went through the door into his bed and with a very satisfied smile on her lips, went to sleep.

At breakfast they discussed their programme for the day and Freya suggested the first thing they should do would be to get their respective evening dress steamed and pressed as that of Hamish was "A disgrace that even a tramp would refuse to be seen dead in!" was her, not to be challenged opinion.

Freya told Hamish about her time at Scotts and the matters discussed, with a few exceptions. When commenting on the plans for Sarah's future after her boss retired, Hamish simply asked. "Is she making her 'Thatched cottage with roses around the door' into another smaller Sunny Patch?"

"Guest's by invitation only and no sleepovers I expect," she told the less than impressed Hamish then added. "Sarah is keen for you to attend her next soiree. I explained that you were conscious of your scarring and you were hesitant about coming with me because of that. She also mentioned that Joy wanted to renew your 'In-depth chats' that she'd so enjoyed."

Just to tease Freya, Hamish, tongue in cheek, replied. "Oh, in that case, I will make a special attempt to come and see dearest Joy and resume our 'In depth' chats. Yes, that will be so special. I will enjoy that."

Making what turned out to be a badly aimed kick at his shin and missing, Freya succeeded in upsetting the contents of their cups into the saucers as her foot pulled on the tablecloth as she withdrew it from the general area of the leg of Hamish.

She refrained from using an expletive with the arrival of two waiters to clear up the limited mess.

All she gained from her shin kicking exercise was a broad smile from Hamish followed by a single word "Missed!"

Their stay in London was completed with a walk along the Embankment and a photograph taken by one of the 'tourist hunting' photographers. Hamish gave the address of the police HQ for it to be sent to with the title of the address as 'Miss Sarah Dodds-Younger. The Office of the Assistant Chief Constable'. It did ensure that their, or rather his, money would not be wasted.

A couple of weeks later Freya took him to Sarah's Soiree, the film night.

Before the start, at the interval and after the end of the film Hamish and Joy were very much in deep conversation. Other than the enjoyment of the film by the guests, Sarah with Joy's husband, had their principal enjoyment in watching Freya trying her best to ignore Hamish and Joy and judging by her frequent looks towards 'Her Man' she wasn't ignoring him for longer than a few minutes at a time.

The conversation in the Bristol as she drove Hamish home is best left unrecorded except to say that he had to kiss her icy cheek and countenance goodnight rather than her gently kissing him!

Freya went back to her Home Office visits, Sarah went back to her secretarial work and Ron Wilkins went on with the tidying up of the murder case. The prisoners went before the magistrates and were remanded in custody for their case to be heard at the Spring Assize sitting. At headquarters, Mr Gaunt was dealing with the political fall-out from the arrest of one alleged Russian citizen on charges of murder with espionage thrown in if the Home Office with their intelligence services provided the evidence.

The stumbling block for Mr Wilkins was the character, Mr Lambourne. Ron wanted a better charge than 'Assisting an offender' as the evidence depended on proof of even that charge and the facts so far did not prove beyond doubt that he knew of the misdeeds of his lady friend. The magistrates were satisfied with the charge but a jury was harder to please so Ron was still digging and hoping that MI5 would help out in handing over decent evidence that he could use in front of a jury.

He asked Freya if she had a good source of intelligence from anyone. She referred him to Mrs Erricksen with herself as the go-between.

Ron's other stumbling block was Mrs Briggs. Whilst it was not a 'Given' that she would be called as a witness, he had to be prepared.

To this end, Ron decided to film Mrs Briggs telling the camera, with a magistrate at her side, and in the shot, what she knew, what she saw and what was the nature of her participation in the photographic proceedings. All done in the hope that the defence and particularly the judge would accept her non-controversial filmed evidence rather than calling her; necessitating her appearance in a strange and even for most policemen, a forbidding place, the witness box.

"What are your plans for Christmas this year?" Freya asked Hamish. He thought for a while then told her.

"It must be about ten years since I was not on duty over Christmas," he replied. Then went on to say, "It was an unwritten rule that we bachelors would always do the three tours over Christmas to allow the men with children the time off to be with their families.

If there were not enough bachelors to cover then married men with no children would step into the breach. The year that I had off was, believe it or not, overwhelmed with bachelor's. I went up to Ballantrym and it was the first time as an adult that I'd been there for Christmas. It was truly bloody awful, dark, dank and miserable. That was my parents and the castle was much the same.

If they want me for station duties I will work back at 'D' Division for Christmas and Boxing day. You can let 'Old King Cole' know if you speak to him."

"Why not come home with me for Christmas," Freya asked, then waited for the reply with some trepidation.

Will your family be there?"

"No, just you, me, housekeeper, cook, and the housemaids. Oh, and the very ancient butler, so we will be quite alone," she mischievously explained.

"What else will I be expected to do?" he asked.

"Christmas eve we attend midnight mass and matins on Christmas morning. After that, you a join me on a walk around the estate and visit a few of the Estate workers. In the early afternoon, we serve the household their Christmas dinner and wash up.

On boxing day, we visit a couple of the tenant farmers. That's all except to enjoy each other's company. On New Year's eve, we join the farmers and the other tenants and the household in the Estate hall for dance and copious amounts of cider to toast in the New Year."

"I'm not too sure about dancing but just for you and on the condition that your family is not there. Thank you for the invitation, I'll look forward to that. Do we go down to your home together or separately?" Hamish asked.

"Separately," she replied, adding "If I am called away I will leave you there until I return. If you don't have a car you will be stranded otherwise."

Rain and sometimes sleet accosted Hamish as he made his way to the west country to join Freya.

He had not been inside her home before, and on arrival, the staff fussed around him. Some of them had seen him when he was at church with Freya at Easter, but to others, he was a new face, including the very epitome of a film version of a very ancient butler.

Plainly the said butler considered Hamish to be quite 'Below the salt' to be in the manorial home of his master and even worse, in the company of Lady Freya.

Hamish looked long and hard at the butler when he deigned to enquire "Would you want any refreshment?"

Hamish replied, "Sir would want to be refreshed with three fingers of Guiana rum if you would be so kind, old chap."

Hamish thought to himself that it was unfair of him to take a rise out of this ancient being trying to emulate what other ancient butlers did.

They in turn would have passed on the butlering habits from the butler to Queen Victoria era. The same type of butler was to be found holding court at his ancestral home in the Highlands.

Hamish did his best to maintain his dour face as the butler returned to inform Hamish that, "Rum is not consumed in this household."

"Do not concern yourself." Hamish told him "I will have water which I take it, this house does consume," then enquiring, "Your name if you please?"

"Jennings," the butler told him dismissively, as he went for water. Hamish decided if the butler returned with water he would not drink it as it would probably be deliberately adulterated.

No sooner had his water arrived than he heard Freya's voice. As the staff assembled in the huge hall to greet her. Hamish thought it better to wait for her appearance before attempting to greet her.

Other than moving themselves for dinner and Freya introducing Hamish to Jennings as the Hon Hamish Ciaran-Fergusson, a calculated step by Freya to assimilate the position in society of Hamish; for no better a reason than to simply satisfy the class conscious values of the butler Jennings, neither Freya nor Hamish did little for the rest of the day.

It was not surprising, in fact predictable, that the attitude of Jennings to Hamish abruptly changed from one of forced tolerance to a guest of Freya to abject servility, simply by the word 'honourable'.

On Christmas eve a knock on the door brought Hamish to his senses and he turned over in bed to see Jennings putting a tray down on the table in the bay window.

"Thank you, Jennings," Hamish said as Jennings pulled his curtains back.

"Shall I return to lay out sir's clothes?" Jennings asked in his best 'Plummy' ingratiating voice.

"No, thank you," Hamish replied. Adding, "I was a mariner Mr Jennings and in my habits I still am. I look after myself in washing bathing and dressing but I would appreciate my dress shirt being 'seen to' later this day if you please."

As Jennings was about to close the door Hamish heard Freya's voice say. "Good morning, Jennings, please hold the door for me, I'm going in."

As she came through the doorway, most unusually, in the experience of Hamish, in a nightdress carrying her cup of tea the face of the butler was a picture without words as he attempted to, but failed to avert his gaze from his mistress within the confines of a doorway.

From his 'Roman' nose, a loud sniff was audible as he noisily closed the door behind him.

Freya went to the tray and poured out a cup of tea for Hamish then climbed into bed with him.

"Poor Jennings," she said. "I've not had a male friend to stay here before and now Jennings has not only seen me in my nightie but, horrors upon disgraceful horrors, in a man's bedroom as well."

"If he returns and sees you in my bed it could cause a heart attack. He looks as if he liberally partakes of the master's best vintage Port. That fact will help to put him in the infirmary if the sight of you in my bed doesn't." Hamish suggested.

After a giggle or three, they got down to the programme for the day until eleven fifteen and then be ready to celebrate midnight mass at 11:30.

After dinner, the pair of them played cards before heading through the parkland on foot in the clear starlit night to the medieval church bathed in floodlighting with the 'new' eighteenth-century tower standing tall in the glow of the lights.

Hamish remarked on the lights even before they went through the gate into the churchyard.

Freya said, "They cost father a packet to put in and a greater packet onto his church electricity bill which has a feed from the estate office."

As they emerged into the churchyard so Freya pulled on his arm and said. "Wait a bit, slow down. There are a few latecomers to get inside before we turn up. It's bad form for us to be in before most, if not all of the congregation."

"Much the same as at our estate Kirk," he said as he studied the shadows made by the tombstones from the lights played on the mellowed stone of the church.

"Right," Freya said as with a quicker step they went to the church porch to be greeted by the rector.

The communion procedure part of the service went as on the last occasion that Hamish had been there with the pair of them occupying the centre of the altar rail while the rest of the communicants waited in line until they had finished.

As before on Easter Day, after the bread and wine, the priest put the cup on the altar, walked forward and laid his hand on their heads and whispered his benediction "Bless you, my children. God be with you always."

As Freya, arm in arm with Hamish, led the congregation out of the church to the sound of the mighty, rather pretentious organ for a village church playing the tunes of carols, Rector Smythe gravely shook hands with them and in return received a kiss on the cheek from Freya.

As they approached the gateway into the estate Freya stopped and turned to Hamish and said.

"At this very place on Easter Day, we parted without a word being said. For me, it was a defining moment in our long association. I had a feeling in my being that I have never experienced before.

As we parted then I knew that we were destined for each other. Sentimental fool that I may be, but it is so significant for me that this time you are coming through the gate with me.

Like it or not, to me this is a symbolic moment for both of us." Freya disengaged from his arm and threw both arms around Hamish and kissed him with a passion that surprised even her. Hugging her tightly to him he returned the kiss.

Hand in hand they went through the gate. They had only gone a few feet into the estate when they heard the sound of the squeaky hinge of the gate and looked behind them to see the outlines of the estate workers returning to their homes from the church. The happy couple then realised that the people had witnessed the whole scene.

As they got to the fork in the drive and turned to walk to the house so the workers took to the other path with a chorus of "Happy Christmas M' Lady and sir," echoing through the bare branches of the ancient Beech trees lining the drive.

The pair stopped and Hamish returned the greeting with a voice trained on the forecastle in a force nine gale. "And a very happy Christmas to you all. May it be a peaceful one."

"Thank you, sir," came the ever fainter reply with a distinct male voice saying, "not as 'appy as you be. "Lucky bugger." was the last words heard except for a faint "Shuss," from the all-enveloping darkness.

The butler opened the door as they arrived home. Jennings went to take Freya's coat but she told him.

"Thank you for waiting up for us, Mr Jennings, and a very happy Christmas to you. We will see to ourselves. Is a fire still in there?" asked Freya as she pointed to the library door?

"Only the embers, m'lady. I will put logs on," Jennings told her.

"Please don't, we will see to that," she told him. "However, could you just provide a Scotch and ginger for me and a straight three fingers for 'Sir' on your way to bed, oh, and could you also see that my morning tea is delivered to Sir's room. I will join him there. But I will still want a call as usual when the tea is delivered."

With a formal nod and a whispered 'm'Lady', Jennings went off to find ginger as the Scotch was already decanted and probably sampled as well.

After yet another loud sniff from Jennings, he delivered the required ginger then asked Freya if he should serve her the whisky and ginger.

"I'll see to myself thank you," she told her butler and added as a mother would to her child, "now off to bed, it's been a long day for you dear Jennings."

May I respectfully wish you a happy Christmas too, m'lady.

Hamish bit on the inside of his cheek to successfully stop himself from laughing at the butlers, no doubt, genuinely meant words but it was the manner and tone that he had delivered them.

They went onto the library, made up the fire and settled down with their late 'Nightcaps'.

"How come it is still quite warm in here?" he enquired.

"When father inherited this place along with grandpa's title the second thing that he did was to commission a refurbishment of the place and the installation of central heating all disguised as original panelling. Did you not notice this morning how warm your room was?" she asked.

"No, I didn't, I had a bed warmer in with me. It's a pity that my father would not do the same plumbing at Ballantrym.

Even with a hearty fire, it's bloody cold everywhere including in the summertime.

It's almost impossible to draw water from the taps as they are mostly frozen. People look at the Laird and his entourage with envy. If they had to live in a Scottish castle in winter they would think quite differently. A three up and down is a damn sight more civilised."

"What's the programme for tomorrow?" Hamish enquired. "Tomorrow is today," she gently explained as he poured another manly drink of 'Highland Mist'. She reminded him that he had been told all of this yesterday and repeated; Church at eleven. Back here at 12:15, lay the table in the great hall, serve the staff their Christmas dinner and wash up afterwards.

By then it will probably be about four and you and I have a cuddle here for an hour then dress for an early dinner so that the staff can have an evening to themselves and we look after ourselves.

On boxing day, we have a morning of me taking you around the estate. After lunch, we go to the Estate hall where we entertain the tenant farmers, their families, the estate workers and their families to a stand-up buffet and then we hand out gifts on behalf of father and mother.

The estate manager, his wife and their senior staff buy all the gifts and we simply dish them out with genuine and heartfelt thanks for all each man and woman do for us.

You can be sure that you will be the centre of interest and gossip, particularly after your church visit at Easter and again last evening. Don't moan at me if I play up to them, just a teeny weeny bit."

"Have your bit of fun, my dear. Being with me you deserve it," he told her.

Freya thought about what he had just told her and decided that he would probably regret his largesse when it was all embarrassingly for him, over.

"How different it is at home," Hamish told her. "Other than a visit to the Kirk and a cheap card to the household staff that's Christmas done. At Hogmanay, the old man would send a bottle or two to the estate office and that was that."

The clock chimes for 3:00 a.m. was the signal for them to take to their beds.

A knock at the door and a very loud sniff announced the arrival of Jennings with a tray containing two cups with the tea-pot, sugar and milk. "In view of the lateness of the hour this morning, sir," Jennings announced, "I have taken the liberty of allowing you one extra hour of sleep before delivering your morning tea sir.

It was very obvious that Jennings was taking a noticeable interest in the bed. Hamish, though the morning fog in his brain decided to play up to Jennings.

Throwing back the bedclothes, Hamish announced to Jennings, "D'you see Mr Jennings, no one here but me!"

Jennings replied as he made for the door, "I'm quite certain that it is of no importance to me who might or might not be in your bed… sir."

"Well said, Jennings, nothing less than I expected from you." As his bedroom door was closed Hamish, as anticipated, heard a loud sniff of disapproval.

Later when Freya and Hamish walked along the church path they looked around them in case there was anyone else heading for church. Not a soul could be seen so they continued to the porch while the bell rang out into the valley below. After being greeted by the rector they entered the church.

It was noticeable the different sizes of the congregation in comparison to the midnight service. After their prayers, Hamish remarked on the disparity between the two congregations. Freya whispered, "It's that people not as privileged as we are, have to cook their own Christmas meal. They can't be in two places at once. "The point well-made and understood," he agreed as the service began.

The sermon was noticeably shorter than at a normal morning service. Plainly, the rector wanted to be in his home rather than his place of work.

As they led the congregation out again to the sound of the bells so Hamish suggested, quite to the surprise of Freya, that they might have a walk around the churchyard. They slowly perambulated around the church pathways ending up at the west door as the bells stopped.

When Hamish led Freya into the west porch he explained that he wanted to pray without an audience or any distractions. "What a surprise, I didn't expect prayer to be so important to you," she said as he lifted the clasp of the door.

As the door was opened Freya, Hamish and a lady holding a giant key jumped in surprised as they unexpectedly met.

"Are you locking up Mrs Cowles?" Freya asked. The lady gave Freya a little bob and told her that she was in fact doing just that.

"Is anyone else in here?" Freya asked. "No, M'lady, only the rector and he is going out the north door." Mrs Cowles told her.

"We will lock up for you and I'll drop the key in your letterbox when we leave," Freya told the sexton.

Picking up her handbag and turning off the lights as she went out of the south porch Mrs Cowles left the pair to what appeared to be an empty church.

Freya and Hamish went back to the family pew and both knelt and clasped their hands in prayer. Unseen by either of them stood an ethereal like figure by the altar rail.

As Freya pulled herself back onto the seat. From his kneeling position and in the confines of the pew, Hamish turned, clasped her hands and asked.

"Lady Freya Douglas Gore Hamilton would you do me the honour of becoming my w…?"

The rest of his words were lost in the deafening, stone-shuddering thunderous sound from the tower as the eight bells rang out again to celebrate the birth of a very special boy. The occasion was symbolised by the wondrous peal of their joyous, melodious, soul-stirring ringing Methods to the people of the village and the valley below them.

In the tumult, the now smiling apparition moved from the altar, lifted the right hand making a silent gesture of benediction then, with the briefest show of white surplice, seemingly disappeared, as would a wraith, into a concealed alcove in the chancel wall.